THE
SILVER LINING
BETRAYALS

S. J. FAIRCHILD

ACKNOWLEDGEMENTS

There are many people to thank: family, friends, and business colleagues.

Katherine—my dear wife—read, reread, edited, and most importantly, guided my writing journey. She taught me the art of saying more with less. Lyn and Antonia, my accomplished artistic daughters, encouraged my nascent writing instincts. I trust that I did not disappoint these three beautiful people.

I am grateful to my parents, Fred and Madelyn Fairchild. I learned many valuable lessons as they guided a family enterprise. They taught me to recognize family problems that interfere with rational business decisions.

Carl McKinzie and Clinton McKinzie provided guidance concerning patents, jury trials, and murder investigations. Michael Buescher offered valuable insight on 1985—1995 computer and Internet intricacies. Thanks to my beta readers—Carl McKinzie, Dan Marovich, Denny Holland, Randy Yale, Larry Ross, and Antonia Fairchild—for your excellent suggestions.

Albert Haussener, you introduced me to the world of international business involving innovations, patents, and commercializing technology. I learned the importance of balancing technology and politics when introducing new products to the marketplace.

A special note of appreciation goes to Elizabeth Simmons for completing the final editing work and to Streetlight Graphics for the cover design and formatting.

To all of the above, I am indebted to you for your support and encouragement.

PART I
THE ASCENT
(1986–1994)

1986
SAN MATEO, CALIFORNIA

"I'VE BEEN PEARL HARBORED!" PUG James yelled as he stormed into the kitchen. He threw his briefcase at the linoleum. It slid to Marcy's feet. She jumped back.

"Honey, be careful! You'll wreck something!"

He ripped off his suit jacket and tossed it on the table. "Who cares? I'm gonna remodel this dump!"

Marcy sighed. Pug had uttered the dreaded word that was synonymous with endless do-it-yourself home improvement projects.

"What do you mean 'Pearl Harbored?'"

Pug yanked open the fridge door, grabbed a Budweiser and grimaced; a sharp pain—a souvenir from Vietnam—radiated from his shoulder into his back.

"The company's Jap attacked me!" He popped the cap and took a long gulp.

Marcy poured generous Jack Daniels over ice. "Sweetie, wasn't January's sales meeting to celebrate your million-dollar order?"

"Doug Aldrich screwed me! Invited a sake-sipper to my meeting just 'cuz he got a bigger order!"

"But isn't that great for MatraScience?"

"Aldrich blabbered about politics and patents and barely mentioned my order! He slobbered all over the slant eyes."

"Next weekend's family reunion will take your mind off MatraScience," Marcy said, trying to change the subject.

"Aldrich suckered me to join MatraScience with his techno-babble and Guadalcanal Silver Star bullshit. How can he trust Japs?"

Marcy bit her lip. With Pug in this mood, it was no good to defend Doug Aldrich, the company's CEO, or to remind Pug how much he admired him. Doug had founded MatraScience in the late sixties relying on technical brilliance, entrepreneurial instincts, and appetite for risk. Under Doug's leadership, MatraScience grew from zero to $500 million. A well-respected company, MatraScience developed and commercialized proprietary materials and products for various industrial markets.

"Dinner's almost ready."

"Screw it, going out!" He grabbed his suit coat and slammed the door. The kitchen shuddered. Marcy sighed and refilled her glass. *Another evening with Jack.*

Pug drove north on Bayshore Freeway to the Velvet Turtle, his favorite watering hole. The dim lighting, soft Sinatra ballads, and plush décor calmed him. He settled at the ornate bar and nursed a Bud. His eyes followed cute waitresses wearing skimpy green velvet. It was a slow evening, and there was a cooking show on the bar's TV. It featured an Italian chef.

Pug signaled for the bartender. "Another Bud, and, hey, can't you turn on a better channel?"

The bartender placed another brew in front of Pug. "Got it on PBS. All the other channels are bashing President Reagan about Iran-Contra. And we're not un-American in this bar!"

"Good one! I'll drink to that!"

As he stared at the TV, Pug's thoughts drifted back to last week's meeting with a Pacific Gas & Electric engineer.

"Pug, we like MatraScience's technology. But until you guarantee PG&E a watertight system to protect our network, I'm staying with our current supplier."

"You guys never change. I can't do this."

"Pug, if you say you can't do it then you're right, you can't do it."

Pug slid the empty bottle toward the bartender. "Gimme another!"

He glanced up and watched the television chef roll pasta dough around sausage, pour olive oil into the pasta wrapper, and then tie each end with string. The chef massaged the roll to spread the oil.

Pug breathed out, "Sonovabitch!" He grabbed bar napkins and sketched electric cable connection points. Around them he drew a pasta-like wrapper. *Now pour PG&E's liquid cement into the wrapper, close it, and seal it with MatraScience's patented plastic.*

He leaned back in the bar stool and grinned. *I solved it! Goddamn it! I can do it! I invented the perfect watertight system for power connections!*

The scent of Chanel interrupted his self-congratulations. He looked to his right and beheld a genuine beauty: shiny blonde hair, big blue eyes, creamy skin, and full lips. A snug sweater dress hugged nice curves.

"Hey, you're Miss San Jose!"

She smiled, her look direct and interested. "I was."

He extended his hand. "Name's Pug James. Buy you a drink?"

"Tiffanee Anderson... thanks."

Gotta order something expensive, impress this broad. "Bring me Cakebread Chardonnay and two glasses," he told the bartender.

"So, Tiffanee, subsize your life for me."

She giggled. "Subsize? You mean summarize?"

He smiled. "Isn't that what I said?"

She giggled again. "Well, if you want numbers, it's ten beauty pageants and one win."

"Guess I was interested in your other stats," Pug said with a wink. He watched her eye his new Brooks Brothers suit, a birthday gift from Marcy. She took in the rest of him, the way ladies do when they don't think a guy will notice.

"Oh, I don't share secrets," she laughed. "So, what are your stats?"

"Six three and two hundred soaking wet!" *Hey, what's an inch or two, a little exaggeration?* "So, you in school, or what?"

"Just finished my marketing degree at San Jose State. Tough finding a job right now."

"How 'bout MatraScience? We can always use new marketing talent."

"MatraScience? How long have you worked there?"

"Almost eight years." *Her voice says job search, but those eyes say strip search.* "Got promoted to sales 'cuz I got a lot done in manufacturing. Already got three patents. Now I'm in charge of solving customer problems."

Pug took a gulp of chardonnay and pointed to the napkin drawings. "See my sausage on this napkin? It's my latest invention."

She looked perplexed. "That's... nice. Um, could you let me know when they interview, or give me someone to contact?"

"No sweat. Gimme your number."

5

She jotted it on a bar napkin. "Well, it's getting late. Looks like my friend isn't coming after all."

"Right, your friend." Pug smiled. That was what they all said when they were on the hunt.

"Thanks for the drink." Her smile told Pug she expected a call.

"Sure, anytime," Pug replied. He watched her walk away. *That's one fine ass!*

He finished the bottle then headed home. When he crawled into bed, Marcy threw back the blanket and said, "It's late. I was worried."

"You won't believe what happened!"

She rolled over to face him. "What?"

"I solved PG&E's problem! Can't wait till the development gang sees my idea."

She yawned. "Get some sleep. You got a busy weekend. Finish remodeling the bathroom. I want it back."

"I'll get those tiles replaced in no time." He prodded her side. "Say, how 'bout a roll in the hayloft like old times?"

She groaned. "Honey, Jack gave me a terrible headache." She turned away and pulled the covers around her.

Pug smiled to himself. *Okay for you. I got me Tiffanee's number.*

FARM RIDGE, COLORADO

The James and Decker families held their annual winter reunion at Paul Decker's farm, a two-hundred-acre spread that had been in the family for over a century. In 1938, Darin James, Pug's father, married Paul's daughter, Amelia Decker, and they produced two sons: Pug, born in 1944, and Rich, born in 1960. Every year, Pug pressured Marcy to accompany him to the reunion. She despised the event but always relented at the last minute.

As they drove to Farm Ridge from Stapleton Airport, Marcy complained, "Your dad makes everyone miserable at these reunions. Never a civil word."

"Your family's no better. If I hadn't married you, you'd be stuck in Farm Ridge. You owe me big time."

"Oh please, who's the lucky one? Do me favor and make sure we sit far away from your cousin Darin. Last reunion, he was worse than your dad... like uncle, like nephew."

Pug laughed out loud. "Yeah, my cousin's ego's so big, he yells his own name during sex."

"I do enjoy seeing Rich. Aren't you proud of how he's matured?"

"Yeah, and with no thanks to Dad who was never around after Mom died."

"You promised your mother you'd take care of him, and you raised him like a son."

Pug sighed. "With his athletic ability, he coulda had a football scholarship to Colorado State. His grades sucked."

"At least he went to community college and got some technical training. With his street smarts, work ethic, and personality, he'll land on his feet."

"Hope you're right, sweetie," Pug said.

They arrived at the Decker farm and parked the car in front of the dilapidated old farmhouse. Before getting out, both stared ahead at its weathered shutters, peeling paint, and buckled shingles. Wide steps to the front porch sagged. The roof's lightning rods leaned at crazy angles.

Pug shook his head. "Sad. Used to be a real nice place."

A rustic milk barn and silo—in great disrepair—stood behind the house and brought back memories for Pug and Marcy. As teenagers, they'd spent many summer nights in the barn's hayloft.

At the farmhouse dinner table, they joined Pug's dad, Cousin Darin, his wife, Sylvia, Rich, and Rich's pregnant girlfriend. They washed down burgers, potato salad, and baked beans with lots of Coors beer. As they tucked into apple pie and coffee, Pug's father glanced around at the faded wallpaper on the dining room walls. He tipped his head down to examine the dull and worn oak floor. "Just look at this shit hole!" the old man groused. His scowl, ill-fitting toupee, and thick eyeglasses matched his sour attitude. "Stupid Pecker cousins let it go to hell! Never happen if I owned it."

Marcy rolled her eyes at Pug who just grinned and whispered, "Dad's still pissed that Mom died before Grandpa Decker did."

Marcy took a sip of hot coffee and grimaced, "Can you tell him to stop using the word 'pecker?' It's disgusting."

Pug threw an arm around her and raised a beer can in a toast. "Boy, could I remodel this place!"

She frowned, whispering back, "Enough with remodeling."

Pug's cousin Darin ran his tongue over piecrust clinging to his mustache. "You wait, Uncle Darin! I'll buy this farm one day!"

"Hear that, Puggy? My favorite namesake's getting my farm back!"

As Marcy registered disgust, Pug spoke loudly, "Why don't you just do that, Ted?" Darin's resemblance to Ted Turner: razor-thin silvery moustache, dimpled chin, and nasal voice is what inspired Pug to call him "Ted." Seething, Pug continued, "And get over it, Dad! Grandpa Decker left it to the Decker cousins!"

"They changed the old coot's will. Shoulda sued 'em!" the old man growled.

"Yeah, like suing'll fix everything. Changing the subject!" Pug turned to Rich. "So what are your plans, bro?"

"Got me a production job at Appliancorp. Start in August."

"Appliancorp's growing. Lotsa good jobs," Pug said.

"Rich, be sure and call if you need anything," Marcy said. "You know we're always here for you."

"Thanks, don't know what I woulda done without you guys."

Darin interrupted, his nasal voice at its grating best, "Yeah, Rich, what have they done for you lately?"

"Helluva lot more than you ever did," Pug snapped.

That night in bed, Marcy snuggled close. "Honey, I'm really proud of what we've done for Rich after your mom got sick."

"She knew she couldn't trust Dad. Now you understand why Grandpa changed his will."

"I'm worried Rich is too influenced by your cousin Darin."

"Dad encourages it, and I don't understand why. But how do you understand crazy? Mom told me he was never the same after he came back from fighting the Japs. Maybe he's got a case of post-dramatic stress order."

Marcy chuckled, "You mean post-traumatic stress disorder? That could explain it."

"Whatever, look, next year we're sitting with the Deckers. No more Dad or Ted. They don't give a flyin' fig about me. Did you see how they dissed me when I mentioned my million-dollar order?"

Marcy sighed. She caressed his thigh and nuzzled his ear. "Enough about them. Let's pretend we're back in Grandpa Decker's hayloft."

"You got it, sweetie."

TOKYO, JAPAN

In February, Kenji Kobyashi, Japan Technologies's CEO, and his closest friend and business associate, Shiganari Okazaki, Hondoya Appliance's CEO, met at Takamura, their favorite Tokyo restaurant. Since 1947, they collaborated in rebuilding Japan's appliance industry.

Kenji wore a custom tailored, charcoal-gray suit accented with a maroon tie and matching pocket handkerchief. His coal-black hair, trim physique, and erect posture belied his age. Shiganari, taller and white-haired, dressed modestly—no match for the fashionable Kenji.

Two hostesses bowed and escorted them to a private room. The gentlemen removed their polished shoes and sat cross-legged on the tatami. A geisha entertained with song and sophisticated conversation while Johnnie Walker Blue flowed, and cigarette smoke fogged the intimate room.

After dining, the ladies left and closed the screen.

Shiganari lifted his glass. "My esteemed friend, I salute your sixty-first year, an auspicious milestone."

Kenji nodded. Each refilled the other's glass.

Kenji raised his. "Tradition requires we honor our respected American mentor. Patrick Hafferty launched our business careers."

"And fortunes!" Shiganari exclaimed.

"As General MacArthur's industry liaison, Hafferty-san mentored us for our current roles. We are indeed grateful."

"Hai! And never forget his wisdom: compete locally, cooperate internationally, and nurture political relationships! The keys to Hondoya's global domination!"

"Hai! Very wise advice."

"Kenji, Hafferty-san would be very proud of your leadership of the Thermal and Acoustics Device Association. TADA has allowed Hondoya's keiretsu to maintain our market and technical leadership in Japan's appliance industry."

Kenji nodded and refilled their glasses. They toasted each other.

"For Hondoya to overtake America's Exeter and General Appliance, we must search for best technologies and combine them with appropriate customer relationships," Shiganari said. He downed his glass of scotch.

"Shiganari, that is why TADA's North American-based consultants continually search for new technologies and customer contacts." Kenji swirled his scotch. "Our American colleague, Marken-san, serves as our eyes and ears for this region."

They again refilled each other's glass and lit cigarettes. Slurring words, Shiganari asked, "What does Marken-san report about Seamus Hafferty?"

Kenji inhaled deeply and exhaled slowly. "Seamus's problem continues."

Shiganari shook his head. "Very disappointing. We accepted responsibility for Seamus after Hafferty-san died."

"Hai! And we must not fail in our obligation."

Toasts and conversation concluded. Chauffeurs arrived.

"May you live another sixty-one years, Kenji."

They exchanged bows and staggered to their limos.

BURLINGAME, CALIFORNIA

During February, MatraScience's development staff generated working prototypes from Pug's sketches. Thirty days of system testing followed to simulate product performance over a thirty-year life cycle. MatraScience had developed a proprietary watertight connection system called MatraConnect 5000.

Jackson Huntley, MatraScience's intellectual property attorney, filed the patent application. He possessed an undergraduate metallurgy degree and spent three years as an examiner at the United States Patent and Trademark Office (USPTO) before joining MatraScience.

Pug organized April field trials for MatraConnect 5000. By June, PG&E approved the product and placed a $3 million order. Pug's increased workload required assistance. Several dinner interviews at the Turtle convinced Tiffanee to become his marketing assistant.

Doug Aldrich's Marine buzz cut had not changed since World War II, except that his dark hair was now silver. His lean physique testified to his racquetball passion, and his weathered, suntanned skin showed his love of sailing. He maintained a fifties engineer's look: short-sleeve white shirt with pocket protector and always-present slide rule attached to his belt. His engineering accomplishments included twenty-four granted patents for MatraScience.

He summoned Pug to his office. He cleared his smoker's throat. "Pug, MatraConnect 5000 has successfully launched. Development's effort and your sales work with PG&E has opened a multi-million dollar market at power companies. It's been a tremendous team success."

"But my name's not on the patent."

"In the rush to file, the development gang didn't give Jackson all the details."

"Can't he add my name?"

"Look, Jackson is a first-class, Harvard-trained attorney. He'll add your name when he files for additional patents. You know, where we revise the original patent with additional claims. With his work experience at the United States Patent and Trademark Office, he knows how to work the system. Next time you have a brilliant idea on a bar napkin, be sure to sign, date, and have someone witness it."

Pug looked unconvinced. "But it's not the same."

"Pug, Jackson says adding names now could delay approval. Anyway, you did the most important job: greasing customer politics. Without solid customer relationships, there would be no commercial success."

"All I did was book tee times at Pebble Beach to get PG&E honchos to sign off."

Doug gave him a stern look. "Next time we play racquetball, I'll tell you how Maurice Oshima really got that ten million dollar order at Japan Electric Power. Technology has its place, but so does politics. In Japan, it means getting in bed with cartels that control customer politics and relationships. Never forget that!"

Pug frowned. *Always praising the slant eyes!*

Doug continued, "Let me get to the good news. First for the appetizer, with your increased workload, I let you hire a marketing assistant. Your gal Tiffanee is one gorgeous babe— my kind of assistant—and you know what I mean." Doug grinned. "Now for the main course, I want you to be national sales manager for the Power Division. This new role will develop your management skills and customer relationship smarts. Think you can you do it?"

Pug blurted, "Can I do it? You betcha!"

"Pug, there's one key consideration, the job's in Chicago. How will Marcy feel about moving?"

"She hears about my promotion, it's Marcy-bar-the-door!"

"Great! Take a few days. Visit Chicago before deciding."

That night at the Turtle, Pug broke the news to Tiffanee. Tearful, she whispered, "Pug, I don't want you to leave California."

"Sweetheart, you'll always be my marketing gal." He gave her a mischievous wink. "My heart's not leaving Burlingame."

"You're so sweet."

"Let's finish our dinner. I got a bottle of the best champagne on ice back at our hotel."

CHICAGO, ILLINOIS

Pug and Marcy moved to Chicago in July and enrolled their sons, Skip and Dave, in school. The next nine months involved extensive travel, endless meetings, weekly management reports, and corporate bureaucracy. He spent zero time solving customer problems.

The family, unhappy and not adjusting, felt abandoned in an unfamiliar city. Rumors about Pug and Tiffanee drifted back to Marcy.

On a cold April day, Doug called Pug at home. "What's this I hear about you leaving Chicago?"

"I'm traveling all the time, Marcy and the kids hate it here! Never shoulda left California."

"I told you not to move until the office construction finished."

"I don't care! We're coming back as soon as school's over."

"Pug, you do that and you'll regret it."

"You mean like regretting puny bonuses for all my inventions the development guys stole, and my PG&E three million order?"

Doug ended the call.

1987
BURLINGAME

DOUG INVITED MICHAEL FIELDS TO stop by his office in late April.

Michael had joined MatraScience in 1978 after six years with the United States Air Force. His first years at MatraScience focused on procurement and later sales management. His energy, enthusiasm, and sense of humor invigorated his colleagues. At forty-one, he was tall and fit with streaks of gray in his dark brown hair. Ellie, his spouse, often joked, "If you ever need a 'real job,' you can model for GQ in your Hart Schaffner and Marx."

Doug greeted Michael with his usual firm handshake. "Michael, I'll get right to it. I'm reorganizing the North American Power Division. I want a seasoned, balanced, flexible manager; someone who sees the big picture and fosters teamwork. This new position oversees sales, marketing, and development. Job's in Chicago. Need you there."

"Doug, why isn't Pug James the logical choice?"

"Pug's a brilliant engineer, very inventive. His latest idea opened up a multi-million dollar market. But he's a technical renegade." Doug chuckled. "Reminds me of myself at his age: we're both engineers, ex-military, entrepreneurial." He grew serious. "But Pug needs to learn the art of balancing technology and politics when commercializing new products. He's got the brain, but not sure about personality and patience. He needs rehabilitation time, and that's where you come in. Think you can do it?"

"Rehabilitate Pug James? I'll need to brush up on my people skills..."

Doug smiled, "Look, Michael, you've done a great job handling all kinds of difficult people. You know, the ego and asshole mentality. If anyone can handle Pug James, it's you."

"Thanks for the vote of confidence. Looking forward to it."

"Great! One more thing, a while back I visited Lockheed Aircraft in Southern California. They let me tour their secret development lab. It's a unique concept that keeps corporate bureaucracy out of innovation. I'll put you in touch with Lockheed so you can learn more about its 'skunk works.' Pug might thrive in a similar environment. This may be a way to retain him."

Michael called Ellie and arranged to meet her for lunch at Casa de Margaritas in Palo Alto.

When Michael arrived, Ellie had already ordered margaritas.

"What's the occasion, given the short notice?" she asked.

"An opportunity to move back to Chicago."

"Seriously? That would be wonderful! The girls will be thrilled."

Michael paused. "Are you okay with giving up your position at Orlio & Associates? You're up for partner next year."

Ellie thought for a moment. "I'm pretty sure Gordon Orlio would let me work offsite and with his Chicago affiliate."

"He should, based on all the great securities work you've done for his firm these last five years."

"Tell me more about your opportunity."

"Doug offered me a great career move. It'll enhance my experience. I'll have full P&L responsibility for the North American Power Division."

Ellie took a slow sip of her margarita. "Everybody knows you're a good manager, why else do you think Doug wanted you?"

"He said he'd read my graduate thesis on Japan's restructuring after World War II. That surprised me. He was especially interested in the role of the keiretsu in economic growth."

"How relevant is that for doing business in the US?"

"Doug said my analysis shows I understand the importance of developing customer relationships in order to commercialize technologies. Applies to any geographic region."

"Sweetheart, I'm very proud of you. Looks like all that education finally paid off!"

"Hope you're right. There's one unique challenge... "

"And?"

Michael described the rehabilitation project. After listening to the details, Ellie concluded, "With your people skills, that'll be a slam dunk."

"Doug wants to save Pug and his technical talent."

After a whirlwind visit to look at houses and private schools, Michael accepted Doug's offer, and Ellie took a leave of absence from the law firm.

SAN MATEO

Pug's family returned to California in July. A San Mateo real estate agent struggled to find Pug a bargain "fixer-upper." He settled for a foreclosure property needing a carport, a new kitchen, pool renovation, and major landscaping. Marcy referred to the house as "the wreck of the century."

Tense and not speaking, Pug and Marcy unpacked moving boxes. The phone rang but neither answered. Pug listened to Doug's curt message. "Michael Fields will contact you about your new assignment."

Pug shrugged. "You believe that? Doug's making me work for a purchasing slug who knows nothing about technology!"

Marcy ignored him. She was in no mood to discuss his problems. The Chicago experience had obliterated her vivacious personality. She was exhausted; dark rings circled her blue-gray eyes. As she unwrapped a favorite hand-painted vase, a gift from Grandmother Decker, it slipped from her hands, fell to the floor, and shattered.

She gazed down at the scattered shards. She tipped her head up, and with trembling hand, drew blond hair from her face. Her eyes were wild. She exploded, "That's it! I'm filing for divorce!"

"Goddamn it! I moved us back because of your bitching!"

"I never wanted to move in the first place!"

"Oh, it's my fault I got promoted!"

"I'm sure 'Miss Tiffanee' was thrilled about that!" She kicked the box in his direction. She spat out words. "Get the hell out of this house!"

Startled, Pug's mouth fell open. Suddenly, he spun on his heel and yelled, "You got it!" He slammed the door; the house shook.

Marcy fell to her knees and sobbed.

FARM RIDGE

During his annual summer vacation to Colorado, Darin visited his cousin Rich. They sat on Rich's back porch with its spectacular view of the Rockies. They drank Coors, a welcome treat on the hot, dry day.

Holding the bottle at eye-level and staring at the pale liquid Darin asked, "Why does Puggy like Budweiser?"

"Haven't you heard? He's switched to Pat Henry 'cuz it's a rebel beer."

"Like your dad... never satisfied. Speaking of, you sounded worried."

"Dad's heading downhill fast ever since he retired. Eyesight's failing, hearing's gone. Complains every day about aches and pains."

"Hey, he's old."

"His mind's getting goofy. Accuses people of stealing his ideas or his latest invention."

"He's always imagined things, not to mention his exaggerations."

"I got promoted to production supervisor at Appliancorp for heat dissipaters. I don't have time to nursemaid him."

"Get Puggy to visit more."

"And start World War III? They've never got along. 'Sides I can't ask Pug to do that after all he and Marcy did for me."

"Yeah, yeah. Say, I got a better idea. Let's send your dad to Puggy! Puggy and Marcy have split. Uncle Darin will jump at a free San Francisco vacation. I'll buy the plane ticket. Puggy provides room, board and companionship. And best of all, you get a break."

"'Cuz, you're a genius!"

"Done deal. Say, I hear the Decker cousins are in trouble."

"Yeah. Blew through the inheritance. Bank's foreclosing on the farm."

As they got into Rich's truck, Darin bragged, "My company's going gangbusters. If Boeing keeps ordering, I'll do 15 mil this year."

"You'll need money to expand."

"Duh, why do you think I'm doing my IPO?"

CHICAGO

Settled into his new office, Michael reviewed the Power Division's financial results for fiscal year ending June 30, 1987. He analyzed the fiscal 1988 financial plan and upcoming challenges. He thought about information obtained from Pug's former direct reports.

– – Fiscal 1987 revenues of $20 million—a record—due to MatraConnect 5000 sales to PG&E. No other power companies had bought the product because of increasing economic uncertainties. External data indicated power companies were adopting conservative capital spending.

– – Pug had hired fifteen new sales engineers to support a planned $38 million revenue forecast for fiscal 1988. He projected each new salesman would produce at least $1.0 to $1.5 million in his first year. (Unrealistic? New salesmen undergo six months of training before selling. History shows it takes 12-18 months before a new salesman produces a million + revenues.)

– – Pug's direct reports complained about his missed meetings, inconsistent direction, and constant distractions due to marital problems.

– – Fiscal 1988 looks like an unfolding disaster. Need a rescue plan.

The next few months, Michael focused on people and applied his management and team-building skills. Despite colleagues' concerns about his reputation for over-analysis, they found Michael a refreshing change from Pug's chaotic style.

Over dinner at a neighborhood trattoria, Ellie listened to Michael's summary. She asked, "Is Pug a keeper?"

"I'm optimistic he can be saved. I just hope I can devote enough time to him."

"But if he drags you down..."

"Look, I already reduced his management scope. Once I understand the business, the organization's strengths and weaknesses, I'll decide his longer-term role. Just need to find the right time and project to get Pug's innovative juices flowing again."

SAN MATEO

Marcy enrolled the boys in San Mateo schools in August. Skip started his junior year, and Dave entered ninth grade. She found employment at an interior-decorating firm. Her boss coached her to assist customers with fabric and color decisions. She felt validated, and the extra income eased the family's financial worries.

She and Pug spoke each week by phone to update him on the boys' progress.

In mid September, Marcy announced, "The school suspended Dave for bringing alcohol to class."

"No big deal," Pug yawned loudly.

Her voice grew curt. "He and Skip fight all the time. Skip's eyebrow needed four stitches."

"Just like I gave Cousin Ted."

Marcy shouted, "And I found marijuana in Dave's bedroom!"

"Well, cut his allowance."

"That's your solution?"

"And you don't spoil him? So what's my number one son up to?"

Marcy swallowed anger. "Found another used condom in his jeans. Let's see... where'd he learn that? You better talk to him."

"Yeah, yeah, I'll get him to practice for that tennis scholarship. More court time will delude his urges."

"Speaking of diluting urges—give Tiffanee my regards." She slammed the phone.

Pug's financial problems mounted: two mortgage payments, apartment rent, unreimbursed moving expenses, and rising credit card debt. His addiction to stock market gambling compounded the mess.

Despite serious reservations, he hosted his dad for a few weeks during September. One evening, they watched televised baseball with the San Francisco Giants playing the Cincinnati Reds. Pete Rose, the Reds manager, was arguing an umpire's call at home plate.

"Like me, Charlie Hustle never gives up!" Pug boasted.

"Harley's muscle? Puggy, what the hell you talking about?" The old man rubbed his neck and groaned.

Pug lowered the volume and yelled, "You've bitched about neck pain for the last two weeks. Taking you to a doctor."

"Don't need no goddamn doctor. The air in this damn state gives me headaches!"

"Your toupee strangles your brain."

"Mangles a train? What the hell, Puggy?"

"Stop calling me Puggy."

"Puggy's your name, and your mama's to blame! She started it all when she named you Paul!" The old man cackled and slapped his knee. In an instant, his mood turned angry. "She never showed me no respect! I wanted to name you Darin, an' she wouldn't let me."

"You didn't deserve her respect after the way you treated her! And if you're not better tomorrow, you're seeing a doctor! This ain't no fuckin' democracy while I pay the bills!"

"Huh? What truckin' bureaucracy?"

The next day, Pug contacted the veteran's hospital and arranged an appointment with Dr. Tower, a geriatric psychiatrist.

"Not going to no damn doctor! You need one 'cuz Darin says you dipped your dick where Marcy ain't."

"He should talk; already dumped one wife."

Three days later, Pug drove his dad to the Menlo Park VA hospital. At admissions, Pug restrained him as he yelled, "I don't want no fucking examination!"

A nurse and Pug struggled to get him into a hospital gown.

"Cooperate with Dr. Tower!" Pug ordered. His father glared at the floor.

Pug shoved a magazine toward him. "Read *Playboy*. Maybe there's life still left in your dick."

Pug returned to the waiting room and scanned *Remodeling Digest*. He sketched carport designs and made notes for remodeling projects.

A few hours later, Dr. Tower appeared. "Mr. James, today's tests are finished."

"What's the prognosticate?"

The doctor chuckled. "You've coined a new medical term. No

prognosis yet, but I'm working on a diagnosis. First impression: your father suffers from paranoid delusions."

"Delusions?"

"He claims people steal his discoveries, says 'everyone's out to get him.' When I ask for specifics, he becomes very agitated and irrational. It's possible that his World War II experiences contribute to his mental health problems. Today we call that post traumatic stress disorder."

Pug rubbed his forehead. "Sometimes he acts just plain nuts. How 'bout his pains?"

"He denies having pain but shows evidence of short-term memory loss. I'll order an MRI and CT scan and have a neurologist evaluate for stroke. We'll do blood work, other tests, and conduct more interviews. Your father should stay two more days."

"Then what?"

"Depending on findings, it could require commitment for therapy and medication. At his age, physical condition, and uncooperative attitude—treatment could take time."

Pug stopped by his dad's room. "Dr. Tower's gonna do more tests."

"You can't fool me! You're in cahoots with the bastards so they can steal my theories!"

"Calm down and get some rest! I'll be back tomorrow."

As Pug reached the door, his father yelled, "You and Amelia screwed me!"

"She's been dead for twenty years! I don't deserve this shit! And where were you when Rich needed a father? Nowhere, that's where! That's why I raised him!"

The old man grew silent and stared at the floor.

Dr. Tower confirmed the preliminary diagnosis. He recommended drug therapy, counseling, and confinement for four months. Rich quickly consented and let Pug organize the convalescence.

When Marcy heard about Pug's dad, she called and agreed to meet at a restaurant in Menlo Park.

"How's he doing?" she asked.

"Not good. Doc Tower said he's had a small stroke; he's got serious mental problems, probably from his war experience. Won't cooperate, won't take his meds. They gotta isolate him; he fights with other patients. Doc says he's a danger to himself and others."

"I'm so sorry. He's a handful; he never treated you well."

Pug slumped forward and held his head in his hands. "Sweetie, my world's crashed. Our marriage's a wreck, my job's disappeared, my boss ignores me, finances are in the toilet." He looked up at Marcy, his blue eyes sad and tearful. His voice cracked. "My sons don't wanna see or talk to me; my dad's crazy." He sighed and leaned back. "For the first time in my life, I feel really alone with no one to turn to."

Marcy took Pug's hands in hers; tears rolled down her rosy cheeks. "Honey, why has it come to this? Skip and Dave need their father. I want my husband back. Can we start over?"

Pug, his face wet with tears, squeezed her hands. "Sweetie, I don't wanna divorce. I've done dumb things. I'm sorry. Forgive me?"

She paused and looked directly into his eyes. "Give up Tiffanee."

"We're finished. She left the company, wants no part of me."

"Do you love her?"

"No."

"You'll be faithful from now on?"

"Please give me another chance."

Pug stood and pulled her up from her chair. She leaned into him, and he wrapped his arms around her. They held onto each other and wept.

1988
CHICAGO

B<small>Y JANUARY, EVERYONE IN THE</small> Power Division knew fiscal 1988 sales would only reach 20 million—far short of Pug's projection. Michael had split the organization into three sales regions and relieved Pug of all direct management responsibilities. He gave Pug only one project: evaluate the impact of new technologies for power companies.

For the next eight months, Pug kept a low profile; and Michael's diverse duties meant minimal oversight. Pug spent weekday mornings researching and conducting stock trades. He heard rumors about MatraScience's deteriorating financials and noted increasing trade volume in options and short selling. Borrowing from MatraScience colleagues, he purchased put options. When MatraScience announced disappointing quarterly earnings, its stock price plummeted. Pug reaped substantial profits and promptly expanded his trading activity beyond MatraScience.

In September, after visiting several Midwest power companies, Pug burst into Michael's office.

"Fieldsy, my man! Power companies have no balls for risk!"

"Pug, slow down, take a seat. Explain." Michael's neat slacks, starched shirt, and shined shoes contrasted with his cluttered office. "File piles" covered every flat surface. A bookcase held a collection of Asian World War II histories, most on post-war Japan's economic restructuring under General MacArthur.

Pug plopped down in a chair. "Power companies are spending more on maintenance, less on new construction and wanna stay with known technologies."

"So, what does MatraScience do?"

"Chase the easy stuff. They always got maintenance problems and need solutions now, and we got known technologies."

"Got enough facts to persuade Doug?"

"You bet your butt!" Pug pulled a paper from his pocket. "Lemme use your flip chart."

"Uh, oh, another bar napkin moment?"

Pug scribbled an equation on a blank sheet:

$NP + A + SWS = \$\$\$.$

"My formula for big bucks! Network Plant + Analysis + Skunk Works Solutions equals $\$\$\$\$$."

"Great, Pug, but I'm short of time. Give me a detailed memo and we'll discuss when I'm next in California."

Pug scowled. "Hey, Fieldsy, this is important! Solving customer problems here!"

"I get the message, Pug, but I have priorities too! Do the memo, and I'll get back to you ASAP."

Angry and disappointed, Pug stormed out. That night from the hotel in Chicago, Pug called Marcy and vented. "I had a terrible meeting with Michael this afternoon."

"Honey, what happened?"

"Wanted to explain my idea on how MatraScience can use a skunk works development lab. How I could invent new products using the company's existing technologies. Michael wouldn't gimme ten minutes to explain how it'd work. Said he's too busy, told me to shoot him a memo instead. And he's the one who suggested I start a skunk works lab!"

"Are you going to send him a proposal?"

"Yeah, don't expect anything to happen."

"Honey, get a good night's sleep. Things'll look better tomorrow."

"Tell ya one thing, sweetie, they'll be sorry they blew off my idea!"

1989
TOKYO

KENJI AND SHIGANARI MET AT Shiganari's Tokyo apartment in late January. Kenji, sipping Johnny Walker Blue, studied Hondoya specifications for its new appliance models including ovens, dryers, water heaters, and HVAC systems.

"Shiganari, this means Hondoya's new models require major improvements in dissipater performance metrics: thermal, noise, weight, space, and environmentally acceptable materials."

"Hai! Asbestos and fiberglass are no longer acceptable. Also, we need dissipater materials that will prevent electrical wiring fires in appliances."

"Understand. TADA will ask Marken-san to assign our best consultant to find companies that possess better technologies and individuals who can invent them."

"Excellent! Tell Marken-san to have the consultant look for companies in both appliance and non-appliance industries."

SAN MATEO

Pug bent over his workbench, sanding a wall cabinet for the family room. Marcy, working hard at their reconciliation, brought a cold Pat Henry.

"Sweetie, the cabinet looks wonderful. But... you don't look pleased."

"Michael still hasn't read my skunk works memo." Pug shoved the sanding block back and forth as if rubbing away anger. "Worse, I got a piss-poor bonus of five grand. You know, I can't make real money at this company."

"Honey, you need to be patient."

"You don't get it! Ted's company's going public at the end of March!"

"What's that got to do with MatraScience?"

Pug slammed the sanding block on the workbench. "Forget it!"

SAN FRANCISCO

In September, Pug and Marcy drove into San Francisco and parked on Chestnut Street in Cow Hollow. As they strolled to their favorite trattoria, they encountered a dozing homeless man. As they stepped around him, Pug said, "Hey, bum's got it figured! Stole a hotel luggage cart, organized his junk with the mattress on top, covered it with plastic. He could patent his mobile all-weather homeless shelter!"

"You always want to patent something," Marcy said, laughing.

Ristorante Sienna was warm and inviting. Frescos and vintage family photos added to the charm. A nine-foot-high rack holding many of Pug's favorite wines ran the length of the room.

Marcy smiled knowingly as he took out a notepad and sketched. "I'll license my earthquake-proof rack for free meals!"

"*Buona sera, Signore James, Signora James. Come stai?*" Giacomo, the owner, greeted them.

"Do my ears hear me? Are we in Frenzy?"

Marcy whispered, "Giacomo, he means 'Firenze.'"

"I have your favorite-a table for you."

"You're so sweet," Marcy said, hugging Giacomo.

He planted a kiss on each cheek. "Signora James, you looka like that-a pretty actress Sandra Dee."

He turned to Pug. "Signore James, you look-a like that tough guy, what's his-a name? Aaah, Harvey Keitel-la." And with a hearty laugh, he announced, "Now, I get you vino and-a Pellegrino!"

As Giacomo departed, Marcy asked, "I look like Sandra Dee?"

"Yep."

"He's got the right generation."

"I look like Keitel?"

"I see some resemblance. You definitely have his attitude."

Giacomo returned with Ruffino Riserva Ducale, Chianti Classico 1980. He poured glasses for Pug and Marcy and one for himself. "Salute! I order for a-you!" Yelling in Italian, he strode toward the kitchen.

Pug smiled at Marcy and raised his glass. "Babe, here's to my future. I got myself a half million bucks from some smart stock trades."

"I can't believe it! This means we can finally get out of debt and save for the boys' education."

"Yeah, yeah, but I gotta better idea that'll make even more money."

DENVER AND SAN FRANCISCO

Prior to attending an October family wedding, Pug visited Wallace Decker, an uncle, who owned a small materials job shop in Denver. They chatted in Wallace's dusty and cramped office.

"So Uncle Wally, how's business?"

"Getting too much at my age."

"Whadya gonna do?"

"Sell."

"How much you lookin' to get?"

"Least a million."

"Pretty pricey; that's one times revenue. You got lotsa competitors and no technology."

"Don't care! Broker says it's a seller's market."

Later that evening, Pug told Marcy, "You believe in chaotic theory?"

"You mean chaos?"

"Here I wanna buy a business, and it's right under Uncle's Wally's butt."

"You always said his business was worthless!"

"I'll fix that. 'Sides it's my ticket to freedom from MatraScience."

"Why Colorado? Oh no! We're not moving back!"

"Colorado is my first step to Oz."

"Oz?"

"South San Francisco. Already got a place picked out."

"You're not making sense."

"Look, I got enough for the down payment! I'll get Uncle Wally to lower the price and make him take a note for the balance."

"Sweetie, he's never opened his wallet for anyone."

"I'll convince him. 'Sides he's family."

Pug announced his interest in late October. He and Wallace agreed on a price of $950 thousand with $500 thousand down and a five-year, 14 percent installment note. Wallace's lawyer prepared the documents, which included a conditional balloon payment clause.

After signing the contract, Pug and Marcy celebrated with the sons at Ristorante Siena. Pug raised his wine glass. "Uncle Wally's company now belongs one hundred percent to me. The future is now!"

"Pops, what'll you call the company?" Skip asked.

"IPS," Pug declared. "Stands for 'International Protected Solutions.'"

"That's neat!" Dave said. "Your company's international and uses patents to protect product solutions for customer problems!"

"See Skippy, Davey read my brain!"

Skip glared at Dave and mouthed, "Suck-up."

Giacomo arrived with the first course. "*Buon appetito!*"

OSAKA, JAPAN

Kenji watched Nani graduate from Osaka University on December 1. She received a business diploma with honors. Fluent in English, she had matured into an accomplished young woman. Her striking beauty—dark auburn hair, fair skin and green eyes—indicated *konketsu*.

Ceremonies completed, they drove to a restaurant. Nani wore an emerald green silk dress; a necklace of pale green beads complimented her eyes. Heads turned as she entered the restaurant. Her distinctive features always evoked attention. Kenji's security aide remained close and guarded against over-zealous admirers. A hostess escorted them to a table in a private room.

"My dear Nani, what are your plans?"

"To gain experience using my diploma in hotel and restaurant management."

Lighting a cigarette, Kenji smiled. "I have arranged a position at our Comfort Station restaurant. With experience, we can plan your next steps."

"Thank you! I am most grateful."

"Follow my instructions at all times. You will start next week. Show initiative, work hard and your future success will be assured."

"I will not disappoint, Kobyashi-chan!"

Kenji's time with Nani was always bittersweet. Her elegance and purity lifted his spirits, but memories of her birth fell heavy on his heart.

Dinner concluded and goodbyes said, Kenji watched his chauffeur open the limo door for Nani. She waved as the car pulled away. Trailed by his aide, Kenji walked slowly to his apartment.

Nani's future and his business legacy occupied his thoughts. He recalled an earlier conversation with Shiganari:

"Kenji, you are to be congratulated for raising Hafferty-san's grand-daughter, the lovely Nani."

"I wished to honor the memory of Hafferty-san."

"Nani is the link to your legacy."

CHICAGO

The cold December weather weighed on Michael. He sat in his office pondering his next assignment when the phone rang. He heard Pug shout. "Fieldsy, adios amigo!"

"Pug, what are you talking about?"

"It's goodbye MatraScience!"

"Wait a minute, Pug… we need to talk."

"Too late. Bought me a business, and the seller cashed my check. 'Sides my career at MatraScience is kaput. Doug never gave me a fair chance."

After the call, Michael contemplated Pug's decision. He reached for the file containing Pug's proposal. He recalled discussing it with Doug.

Pug's idea was brilliant—an independent development group would collaborate with customers to solve their current power network problems using existing MatraScience technologies. The group would propose proof of concepts, develop and test prototypes and seek continual customer feedback. Once new product solutions were accepted, development would finish. Commercialization would follow. Pug's clever roadmap balanced customer politics and MatraScience technology.

Doug told me, "Michael, I love Pug's innovative concept, but corporate profits are terrible. The stock price has tanked. I'm cutting all R&D spending."

And I told him, "Doug, we'll regret not funding Pug's concept."

MENLO PARK, CALIFORNIA

Before the Christmas break, Michael hosted a farewell party and invited Pug's colleagues from ten years at MatraScience. The group celebrated at an upscale restaurant on El Camino Boulevard. A long evening ensued: six courses, each paired with a different wine. After the main course, Michael stood and clinked his glass.

"Tonight we bid goodbye to an innovation dynamo whose creative talents have found a new outlet. Pug, MatraScience will miss you! Best wishes for your new venture."

Everyone stood and shouted, "Hear! Hear!"

Jackson tapped his glass. "As Pug's patent attorney of record, I can attest to his inventive brilliance."

Pug hollered, "Yeah, if I'd done the skunk works project, you woulda developed patentitis from all my patents!"

Jackson chuckled. "And we'll miss your smart-ass 'Pugisms.'" He handed Pug a framed picture.

Pug grinned at a cartoon of an alligator head. He read the inscription out loud: "To Pug with affection from his MatraScience pals. We'll miss your alligator mouth." Everybody howled.

Jackson continued, "Along that same line of thought, Pug, here's a gift from me to you." He handed Pug a book.

Pug read the title out loud, "*All Lawyers are Gators*." Laughing, he said, "And Jackson, you'll always be my favorite gator. Thanks!"

At evening's end, a colleague told Michael, "I've invested in Pug's company."

"Think it's a good long-term investment?"

"Pug owed me 50 thousand dollars. Gave me IPS stock instead of cash. Choice was stock now or cash later... or maybe never."

1990
DENVER

Doug requested Michael take a senior position in MatraScience's international division. He and Ellie regretted leaving Chicago, but they looked forward to relocating to Korea in June after a brief stay in San Francisco.

On one of his business trips, Michael passed through Denver to visit Pug. From Stapleton Airport, he headed towards the Denver-Boulder turnpike. After 45 minutes, he exited into a shabby industrial park and found a dilapidated building with a brand new sign. He surveyed the facility and thought, *Wow! Pug loves remodeling projects, but this is ridiculous.*

Pug met him at the front entrance. "Hey Fieldsy, good to see ya!"

They walked through the factory while Pug described manufacturing processes for various materials. The facility comprised 40,000 square feet of crowded, poorly lit, musty space.

Michael coughed. "Pug, what's in the air?"

"Ceramic fibers. Ventilator's broken."

"OSHA will shut you down. The employees should wear masks."

"Always the anulytical, ain't ya?"

Michael laughed. He missed Pug-speak. They returned to Pug's office where Michael surveyed the surroundings. "Looks like furniture from your old MatraScience office."

"Yep. Doug made sure I paid top dollar for this."

Pug looked up as the office door opened. "Come in, Ted. Fieldsy, meet my cousin."

Michael extended his hand. "Good to meet you, Ted."

"Name's Darin!"

"Ted's on my board," Pug said.

"Puggy, gotta get going," Darin interrupted. "Send the IPS stock certificates to my business address; Sylvia doesn't need to know." He headed out the door.

"Yeah, see ya at the next board meeting," Pug called after him.

"Is his name Ted or Darin?" Michael asked.

"Both. He's named after my dad, but I call him Ted. Owns a business in Seattle that just went public; figured his experience'll help me do the same."

"So, tell me about IPS."

"What you saw today is temporary. When I invent new technologies, I'll replace obsolete processes with high-tech machines. Several MatraScience guys already invested in IPS. One guy's done fifty thou. I'm offering pre-public stock at a buck a share. Arthur Hansen prepared this private placement memorandum. Pass it around to your friends."

"Can IPS afford big-eight accountants?"

"When I go public, I'll need big bean counters."

"I'll read it, but with my job change, the timing isn't good."

"Fieldsy, the future is now! Get on my ship before it sails!"

Thank god you don't owe me any money.

SAN FRANCISCO

In California, Michael called the MatraScience people Pug mentioned. Several confirmed they had bought shares. Ellie reviewed the memorandum and said, "Those investors based their decision on a hope and a prayer. Hope Pug's forecasts materialize, and pray he survives."

"Why don't you give Gordon Orlio a copy?"

"No way! You know he's still upset about Pug not paying him."

"Pug claimed Gordon overcharged him for his legal services."

"Gordon got Pug out of that insider trading lawsuit and saved him considerable money and agony. The other defendants weren't that fortunate."

"Pug claimed MatraScience's legal counsel was intent on roping him into the lawsuit along with Doug Aldrich and several others."

"Whatever. My point is that Pug was lucky to have Gordon in his corner."

DENVER

Every alternate year during August, the North American Appliance OEMs and their Tier 1 vendors assembled at Denver's convention center for the Mountain States Appliance Exhibition. Pug stopped at Appliancorp's booth. The company supplied dissipater systems to American OEMs, and it was introducing a new material, Applianshield. This material—comprised of polyester, fiberglass, and ceramic—shielded sensitive components from an appliance's hot temperatures.

"Hello, I'm Dr. Sean O'Leary. I see you're admiring Applianshield."

Pug glanced up at a six-foot-six-inch frame topped by thick rust-red hair and rimless glasses. *Looks like a nerdy professor. Weird green eyes behind those coke bottles.*

Pug introduced himself. "You a salesman?"

"No way! I'm the one who invented this material."

"Engineer?"

"I have a doctorate in metallurgy from Colorado School of Mines."

Pug scanned the Applianshield brochures. *Big fuckin' ego, too.*

"Why does a metallurgist invent a non-metal material?" he asked.

"Do you understand technology?"

"Try me. I'm a mechanical engineer. Gimme the scoop on this Applianshit."

"Applianshield," Sean corrected. He lowered his voice. "I have a hunch you might understand thermal transfer mechanics. Appliancorp wouldn't let me use my knowledge of conductive alloys, so I invented a second-rate alternative."

Pug glanced at the material's specs. "Says here the product has great performance metrics and a patent pending. Stuff looks pretty good compared to what's on the market. Hey, can I buy you a cup of coffee?"

"Why not? My booth shift's done."

At a nearby snack bar, Sean lit a Marlboro and studied Pug's business card. "Tell me about IPS."

"We process materials for lotsa applications."

"What types of materials?"

"You name it, we process it: polyester, asbestos, ceramics, aluminum, stainless steel, fiberglass, acoustic foams, plastics, cork." Pug took a swig of coffee. "So, Sean..."

"It's Dr. O'Leary."

Pug suppressed a laugh. "So Doc, you interested in full-time work?"

Sean sipped coffee and took a slow drag. "Prefer freelancing. What does IPS stand for?"

"International Protected Solutions."

"Company has patents?"

"Stay tuned!" Pug looked at his watch. "Doc, enjoyed yakking, but I gotta catch the other exhibits before they close."

At his cousin's insistence, Pug hired Rich to supervise IPS's production starting in September. Rich had left Applianshield three months earlier. In return, Darin persuaded Bob Kenton, a Seattle aerospace colleague, to invest $25 thousand in IPS: enough to fund a six-month consulting contract for Dr. O'Leary.

Pug met Sean O'Leary at McCormick's Steakhouse in Denver's LoDo to finalize the agreement.

"So Doc, you home grown?"

"Pretty much. Grew up in Denver, graduated Regis High and School of Mines."

"Tell me about your doc theorem."

"Thesis? I researched a conductive alloy with unexpected thermal and acoustical properties. The commercial possibilities are exciting."

Sean signed the agreement which included renewal options and a start date of October 1.

Later, Sean left a voice mail at a Chicago number. "Check out a Colorado company called IPS... a potential client for Mile High Bank and VenCapOne."

During early October, Pug prepared the company's 1990 requirements for its vendor, a North Carolina-based textile mill. IPS needed a long-term, low fixed-price contract for various acoustics fibers. After meeting the company's CEO, he returned to Denver and rushed to the development lab.

Rich and Sean joined him. "What's the problem?" Rich asked.

"That textile CEO's a moron."

"What happened?" Sean added.

In Pug's best redneck drawl, "Uh... well, Mistuh James, suh... that wuz a very fine pres-in-ta-shun. I am im-pressed with I-P-S progress in the a-pliance worl'. We look fo'ward to being your ven-duh for sev'ral years.' Blah, blah, blah. Then the bastard says, 'Suh, my company has to raise material prices fo'ty percent, effective in si'ty days. Sorry to do this to y'all, but our base costs rose, an' we hafta pass a-long these in-creases.'"

"What did you tell him?" Rich asked.

"That I couldn't charge those increases to my customers."

"Sounds like he's firing IPS," Sean observed.

Pug grabbed a piece of the vendor's material. In a fit of frustration, he yanked the ends, ripped it, and yelled, "How do we make this shit go further?" To everyone's surprise, it separated into two identical thinner segments. He yanked again. Two became four. His blue eyes sparkled. "I can reduce this expensive shit!"

"Wait a minute. Less material hurts performance—right, Dr. O'Leary—sir?" Rich asked. Sean sensed Rich's mocking tone but did not respond.

"Think about it over the weekend," Pug insisted. "We'll rainstorm ideas on Monday."

Rich said, "Doc, he means brainstorm."

"Got it." *Asshole!*

That weekend, Pug and Dave installed fiberglass insulation in the basement walls. Dave loved remodeling projects, a welcome break from school homework. Skip avoided these events.

"Dave, see this stuff?"

Dave examined the insulation. "It's got a thin silvery metal-alloy sheet glued to a fibrous layer. Looks like a backing material."

"Maybe so, but this silver lining gives me a terrific idea!"

On Monday, Pug summoned Sean and Rich to the lab.

"Okay guys, gimme your solutions."

"Didn't think about it. Babysat Dad all weekend."

"Doc, what about you?"

"Sorry, Pug. Played in a golf tournament."

Shaking his head in disgust, he handed each a piece of fiberglass insulation. "Whadya think?"

"Standard house insulation," Rich said.

"You're denser than this material. Doc, whadya see?"

"A material like the conductive alloy in my doctoral thesis!"

"Your metal learning finally paid off!"

Rich muttered, "Huh?"

"What if we took a thin layer of the alloy and put it between thinner layers of the moron's material?"

"The alloy adds good thermal properties and minimum width," Sean replied. "My hunch is the alloy-fiber combination provides better thermal dissipation without degrading the acoustic properties."

Pug grinned. "Let's test some prototypes." *Bastard read my brain. My kinda guy.*

A technical frenzy swirled for days as they analyzed multiple configurations. The best solution contained four-layers alternating between metal alloy and acoustical fibrous material. Sean and Pug realized this would be perfect for noise and heat reduction for interior appliance applications. They sent test data, samples, invention notes, and Rich's manufacturing ideas to a local patent attorney.

A few days later, the attorney called. "The prior art search found no obvious issues. I'll file the application. What do you want to call this?"

"IPS should be in the name. It's the first patent," Sean suggested.

Pug proclaimed, "I'm calling it IPS 100 'cuz it's a hundred times better than Applianshit."

"Applianshield," Sean muttered under his breath.

"Easy Doc, just joking," Pug laughed. "Don't get so uppity."

Once the application filed, Pug called his father. "Hey Dad, my company got its first patent!"

The old man snorted, "Darin's company went public. Always knew he'd do good!"

"Yeah, Dad, thanks for the support." Pug slammed the phone. "Didn't hear a damn word. Thinks more of his nephew than his own sons." He looked skyward. "Mom, what'd I do to deserve this?"

Cramped and uncomfortable, and unable to stretch his long legs, Sean maneuvered his Nissan sedan through Denver traffic. He wanted nothing more than to decompress, to enjoy a relaxed weekend after the IPS 100 invention whirlwind.

The radio reported a serious accident stalling traffic for miles on Interstate 70.

"Damn! Right at my exit!" He squinted into blinding late-afternoon sun. "Son of a bitch! Left my shades at the office!"

He lit a Marlboro and inserted a book tape, *Rising Sun,* by Michael Crichton. The narrator began, "There is an old Japanese motto: Business is war."

"Amen!" Sean added. "Couldn't agree more."

Passing the Sheridan exit, he glanced at Willis Case golf course where he spent many enjoyable hours but never broke 85. Nearing the accident, he saw an American sport coupe demolished by an unscathed Toyota.

"Another victory in this 'war of business.'"

Turning onto Wadsworth Boulevard, he drove north. He entered the driveway of his small white-frame 1920's house in Arvada. Knees aching, he climbed the back steps and hurried to relieve a full bladder. The phone rang. The answering machine recorded, "*Konban wa. Ogenki desu ka?*"

"Guess they want a status update."

He grabbed a Sapporo and headed to his office at the rear of the house. Unlocking the door and then his desk, he opened a notebook and wrote bullet points.

– – *Appliancorp consulting work completed; it's sayonara time.*

– – *Sending report and samples of Applianshield material.*

– – *Learned Lawrent Appliance, an Appliancorp vendor, has deep politics with General Appliance's procurement. Will investigate opportunities to establish commercial relations.*

Sean finished his thoughts and put the notes into an envelope with a Chicago address. He opened another Sapporo and inserted a mail-order movie into the VCR. Reclining on the sofa, he watched *Kabuki Coitus.*

Natsuko… I miss you so much. Where are you? Why did you leave me?

SAN FRANCISCO

Driving the Bayshore freeway toward San Francisco, Pug raced past the Velvet Turtle exit.

Marcy asked, "What's bothering you?"

He sighed. "My life in 'Nam. There you knew the enemy, the one shooting at you. At IPS, enemies pop up everywhere: customers, employees, the bank, that asshole vendor!"

"But the vendor's price increase caused you to invent IPS 100."

"You don't get it! Crooks are everywhere!"

"Honestly, sometimes you sound just like your dad. Maybe you should have stayed at MatraScience."

"Yeah, right. All my sacrifice for Doug and what do I get? Nothing!" He swerved into the far left lane almost hitting a Honda sedan. He accelerated. "Should drive all Jap cars off the road!"

Marcy gripped the door handle with one hand and grasped at her heart with the other.

A few minutes later Pug yelled, "There's Candlestick—home of the Bay Area's immaculate reception—you know, Joe's pass to what's-his-name?"

"Dwight Clark?"

"Just a receptacle—in the right place at the right time. Joe had the arm technology."

"Pug, slow down! You'll get a speeding ticket!"

As they continued north, South San Francisco, with its hills and pastel-colored houses, emerged in the hazy sunset like an impressionist painting.

Pug smiled. "Don't you love this? These houses look like poppies in *The Wizard of Oz*. Someday I'll put my company here."

Marcy relaxed. *One minute... furious. The next minute... fantasy. Never a dull minute with this guy. Guess that's why I love him so much.*

Giacomo, the restaurant's owner, greeted them. "How you-a this fine-a November evening? I got-a good Chianti for you!"

He poured wine. Pug swirled it in his mouth and nodded. "The usual, Giacomo." He leaned toward Marcy and twirled his glass. "Well,

Sandra Dee, here's to another last supper. I've owned IPS a year and meeting payroll means I never get paid."

"Why's the company always short of cash?"

"Might have to declare bankruptcy."

"We can't afford bankruptcy! IPS is our sons' future!"

"Can't afford bankruptcy!" Pug laughed. "You sound like me!"

"Been around you too long, sweetie."

"Don't have cash for Uncle Wally's next payment. He accelerated the balloon clause 'cuz I sold too much stock."

"Can Darin help?"

"Ya think? Ted says he's short of cash yet he somehow found money to buy Grandpa Decker's farm."

Giacomo brought antipasto. Pug stared at the delicious array: roasted red peppers, marinated artichokes, grilled eggplant, Parma ham, and olives.

"Things will get better," Marcy sighed. "Remember 1986?"

"My year from hell!" Pug shoveled food onto his plate. "Say, how much credit's left on your American Express?"

"About fifteen thousand. Why?"

"Let's take the boys to Japan for Christmas break."

"Japan? We don't have money."

"Who needs money when you got credit? Besides I'll cash in all those unused MatraScience air miles! With your fifteen-K, we can survive for a week."

"And who pays the credit card?"

"Details, details—personal bankruptcy, whatever."

"Get serious. But why Japan?"

"Found me a Jap company who'll buy IPS 100. If American companies like IPS 100, Japs will too."

She brightened. "Maybe Michael and Ellie would come from Korea and join us!"

"Great idea! Call them tomorrow."

Giacomo brought the pasta course then veal piccata. He tempted them with tiramisu and double espressos. At the end of the meal, he sensed a happier, more relaxed couple.

As they opened the door to Steiner Street, Giacomo yelled out, "Ciao!" Marcy called back, "Thank you, Giacomo!"

FARM RIDGE

After their annual fall hunting trip, Darin and Rich returned to Farm Ridge. Enjoying the mild weather, they relaxed on the front porch of the Decker farmhouse and watched the sun disappear behind brown foothills. The classic 1884 house overlooked a broad lawn, and its backyard blended into now-dry cornfields. Darin had negotiated an attractive lease-purchase option and would exercise it after selling some shares from the company's recent IPO. An architect had designed a $500 thousand renovation.

Enjoying the early evening's quiet, they sipped Coors malt.

"You look pleased," Rich said.

"Things couldn't be better: good hunting, getting this farm, going public. So what's new at IPS?"

"Puggy ordered me to hire Skippy."

"How come?"

"Flunked out at Buffalo U."

They watched a purplish haze emerge on the horizon.

"Puggy coddles him too much," Darin said. "Now you have to babysit him?" He took a long sip of beer. "Hey, you gonna work for Puggy the rest of your life?"

"I owe Puggy a lot. He and Marcy looked after me after Mom died."

"Yeah, like I said before, what's Puggy done for you lately? He'll hold you hostage as payback. If it weren't for me, Puggy woulda never hired you after you got fired from Appliancorp."

"What the hell you talking about?"

"Puggy demanded I invest twenty-five thousand dollars in his company before he offered you a job."

"He never told me that."

"There's a lot of things he won't tell you. Your dad asked me to look out for you. Stick close to me, and I'll see you're taken care of."

DENVER

Mile High National Bank's CEO received a call from Chicago.

"Hey Walter, how are you? How's business?" the CEO asked.

"I'm fine, and the appliance business is great!"

"What can I do for Mile High's major stockholder?"

"I have a new client for your bank and your venture capital affiliate."

"What do you know about this company?"

"Privately owned and just developed some proprietary technology. It's definitely a ground floor opportunity and fits your bank's small business loan portfolio."

"How much due diligence and initial funds?"

"Handshake, start with one-hundred thousand dollars. Let's see what happens."

"I'll get Robby Benton on it," the CEO replied.

NARITA AIRPORT

On December 10, Pug, Marcy, and Skip waited in the visitor's lounge in Tokyo's Narita Airport.

Skip asked, "How much longer before Mr. Kamikaze arrives? We'll miss the Kyoto train!"

"Patience, sweetie," Marcy said, weary from the long flight.

Skip ambled toward a snack bar. His six-foot-five athletic frame, blond hair, and deep blue eyes drew stares.

"I pray he returns to school," she sighed.

"With his grades? Two-and-half friggin' wasted years."

"Why are you so hard on him? You treat him just like your dad treated you at the same age."

"So, I turned out okay. This airport sucks! No signs in English. Goddamn it, we won the war!"

"Speak softer," Marcy whispered.

"Mr. James? Konnichi wa."

Pug turned and saw an exquisitely dressed Japanese gentleman. "Whadya say?"

"Allow me to introduce myself. My name is Kenjiro Kobyashi. We have an appointment."

Pug shook his hand with gusto. With both hands, Kenji presented his meishi positioned so Pug could read it. Pug grabbed the business card and shoved it into his pocket. His faded jeans, sweat shirt, and dirty sneakers contrasted with Kenji's elegant attire.

"Been waiting an hour." *His coal-black hair looks fake.*

"I apologize for the unfortunate delay."

"Marcy, go join Skip."

Embarrassed, Marcy turned and walked away.

"Your wife, Mr. James?"

"Yep, I was told women don't participate in business discussions in Japan."

"Do you have sons?" Kenji asked.

"Two." Pug pointed towards the restaurant. "That hunk over there, my oldest."

"You must be very proud, Mr. James. Would you join me for a drink?" He politely directed Pug to a bar and found a small table. A waiter approached.

"Mr. James, what would you like to drink?"

"Pat Henry. Best damn beer in the U S of A."

"If you permit, I will order."

The waiter brought two large Sapporos. "Allow me." Kenji poured the golden liquid into Pug's glass.

Pug grabbed the other bottle. "Never use glasses. Drink from the bottle. Much cleaner."

"As you wish."

Kenji raised his glass. "Kampai, Mr. James."

"Cheers! Hear ya wanna buy some IPS 100."

"Mr. James, I have not seen IPS 100. I would be pleased if you provided samples."

"No problem-o!" Pug opened his briefcase and handed him two.

"Very interesting, Mr. James." Kenji stared at the shiny metal alloy sandwiched between polyester layers. "What are the benefits of this material?"

Pug launched a fifteen-minute pitch describing the invention and customer reactions.

"Mr. James, can you be more specific about these metal layers?"

"It's a special alloy I discovered. Dissipates heat better. And my acoustics fiber improves the noise control. It's perfect for dishwasher and washing machine applications."

"You must be very proud of your invention. I realize your time is short. With your permission, I will take these samples to our engineers. Do you have thermal and acoustic test data and examples of customer applications?"

"I'll send ya some."

"Excellent. I must leave for an appointment. It has been my pleasure. You must visit our Osaka facility at your earliest convenience."

They shook hands. Pug watched Kenji rush to the taxi stand. Out of view, Kenji entered his limo and called Jun Ashi, Japan Technologies's general manager.

"Is Dr. Yamura's report on the James Family ready?"

"Hai, Kobyashi-san. It is on your desk."

"Excellent!"

Marcy and Skip returned. "How was your meeting?"

"Okay. Nice guy: polite, okay English."

"Did he like IPS 100?" she asked.

"You bet! Invited me to Osaka. Damn, we got less than forty-five minutes to get to the train."

"Told you we'd be late, Pops."

"Race ya to see who gets there first."

Pug and Skip ran as Marcy scrambled to catch up.

TOKYO

The silver-gray Shinkansen train sped towards Tokyo from historic Kyoto after brief stops at Nagoya and Yokohama. Three frustrating days in Kyoto exhausted Marcy's patience.

"You had to rent a car and self-guide us. We missed eighty per cent of the shrines!"

"Big frigging deal! Kyoto is ancient history! This country's so screwed up, they even drive on the wrong side of the road!"

They stared at the passing landscape. The only spoken words came from attendants offering drinks, sandwiches, and candies. Finally Skip asked, "Pops, do I really have to work for Uncle Rich?"

"You flunked the fuck outta college."

"That's unfair!" Marcy snapped.

"You ain't got a vote while I pay the freight!"

At the Tokyo station, Marcy opened her book of English to Japanese expressions. She told the taxi driver, "Teikoku Hoteru!"

"What'd you say, Mom?"

"I told the driver our hotel, the Imperial. It's near the palace."

At hotel registration, they received directions to the restaurant Inakaya, which was a 25-minute walk from the hotel.

Marcy said, "I'm taking a taxi. I'm not keeping Michael and Ellie waiting. Be my guest if you do your self-guided walk."

"I'm hitting the Pachinko parlors," Skip said.

At the Roppongi restaurant, Pug and Marcy heard Michael shout, "Pug! Marcy! Over here!" Marcy hugged Ellie. Pug's handshake crushed Michael's hand.

"Fieldsy, what's this noisy place?" They took seats at a horseshoe-shaped counter amid shouting waiters.

"Waiters just announced we're sitting down. Get ready for *robatayaki*-style dining."

"Robo what?"

"It means 'cooking at fire side.'"

In the room's center, two chefs—each wearing a blue and white bandana—kneeled in front of grills. They were surrounded by food: wicker baskets filled with colorful vegetables and blocks of ice piled with whole fish, giant prawns, and meats. They rapidly and expertly prepared orders shouted to them. The aroma of grilled meats tantalized, and the bustling scene amazed.

"See those long paddles?" Ellie said, "They're for serving drinks and food."

A waiter appeared behind them. Michael ordered four Sapporo O bins. The waiter shouted to the chef. Soon four tall bottles arrived by paddle.

"Wow, bartender and cook all in one!" Pug exclaimed.

"*Kampai* everyone! Welcome to Tokyo!"

"Fieldsy! You speak Jap yap?"

"Passable. My Korean is better."

"You speak kook too?"

"You should trademark your words," Michael laughed. "But be careful about using them in public. It will offend the locals."

Marcy noted that Ellie frowned and nodded in agreement.

"Dave speaks Jap."

"How would you know?" Marcy asked in a sharp tone.

"'Cuz he's got my DNA."

"Dave can get a good job here because companies look for gaijins who speak Japanese," Michael said.

"Yeah, to steal American technology quicker."

"Pug, Japanese are cautious about outsiders."

"Yeah, yeah… hey, look at that cook!" Pug shouted. "Never stands up."

"Ellie, how does he keep track of the orders?" Marcy asked.

"One of many mysteries in Japan."

"Mystery huh?" Pug interjected. "That why Japs drive on the wrong side of the road?"

"You mean the left–hand side?" Michael asked.

"Yeah, the wrong side."

"They got that from the British."

"Figures. Explains why I saw no American cars."

"American auto companies haven't learned how to sell here."

"What's so hard?"

"They don't have patience to meet Japanese standards."

"I'll show 'em with IPS 100."

"Pug, how's IPS doing?"

"Cash's tight. Appliance business sucks."

"You miss MatraScience?"

"You kidding?"

Michael ordered the main course; the waiter shouted to the chef who repeated it. The foursome watched as the chef deftly grilled and sautéed. Soon, he extended the paddle with grilled snapper, Kobe beef, and vegetables. Fresh strawberries were the finale. The noise level made conversation impossible.

Michael shouted, "Let's go to MatraScience's club."

"MatraScience has a private club?"

"Our Japanese country manager's a member. Remember Maurice Oshima?"

"The asshole who sabotaged my sales meeting?"

"What a memory!" Michael laughed. "Maurice became country manager after building a successful power business. Plans to retire soon. If IPS ever needs a senior consultant, he's your man."

"As Buddy Holly said, that'll be the day I hire a Jap consultant."

As the four stood, the waiters announced, "The customers are leaving!"

They taxied to the Ginza. The intimate, quiet bottle club with its subdued lighting, soft music, and hushed voices was inviting and comfortable. As they walked to a table, Michael pointed out glass cases containing members' private liquor stashes. "Look at that one," Michael said, "a dozen bottles of Johnnie Walker Blue."

"Whoa!" Pug breathed. "Somebody knows great scotch." He squinted at the nameplate with the initials KK.

They relaxed and enjoyed cognacs. Guests at other tables smoked pungent Japanese cigarettes.

"Will Japs ever stop smoking like chimneys?"

Michael replied, "Not in your lifetime."

"How do you like living in Korea?" Marcy asked.

"Very much," Ellie replied, "I've learned a lot. I'm studying international securities law at Seoul University."

"I like the business challenge," Michael added. "Different cultures require adjustments. American 'in-your-face' approach never works in Asia."

"Hard to get in their face when they won't talk English like Europe!"

"You mean like they do in France?" Michael joked. "When we first visited Kyoto, we got lost. A local asked in clear English if he could help. Went out of his way to escort us to the correct train station. Japanese are very considerate and many speak excellent English."

"Yeah, well, I couldn't find those guys in Koto."

"You never gave Kyoto locals a chance," Marcy said.

"What brings you to Japan? Vacation or business?" Ellie interjected.

Pug answered, "A sake-sipper's gonna buy tons of my IPS 100. Exporting to Japan will offset the trade deficit caused by Americans buying Jap cars."

Michael chuckled. "Pug, you need to learn the economic laws of comparative advantage and free trade."

"You some kind of economy?"

"Yes," Ellie answered. "Michael has a degree in economics."

"I'll be damned! Anyway, besides doing some business, we wanted one more family fling before IPS crashes."

Michael and Ellie looked puzzled.

"Hey, just kidding!" Pug grinned.

"You better be," Marcy said, not smiling.

"Once IPS 100 takes off, we'll be fine."

"Pug, don't depend on Japanese customers. It took MatraScience five years to book its first order."

"IPS technology will impress the slant eyes."

Ellie's smile froze. *If I hear one more racist remark...*

Michael warned, "Pug, be careful. Don't confuse politeness or silence with agreement, or you'll spend all your time translating lies."

"My technology will open their komotos."

"Maybe, but opening Japanese kimonos requires respecting their culture. Tradition requires allegiance to the common good; teamwork is crucial. Most important, avoid confrontation."

"Hey Fieldsy, this place sounds boring as hell."

"Okay, enough business talk!" Ellie said. "How long are you here?"

"We're leaving in two days," Marcy answered.

"Next time you visit, plan to come to Seoul." *But leave Pug at home.* Two more rounds of cognac, and they returned to the hotel.

"Pug hasn't lost his naiveté and can-do optimism," Michael said as they readied for bed. "He's passionate about technology, but you know what I like most about him?"

"His obnoxious and racist comments?"

"He doesn't mean those things. He always talks crazy. I love his 'Pugisms.' He's fun to be around. His energy, humor, and work ethic are contagious. And that innovative brain... did I ever tell you about his..."

"At least twenty times. If he spouts his opinions to Asians like he did with us, he'll offend everybody."

"He's got a generous heart. He raised his brother Rich after their mom died."

"I do like Marcy. She's sweet, proud of her sons. She's a saint to live with that motor mouth. Did you see her wince after some of Pug's comments?"

"You have to cut them some slack. They've been through a lot and managed to survive."

"Michael, don't forget you played a role in helping him during those difficult times."

"Maybe. I regret not devoting more effort to keeping him at MatraScience."

1991
OSAKA

"**H**AVE A GREAT TRIP, SWEETIE," Marcy cooed as she double-parked at San Francisco Airport. She kissed Pug on the cheek. "Tell Mr. K to buy lots of IPS 100."

The cold, rainy March weather aggravated Pug's arthritis. He waved a half-hearted goodbye and shuffled to economy check-in. Passengers snaked forward in a cloud of cigarette smoke.

Oh great! A line of slant-eyed smoking sake-sippers!

Pug's foul mood was compounded by congested sinuses and a stiff neck. Forty-five minutes later, with garment bag slung over one sore shoulder and a heavy briefcase pulling on the other, he boarded his flight.

The only reason I'm taking this goddamn trip is Kenji keeps beggin' me to visit Jap Tech. Said if American customers like IPS 100 so will their customers.

Sean gave me books on doing business with Japs. Learn easy words like hello, goodbye, how to bow, keep your jacket buttoned, show respect... and other face-saving shit!

Pug eased into the narrow seat. He had ignored Sean's advice to fly business class. His search for the cheapest ticket resulted in booking a last row, middle seat on an aging Boeing 747-300.

After inhaling dinner, Pug watched the film, *Rising Sun*. At the end, he pushed two sticks of Big Red in his mouth. He caught a seatmate's annoyed stare.

"So whadya think of Sean Connery's character?"

"He knew his way around Japanese culture," the passenger replied.

"Gimme a break! How do they get anything done with that bowing, seniority-is-everything stuff?"

"You have to respect their culture and traditions," the man said wearily.

"Are they all corrupt like the movie says?"

His seatmate yawned. "Unlike Chinese and Koreans, Japanese value intellectual property." He closed his eyes, ending the conversation.

Jun Ashi sat in Kenji's office. Jun had joined Japan Technologies after Patrick Hafferty's untimely death. Kenji groomed him to become managing director of operations and trusted assistant.

Kenji's secretary placed a tray in front of them. They sipped hot tea and scanned a report prepared by Dr. Yamura, Kenji's personal attorney and chief counsel for Japan Technologies and for TADA.

The report highlights included:

– – *Pug James's mechanical engineering degree from University of Colorado, graduation with honors and earning a ROTC commission.*

– – *His four-year military service in Viet Nam with Green Berets and awarded three Purple Hearts.*

– – *His role in a controversial general discharge of Sergeant Joseph Sacker.*

– – *Employment at two Colorado Springs-based engineering firms before joining MatraScience.*

– – *His technical accomplishments, including seven granted patents at MatraScience.*

– – *His marital separation and recurring financial problems.*

– – *His father's commitment at a Menlo Park mental hospital.*

Kenji lit a cigarette, exhaled, and leaned back in his leather chair. "As usual, Dr. Yamura has done comprehensive research. Mr. James is a most interesting talent."

"Hai! Dr. Yamura was very impressed with Mr. James's role in launching the connection systems market for MatraScience. It now sells over one hundred million dollars annually."

"Yes, Jun. He excels at solving customer and vendor technical problems with proprietary solutions. That talent can be useful for TADA."

"Hai!"

"Ask Dr. Yamura to research more about Sergeant Sacker and his discharge from the Green Berets."

Jun nodded.

Two hours after arriving in Japan, Pug relaxed aboard the Nozomi Shinkansen express from Narita Airport to Osaka. Clean and quiet, the sleek silver train sped at 200 kilometers an hour. Pug watched the countryside flash past. He marveled at the well-designed buildings, highways, and neat farms.

Kenji had booked him at Hotel Osaka. The staff accorded him every courtesy. He showered and, while shaving, studied the toilet's electronic features. Room service delivered Kobe steak and eggs, which he washed down with a pot of strong coffee.

A taxi waited at the hotel entrance, and the bellman gave Pug's destination to the driver. The driver, dressed in suit and tie, wore a mask.

From the back seat, Pug yelled, "What's with the mask?" The driver eyed him in the rear view mirror. "Oh, yeah, forgot... no speaka da English."

After fifteen minutes in heavy city traffic, the taxi turned into a broad avenue lined with impressive plantings and trees and leading to an industrial park. The driver slowed as they passed a sign with Japanese symbols and the letters *JT* below. Beneath were more Japanese names and the letters, *NTOOL*, *RAD*, and *GN*.

Whew, a real alphabet soup!

The taxi parked in front of an ultramodern glass and steel structure. The driver pointed to the meter. "Want some yen, do ya?" Pug asked.

He entered the building and found Kenji waiting in the lobby.

"*Ohayou gozaimasu*, Mr. James."

"What?"

"I said good morning."

"Oh, yeah, morning to you too." Pug squeezed Kenji's hand, put his left arm around Kenji's shoulder and gave him a firm back slap. Kenji flinched.

"Mr. James, a pleasure to see you. I trust you had a satisfactory flight?"

"Call me Pug. Say Kenji, what's the deal with the masked driver?"

"It is precautionary to prevent spreading colds and flu."

"Trying to figure out this alphabet soup, Kenji. I guess 'JT' stands for your company?"

"Correct, Mr. James."

"So what the heck's NTOOL and RAD and GN?"

"NTOOL stands for Nippon Tooling, RAD is Research Appliance Devices, and GN is Gano-Nippon. Mr. James, allow me to show you our company."

They entered the state-of-the-art manufacturing facility. They paused on a mezzanine to survey the plant floor. The operations were first class: organized, clean, machines operating in perfect harmony. The workers wore identical hats and white uniforms. Pug noticed framed certificates on the wall.

"What are these?"

"Quality awards earned by the company from customers: Hondoya, General Appliance of Japan, and Niota."

Among the plaques, Pug saw a photo of Kenji shaking hands with a tall, elderly, bald-headed American. "Who's that?"

"Mr. Edward Demming. He taught us quality in the 1950s. He said quality is the key to better productivity and profits. It requres discipline and patience."

"Bet the geezer never invented a single thing. Impatience is key to innovation."

"Geezer? Please explain."

"Old folks, you know, anyone over sixty."

Kenji led Pug to the tool-making area. "Please meet chief tool engineer, Tanaka-san. He designs tools for our dissipater products."

"*Hajimemashite*, Mr. James."

Pug looked at Kenji. "Huh?"

"He is pleased to meet you. Tanaka-san, please speak English."

"Excuse me. Welcome to Japan Technologies. It is my honor to show you tooling department."

Pug surveyed the room. *This is a first-rate operation.*

Pug and Kenji arrived at the reception area leading to Kenji's conference room. While Kenji conferred with an aide, Pug eyed framed photographs on a credenza. In one photo, a younger Kenji posed with an American couple and a boy; in another, Kenji stood with three men wearing 1950's business attire. The last showed an attractive young woman.

"Your daughter, Kenji?" *She a Jap? Looks different.*

"No. May I ask, Mr. James, your first name, does it have special meaning?"

"Long story, Kenji. My mother named me Paul. My dad hated it, so he called me Pug. Told me I was like a pugilist, you know, a fighter. I kinda like that."

"Very interesting, Mr. James."

They entered the impressive room where five men stood around an enormous glass conference table. Pug had never seen an office like this. Three walls of glass, floor-to-ceiling, provided a spectacular panorama of distant mountains and a nearby lake. Gleaming furniture and high-backed leather chairs projected wealth and strength.

Kenji introduced each gentleman, moving clockwise around the table. "Mr. James, please meet our managing director of operations, Ashi-san." Jun, thin and stooped, presented his card to Pug. In quick succession, Pug met the others, each showing a card with the company logo. Kenji announced impressive sounding job titles, and everyone's name ended in *san*. To Pug, all names and cards blurred.

Pug surveyed the attendees. *All part of the San family?*

All remained standing until Kenji sat. Pug noticed ornate hand-carved figures at the center of the table. "You play chess, Kenji?" Pug asked.

"Chess is one of my passions, a game rewarding strategy and foresight," he replied.

"Checkers's my game."

"Interesting," Kenji said with a slight smile. "Mr. James, we are most impatient to learn about IPS 100."

Pug launched a rapid thirty-minute pitch emphasizing IPS 100's features and benefits. He paused to show examples of test results and pictures of applications.

Pug concluded, "So, IPS 100 technology revolutionized the appliance industry. Manufacturers will no longer use fiberglass and mineral wool for dissipaters. They get real technical and economic improvement by using IPS 100. IPS needs a sales rep in Japan. Can your company handle it?"

Pug looked at the audience. *They've really paid attention. Not one interruption.*

"Mr. James, please excuse us," Kenji said. "It is much easier if we discuss your informative presentation in Japanese."

"Take your time. Gave ya lots to chew on."

After a few minutes of spirited discussion, Kenji spoke. "Mr. James, IPS 100 is most impressive. American customers must be pleased. How much does your company currently sell?"

"Current projects are worth several million dollars."

Kenji spoke in Japanese. "Very optimistic."

Pug heard a collective but muted "hai, hai."

Pug wondered, *What's with these hi's?*

"Mr. James, IPS 100 is very similar to Japan Technologies's fiberglass composite products. The only differences are these metal layers. Even if your material performs better, the economics make no sense. Allow me to explain. The manufacturing and logistics costs from your American plant combined with our expensive sales and distribution costs in Japan require charging more than Japan Technologies's current prices. We would lose market share. Therefore, we see no near-term opportunities for selling IPS 100."

Kenji continued in Japanese. "IPS 100 material is a clever improvement. It could lead to more innovative solutions for our dissipaters."

Pug interrupted, "Looks like we can't do business. Call me a taxi." *You polite sons-a-bitches... didn't understand one technical point. Thought you were engineers.* He packed his briefcase and snapped it shut.

Kenji took a dissipater from a nearby table and handed it to Pug. "Mr. James, we make and ship five thousand of these each day for Hondoya's current water heater models."

Pug dropped his briefcase and examined the dissipater. *Fuck, at that rate, annual volumes are over a million units a year!*

"We sell each dissipater for five hundred yen," Kenji continued.

Pug's digital mind converted yen to dollars. *Holy shit! Five and half million dollars a year! This one application is bigger than IPS!*

Kenji enjoyed Pug's stunned look. He handed Pug a thick spiral-bound volume. "Hondoya has issued new specification for dissipaters. If we can meet the requirements, we can supply new products for Hondoya's new models. Mr. James, Hondoya will produce one and a half million appliances per year with multiple dissipaters on each."

Pug's eyes widened. *My god, what an opportunity!*

He flipped through the 45 pages. "You got this in English...?"

"Please study it," Kenji said. "Give us your ideas. If you cannot, we will find someone who can."

Kenji hosted dinner at the "Comfort Station." The building, dating to World War II, once housed Korean prostitutes for Japanese soldiers. Now a restaurant, it was famous for its Kobe beef.

Kenji invited Pug to a private room where they settled cross-legged on to the tatami. Two attractive hostesses caught Pug's eye. They wore kimonos with brightly colored *obis* wrapped tightly around their tiny waists. They carried drinks on lacquered trays.

Pug stared as they served sushi and sashimi. *Gorgeous gals!*

Kenji invited Pug to try the first course. Pug fumbled the chopsticks, finally resorting to fingers.

"What's this duct tape around these rice balls?" Pug asked, his mouth full.

"Mr. James, it is seaweed."

"Real tasty." Soy sauce dribbled down his chin.

For the second course, Kenji ordered drunken prawns and sake. As Pug watched live prawns struggling to escape boiling alcohol, he missed Kenji's comment: "Observe the futile struggle."

Dinner finished, Kenji escorted Pug to his private izakaya bottle club in the Osaka business district. After sitting on tatami mats at the restaurant, Pug welcomed a comfortable chair. An attendant brought Johnnie Walker Blue. Two ladies appeared, and Kenji invited them to join.

"Mr. James, allow me to introduce Nani and Suzi. If you recall, they served us dinner."

The elegant young women now wore stylish and form-fitting dresses. Suzi joined Pug while Nani sat near Kenji.

Pug was delighted. *Suzi's one cute Jap! Tiny but stacked! But Nani's different: her round green eyes, reddish hair... something familiar about her.*

After a short and pleasant conversation, Kenji and Nani said good night and departed. Suzi poured more Johnny Walker Blue and convinced Pug to try karaoke at a nearby club. Late into the night, they drank, laughed, and sang. At four a.m., Pug finished with "Always Look for the Silver Lining." Suzi thanked him for a pleasant evening and excused herself.

Kenji insisted Pug stay an extra night in Tokyo as a guest of Japan Technologies. His secretary arranged a room at Ginza's Dai-ichi Hotel. The concierge gave him maps and directions to the Imperial Palace. Pug walked along a street parallel to railway tracks. The tracks sat above the street on a brick infrastructure, resembling a series of brick pizza ovens. Under each archway was a different type of restaurant all with ceilings with silver-like finishes.

What if I put the metal alloy in pizza ovens? Or in appliances with big exhaust hoods?

Pug walked for hours and shopped in the Ginza district. He returned to the hotel for an early dinner and ended the evening with a beer in the hotel's nightclub. The choking cigarette haze and loud conversation brought a quick headache. He went to his room and phoned Marcy.

"Sweetie, flying out tomorrow."

"How's Tokyo?"

"Great! Walked about ten miles, had a nice dinner, got an idea for a new invention."

"How's the hotel?"

"You should see the toilets."

"What?"

"A toilet's for taking a crap, but here you can have a douche, get your butt warmed, and who knows what else. If I'd invented this, it would wipe too!"

Marcy laughed. "Always inventing; go to bed."

Pug turned on the TV. "Since the Jap's paying, why not?" He laughed himself to sleep watching a porn movie, *Nippon Delights.*

DENVER

On his return flight, an agitated Pug scowled and sulked. As the plane ascended, his thoughts raced. *Bastards rejected IPS 100. Why the hell...? But if I solved the new spec, it'd mean lotsa of bucks! At least I got Suzi's number.*

Pug changed planes in San Francisco and headed to Denver. When he arrived at the IPS facility in the aging industrial park, he thought, *When I get some cash, this shit hole is history.*

Pug's office, at the center of the main building, gave him instant access to Sean, Rich, and Bruce Hargett, IPS's new accountant. Bruce had earned an MBA at Colorado State and completed his CPA with Arthur Hansen. Capable and efficient, he followed Pug's instructions without challenge. Rich called him "Puggy's go-fetch fag."

Pug's voice boomed down the hallway, "Got a minute?" To all, this meant "get to my conference room now!"

Rich, Sean, and Bruce gathered around Pug's teakwood table.

"Anybody know Jap yap?" Pug dropped the thick specification binder on the table. Bruce scanned and slid it to Rich.

"What the hell's this mumbo jumbo?" Rich demanded.

"Hondoya's new appliance model specs."

"We've got plenty of American specs and in English!"

"I'll make some calls," Bruce said. "Translating could be expensive."

Pug frowned at Rich. "Wish you had Bruce's can-do attitude. He acts while you bitch. Old Kenjikaze asked me to solve this. The business is worth at least fifty million a year!"

"So Japs move faster than Americans," Rich snarled. "Another Puggy-Hail-Mary-bullshit project!"

Bruce returned thirty minutes later. "Three quotes. Expect to pay three to five thousand dollars. Cheapest is University of Colorado."

"Doc, is it worth it?"

"Sounds like we can't afford it," Sean replied.

"What the hell!" Pug sighed, "Get it translated."

As they left the conference room, Sean asked, "How was Japan?"

"Almost got hit by a taxi. Bastards drive on the wrong side. Got a good one for you. I watched a Jap porn movie. What a hoot! The naughty parts were blocked out."

"What was the title?"

"Don't remember." *Why would you care?*

On April 14, the translated spec arrived with a $4,500 invoice.

Pug ordered, "Sean and Rich, read this damn thing! We meet in an hour." He fumed to Bruce, "Put this shitty bill on the bottom of the payment pile."

When they re-assembled Pug announced, "Dave's here on school break, and I want him to watch and learn."

Pug thumbed the 45-page document. "Like I told my soldiers in 'Nam, the mission is simple…"

"Quiet everybody, General George Puggy speaks." Rich smirked.

"Bruce, take notes and get a camera to film this. Listen up! We need a recyclable material that meets or beats tough heat and noise criteria within tight dimensions."

"Recyclable means no materials like fiberglass, polyester, asbestos, ceramics, etc.," Sean added.

"That's why Kenji rejected IPS 100. Besides it can't pass the spec's higher temps."

"American customers don't need recyclable shit, and we know shit-all about Japan," Rich snapped.

"Shut the fuck up!" Pug yelled. "Now, what are acceptable materials?" He approached the whiteboard and listed six possibilities along with Sean's suggestion: the IPS 100 metal alloy. Pug and Sean sorted the candidates into operating thermal ranges. They narrowed the list to three, which passed the 250 degrees Celsius criterion.

Pug jabbed his finger in the air. "Let's test prototypes!"

They crowded into the development lab, IPS 100's birthplace: a small, windowless and musty room, crammed with antiquated test equipment except for a new $90 thousand thermal imaging camera.

"Rich, get a table for making samples."

"And where do I put it? On top of your new toy?"

Pug ignored him. "Doc, set up test rigs with the propane thermal source. Dave, get enough thermocouples to measure temps. We'll measure twenty-five different locations above, between, and below the material layers. Doc, position the camera to take temperature images from different angles."

"Pops, I'll help Dr. O'Leary with the camera," Dave said.

"Okay, get crankin'!"

"Pug," Sean said, "you remind me of General Patton directing traffic at that crossroads with the tanks and trucks stuck in the mud."

"Pug'll court martial us for invention fatigue," Rich muttered.

"If we don't have an invention in ten days, I'll discharge you like I did Sergeant Sacker in 'Nam."

Sean asked, "Who's Sergeant Sacker?"

"Some guy who crossed Pug in Viet Nam," Rich added.

That evening, Pug and Dave ate at a sports bar on Larimer Street. "So Davey, have fun today?"

"Is work always chaotic like this? Uncle Rich argues, Dr. O'Leary's arrogant, and Bruce takes notes."

"My chaos stimulates creativity! I want a written record of my brilliance. Bean counters take good notes."

Each morning, Pug's mini-army reviewed the previous day's progress. Pug generated experiments requiring new prototypes and more testing. By day eight, the material candidates narrowed to one.

"Well Doc, your metal alloy survived."

As if thinking out loud, Sean said, "We know this alloy conducts heat, but can it insulate?"

"Wait a minute! I got it!" Pug shouted. "If we use multiple layers and separate them, you get radiation and convection as well as conduction—trifecta! For more insulation, add more layers."

Sean made a mental note. *Later I'll add acoustic materials for noise reduction.*

Rich sketched layers of metal alloy separating the thermal source from the protected object. "When heat hits the first layer, what happens?" he asked.

"Easy," Sean replied. "The closest alloy layer to the thermal source reflects eighty percent of the heat back toward the source; that's radiation."

"But what happens to the twenty percent?" Rich asked.

"Stupid question!" Pug interjected. "Why'd ya think I said multiple layers? The second layer reflects eighty percent of that heat, ditto for the third, fourth and so on. If we keep space between the layers, you have the best of all insulators—air!"

"Now you got convection working!" Sean added.

Rich looked skeptical. "What happens to the heat trapped between the layers?"

"Davey, tell Uncle Richie what I taught you."

"Radiation, convection, and conduction. This alloy hasn't lost its conductive properties. It's one of the best, second only to copper. The heat will flow horizontally along each layer's surface to its outer edges."

"Richie, Davey's only twenty and knows more than you. Let's build some more samples and test my theories. If it doesn't work, I'll sue Doc for mispractice."

Bruce asked, "Don't you mean malpractice?"

"That's what I said."

They conducted more thermal experiments with varying sample sizes. With the thermal source on one side and thermocouples attached to the alloy layers, it was easy to measure temperature reduction. The thermal camera captured exact images of the hotter and cooler portions. On the thirteenth morning, the latest samples still failed the specification.

"Doc, your material sucks. Too much heat gets through the layers. Back to the drawing board! Your theorems stink," Pug barked.

"Not so quick! I re-read my doctoral thesis last night. Two of the three elements work: radiation and convection. We've proved it with the thermal images, but conduction doesn't."

"Wait a minute," said Rich muttered, his head down. He sketched furiously. "It must conduct heat somewhere."

Pug's face lit up. "You're right! The heat has to get deluded."

"And diluted too, or better, dissipated to a place pulling the heat," Sean added.

Rich sketched several layers but with an important change. He shaded in the area around the layer's edges. He held up the drawing and pointed to the shading.

"What's that?" Pug asked.

"Compressed edges... to suck heat away from the center of each layer."

"Brilliant!" Sean said. "And if this compressed edge is attached to another structure, then the heat dissipates into it. But you forgot one item."

"What?" Pug asked.

"How do you keep the individual layers separated to allow convection principles to work? Our prototypes are jerry-rigged for testing. We need permanent gaps between layers."

The group sat in silence and stared at Rich's sketch. Dave glanced around the room, then up at rectangular grids covering the fluorescent ceiling lights. Like oversized ice trays, the units had distinct horizontal and vertical patterns. Dave pointed up.

Pug's eyes moved upward. He stood on his chair and pulled down a grid. They inspected the three-dimensional pattern.

"And Davey Edison said, 'Let there be light!'" Pug announced. "If we take each individual alloy layer and alternate the dents then..."

"Or you could put an extra layer between each standard layer to do the same thing," Sean said. He scribbled a note: *Defensive patent— Thermal Acoustic Integrator (TAI).*

Pug laughed out loud. "Doc, that's the dumbest thing I've ever heard."

"Regardless, each layer won't align allowing permanent space between," Sean insisted.

"To the lab!" Pug ordered.

After two more days, the overworked team discovered an elegant yet simple solution. Sean's theories, Rich's practical mechanics, and Pug's manic energy converted a conductive metal alloy into an insulation dissipater. It surpassed all spec requirements. Rich sketched the manufacturing process for indenting the material and creating the compressed edges. Pug named the product IPS 10000.

"Why 10000?" Dave asked.

"'Cuz it's a hundred times better than IPS 100!"

"You should call Mr. Kobyashi," Sean said.

"Remember what President Reagan said? Verify then trust."

"That's backwards," Rich replied.

"Patent first, then trust."

That evening, Pug headed to Denver's Monte Carlo Hotel. Exhausted, he skipped his usual nightcap and called Marcy. "Sweetie, I solved Hondoya's spec. Once I file for a patent, it's Kenji bar the door! What time is it in Korea?"

"Early morning. Why?"

"Talk to you tomorrow, sweetie." Pug dialed Michael's number. "Fieldsy! How ya doing?"

"Pug, a voice from the past! What's up?"

"Things are really popping! Invented IPS 10000, a hundred times better. Get it?"

Michael laughed, "You've used that logic before."

"Need to file a patent. My local gator quit on me. Know any moonlighters at MatraScience's legal group?"

"You remember Jackson?"

"Hell, yes!"

"Here's his number. He's a partner at Dexter-Foresmen, a first-rate San Francisco IP firm."

"Thanks, Fieldsy."

At the end of the month, Jackson Huntley flew to Denver and met Pug in IPS's lobby. Pug had forgotten how thin and gaunt Jackson looked. Then he remembered: triathlon.

"Jackson, you and me are soul mates! Fieldsy told me about you and Isaac. That guy still mucking things up at MatraScience?"

"You mean my legal acid reflux? He's the reason I left MatraScience."

"Asshole tried to screw me over with a lawsuit for insider trading. I did real good with puts and calls. Got me one tough gator, Gordon Orlio, and I sued back. Isaac ran with his tail between his legs. But, hey, you're here for more important stuff! Lemme give ya a quick tour."

After Pug had taken Jackson through the plant and the lab, they sat in Pug's office. "Whadya think?"

Jackson hesitated. "It's uh…"

"What you saw is a temporary delusion. I got big plans." Pug launched into a description of the 10000 invention, showed prototype samples, and spouted ideas for more inventions. His enthusiasm reminded Jackson of their past collaborations.

Jackson studied the spec and examined test results.

"I'm under time pressure here," Pug said. "Kenji wants Hondoya to see it."

"Sign a confidentiality agreement. That'll protect your ideas."

"A patent gives more protection."

"Pug, the US Patent Office will never grant a patent."

"Why not?"

"All you have are layers of common metal alloy connected by edge compressions. Must be considerable prior art; and besides, this invention is too obvious for someone skilled in metallurgical art."

"Jackson, there's a sixty million-a-year opportunity here!"

The next two days Jackson interviewed Rich, Sean, and Bruce to understand the invention. Bruce's notes and video documented the creative process. Sean explained the test results. Rich described the manufacturing processes. Back in California, Jackson's initial search revealed no prior art. He drafted comprehensive patent claims, reviewed them with Pug, and filed.

He called Pug. "To cover all bases, I've filed documents with the Japanese patent office to establish provisional disclosure priority.

If a US patent grants, we'll file in every country IPS plans to sell or manufacture. I listed three co-inventors."

"Three?"

"The patent procedures are very clear; everyone contributed. You and Sean had the original ideas how the multiple alloy layers work, and Rich reduced the idea to practice especially the method for integrating the metal alloy layers."

"If I hadn't kicked everybody's ass, there wouldn't be no invention."

"Think of it this way. IPS will own the patent and you..."

"Own IPS!" Pug laughed out loud.

In Tokyo, a clerk at Japan's national patent office copied and distributed the disclosure filing for IPS 10000.

In Singapore, MMc Ltd. filed for a patent called Sing 1000 with a disclosure date two months prior to the filing of IPS 10000. The patent filing incorporated the novel concept of integrating acoustics materials with metal alloy layers.

DENVER

"Sake time!" Pug hollered in the hallway. "Ol' slant eyes wants samples, but...!"

Sean responded, "But what?"

"The P in IPS stands for 'protected.' I faxed him a confidentiality agreement."

"But the patent's filed."

"Why use a condom when your wife's on the pill? Extra protection!"

"What did Mr. Kobyashi say?"

"Some Jap yap about trust, blah, blah."

Kenji returned the agreement within forty-eight hours. Pug waved the fax at Sean.

"Kenji knows I own the silver, and I make the rules! Send him a package with a letter telling him no can show it until I get there."

Sean shook his head. "A letter adds more insult."

"Tough! Anyway, I got me a scheme: Someday, all customers will use IPS 10000 for dissipaters, thermal and acoustics." Pug gestured as if orating. "I'll invent multi-dimensional shapes and produce low cost products in large volumes. IPS will be the Johns Mansville of dissipater insulation. I'll license everyone! How 'bout them apples?"

"Interesting." *And visionary.*

In mid-May, Kenji phoned Pug. Sean sat in Pug's office and listened to the conversation.

"Mr. James, Hondoya invites you to visit Tokyo."

"Geez, Kenji. Short notice!"

"Mr. James, very important officials will attend. If you cannot come, Japan Technologies will represent IPS. We must not disappoint Hondoya. Our competitors have already presented acceptable solutions."

Pug muted the speakerphone and leaned toward Sean. "Means cancelling Chicago visit and leaving this Friday."

"Pug, I'll cover Chicago for you."

Pug engaged the speaker. "Okay Kenji, I'll be there Monday."

"Mr. James, a wise decision."

As Pug ended the call, he told Sean, "Doc, forgot to say... last week some venture capitalist named Robby Benton contacted me. Looking to invest in firms with new technologies. When I told him about IPS 100 and 10000, he couldn't wait to invest. He's a wannabe engineer."

"How much?"

"Hundred K, and the best part he's a handshake type-of-guy."

"That's great. IPS could use the money."

"Who's talking IPS? I sold him some of my personal shares."

TOKYO

On the plane to Tokyo, Pug sat next to a Japanese mother with a colicky baby who without warning, vomited on him. In spite of efforts to clean up, the odor persisted making the long flight miserable. A headache, dry sinuses, and upset stomach compounded his discomfort. He was in a foul mood by the time he checked into the Dai-ichi Hotel.

Next morning, he walked three blocks to Hondoya's headquarters. Pausing at an intersection, a wet substance hit his scalp. *Fuck! Bird shit and no handkerchief!*

Kenji greeted Pug in Hondoya's lobby and escorted him to the men's room. "This is your good fortune, Mr. James. A Japanese proverb says encountering a bird before an important event signals success."

The meeting commenced in Hondoya's main conference room. The walls of the huge room displayed elegant paintings and Japanese scrolls.

Kenji opened the meeting. "Mr. James, may I present Okazaki-san and his staff. His staff approves all new thermal and acoustic materials for new models of home and commercial appliances."

Each gentleman presented his meishi with both hands extended. Pug reversed each unable to locate English translations. None of the attendees spoke.

Kenji continued, "Mr. James, kindly speak slowly, so I can translate."

Pug's discomfort increased at each translation pause. Midway through, Pug stated, "IPS 10000 exceeds each Hondoya spec requirement."

"Mr. James, please stop for one moment. We must confer."

In Japanese, Shiganari said, "Hondoya's tests confirm Mr. James's claims for thermal improvements, weight and space savings. Our cost analysts estimate this material can reduce dissipater component costs by fifty percent."

"Nippon Tooling confirms tooling costs will decrease by seventy-five percent," Kenji added.

Shiganari concluded, "IPS 10000 is environmentally acceptable. Kenji, Hondoya will designate this project as priority one for our keiretsu."

"TADA will undertake extraordinary actions to perfect, engineer, and market! Considerable work remains to introduce, price, and control this new technology," Kenji said. "Market stability, sustained profits, and proprietary protection are paramount."

Pug watched the animated discussion. *Boy, musta said something that jazzed the slant eyes.*

Kenji invited Pug to resume his usual 45-minute pitch. Three hours passed.

Shiganari stood and announced, "Kenji, tell Mr. James to provide more product samples." He shook Pug's hand and exchanged bows with Kenji.

"Mr. James," Kenji said, "Okazaki-san informs me it takes nine months for engineering tests and economic analyses."

"I thought Hondoya was in a big hurry."

"Hondoya does not permit haste."

"Yeah, no wonder nothing gets invented here."

Ignoring the comment, Kenji extended his hand. "Safe journey, Mr. James."

Pug returned to the Dai-Ichi to check out. He had five hours before departure. Suzi did not answer his call. In a glum mood, he taxied to Narita.

DENVER

Back in Denver, Pug summoned Sean and Rich. "Fell on my sword again. Flew cattle-car and a crying, slant-eyed baby puked on me. Then a bird crapped on my head."

Pug described the meeting and Hondoya's request. Rich exploded, "We've blown 50K in labor and materials with nothing to show for it!"

Sean's pale face reddened. "Rich, Japanese are cautious, methodical, avoid mistakes, never make false promises, think in years and decades, and build things that do not fail. Until you understand this…"

"How would you know?" Rich glowered.

"I read books."

"Rich, send more samples to Hondoya," Pug demanded. "They don't trust your test data."

"My data?"

"Do it, damn it!"

Rich, cursing under his breath, stomped out.

Pug turned to Sean. "Doc, the Japs will take to long. We gotta get IPS 10000 into Chicago, pronto!"

"We need full-time local sales presence."

"Can't afford full-time guys."

"So what's your plan?"

"At MatraScience, I hired sales reps. Costs nothing till they produce."

"I know some rep groups in Chicago."

"Check 'em out, but remember I decide."

As Sean was leaving, Pug added, "Kenji said bird shit is good luck. You believe that?"

"You could use some luck about now."

A few days later, Sean and Rich waited in Pug's conference room. "IPS teeters between insolvency and bankruptcy," Rich said. "Not sure IPS will survive before this year's out."

With Bruce at his heels, Pug entered and announced, "Bruce ran out of cash... again."

"Pug, that's not fair," Bruce said, nervously adjusting his bow tie.

Pug enjoyed teasing Bruce but respected his work ethic, dedication to IPS, and solving the accounting mess left by the former bookkeeper.

"Damn it! I never get a friggin' break. Vendors and customers always screw me."

"Then quit chasing crazy ideas—like Hondoya," Rich said.

"If you don't like it here, take a hike!"

Rich stood and threw his keys at the table, scratching the surface. "Fuck you, I quit!" He stormed out.

Pug shrugged. "He'll be back after a night on the town. Wants an excuse to gamble, drink, and..." Pug smiled and jammed his right middle finger into a circle formed by his left hand. "He had a tough childhood. Mom made me promise to look after him."

"How many times has he quit before?" Sean inquired.

"Who knows, I've lost count."

"Pug, we don't have cash to meet the next payroll," Bruce said.

"You know what to do. Stiff the vendors!"

"When they put IPS on C.O.D. and the plant shuts down, don't blame me. And Farm Ridge National Bank started last rites."

"Got any more good news?"

Bruce's lips tightened. He stifled a reply and stared past Pug.

"Hey, loosen up! I'm kidding! Go do a six-month cash flow projection."

Bruce returned to his office and slammed his note pad on the desk. "I'm nothing but an accounts payable clerk!"

The following month, Pug and Sean studied Bruce's forecast containing numerous footnotes and exhibits. The phone rang. When Pug heard Kenji's voice, he switched on the speakerphone. "*Konnichi wa wa*, Kenji."

"Good morning, Mr. James. Attempting Japanese, I see."

"*Hi*! Sean's with me." Sean stifled a smile.

"Good morning, Dr. O'Leary."

"Hello, Mr. Kobyashi."

"Mr. James, Hondoya's engineers tested IPS 10000. They think it may work, but…"

"Wait! You told me it would take nine months."

"Hondoya reorganized, priorities changed, and the new model testing accelerated."

Pug's mind raced. *This means IPS 10000 for everything…*

"Mr. James, Hondoya's 'just-in-time' policy prevents import of critical components."

Pug's whispered to Sean, "What the fuck is 'just-in-time?'" He raised his hands in exasperation.

Sean shrugged his shoulders in agreement.

Pug's mind flashed. *Haven't got time to set up manufacturing and marketing in Japan.*

Kenji continued, "Japan Technologies desires a license to manufacture and market IPS 10000. Mr. James, please come to Osaka immediately."

"Kenji, lemme get back to you."

"Very well, do not delay. Goodbye, Mr. James."

Pug stared at Sean. "You believe this? Once Hondoya uses IPS 10000, it's Kenji-bar-the-door!" He high-fived Sean. "Thank god for reorganization. Ain't chaos wonderful? Bird shit's good luck. You're coming with me to sakeville."

Sean nodded, "Let's look at Bruce's cash forecast."

"Forget it. We'll do our own. What do we use for the six month's sales?"

"Take the current order rate and bump it five per cent."

"Too low! With a Chicago sales rep, orders'll increase at least fifteen per cent."

"Pug, too optimistic! Let's do eight per cent, max."

"You got no balls! We need fifteen per cent to make my numbers work. With a rep in place, the IPS 100 orders increase, and the IPS 10000 introduction goes faster. Here's more good news: IPS 10000 profit margins are super."

After several back of the envelope calculations, a profit-and-loss statement emerged.

"How about the cash projection?" Sean asked.

"With net income, all I gotta do is add depreciation and bingo! There's the cash!

How much will Kenji pay for a license?"

"With no patent, I'm not sure. But if Hondoya likes the technology and Japan Technologies sees near-term business, maybe half a million."

"I need two million to wipe out the debt and get some breathing room!"

"Pug, let's do some market research to see how large the Japanese market is. Maybe we can ask for more than two million."

"Damn it! You're not listening! I don't have time for research shit!"

OSAKA

Three days later, Sean left an urgent voice mail. "Pug, I'm in Asheboro, North Carolina. My sister had a terrible car accident. I'll let you know when I can get back to the office. Sorry I can't join you."

Pug changed his plans. *Never mentioned a sister before... but with no Doc expenses, I'll book business class and leave earlier.*

In Osaka, he checked into his hotel, showered, and splashed on Old Spice. He taxied to the Comfort Station.

"Welcome to Osaka, Mr. James. It is my pleasure to see you again." Suzi's low-cut kimono teased.

Pug held her soft delicate hands and gazed into her smoky eyes. "Suzi, call me Pug."

She took his arm and led him to a private room. She closed the screen and kneeled on the tatami. Pug sank onto the floor pillows.

A server brought a tray of appetizers. "We wish enjoyment for special guests," Suzi whispered as she draped a napkin over his lap.

With chopsticks, she deftly placed a morsel in his mouth then caressed his lips with a warm moist cloth.

"Is it to your liking, Pug?"

Pug smiled, his eyes closed. *Never knew food could be so sexy.*

She poured more beer. He sat back, took a sip. "Suzi, when we first met, didn't you work here?"

"Yes, while attending university. Now I work at Hotel Sakura. Perhaps you stay there next time?" More beer and food arrived. He lost sense of time, and she showed no urgency to conclude. Four hours passed.

"Suzi, I got an early meeting tomorrow." He rose to his knees and fell back onto the cushions. "Whoa... jet lag's got me!"

She wrapped her arm around his waist and steadied him as they walked to a taxi. At the hotel, she said, "I will assist you to your room."

Fumbling and finally unlocking the door, he said, "Night, Suzi. Had a great..." She kissed his cheek. Instinctively he pulled her close and then into the room.

Not since Tiffanee had he felt such ecstasy. At 4 a.m., completely spent, he did not hear the door close.

At the front desk, Suzi booked a 6 a.m. wakeup call and left a package.

The wake-up call jolted Pug. He showered, dressed and drank three cups of coffee. When he arrived at Japan Technologies, a receptionist escorted him to Kenji's office.

"Mr. James, you look rested," Kenji said.

"Slept like a log."

"Mr. James, I apologize, but I must attend to a crisis which needs immediate attention. Ashi-san will begin discussions."

Kenji left. Jun nervously lit a cigarette; sweat beaded on his brow. In a weak voice, he said, "Japan Thermal and Acoustics Technologies requests International Protected Solutions grant a license to manufacture and market IPS 10000 for Japanese appliance markets. What would you consider a fair price, Mr. James?" He lit another cigarette before finishing the first.

Without hesitating, Pug blurted, "I want two million dollars for the license rights... plus... plus an annual royalty of five per cent on all IPS 10000 sales." *Got this cigarette-sucking sap by the short hairs.*

"With much respect, Mr. James, how can you justify two million?" Jun stuttered, "I... I... IPS has no patent."

Pug raised his voice. "Jun, when it issues, the price of poker goes up."

Smoke encircled Jun's head. "I do not understand. What does poker... have to do with patent?"

Pug laughed. "Act now, or I'll want four million when the patent comes."

"Mr. James, Hondoya will never allow Japan Technologies to include such excessive license costs in its prices."

"Jun, that's your problem. Hondoya engineers love the technology, so price ain't important."

"Mr. James, Hondoya's engineers claim IPS 10000 barely meets its specification. Cost analysts see no justification for a price premium. Without a price premium, we cannot fund manufacturing start-up and expense of sales and distribution, plus the license cost unless..."

"Unless what?"

"Unless IPS shares the economic costs."

"Jun, that's the licensee's responsibility!"

"Mr. James, my analysis indicates it costs at least one million dollars for equipment plus considerable marketing expenses."

Pug did not react. *His million matches Rich's.*

"We can offer five hundred thousand dollars in four installments, payable as commercial business develops. All parties must share economic burden when introducing new technology." Jun lit another cigarette.

Pug's mind raced. *Jap Tech pays one and a half million: a half million to IPS and one million for its capital.*

"I thought you guys... uh... think long-term. Where's the long-term vision Kenji yakked about?"

"Mr. James, vision without strategy creates chaos."

Pug barked, "The price is two million. Take it or leave it! I'm not giving away my technology for a puny half million!"

Jun exhaled then emitted a hoarse cough. Speaking in a quiet monotone and engulfing Pug in secondhand smoke, he argued for a reduced fee. Two hours passed; Pug struggled to stay awake.

Jun looked at his watch. "Mr. James, I suggest a break. Let us meet in three hours."

"Okay, but rethink your insulting offer."

"Mr. James, I mean no disrespect."

"Then up the ante!"

Pug returned to his hotel room and slept. He awoke suddenly after two hours. *Gotta make a deal! I'll split the difference... one point two-and-a-half million dollars up front for a non-exclusive license.*

When they reconvened, Kenji appeared.

"Mr. James, Ashi-san informs me you drive a hard bargain. It's what you Americans do, yes? Although IPS has no patent, we will attempt to work with your number. Jun will instruct my attorney to draft an agreement."

A broad smile covered Pug's face. "Kenji! Let's shake on it!" He crushed Kenji's hand. *Wait 'til I tell Doc! And look at Jun's face. He knows I whipped his ass.*

Kenji and Jun accompanied Pug to the lobby, thanked him, and said goodbye. They returned to Kenji's office and relaxed with cigarettes and tea.

"I trust golf went well?" Jun asked.

"Hai! I have photos to show you."

CHICAGO

Sean and Rich met in Chicago to visit appliance companies and Tier 1 suppliers. They relaxed in the hotel bar.

"Puggy told me about your sister. How's she doing?"

"Out of intensive care. Her fiancée's with her. Doctors are optimistic."

"Glad to hear," Rich said. He ordered another Coors. "So what's up for the next three days?"

"We pitch IPS 10000 at Exeter, General Appliance, and some suppliers. Pug wants us to check out Marken and Associates; he heard they're good sales agents."

After several routine sales calls, Sean and Rich arrived at the impressive offices of Walter Marken. Walter described the firm's extensive commercial and political connections with OEMs and Tier 1 suppliers. His experienced team outlined selling strategies and listed accomplishments. Walter hosted lunch at the downtown Athletic Club and introduced them to senior appliance executives from Exeter and General Appliance.

On the plane to Denver, they compared notes. "What do you think of Marken?" Rich asked.

"Their connections can get us introduced and IPS 10000 approved. Their political muscle and boots on the ground will compliment Pug's technology. Glad Walter accepted your invite."

"Yeah, he'll come to Denver in a few weeks to get Puggy's blessing."

DENVER

Pug and Suzi enjoyed three relaxing days in Kyoto. On his return flight home, he upgraded to first class. The attentive flight staff offered him Dom Perignon and caviar. Filet mignon and an excellent cabernet sauvignon followed. As he savored after-dinner cognac, he thought, *Boy, October ended on a high note.*

Then it hit.

Shit! Two million dollars is not enough! Damn, I need two million after taxes.

Back in Denver, Pug told Sean and Bruce, "Whadaya want first? Good or not-so-good news?"

"We need good news. Farm Ridge National called; we got forty-five days to find a new bank," Bruce said.

"Old slant eyes popped for a two-million-buck license!"

"Congratulations!" Sean said.

"And the not-so-good?" Bruce asked.

"After the taxman screws me, IPS nets only 1.2 million."

Bruce shook his head in frustration. "My analysis showed IPS needed two and a half million pre-tax to get through six months. My footnotes clearly..."

"Bruce, I never read your fuckin' footnotes!"

"Bruce, is a stock purchase a taxable event?" Sean asked.

Pug laughed. "Hey! The red-metal-headed PhD's a CPA too!"

Three days later, Pug called Kenji. "I got some new ideas about our agreement."

A long pause ensued. "Mr. James, we shook hands."

"I'm making the deal better!"

Pug heard muffled Japanese. Kenji replied, "Mr. James, I do not understand."

"Listen, a licensee is like a partner or, let's say, an investor in the company's technology. That make sense?"

Kenji remained silent.

"Why doesn't Jap Tech invest the two million dollars in IPS stock? Then you're a long-term technology investor."

"Mr. James, does the price of the IPS 10000 license remain the same?"

"Absolutely! You got my word!"

"Mr. James, I must consult my lawyer."

That evening, Pug and Skip ate at a BBQ joint near the plant. Skip complained about how Rich mistreats him.

"Too fucking bad," Pug said through bites of a saucy rib. "Now you know how my dad treated me. Get used to it."

"How long do I have to work here?"

Pug rubbed his hands with a napkin. "Call my real estate agent. Here's his number."

"I don't need a house."

"He's got a job for you."

"A job?"

"Needs sales agents. He'll train you to work in the Bay Area."

"Geez, I'm not sure..."

"Look, you flunked college. You're shitty at blue-collar work. Only thing left's an office job."

"But..."

"But nothing. You get women to take off their panties... so get 'em to buy real estate."

"Uh... I don't have to stay in Denver?"

"Unless you screw this up."

Thanks for the vote of confidence, Pops.

A FedEx package arrived on November 12. A cover letter introduced Dr. Yamura, a Tokyo lawyer and chief legal officer for Japan Technologies. A heads of agreement (HOA) document stated Japan Technologies (or a party to be named) would purchase two million dollars in IPS common stock for an ownership interest to be defined (subject to due diligence). In addition, IPS would execute an exclusive license for Japan Technologies to manufacture and to sell IPS 10000 products for all markets in Japan and for Hondoya appliances worldwide.

Pug shoved the documents at Sean and Bruce, "What the hell's a 'heads of agreement?'"

"Maybe like a pre-nup?" Sean suggested.

"Or a memo of understanding?" Bruce added.

"Notice how Japs now talk American?"

"These guys are difficult to understand," Bruce remarked. "I'll ask Jackson to review this."

"No! Get a local gator to look at it."

"But we're talking about licensing," Bruce argued.

"Farm Ridge National won't wait for Jackson's review!"

The local attorney recommended IPS send financial data once Japan Technologies signed a confidentiality agreement. Bruce faxed three-years of financial data and year-to-date results after receiving the executed document.

Dr. Yamura's proposal arrived ten days later. It stated:

An offshore company would invest $2 million for a 25 percent equity stake.

The investment had minority rights: veto power over specific future transactions and a permanent seat on the board of directors.

IPS would grant Japan Technologies exclusive license to manufacture and to sell IPS 10000 products for all markets in Japan and Hondoya Appliances worldwide. Japan Technologies could sell IPS 10000 products in other Asian countries on a non-exclusive basis.

Japan would be the legal domicile for all dispute resolutions.

There were two copies for Pug's signature, one in English and one in Japanese.

"Pug, I'll get the Japanese version translated," Bruce offered.

"And pay another forty-five hundred dollars? No fuckin' way!"

On reviewing the draft, Pug disliked "minority rights" and the 25 percent equity dilution. He wanted 10 percent. IPS's lawyer disagreed with the domicile location. Pug argued with Kenji while the lawyers exchanged comments. Kenji and Dr. Yamura remained firm. Frustrated, Pug called Sean, who was visiting his sister in North Carolina.

"Why is this SOB so stubborn?"

"He's probably being very cautious. Maybe he doesn't trust you," Sean said. "You forced him to sign secrecy agreements before showing the IPS 10000 solution and financial information."

"That was proprietary stuff!"

"At this point, it doesn't matter because time is not your friend."

That evening, Pug called Marcy, "If I give Sake Breath twenty-five percent, then my ownership goes below fifty percent."

"Honey, with all your MatraScience friends plus Robby Benton and Darin, you still control more than fifty-one percent."

"Sweetie, I love your math."

The next morning, Pug faxed the signed HOA.

On day forty-five, Brunei Trust wired two million dollars to IPS's account. Bruce alerted Farm Ridge National who extended its deadline by fifteen days.

The following week, Sean phoned the Mile High National commercial loan officer. "Did you look at the financial data I sent?"

"Yes," the loan officer replied.

"IPS needs to change banks."

"But why change now that IPS has a stronger balance sheet?"

"Farm Ridge National wants larger clients than IPS."

"So IPS wants a working capital line of credit secured by receivables and inventory. Anything else?"

"There's one more item. Pug James needs a personal loan of five hundred thousand dollars. He has to pay off a personal note to Farm Ridge National."

"Send me his financials. I'll take a look."

A few days later, Sean announced, "IPS has a new bank."

"Great! But how 'bout my personal loan?"

"IPS has to provide monthly financial data and keep its credit line within collateral parameters."

"With my plans, Mile High will beg me to increase the loan. So, how 'bout my personal loan?"

"Mile High can't do that."

"Fuck 'em! I'll find another bank!"

Sean feigned a cough. "Pug. I'm pulling your chain. Mile High will loan you half a million, renewable annually. You have to pledge your IPS stock and sign personal guarantees. You and Marcy okay with that?"

"When do I sign?"

"Next week."

Buoyed by the news, Pug called his dad. "Got me two million bucks for my new invention!"

"When's IPS going public? Darin gave me 50 shares of his company for my birthday."

"Look, when IPS goes public, I'll give you a 100 shares... worth a helluva lot more!"

Pug slammed the phone. "Darin this, Darin that. Why do I bother?"

SAN FRANCISCO

For Skip, real estate training was fun. He loved meeting new people, showing homes, and missionary marketing. But he hated the paperwork, follow-up, answering tough questions, and closing the sale.

Skip's fraternity brother recommended he contact Michelle Burkett who wanted to purchase a condo. She had a master's in computer science and worked as a software engineer in Sunnyvale. Her sparkling personality meshed with Skip's, and he soon leveraged this into dates and frequent overnight stays. Five months later, they married.

Kenji's investment allowed Bruce to pay vendors' overdue bills while Rich ordered new manufacturing presses. Sean bought new thermal, acoustics, and vibration lab equipment.

Marken introduced IPS to contacts at Exeter and General Appliance. Thermal and acoustic dissipater engineering groups quickly approved IPS 10000 products. Orders flooded in.

Jackson's phone call added more good news.

"Pug, the US IPS 10000 patent issued! Congrats!"

"About time!"

"And the Japanese patent office granted provisional approval."

"Provisional?"

"IPS can practice the technology until the actual patent grants. I'll file for an Asian patent to cover the entire region. It's expensive, but IPS needs coverage in every major market."

"Do it!" Pug proclaimed.

In his office, Pug hung a painting of a Central City, Colorado silver mine. Beneath it, he placed a silver-framed copy of the two-million-dollar wire transfer. Marcy gave him a silver music box that played, "Always Look for the Silver Lining." Listening to the melody became Pug's morning ritual.

Marcy decorated his office with a silvery-gray carpet, silver frames holding family photos and the MatraScience farewell gift, and stainless-steel bookcases. Silver Baoding balls, a gift from Darin, rested on his desk.

1992
SAN FRANCISCO

KIP ENJOYED CONSIDERABLE FREEDOM WITH little sales accountability. His no-pressure schedule allowed frequent visits with Marcy during commutes between Sunnyvale and San Francisco. She relished their morning chats without Pug's presence.

One February morning, Marcy asked, "Sweetie, how's Michelle's work going?"

"She refused a promotion."

"Really? How come?"

"She wants to quit and start our family."

"Honey, that's wonderful! All women her age think about motherhood."

"I know, but my salary is based on commissions, and the real estate business is so uncertain. We need her salary to make ends meet."

"Let me talk with Daddy. We'll figure something out. You know how much he wants a grandson."

"Thanks, Mom. Knew I could count on you."

Two months later, Michelle announced her pregnancy. By that time, Skip had not closed one deal, and his commission income remained zero. His boss told him his future in real estate looked bleak; he needed to find another career. Skip met with Pug in late March.

"Let's see if I got your story straight. You knocked up your wife, she's quitting her job, and now you got fired from the job I got you. Did I miss anything?"

"Pops, that's totally unfair. My boss is an asshole; his ethics suck. He messed up five of my deals. It's his fault I lost my commissions."

"Don't give me your lousy excuses! You got your wife pregnant, so now I can't ship you back to Rich cuz I gotta worry about my future grandson. You wouldn't even have a place to live if I hadn't got a second mortgage on my home, so you could buy your goddamned Sunnyvale house!"

"What should I do?"

"I'll figure something out like I always do. Now get outta my sight, you worthless piece of shit!"

That evening, Pug and Marcy sat in their kitchen. Pug popped open a Pat Henry, and she poured a Jack Daniels over ice.

"Honey, we have to help Skip and Michelle. They're in deep financial trouble, and Skip has no employment prospects. Can't you do something?"

"I should send him back to Rich."

"Not funny, please be serious. We're talking about our son and family."

"Lemme think about it."

Two weeks later, Pug leased a San Francisco office space and hired Skip to do marketing research. His starting salary was $45 thousand, and he got a 1992 Buick sedan as a company car.

DENVER

At the first board meeting after Kenji's investment, Pug distributed a one-page agenda.

April 15, 1992
-Welcome and introduction	*P. James*
-Approval of prior meeting minutes	*B. Hargett*
-Financial updates	*B. Hargett*
-Mile High Bank	*P. James*
-IPS 10000 progress	

Pug welcomed Kenji, Darin, and the management team. Bruce reported financial results showing how Kenji's investment strengthened the balance sheet. Incoming order rates indicated 1992 would break even with revenues of $5.1 million. Estimated revenues in 1993 would approach $7.5 million and produce $700 thousand of after-tax profit.

"Mr. Kobyashi deserves an official thank you for his timely investment," Darin said.

"It's a license! We called it equity to save taxes," Pug snapped.

"Puggy, two million dollars is two million dollars. Bruce, let the record show the board's appreciation." Darin nodded toward Kenji who acknowledged the compliment.

"Ted, orders for IPS 100 and 10000 exploded," Pug insisted. "IPS technology is first choice for thermal dissipaters at Exeter and Gen Appliance."

"Without Mr. Kobyashi's help, IPS wouldn't survive to get those orders."

"Enough! Gonna talk finances now. I hired Mile High as my new bank."

"What are its requirements?" Darin pressed.

"Enough working capital to secure borrowing. That's it."

The meeting continued with reports on the state of the business. Rich summarized plant improvements; Sean described the latest development projects and sales progress in the US.

"Marken's excellent relationships at OEMs have opened the right sales doors," Rich added.

"Whoa!" Pug interrupted, "IPS's technology did that!"

"Puggy, you don't get it. You need partners who know market politics to commercialize new technology," Darin argued. "I hear Marken does a first class sales job."

"Japan Technologies uses partners to open the right doors," Kenji noted.

"Kenji, that doesn't work in the U S of A," Pug insisted.

"Mr. James, because you don't take an interest in politics doesn't mean politics won't take an interest in you."

"Sounds familiar, Mr. Kobyashi," Darin said.

"Pericles, 430 B.C."

Pug's face reddened. "Before Ted interrupted, tell us Kenji, why does Jap Tech have zero orders from Hondoya? You promised they'd use IPS 10000 for all the new models!"

Ignoring a no-smoking sign, Kenji lit a cigarette and looked out the window. Bruce scrambled for an ashtray. "If you recall, Mr. James, commercial progress in Japan requires patience to nurture customer relationships." He exhaled in Pug's direction.

"He's right," Darin interjected. "Takes years to build successful relationships."

"Geez, Professor Ted, first finance and now a marketing lecture. With an athletic supporter like you, I know my family jewels are safe."

Darin rolled his eyes.

Pug announced, "IPS's been granted two US patents and five trademarks. Jackson's got fifty-three patent filings in forty countries."

The meeting adjourned. Kenji requested a private meeting in Pug's office. The framed bank wire caught his eye. Then he pointed at the painting.

"Mr. James, what is that?"

"Colorado Silver Mine."

"A silver mine?"

"The painting shows my discovery of the IPS 10000 silver lining. When Hondoya orders, I'll commission a picture of Mount Fushi."

"You refer to Mount Fuji?" With a wry smile, he continued, "Permit me to discuss another matter. IPS 10000 is now introduced in America thanks to W. Marken and Company."

"Kenji, where are the Hondoya orders?"

"Mr. James, may we speak in confidence? Hondoya experienced technical problems with new models. Embarrassing news remains silent until solutions are found. Orders will come. Meanwhile, IPS 10000 is now specified on several models for other OEMs: General Appliance of Japan and Niota."

Pug snapped, "Hondoya is the big kahuna!" When Kenji looked

puzzled, he added, "You know, the big prize. You gotta put more resources on Hondoya!"

"I will ask Ashi-san to study your request."

Kenji lit a cigarette and glanced at the wire transfer. He exhaled, the smoke curling above his head. "When you asked me to invest in IPS, you mentioned a technology partnership. Why not operate IPS as a business partnership? You concentrate on American markets while Japan Technologies focuses on international markets. If twenty-five per cent of the company is worth two million, then fifty percent is worth four million." He tapped cigarette ash. Pug watched it flutter to the silver carpet. "I will invest enough funds to buy shares for fifty per cent. Your endorsement would help convince other shareholders to sell. As partners, we can expand IPS technologies worldwide. Do you agree?"

Pug was momentarily speechless. "I dunno."

"Mr. James, IPS has 'know how,' and Japan Technologies and Marken have geographic 'know who.'"

The receptionist interrupted. "Mr. Kobyashi, your limo's here."

As Kenji rose to leave Pug said, "Kenji, lemme sleep on it."

"We can have a profitable partnership. Sayonara, Mr. James."

Pug yelled for Sean. He summarized Kenji's offer, "What's slant eyes up to?"

"Not sure."

Pug reclined in his chair and rotated the silver Baoding balls in his right hand.

"Pug, have you finalized my option grants yet?" Sean asked.

"Ted did some analysis. He recommended you for forty thousand shares at four dollars a share. When IPS makes a profit in 1993 and 1994, you'll be one hundred percent vested. When we go public, you'll be worth a ton of money. Wanted to do more, but Ted said no. Think of the options as incentive to sign on full-time."

Before his departure to Japan, Kenji waited in the airport lounge and returned calls. He spoke with Dr. Yamura.

"What have you learned about the sons of Mr. James?" Kenji asked.

"Both attended the University of Colorado at Boulder. Skip James quit because of an unsatisfactory academic record. He failed at his first employments."

"When the eldest son fails, the father is embarrassed. And the other son?"

"Dave James is a second-year computer science student. He excels at computers and language. The full report awaits your return. Did Mr. James accept your offer?"

"Not yet, however, we must be ready should he reject."

Two weeks later, Pug called Kenji. "Sean and I discussed your proposal."

"Mr. James, I thought our conversations were confidential."

"Kenji, I trust Sean. Anyway, he claims your offer gives IPS no new money, since shareholders sell to you. With a low book value, they won't get much premium. For many, the price could be less than their original cost."

"Mr. James, you speculate. No price has been established. In fact, different prices can be negotiated for different shareholders. For example, what price could be acceptable for those owning 10,000 shares or more?"

A long pause ensued. "IPS is going great guns! Twenty times book value—absolute minimum!"

"Twenty dollars per share is quite generous given IPS's history."

"Kenji, the future is now. History don't interest me."

"Unwise to ignore its lessons. Mr. James, think about this. With only two shareholders, we can increase IPS's flexibility to respond to special opportunities."

"Uh… whadya talking about?"

"Global relationships will be more critical to future success in appliance markets."

"Kenji, IPS's technology is the only relationship that counts."

"I am disappointed you feel that way."

Kenji penciled a note to Jun. *Instruct Dr. Yamura to execute Japan Technologies's sub-license agreements.*

Pug rose from his chair, rotated his sore shoulder, and ambled to Sean's office. "Kenji pulled the plug on his stupid offer. Claimed timing's bad.

All he talks about is relationships. He couldn't relate to technology if it bit his dick. If his special relationships are so damn good, why hasn't Hondoya ordered IPS 10000?"

"Fair point."

"You decide to become an employee?"

"Given my options, I have no choice."

"Bruce'll do the paperwork. Keep this quiet. Don't want Rich to know."

Sean nodded. *Darin never talks to Rich?*

ARVADA, COLORADO

Later at home, Sean opened a beer and penned a reminder:

– – *Confirm Pug's statement about offer withdrawal.*

– – *Still resents the original investment/license.*

– – *I'm hostage to his unpredictable behavior.*

He watched "Lusty Thighs," a new video received from his Asian distributor. *This is a moneymaker, ready for gaijin distribution...*

Suddenly, he felt a heaviness in his chest, a heartache so profound it caused him to double over.

Natsuko! Why do I do this? Natsuko, I'm sorry... this does not honor your memory. I still love you, miss you so... Natsuko... why did you leave me?

1993
ASHEBORO, NORTH CAROLINA

I N EARLY SPRING, LARRY JUDSON, CEO of Lawrent, Inc., returned to his North Carolina headquarters. Lawrent had dominated the North American thermal dissipater market for years. Now, throughout 1993, a company called IPS threatened Lawrent's market share and financial viability.

He reviewed notes from his recent Chicago meeting:

– – *Met Dan Teller (technical manager for General Appliance's thermal dissipaters) and Jay Watson (purchasing officer for thermal and acoustic dissipaters).*

– – *Walter Marken bypassed Teller and Watson and convinced senior executives to stop purchasing Lawrent's dissipaters.*

– – *IPS 10000 products superior to our products.*

– – *Discussed production economics and licensing alternatives to regain market share.*

– – *Teller establishing a Thermal Dissipater Committee to write new specs. All vendors must re-qualify.*

– – *Teller hiring experienced consultants to assist vendors' compliance.*

– – *Teller and Watson expect better incentives.*

CHICAGO

After secret meetings over three months, Sean accepted Teller's offer to consult for General Appliance. Working evenings and weekends, he developed new thermal dissipater standards. He watched a video feed of General Appliance's vendor meeting where the new specifications were announced.

Dan Teller spoke, "Gentlemen, welcome to Chicago. Each supplier attending today expressed interest in adopting General Appliance's new standards for thermal and acoustic dissipaters. This new specification will address thermal protection, tighter dimension tolerances, noise abatement, and mandatory use of recyclable materials. All vendors must meet these standards before quoting and supplying products for new models and any running changes. Our technical consultants will assist your qualification process."

Dan explained the standards in detail and opened the session for questions and answers. Afterwards, he introduced the consultants and matched them with vendors who requested assistance.

Within three months, Lawrent developed a new product: a special metal alloy dissipater with unique internal geometry. It incorporated extra mesh layers to facilitate convection, an innovative edging technique for thermal banks and added materials for acoustic benefits. These new features allowed for a patent filing. It was the only technology that passed General's specification/criteria.

In a follow-up phone call, Larry asked Dan, "What do you think of Lawrent's Thermal-Acoustic Integrator. We call it 'TAI.'"

"Clever, but Purchasing worries about Lawrent's prices."

"No problem. Current competitor prices provide enough cushion to lower our prices and still earn acceptable margins."

"Good. Jay will let you know when to supply."

"Thanks, Dan. I trust financial matters are satisfactory."

"Lawrent's generosity exceeded our expectations."

1994
CHICAGO

1 993 FINISHED WITH IPS REVENUES of $7.35 million, gross margins approaching 65 percent, and profits of $695 thousand. Business expanded at both Exeter and General Appliance.

In February, Hondoya introduced its new models at Chicago's Appliance Show. It showcased its latest home ovens, refrigerators, furnaces, water heaters, and dishwashers. Press and appliance experts were impressed; they stated Hondoya posed serious challenges to American OEMs. They praised Hondoya's advancements for thermal management, acoustics abatement, consumer safety, and use of recyclable materials.

IPS exhibited at the show. Visitors to the company's booth complimented Pug on IPS 10000's success. However, rumors circulated that a competitor would soon introduce a new revolutionary material for thermal and acoustic dissipaters.

Pug worked IPS's booth in the mornings and toured other exhibits in the afternoon. He stopped at Hondoya's display and examined the thermal dissipater insulation inside the Hondoya ovens and dishwashers. He raced to a phone.

"Rich get to a Hondoya dealership and look at their new oven thermal dissipaters!"

DENVER

Two days later, Pug returned and stopped by Rich's office.

"Well, whadya find?"

"Hondoya's using IPS 10000," Rich reported.

"Buy some ovens, tear 'em apart, and see what's going on. If it's Jap Tech's material, then Kenji's cheating—or somebody's infringing! Watch 'em for the next few months, and keep Jackson in the loop."

Rich furnished Jackson with evidence of materials infringing IPS 10000. With that information, Jackson obtained a court-ordered injunction against Hondoya for using non-approved materials in their American manufactured appliances.

Revenues were forecasted to double for 1994 and profits to triple over 1993.

Pug shared these results with Robby Benton of VenCapOne.

"It's time to think IPO!" Robby declared.

"You read my brain!"

Pug sent the 1993 financials and 1994 forecast to Robby's investment banker who left Pug a voice mail, "Mr. James, if IPS maintains its '93-'94 profit growth rates, its proprietary position, and access to the multi-billion market potential, an IPO is feasible. Let's meet to discuss."

SAN FRANCISCO

Pug and Marcy headed to San Francisco's Tadich Grill and settled into a cozy high-sided booth. A white-aproned waiter brought kir royales.

"Sweetie, the investment banker says an IPO is locked and loaded once '94's finished. Then I buy Jap Tech. But I need a real CFO."

"What about Bruce?"

"He's a bean clerk. I want Fieldsy, a finance guy who's done operations."

"Can you afford him?"

"Babe, with IPS's growth, salary's no problem. Good reason to raise mine!" Pug laughed and gulped his drink. "Callin' him tomorrow."

"Hey Fieldsy, how's life in Kookville?"

"Fantastic! How's IPS doing?"

"Ninety-three's profitable, and ninety-four'll be Katy-bar-the-door with twenty-four percent net after taxes on fourteen million! I got patents in sixteen countries! And more in the pipeline!"

"Congratulations! When's IPS paying dividends?"

"Don't be a pussy. Think IPO."

"You're kidding!"

"Nope! Hired an investment banker. Going public in '95."

"That's no cakewalk. SEC puts you through the grinder. And once public, you have to follow rules."

"Yep! It's why I need a first rate CFO like you!"

"Pug, I haven't done finance since 1982."

"You know sales, marketing, operations, and finance. I need a businessman, not a spreadsheet jockey."

"Let me think about it."

SEOUL, KOREA

Michael let seven days pass before calling. "Pug, Ellie and I discussed your offer. I'm flattered, but it's not a good time to leave MatraScience. It's taken some effort to navigate Asian market politics, and my time investment is now paying off."

"Fair enough. You never bullshit me."

"Say, doesn't Bruce have an MBA in finance?"

"Yeah, why?"

"Can't he grow into the job?"

"No!"

"Okay, if I can help you recruit someone, let me know."

After Michael hung up, Ellie assured him. "You made the right decision. You're on the fast track for vice president of MatraScience Asia."

Jun Ashi waited at the entrance of the Grand Hyatt. Kenji's limo entered the circular drive and parked in front of the dancing fountain. They exchanged customary bows, entered the hotel's stylish lobby, and crossed the marble floor to a private elevator.

"Okazaki-san waits in the private dining room," Jun said.

"Excellent. Has the room been screened?"

"Hai! Swept for recording devices and all entry points secured. Suzi will serve." Jun handed him a packet. "Dr. Yamura requests you and Okazaki-san review this memo."

Kenji and Shiganari exchanged greetings, and Shiganari poured tumblers of Johnnie Walker Blue. The old friends toasted each other and talked golf and politics.

Suzi refilled glasses, bowed, and departed. Kenji handed the packet to Shiganari who read the summary notes dated March 1994:

– – TADA's 1993 revenues increased by 45% and profits up by 51%. Japan Technologies's licensed 10000 technologies and product spinoffs accounted for 90% of this improvement approximating seventy-five million dollars.

– – Japan Technologies executed sub-licenses for 10000 technologies with Research Appliance Devices, Nippon Tooling, and Akami-Thai.

– – 1993 profits distributed to each TADA participant who, in turn, paid its relationship obligations. Bank Hanjokani monitored all payments and arbitrated all disputes.

Shiganari smiled. "As usual, Dr. Yamura's report is excellent."

"Hai!" Kenji replied. "Excellent in many matters: business intelligence, patents, and TADA communications. He ensures Hondoya's strategic interests are aligned with TADA's."

"Do you think Mr. James has any idea how valuable his technology has been for Hondoya and TADA?"

Kenji lit a cigarette and inhaled deeply. "No, and he must never learn."

"How do we control the growth and success in the North American markets?"

"Dr. Yamura and Marken-san will develop a strategy to address this issue. In the meantime, it is critical to limit IPS's growth while encouraging more innovation."

Shiganari refilled Kenji's glass. "Will we be able to prevent American competitors from stealing the IPS technology?"

"Marken-san's consultant will propose actions for us to consider."

"Can we rely on him given his other problems?"

"For now, yes… but we must remain vigilant."

For the next two hours, they discussed TADA's future plans. At 1:00 a.m., Suzi entered and announced, "Gentlemen, the sauna is ready. Please follow."

SAN FRANCISCO

Pug looked forward to his favorite Sunday show, *Sixty Minutes*. April's lead story profiled Japan's emerging dominance of appliance markets and Hondoya's increased market share. Mike Wallace speculated Hondoya would replace General Appliance as the world's second largest OEM and predicted Exeter could soon lose its top position. The correspondent's aggressive interview of Exeter's CEO angered Pug.

He muted the volume and exclaimed, "Time to bomb the Japs!"

Marcy brought him another beer. "What do you mean 'bomb the Japanese'?"

"Jap Tech hasn't got any Hondoya orders. I need an Asia operation." He took a long gulp. "That sake sipping sucker just sits on his slant-eyed ass."

"Honey, what can you do?"

"One thing I'm not gonna do—no more Jap licenses!"

"If Japan Technologies isn't selling, and you won't license others…?"

"I met a kook in Denver last week."

"You mean Korean?"

"That's what I said. He's with Seoul's Chamber of Commerce. Helps American companies start kook operations, speaks great English. A can-do kook."

"But you want to sell in Japan, not Korea."

"I'll Pearl Harbor the Japs through my kook door! Kooks know how to reverse engineer, and they hate the Japs."

Michael heard Pug's booming voice. "Hello from the Golden Gate!"

"Hey Pug, how's the family?"

"Great! Things are really popping! Just hired Bruce Hargett as my CFO."

"Bruce?"

"Did you know he's a CPA?"

Michael chuckled. "Think he can handle an IPO?"

"He'll learn, and you know the best part?"

"I bet you're about to tell me."

"Hardest working person I know. Totally loyal. Say, you got a couple of free days?"

"What do you have in mind?"

"I'll be in Japan in a few weeks to plan my Asian headquarters. IPS needs sales coverage in kookville and chinkville. You know slant eyes, so join me."

"Pug, you know what free advice is worth. Could use a break from MatraScience."

"Great! I'll send you airline tickets once I got the schedule."

Pug and Marcy settled in at Tadich Grill. His mind was in overdrive.

"When I called Fieldsy, it got me thinking. MatraScience never let me do my skunk works. Got cash now to start my IPS skunk. California real estate's a sure bet."

Marcy leaned over and planted a kiss. "Skip gets a real office. And maybe Dave'll join too!"

"Does this mean what I think it does?"

She smiled. "Hayloft time, sweetie."

OSAKA

Michael noticed Pug had gained weight, looked tired, his complexion pale. They taxied from Osaka airport to Japan Technologies.

"Pug, you need some exercise and serious sun."

"Too much going on. Get ready to rock and roll."

Pug showed Michael the schedule of back-to-back meetings with lawyers, accountants, real estate firms, and government agencies in Tokyo and Seoul.

TOKYO

After visiting Japan Technologies, they boarded the Shinkansen train to Tokyo. This time Pug booked superior class.

"So whadya think of my Osaka slant-eyes?"

"Japan Technologies's a first-class manufacturing operation, very capital intensive. Best I've seen in Asia for its size. Tool department is state of the art."

"I meant Kenji and Jun."

"Odd couple. Kenji's English is excellent. Bet he spent considerable time in the US. Seems to know a lot about American business practices. As far as Jun, he's hard to read… very quiet."

"Only thing I hate worse than a sake-sipper is a quiet smoking sake-sipper."

Same old alligator mouth. "Pug, I get a kick out of your 'Pug-speak' characterizations, but be careful when talking to Asians. If your slurs slip out, you'll offend them big-time."

"Fieldsy, you know I'm just jokin' when I talk like that."

"Yeah, but Asians won't understand your humor."

Pug's face turned grim. "If you saw the kind of stuff I did in 'Nam… you'd understand."

"Pug, just be careful."

"Okay, let's talk business. I put out feelers to Kenji 'bout selling. With my IPO money, I can buy out his slant ass… oops… I mean, butt!"

Michael laughed. "That'll jumpstart your Asian operations."

"Bingo! Our brains are linked!"

Pug briefed Michael on three candidates for administration manager. After the interviews, they relaxed in the hotel lounge.

Michael advised, "Ryo Ito is by far the best candidate, but he's been unemployed for three months. Why not find a good sales engineer first, someone with management potential? Get revenues, then add overhead, like MatraScience's business model."

"Need to plant my corporate flag now." Pug ordered another beer. "How's kookville? I mean, Korea… treatin' ya?"

Michael shook his head. "Jackson's nightmare boss is now my boss."

"Isaac?"

"Afraid so. The guy knows zilch about business, and he micromanages everything."

"Damn, looks like Doug Aldrich screwed you too."

"Yep! Having Isaac for a boss really sucks the air out..."

"Listen up, Fieldsy. The last four days, you've seen my plans. After I buy out Kenji, I'll need a senior guy to run things—right up your alley."

"You offering me a job?"

"You bet your round-eye butt! You can lead my international silver mining team!"

"I'll talk it over with Ellie. Need a couple of weeks to think it over."

Pug phoned a week later. "Hey, Fieldsy, how 'bout you and Ellie join Marcy and me in Japan? We can talk some more."

"Is the job in Tokyo or Osaka?"

"Hey, don't sweat the details."

KYOTO

Two weeks later, they met in Kyoto; they spent four days visiting shrines, enjoying delicious cuisine, and having serious discussions. Afterwards, Pug headed to Osaka; Marcy flew home. Michael and Ellie left for Indonesia to consider Pug's offer.

On the plane, Michael told Ellie, "Pug's one energy bundle."

"Definitely a personality improvement over Isaac but always full of surprises."

"What do you mean?"

"Marcy seemed very upset when Pug announced his last-minute decision to return to Osaka by himself." She looked thoughtful. "You think they're having problems again? Like when he worked for you?"

"Nah, he's just focused on the Kenji relationship."

"Hope that's the real reason. So, what does your head and heart tell you about Pug's offer?"

"I've looked at IPS financials. The turnaround years were 1992 and 1993 so the breakout year is 1994. The company made major progress in sales and profits with IPS 10000 technology. Business will remain solid for years given the life of current production models. Pug's got a backlog of new product ideas, and Jackson said the IPS patents are strong."

"Is Pug a better manager now?"

"Patents, sales growth, profits indicate he's got a winning hand. We had a heart-to-heart about his MatraScience mistakes and the lessons he's learned. Seems more humble."

"That's encouraging."

"And most important, I can add real value to IPS given my international experience."

BALI

They checked into the Grand Hyatt at Nusa-Dua and headed to the beach. Relaxing on the gleaming white sand, Michael said, "Ellie, I'm going for it!"

"It's a big risk given your seniority at MatraScience."

"A lot of good that does with Isaac, the legal beagle. He'll be a major obstacle to my career for at least three, maybe four years. Who knows what happens then?"

"Are you happy with the compensation package?"

"Pug went all out: higher salary, and he stuffed the offer with several thousand options. He agreed to sell me several thousand of his personal shares at a bargain price. When IPS goes public, those options will be worth more than MatraScience's. The investment banker's analysis says the IPO share value could be in the forty to fifty range."

"You okay with the job responsibilities?"

"He'll give me full responsibility and authority to organize and manage all international operations including Japan Technologies and the license relationship. The best part, he'll put me on the board. I know I can help Pug. Always regretted I didn't spend enough time with him when he worked for me."

Ellie stretched out on the beach towel. "Whatever you decide, I'll support."

"We're a helluva team, Ellie. Let's tell the daughters and Gordon Orlio we're coming home."

SAN FRANCISCO

By September, IPS's latest forecast confirmed sales doubling and profits up three-fold. By the end of the year, cash reserves were projected to be $2 million.

Now regulars at Tadich Grill, Pug and Marcy sat at the 1890's-era bar waiting for Dave. The historic eatery's stability and predictability provided a nice respite from Siena's noisy chaos.

"I love this place," Pug said, swigging a Pat Henry. "This restaurant's owned by the same family for over a hundred years, my kinda legacy."

Dave slid into the high-backed booth and glanced around. "Neat place," he said.

Pug ordered an expensive bottle of Silverado Vineyards cabernet sauvignon. "A toast to IPS! We'll celebrate with the mother of all board meetings."

"Where?" Dave asked.

"Vegas!"

"Las Vegas?" Marcy asked.

"It's home to Caesar, king of all valuable metals like…?"

"Silver!" Dave said, laughing.

"That's my boy!"

"Who'll you invite?" Marcy asked.

"The board, the Denver team, Fieldsy, all the wives. Sending Kenji a strong message—inviting all my new slant eyes. Can't wait to see sake-breath's face."

"But honey, that'll be expensive."

"We'll have fun, fun, fun. And, oh yeah, a short meeting to get a tax write-off."

Dinner finished, Dave left for a rock concert at the Cow Palace. Pug and Marcy relaxed with espressos. "Dave's unhappy with his programming job," Marcy said.

"Yeah, wish he'd stayed in college. When I buy the South San Francisco building, I'll take another run at him."

LAS VEGAS

On October 10, Pug and Marcy landed at Las Vegas's McCarran Airport. "Love this airport!" Pug exclaimed as he scanned the ceiling, escalators, baggage carousel, and trash cans.

"All silver!" Marcy giggled. "Just like IPS 10000."

The ceiling, constructed of aluminum and stainless steel slats, formed futuristic, three-dimensional shapes. Squares of silver-looking material filled spaces between each row of slats.

"Those ceiling panels have tiny holes to absorb sound." Pug sketched an idea on his pocket note pad: *Improving IPS 10000's noise reduction features.*

At the hotel, they changed clothes and returned to the airport. They wore western outfits, the fabric a shiny metallic silver. Pug's tailored jacket and slacks hugged his portly frame. Bold stitching above his vest pocket read, "IPS Silver Lining Success." His Stetson, with a silver-dollar hatband, tipped forward at a jaunty angle. Marcy, squeezed into a tight pants suit, wore a silver-dollar necklace and earrings to compliment her silver-tinted hair.

At the VIP lounge, they confirmed catering arrangements for the elaborate welcome buffet for guests arriving from Japan, Seattle, and Denver.

"How much longer 'til Ted gets here?" Pug asked.

"Soon. Let's head to their gate."

"Keep his ditzy wife occupied while him and me talk shop."

At the gate, Darin spotted Pug and Marcy and yelled, "Hey, it's Lone Ranger and his sidekick! Guess what, Puggy? Kenji bought fifty-six thousand of my IPS shares at twenty bucks a share."

Astounded, Pug snapped, "You sold too cheap! Shoulda waited..."

Darin interrupted, "Building my new house next to Bill Gates."

Arriving at the VIP room, Darin flirted with hostesses while Sylvia ordered a double vodka-tonic.

Pug whispered to Marcy, "Starting their usual flirt and drunk fest. Stay here, while I get Kenji."

Pug and Kenji performed their greeting ritual: strong in-your-face handshake versus subdued formality.

"Mr. James, I invited Ashi-san to join me."

"Yeah, right. What's this about buying Ted's—I mean Darin's—shares?"

"He offered a fair price."

"Lemme tell ya, you got more than a fair price."

Pug escorted Kenji and Jun into the lounge and welcomed Sean, Bruce, and Rich and his wife. Darin and Sylvia were into their third cocktails.

Pug shouted, "Hey, everyone! Welcome to my Silver Lining Celebration!"

Marcy, bubbly and excited, distributed silver-leather gift bags. Ladies received engraved silver music boxes and silver dollar necklaces. Men admired their silver Cross pen and pencil sets. Everyone oohed and aahed when they opened silver envelopes containing certificates redeemable for 500 silver dollars at Caesars's casino.

Darin turned to Rich and slurred, "Ya think Puggy's gotta a thing for *silver?*"

The four-day agenda included a Lake Meade cruise, helicopter tours, and golf. For adventure seekers, Pug scheduled bungee jumping, rock climbing, and water skiing. Attendees would enjoy elaborate dinners and front-row seats at popular shows. The fourth day included a brief morning board meeting.

Buffet finished, they boarded a silver stretch limo bound for Caesars Palace. Speakers blasted "Celebration" and "Always Look for the Silver Lining." In their rooms, guests found a gigantic fruit basket, an iced magnum of Dom Perignon, and two-dozen white roses.

Later that day, Michael and Ellie arrived from San Francisco. Ryo and the Korean team flew in the previous day.

The frenetic first day activities concluded with a lavish dinner. Michael offered a toast: "I've known Pug a long time and witnessed his inventions and their commercial success. I'm honored to join his IPS team. Here's to Pug and to IPS success!"

Pug saluted Michael and smiled. With tears in her eyes, Marcy squeezed Ellie's hand and whispered, "Pug's so happy Michael's joined IPS!"

Ellie replied, "Michael looks forward to the challenge and helping Pug."

Darin, inebriated, murmured to Rich, "What an ass-kisser."

"He helped Pug survive that difficult period at their old firm," Rich replied.

"Look, cousin, this guy can only get in our way. Never forget that."

Speaking Japanese to Kenji, Jun asked, "Mr. Fields... problem or opportunity?"

"A problem... for now," Kenji replied. "Maybe a future opportunity. Ask Dr. Yamura to do the usual background checks."

"Hai!"

Sean swirled his wine glass. *Field's a presumptuous sycophant! This guy could disrupt my plans.*

After dinner, Pug escorted everyone to Tom Jones's show at MGM Grand. Tom gave his show-stopping, energetic performance. An international circus at Caesars provided the next evening's entertainment. The stage, an engineering marvel, retracted to reveal a swimming pool. Olympic-style diving and acrobatics awed everyone.

On the third night, Pug showed the IPS 10000-invention video. He announced to all, "I want IPS employees to have energy like Tom Jones. Like the circus guys, IPS'll solve customer problems by taking risks and doing magic. What you just saw in the video, how we invented IPS 10000. Hey, that's just the beginning!"

On the fourth day, a hotel booking error forced the board to meet in a much smaller room. The cramped space soon reeked of Darin's Cuban cigar and of Kenji's, Jun's and Sean's cigarettes.

Pug sat between Darin and Kenji. Bruce sat next to Kenji with Jun and Ryo directly behind. Rich positioned himself behind Darin. Michael and Sean occupied opposite corners.

Pug distributed a one-page agenda. "It'd be nice to get the agenda in advance," Darin remarked.

Pug barked, "Bruce, you're up."

Bruce presented financial statements. His first slide showed the income statement for three quarters of the current year as well as a fourth-quarter forecast.

"These results speak for themselves. Revenue will exceed fourteen million with post-tax profits slightly above two-point-eight million, an astounding twenty-one percent return on sales."

Pug interjected, "Our IPS 10000 sales to Gen Appliance and Exeter blew everyone away. In 1995, we'll do at least twenty million dollars with even better margins. Another fifty percent growth! We'll rake in four million dollars in profit. A twenty dollar share valuation is now kaput." He smirked at Darin. "Continue, Bruce."

Michael smiled. *Still has that manic optimism.*

Bruce started again, but Pug interrupted. "An investment banker's ready to take IPS public. Says IPS shares could go for fifty-five dollars a share."

"How'd you get that pie-in-the-sky number?" Darin sneered.

"Company sales and profit growth support it."

"In your dreams, Puggy!"

"Ignore the family septic. Anyway, IPS is now in the quiet period."

"This is bullshit! With all this excess cash, pay shareholders a dividend," Darin challenged.

Bruce gathered up his slides, sat down, and stared at the table. Presentation over.

Glancing at Kenji, Pug continued, "The due diligence on Jap Tech's almost done."

"What?" Darin asked.

"Sorry, Ted, didn't I tell you? IPS'll buy Kenji's Osaka operations to jump-start the Asia business."

Darin looked at Kenji. "Mr. Kobyashi, I didn't realize you were selling."

A slight smile crossed Kenji's face. "I will listen to the right price."

"We'll make an offer after the auditors finish," Pug added.

"Where's the money to pay for this?"

"Ted, wake up! The IPO!"

Darin's eyes rolled in disbelief. He looked at Bruce whose eyes were closed. The thick haze of smoke grew unbearable.

"This room sucks. I'm gonna subsize the rest of the agenda so you guys can gamble."

Rich laughed, "For you who don't understand Pug-speak, he's summarizing."

"Lemme talk about more growth and investments. You've all met Michael, IPS's international vice president."

Michael studied faces and noted Sean's cynical glare, Kenji's passive stare, and Darin's disbelief.

"To help Michael, I already hired staff in Tokyo and Korea," Pug continued.

Michael was surprised. *I know about Ryo, but Korea?*

Darin began to speak; Pug cut him off. "Now about the US, Sean'll fire Marken and hire direct sales guys. My Chicago recruiter is searching for candidates."

Rich and Sean exchanged *"What the hell?"* expressions.

Darin asked, "Where are the sales projections and business plans for all this new spending?"

"You gotta invest ahead of sales. Customers love our technology. Look at our '94 results; our '92 investments caused this! At MatraScience, sales revenues came 18 months after hiring sales engineers. Right, Michael?" Michael nodded.

"Now for the best news. I'm looking for a skunk works space to invent new products. Stay tuned," Pug said as he folded the agenda. "One more thing: Jackson Huntley says IPS just got its regional patent for Asia. We got full protection throughout Asia. Jackson's lookin' at some infringement by Hondoya and Nippon Tooling." Looking directly at Kenji, he continued, "It's Jap Tech's responsibility to defend Japanese patents."

Kenji lit a cigarette and exhaled without comment.

Michael read his expression. *He disagrees...*

"Jackson says Lawrent Appliance infringes the American IPS 10000 patent. Once he's ready, I'll update the board. Okay, that's it. Motion to adjourn?"

"I second," Darin said. "Let's get to the blackjack tables."

Michael and Ellie rushed to catch their San Francisco flight. "How was the meeting?" Ellie asked.

"I joined at the right time! Pug's full of great surprises. IPS is hitting on all cylinders: booming sales, new people, investments, patents."

"Any concerns?"

"Mr. Kobyashi and Pug have serious issues. I think Kenji values Pug's creativity, but Pug harbors a deep resentment. It'll be a challenge to fix their relationship."

"Any surprises?"

"Didn't realize Pug's younger brother and oldest son worked at IPS."

"Sounds like you work for a family enterprise."

"Yeah, there's one more surprise... Pug wants me to stay in San Francisco."

"What? First we were living in Japan, then Denver, and now San Francisco?"

Michael laughed. "You never know what's in his digital brain."

Pug and Marcy dined at Caesars's Terrazzo Restaurant. "See the VIP lounge over there? It's for high rollers. You can find me there after the IPO!" Pug declared.

Marcy smiled and pointed to the nearby giant million-dollar slot machine. "And I'll play that. Did you have a good meeting?"

"Ted went bonkers about the fifty-five dollar share valuation."

Pug ordered a T-bone steak and a Pat Henry and told the waiter, "Extra rare. Just walk it by the grill."

"What did the board say about the new building purchase?"

"They loved my skunk works idea."

"Did Darin object?"

"Too busy thinking about selling his shares to Kenji so cheap."

"I'm so happy Skip will have a real office."

"So I can keep a close eye on him."

The waiter brought lunch. Pug talked between big bites. "I got Robert Duvall to control Mr. Sake-sipper."

"Robert Duvall?"

"You know, the constigulatoria in *The Godfather?*"

"Oh, you mean Michael's your consigliore!" Marcy stifled a laugh.

Pug took a long gulp. "Don't understand that Jap. Won't lift a finger to defend my patents. Really pisses me off! Once I kick Hondoya's ass, I'm raising his royalty fee."

They ordered double-fudge sundaes and toasted each other with full spoons.

"Having the IPS family in one location with trusted friends is our dream come true," Marcy said.

"Sweetie, when IPS goes public, my ship will sail in an ocean of silver."

Marcy patted his thigh. "What should we name our ship?"

"The USS Silver Lining!"

"You're so clever. Tonight, you can steer my ship."

"You got it, sweetie!" Pug's demeanor changed abruptly. "Just wish mom was alive to see me now."

"She'd be so proud of what you accomplished."

PART II
THE DESCENT
(1994–2002)

1994
LOS ANGELES

S EAN CHECKED INTO THE MARRIOTT Hotel and proceeded to Encounters, the futuristic restaurant at Los Angeles Airport. He liked the Asian décor and the 360-degree view of departing and arriving planes. At the bar, he ordered a tall Sapporo and wrote in his notebook:

October 14, 1994:

– – What a meeting! Kenji and Darin, the enemy of my enemy is not my friend.

– – Pug's crazy "skunk talk."

– – Watch Fields.

– – Babysit Dave?

– – Lawrent lawsuit is one of my annuities. He closed the notebook, checked his watch, and engaged a pocket recorder.

Larry Judson arrived, greeted Sean, and ordered a Stoli and tonic. "So what's new on the IPS legal front?" he asked.

Sean looked thoughtful. "Prepare for war."

"Understood, but we need time to position TAI products at Gen Appliance."

Sean listened intently as Larry outlined his thoughts.

After dinner, they headed to a strip club on Imperial Boulevard for more drinks.

Later in his hotel room, Sean summarized the recorded conversations, then watched pay TV porn for several hours before falling asleep.

LAS VEGAS

Kenji and Darin met at the ornate bar in Nero's Lounge. Kenji nursed a Johnnie Walker Blue; Darin ordered Coors. Kenji lit a cigarette and held the lighter for Darin's Cuban.

"Why did your cousin choose Caesars for this meeting?"

"Puggy couldn't find a hotel named Napoleon or General MacArthur."

Kenji smiled. "Please explain his comment about quiet period."

"Puggy's talking fantasy. I've just taken my company public, battled lawyers, accountants, and the SEC. There's a ton of work before IPS enters any quiet period. Puggy has no idea…"

An attractive server brought more drinks. Darin stuffed a $50 bill in her cleavage and whispered in her ear. Kenji watched Darin give her his room key.

"Mr. James, as we agreed, I will place your stock sale proceeds into my investment company, Brunei Holdings." He handed Darin a business card with a Caribbean offshore address.

"Thank you, Mr. Kobyashi. I look forward to our future relationship."

"I, as well, Mr. James. Tell me, why does IPS need a skunk works?"

"Beats me. The concept worked for Lockheed Aircraft; but at IPS, it's Puggy fantasy."

That evening, Kenji and Jun departed for Tokyo. Seated in first class, Kenji summarized the past four days. "Mr. James had his partnership opportunity. Unfortunate he rejected it."

"Hai! But the lawsuits could complicate our strategy," Jun said.

"Tell Dr. Yamura to organize TADA's response. And tell him to research MMc Ltd. and any licensees for its Singapore patent."

"Hai!"

"I will attend no more IPS board meetings. From now forward, Jun, you will represent my interests."

TOKYO

Kenji's chauffeur greeted him at Narita and drove him to Takamura where Shiganari waited. The old friends greeted each other with bows. After a round of Johnny Walker Blue, the waiter brought a first course of drunken prawns.

"We cannot underestimate damage from lawsuits involving American firms with proprietary technologies. Colorado's senior senator chairs the commerce committee and is an influential member of the foreign relations committee. If he suspects foreign interests threaten a constituent, it creates unwanted political attention," Kenji said.

"Mr. Pug James also plans to sue Lawrent. What will be our course of action?"

"Dr. Yamura will contact Gano-Nippon's lawyers."

"Excellent! Since Gano is discussing an alliance with Lawrent, it is wise to collaborate, but with caution."

Kenji smiled as the prawns grew still.

KOREA

Two weeks later, Michael sat in the United Airlines economy section and studied laptop notes from his recent Korean meetings.

Day 1-2: Visited Japan Technologies's facility to meet Kobyashi (K) and Ashi (A). K unavailable; message received.

– – Met in K's office. Carved Samurai chess set = war mentality. The American in the photo with General MacArthur and Kenji looks vaguely familiar.

– – A's nervous tics and endless smoking are distracting. A didn't host dinner but offered female companionship. Surprised at my refusal; message sent.

– – First official visit unproductive. Understand given Asian hierarchy and my "junior" status. Need to research the K and Pug history. Alluded to a failed partnership (?).

– – Met Ryo Ito in Tokyo. Good sense of humor. Still not sure about his business sense or work ethic. Did Pug even do the due diligence I recommended?

– – Reviewed actions to establish Asian HQ office. Doing everything first class at Pug's direction. (Uncomfortable about this investment with no near-term revenue.)

Days 3-7: Met kimchi gang in Seoul.

– – *Their English is poor. All related: father, son, brother-in-law. Does Pug know? The in-law consultant allegedly has extensive market experience but unrelated to thermal and acoustics dissipaters. I would have never hired these bozos. What was Pug thinking?*

– – *They claimed Pug already met with lawyers and accountants to establish a legal entity. Pug never mentioned this. Somehow they convinced Pug to focus on Handi, fourth largest Asian appliance OEM.*

– – *IPS's office located in Seoul, yet Handi facilities are 250 kilometers away; this makes no sense... except Seoul's where the kimchi gang lives.*

– – *Visited Handi. Our consultant unclear about active projects and has no business development strategy, and worse, no relationships at senior levels. He blamed customer for lack of progress. Strike one.*

– – *Visited local metal stamper. Supposedly, company is local partner candidate. It's a family-owned operation that supplies thermal dissipater systems to Handi. Met in overcrowded office and suffered arrogant owner's excessive smoking. He claimed his special relationships are crucial for IPS success in Korea. Our consultant remained deferential. I smell conflict of interest. Stamper expected exclusive rights to IPS 10000 for little or no cost. Told owner IPS would study his "interesting" proposal. Back in car, told consultant this visit was unproductive. Strike two.*

– – *In Seoul, Ms. Oh, Arthur Hansen accountant, briefed us on legal entity status. She insisted I sign documents "Mr. James already approved." I deferred.*

– – *Met with Ryo before departing. Said Ms. Oh and Pug established a "very close working relationship." Strike three?*

– – *Summary:*

– – *Pug and I need a long talk about IPS strategy in both countries.*

– – *Pug's previous trips probably rushed; decisions didn't consider long-term implications. – I can manage Korea (if Pug doesn't interfere).*

– – *Japan Technologies and K relationship another matter. Keep Pug out of K's face so I can work some diplomacy.*

SOUTH SAN FRANCISCO

In December, Pug called together Michael, Skip, Sean, and Dave to unveil the building for his skunk works. The group toured the glass-and-steel structure located near the intersection of Paul and Silver

Streets in Brisbane Technology Park. From the rooftop on a clear day, one could see from the Bay Bridge to Candlestick Park. The interior of the three-story building, unoccupied for five years, was in horrid condition.

Sean asked, "Do we need all this space just for development?"

"With my plans, IPS'll need more space by the end of '95," Pug replied.

"How much did this cost?" Michael asked.

"Real bargain 'cuz I got a lease/purchase option."

Michael and Sean exchanged puzzled looks. "Needs serious renovation," Sean said.

"Let's get crankin' and get the new digs cleaned up!" Pug handed out hard hats. "First floor's for R&D; second's for offices."

"Let's do it!" Dave shouted.

"You gotta be kidding," Skip moaned.

Over the next few weeks, everybody pitched in to clean the building and set up offices. Pug personally supervised the construction work by electricians, plumbers, and carpenters. Pug commandeered the largest corner office, a triangular-shaped space with two floor-to-ceiling glass walls, a perfect vantage point overlooking Lake Paul. Sean grabbed the other prime corner office, and Skip took an office in between. A small desk in the development lab served as Dave's office. Michael selected a small, unpretentious space soon cluttered with "file piles" and books.

Marcy decorated Pug's office. On the interior wall, she hung the painting of the Colorado silver mine, the framed bank wire, and a directors' picture from the Las Vegas celebration. She created space for Pug's silver-framed patents. She loaded a credenza with family pictures; and on Pug's desk she placed his mother's picture, the silver music box, and the silver Baoding balls.

Pug was admiring the setup when Sean poked his head in. "You brought Colorado to California."

"And you better do the same! I want the labs running yesterday! Start recruiting engineers! My Chicago cousin's waitin' for your call."

"Why not use a California recruiter?"

"Cousin needs the work. Found any prior art on Lawrent's TAI patent?"

"Doesn't the board have to approve the lawsuit first?"

"Board's just window dressing for my IPO."

"Okay. By the way, I need a computer."

"Computers are for secretaries and bean counters."

"It'll help with my patent searches, running test analyses, and reports. With internet access, I can help your relative's recruiting."

"Get Dave's input, and lemme see the purchase order."

"What's Dave's background?"

"Got real talent. Speaks Jap yap so he can help with Jap projects."

"What do you want him to do?"

"Hey, that's why I hired you."

Sean resisted laughing. Pug continued, "Dave's willing to learn, gets bored easy. Don't let him do anything illegal, okay?" Sean's concerned look prompted Pug. "Hey, just kiddin'! Almost forgot, I got you another engineer from Denver."

"Yeah, Rich claimed I stole him from his group," Sean said as he turned to leave.

"Beats me how he got that crazy idea."

Pug flopped into his chair, dialed Jackson Huntley, and left a message: "Hey, Jackson! Need to talk about those Lawrent bastards. ASAP!"

He put down the phone, glanced out the wide window, and stared at the lake. He recalled Rich's and Sean's last meetings with General Appliance purchasing.

"Puggy, General's procurement guy wants cost data on IPS 10000 products."

"What the hell for? Our price is way below Lawrent's."

"General's cost analysts say our prices are excessive."

"Tell 'em to stick it up their asses."

"Puggy, I can't do that."

"I don't share secret cost data!"

"If we don't do something, they'll find other suppliers. Let's counter with some volume commitments and multi-year contracts in return for lower prices. We got enough margin."

"No!"

"What about their request to license other suppliers?"

"I had Sean tell Dan Teller we don't teach competitors our technology."

Pug stood, walked to the window, and shoved his hands in his pockets. He remembered Rich's subsequent phone call.

"Heard General met with all their suppliers—except us. They told everybody to design around IPS's patent. This ain't good news."

Sean rested his long legs on the desk and studied computer magazines. He drafted a purchase order and called Dave. "I need a computer and internet provider. Wrote preliminary specs. Tell me if I'm on the right track."

Dave noted Sean wanted 90 MHz processor speed, 4MB of memory, and 240MB of hard drive capacity, 14.4 Baud modem, and Compuserve as the ISP. Dave recommended 120 MHz Pentium, 16 MB of memory, 420 MB hard drive and an ISDN providing 112 BPS. Instead of CompuServe, he argued for AOL as the Internet service provider.

"These upgrades worth it?" Sean asked.

"Absolutely! Intel's new MMX technology is a third faster. If you need it later, you can add memory or another larger hard drive, but the processor is really hard to upgrade. If you want lots of extra storage, get a zip drive. The ISDN gives your more speed than a standard modem. AOL gives you a real email address not a number like CompuServe. You'll have capability for all kinds of technical analysis, data searches, and enough disk memory and processor speed for large data downloads."

"Appreciate your input."

"When it comes, I'll set it up for you."

"Thanks." *But no thanks.*

Sean finalized the purchase request for Pug's approval. A cover letter described Dave's recommendations. A few days later, Dell boxes arrived.

Pug headed to Sean's office. "Hey, Doc, let's get some ding sun."

"Dim sum? Want me to drive?"

"Taking my car. Don't like your Jap trap. Can't support the trade deficit."

They headed to the parking lot. As Pug started the ignition, a conservative talk show host's voice bellowed. Pug switched off the radio.

"You listen to that conservative wind bag of mush?"

"Whadya talking about?"

"Come on Pug, you love that fat, obnoxious blow-hard!"

"So when you movin'?"

"What's the hurry? You commuted for six years. Besides you sprung this new location with no advance warning. Got lots of transition stuff, especially with our Chicago sales manager and having to argue with Rich about which equipment and tools to transfer. And, I need time for personal stuff like selling my house."

"You telling me you can't do it?"

"Okay, okay, but cut me some slack!"

"Another thing, I want Marken fired yesterday!"

"Huge mistake!"

"If Marken reduces commissions to one percent, then I'll reconsider."

"Wait until our new sales team's in place. Your Chicago cousin hasn't sent any candidates to interview."

"Look, you want me to call Marken?"

At the restaurant, they sat at a small table. Waiters circulated offering various dishes. Sean and Pug made selections. "Don't you love this food? Better than sushi and salami crap."

"I wouldn't know." *Sashimi, you cultural putz.*

"Chinese stuff is as good as Mexican. Speaking of which, we need to talk about our trip. I promised the board we'd open Mexico."

"Why now?"

"Hondoya's regional headquarters is there, and IPS needs global reach."

The server brought tea and fortune cookies. "Doc, listen to mine. 'Behind every obstacle is a silver lining.'"

"Obviously written by an optimist."

As they returned, Pug said, "I convinced Ted to give you 20,000 more options. But you gotta move first. Okay?"

"Okay, Pug. That eases my economic concerns."

Back in his office, Pug called Bruce. "You got the due diligence report?"

"Any day now."

"Tell those slow-poke Jap auditors to get moving. It better be good 'cuz I'm givin' Kenji a Don Corleone offer."

1995
SOUTH SAN FRANCISCO

S EAN SPENT THE SECOND WEEK in January organizing the development lab and setting up his computer. He instructed Dave and the other engineer to study each active project and to prepare a status review.

One of Dave's projects attracted Sean's interest. "Whatever happened with your idea to insulate toasters?"

"Still playing around with it."

"How did you attach the 10000 insulation?"

"Used stainless steel clips. Measured the temps inside and outside of the toaster."

"And?"

"Outside cover temperature declined 150 degrees. I could touch it without burning my hand."

"Makes sense. How many tests have you done?"

"Ten."

"Consistent results?"

"Absolutely. Guess what's the best part?"

"Safety?"

"No! Faster toasting time and better taste. Next I'll try it in ovens."

Sean thought. *That's novel.* "Do more testing, and we'll talk in a few weeks."

"Got it! How do you like your computer?"

"Good so far."

"It'd be great if we had lab computers so we could share info. I wouldn't have to bother you to run our test results."

"Did you take computer classes at school?"

"Yeah, but they were boring."

A few weeks later, Dave stopped by Michael's office. "Things are slow in the labs. Need any help on Korean projects?"

"Sean agree?" *Shouldn't Sean have more work for Dave? Weird...*

"He said check with you."

"Our kimchi gang dropped the ball on the heat dissipater for Handi Appliances. You can help with that. My Korean buddy, a former MatraScience guy, could use some assistance."

After a two-week break working on home and car projects, Pug headed straight to Michael's office. "Don't you know someone who owns appliance dealerships?"

"My friend in Pueblo, Colorado has several, American and Japanese. Why?"

"Just repaired my oven and saw the insulation."

"So, you're thinking why not check out insulations on ovens, water heaters, dishwashers, etc.?"

"You're reading my brain! Ask your pal if we can examine several models. I'll have Rich video everything."

PUEBLO, COLORADO

In February, Michael and Rich met at Denver International and drove to Pueblo. They would spend four long days studying forty different appliance models. Michael explained, "My friend's letting us use his repair shop to examine dissipaters. You film; I narrate."

"Another Puggy crazy idea?"

"Stay tuned."

They checked into the Hilton and met in the lounge for drinks before dinner.

"Why'd you leave Appliancorp?" Michael asked.

"Bastards moved my job to Chicago. Couldn't relocate because of my daughter's medical condition. Puggy needed help, begged me to join IPS."

"Is Puggy a nickname of endearment?"

"You could say that," Rich grinned. "Dad hated the name Paul, so he called him Puggy."

On day five, they drove back to Denver. "We must have filmed the insides of over forty-five different appliances. Lots of fiberglass and other unacceptable materials being used," Michael said.

"One thing for sure, IPS is a minor player. Hell, less than five percent of the dissipater applications are potential for us," Rich said.

"Means we have a great opportunity to grow market share three ways: from competitors, from increased growth, and from new technologies."

"That's Puggy talk! He claims it's a twenty-five-billion-dollar market for appliance insulation."

"Assume five dissipaters per model at five dollars a pop times one billion appliances produced each year, and you can get to twenty-five billion real quick," Michael said. "Pug wants us in Chicago to show the video. At the beginning of the film, insert two letters: *AA*."

"What for?"

"You'll see at the premier."

CHICAGO

Pug, Sean, Michael, and Rich arrived in Chicago for an oven appliance show. Pug and Sean set up the IPS exhibit booth, and Michael arranged for a hotel conference room. On the first evening, Sean opted for a customer dinner meeting leaving Michael, Pug, Rich, and the Chicago sales manager to view the film. The opening credits highlighted AA.

"What's AA?" Pug asked.

"Remember your analysis memo?"

"Yeah, the one Doug sabotaged."

"Think about it."

Pug's eyes sparkled. "Appliance Analysis!"

At the end of the forty-five minute film, Pug asked, "Well, whadya guys think?"

"IPS has no market share and not enough technologies to compete," Rich replied.

"Typical septic thinking. Michael, whadya think?"

"I understand why Rich could be skeptical, but there's huge opportunity to grow."

"Bingo! Michael wins. This film's our roadmap for developing dissipaters for each appliance. New technologies equal more opportunities. So what's the big roadblock?"

No one answered.

"Our material is only two dimensions, length and width. We need multi-dimensions."

Rich groaned, "Oh shit! Here we go again."

"Let's break for dinner. Maybe some carbs will make my pork-ass brother think."

As they took the elevator to the hotel's top-floor restaurant, Michael patted Pug on the back. "Haven't lost your vision."

"It's 20-20!"

"If we apply the AA to Exeter, then we can apply it to…"

"Hondoya… bingo, bango!"

"And have Dave do the AA project."

"What's Jap for 'bongo'?"

DENVER

Pug waited in Bruce's office for a conference call. "What I like about Jackson is his iron."

Bruce arched his brow. "Say what?"

"The book, *All Lawyers are Gators,* talks about lawyers and ethics."

"Iron?"

"Gators should have ethics. This book says they don't."

Bruce smiled, "Oh, you mean ironic."

"That's what I said."

The phone rang; Pug engaged the speaker. "Hey, Jackson! How was the Hawaii triathlon?"

"Finished third."

"Great. How do you like your new plane?"

"I'll give you a ride when I come to Denver."

"You better! I own a piece with all the money I pay you."

"Pug, I reviewed Lawrent's TAI patent. The USPTO granted it

about twenty months after IPS 10000. TAI's appearance, form, fit, and function are definitely similar to IPS 10000. Only the internal construction differs. The material between metal layers creates indentations, but no question it infringes."

"How do we prove it?"

"Through discovery."

"How much'll it cost?"

"Discovery could last six months."

"Can't you gators crawl faster?"

"There's an alternative: Seek a commercial resolution, cross-licensing, or some other arrangement—less expensive, perhaps more profitable."

"No fuckin' way! Sean said Lawrent requested an IPS license. He told 'em to invent their own products."

"I could talk with their lawyers."

"Jackson, the last time I licensed somebody, I got screwed and tattooed and Kenji got twenty-five percent of my ass."

Jackson paused. "Pug, I never saw that agreement before you signed it."

Bruce flashed Pug a "told-you-so" expression.

"My board fully supports this lawsuit. How 'bout Dexter-Foresmen doing this on contingency?"

A stretch of silence ensued. "Pug, our firm rarely does that, but I could run it by our executive committee." Jackson continued as if thinking out loud. "Your estimate of lost market share and profits is significant. If we prove intentional infringement, damages could triple. But I need first-class technical and financial experts. Could be costly."

"Hey, takes money to make money! Get your co-gators on board. Talk to ya later, Jackson."

Pug hung up and turned to Bruce. "Think Dexter-Foresmen'll do it?"

"Jackson sounded non-committal."

"Say, I gotta call Marcy. Tell the crew I'll be back next month."

Bruce closed the door, and Pug dialed. "Hey sweetie, talked to Jackson. He's doing a contingency."

"Contingency?"

"Gator talk for they pay the bills for a piece of the award. Like those TV ads for medical screw-ups."

Two weeks later, Pug returned to IPS's facility like a spring tornado. Chaos swirled as he tackled problems, real and imagined. First stop: manufacturing. With Rich in tow, he stopped at each workstation and greeted employees by first names along with hearty handshakes. A new press was idle.

"Why ain't this operating?"

"Broken," Rich responded.

"Bullshit! I'll fix it! Why am I the one who..."

"Fuck it! I'll get the machinist!" Rich shouted. "We wouldn't have maintenance problems if you'd spend some bucks on this plant instead of your California country club!" He reached into his pocket for a Pall Mall and stomped away.

"Hey! Smoke outside! And Porky, lose some weight!"

Rich hollered over his shoulder, "Look who's talking with that gut hanging over your belt!"

The machinist arrived, and Pug told him, "Here's what I want done..."

Later, he headed to Bruce's office. Pug's continual demand for "what if" analyses taxed Bruce's Excel skills. Besides accounting duties, Bruce monitored patents and managed human resources.

"Last month's profits suck! Already found four mistakes in your numbers."

Bruce adjusted his bow tie. "What's wrong?"

"Material costs are too damn high!"

"We decreased finished goods inventory by a huge amount. We wrote off the prior month's material and overhead. That's why material costs are higher than normal."

"Show me the physical inventory worksheet!" Pug demanded.

After hearing Bruce's update, Pug bounded into Rich's office.

"So what else you find at the dealership?"

"So, I'm fat?"

"Chrissakes, I was kidding. You know I always got your back."

Rich popped a mint in his mouth. "Three more violations."

"Call Jackson!" Moments later, "Hey Jackson, Rich's got news."

"I visited another Hondoya appliance dealer and inspected five different models," Rich said. "Three had separate dissipaters with infringing insulation. Definitely not Japan Technologies's."

"Yeah, we think it's supplied by Nippon Tooling," Pug added.

"Send me samples, photos, and an inspection summary," Jackson said. "I'll compare to the original information, then I'll have a new motion on the judge's desk in a few days."

Pug yelled, "Jackson, get some cash outta those bastards!" He hung up.

"Bro, gimme the story on orders."

"We're losing our most profitable Appliancorp business." Before Rich finished, Pug dialed Sean in California.

"What the hell's going on with Appliancorp?"

"Did you call the sales manager and Marken?" Sean asked.

"He doesn't know shit, and fuck Marken! Call Appliancorp and get me some answers!"

Rich chuckled. *The doctor just got a dissipater shoved up his PhD ass.*

Sean thought about Pug's rant then dialed Larry Judson.

"Sean, good to hear from you. What's up?"

"IPS needs to hire direct sales guys. Any suggestions?"

"Got some Lawrent rejects, but…"

"Send the resumes to Louis James in Chicago but keep the source confidential. One more thing, legal paperwork coming soon."

"Thanks, Sean. I'll get back to you."

Sean clicked off his recorder.

At McCormick's, Pug lunched with the investment banker referred by Robby Benton. Earlier, Pug had sent 1994 financial information and estimates for 1995.

After ordering drinks, Pug wasted no time. "So whadya think of IPS's numbers?"

"Pug, it will be our pleasure to begin the IPO process."

"Do my ears hear me? Now you're crankin'!"

"Send us three-year audited results and well-documented financial projections for the next three. Here's a checklist of other information we need to examine."

"Told the board we're in the quiet period."

"Not so fast, Pug. You have lots of work to do before that begins. What's the latest on the patent litigation?"

"Dexter-Foresmen's filing a second injunction against Hondoya. Jackson says we'll get a nice chunk of cash now that the first injunction was violated."

"Good to hear. If there's any other development on the legal front, let me know."

They finished lunch, rechecked the list, and agreed to talk in two weeks.

Lawrent received the official complaint accusing it (and to-be-named parties) of direct patent infringement. IPS demanded recovery of profits on lost sales and termination of all infringing activity. For Lawrent's willful infringement, IPS sought treble damages and attorneys' fees. IPS requested a court injunction prohibiting Lawrent's continued infringement.

Two weeks later, Lawrent countersued claiming IPS infringed its TAI patent. It further stated IPS's patent was indefinite and unenforceable, maintaining certain claims were invalid. The suit accused Dexter-Foresmen of misleading the USPTO for not disclosing prior art in a timely fashion.

The same examiner had granted both patents, so his opinions were public record. Unless subpoenaed by either party or ordered by the court, he would not testify at trial or give depositions. The discovery process would commence in sixty days.

SOUTH SAN FRANCISCO

Pug called Jackson. "Whadya think of Lawrent's gators?"

"Jason & Jones is first class."

"Just win! As Arthur said, 'There's no victory for substitutes.'"

"You referring to General MacArthur?"

"Yeah. He beat the Japs! Say, why are you guys in trouble with the patent office?"

"Nothing to worry about. We followed all the disclosure rules. Their lawyers are trying to confuse the judge."

"What 'bout Lawrent's claim my patent ain't valid?"

"It's a diversionary tactic."

"You better be right. Say, why in the hell are we getting invoices for the experts? I thought you were paying for experts," Pug said.

"Exhibit A of our contingency contract specifies certain costs as client's out-of-pocket."

"Bruce didn't mention any Exhibit A. Says your experts could cost five hundred thousand dollars."

"We can't win if you nickel and dime the experts."

Sharon Manzi became IPS's latest hire and Pug's personal assistant. With her bouffant red-tinted hair and thick make-up, she appeared older than her thirty-five years. Her snug sweaters outlined a well-endowed bosom. She squinted through oversized lenses as she handed Pug a FedEx package.

"What's this?"

"It's from Arthur Hansen's Japanese affiliate."

Pug skipped to the letter's summary. He yelled for Michael and dialed Bruce in Denver. When Michael arrived, Pug ordered, "Look at this."

Bruce came on the line. "Hey, Pug."

"Michael's with me. Whadya think about the Jap accountant's report?"

"Looks like Mr. Kobyashi wants close to ten million. Did you read Appendix One?"

"No."

"He wants ten million after tax. IPS would have to gross up the purchase price by another five to seven million."

"Shit! That'll take all my IPO cash!"

"It's the least of our problems. Appendix Two describes Japan Technologies's special payments to OEMs' employees and certain government agencies."

"Excuse me," Michael interjected, "I smell bribes."

Bruce answered, "Exactly!"

"It's common practice," Michael said. "Even though the US companies must comply with the Foreign Corrupt Practices Act, it doesn't mean foreign companies do."

"We can't work with Japan Technologies if we know it engages in illegal practices. We should cancel the license agreement," Bruce said.

"Relax! I signed a confidentiality agreement."

"Pug, I can't believe what I'm hearing!" Bruce said.

"Fieldsy, whadya think?"

"Let's study this and find a reason to halt the purchase discussions without either side losing face. IPS can't afford Kenji's price," Michael said.

"What about canceling the license agreement?" Bruce asked.

"I'll take care of this," Pug declared.

A few days later, with Michael listening, Pug phoned Kenji.

"Kenji, how ya doing?"

"Very well, Mr. James. I trust you are ready to make an offer."

"No can do, Kenji. The investment banker stopped the IPO. Said wait 'til we win the lawsuits."

"Mr. James, this is most disappointing."

"It's the banker's call." Pug concluded the conversation and phoned Bruce.

"Bruce, just talked with Kenji. Told him we're good to go." Pug winked at Michael.

"You didn't?"

"Fieldsy convinced me we could ignore bribes. It's how Japs do business. How we gotta do business in Japan."

"IPS must comply with US law!" Bruce exclaimed. He heard bursts of laughter.

"Don't get your beans in a blender! I shit-canned the deal."

Bruce hung up. He was relieved but upset about wasted data preparation and the accountant's bill of $55 thousand.

SAN MATEO

Skip's morning visits with Marcy often included Billy, his two-year-old son.

"Honey, Daddy just left for the airport. Get some coffee while I give my cutie a big kissy kiss." Handing him a stuffed toy, she cooed, "Look what Granny has for you... Skip, what's wrong? You look worried."

"Oh, Michelle's at the doctor again. Mom, I got a customer appointment. Can you look after Billy for a few hours?"

"Honey, happy to. I'll take him home when she returns. Let me know what the doctor says."

"Mom, she's really depressed about money. She shouldn't have stopped working."

"But Skip, look at the beautiful baby you produced. I'll talk to Daddy. How much do you need?"

"Seven thousand. Michelle is three months behind on the mortgage."

CHICAGO

Each May, appliance manufacturers introduced their latest models at McCormick Convention Center in Chicago. Skip scouted the exhibits before stopping at the booth of Mathews Company, the world's largest manufacturer of gas water heaters. The salesman glanced at Skip's nametag. "Welcome to Mathews. What does IPS do?"

"We develop and market dissipaters for noise and heat control."

Skip examined display models, each with cut-away sections. He recognized insulation made from fiberglass composites.

"Mathews happy with fiberglass?"

"No, because it's difficult to handle. Unions complain about work hazards."

Skip asked for brochures and names of technical contacts.

His next stop was Sunshine Toaster. A young woman greeted him. He was transfixed by her ice-blue eyes and pixie-cut blonde hair.

"I... I'm Skip James. This is... uh... quite a display." *God, she's gorgeous!*

"Annie Ramirez. Pleased to meet you." She surveyed Skip's handsome face and lean physique. "Happy to answer questions about our new models."

"Who's your technical manager?"

"You're in luck today." She escorted him to a corner table. "Mr. James, this is Samuel Ramirez, Sunshine's CEO and chief technical officer."

"Pleasure to meet you, sir. I wondered what insulation materials Sunshine uses to address thermal problems."

Skip listened, then gave a ten-minute overview of IPS 10000 and how it could improve toaster performance. Sam invited him to visit Sunshine's technical group.

When Skip departed, Sam told Annie, "His pitch is well-rehearsed. What do you think?"

"He knows his subject."

"I saw the gleam in your baby blues. You know the old joke about a salesman lying?"

"Yes, Father. Whenever his lips move."

"You've been warned."

At the end of second day, Skip had several sales leads. He relaxed at the hotel bar, ordered a drink, and removed his wedding band.

A smartly dressed patron sat next to him.

"Name's Bob Kenton."

"Skip James. Nice to meet you."

"Pretty impressive show."

"Sure is." Skip looked at Bob's nametag. "What does Kenton-Aerocon do?"

"Sales and distribution for aerospace and construction markets."

"Why attend an appliance show?"

"I look for cutting-edge technologies and new applications. Our customers use huge amounts of insulation for thermal and noise control. What does I-P-S do?"

"International Protected Solutions develops and manufactures thermal insulation materials, mostly appliance. Always looking for opportunities outside our traditional markets."

"Interesting, how does IPS sell?"

"Through sales reps. Hey, my date's here. Nice chatting."

"Here's my card. Nice meeting you." Bob watched Skip embrace his companion. *Charming guy... with an eye for good-looking women. Got to thank Darin for the heads up about Skip.*

SOUTH SAN FRANCISCO

The next week, Skip sat in Pug's office.

"Get any orders?" Pug demanded.

"Pops, I was doing market research."

"Yeah, right, but we can't book loafing at trade shows as revenue."

Skip yelled, "That's not fair!"

"Can't take constructive criticism?"

"You got Grandpa James's zero empathy! I'm through with this meeting!"

"Don't let the door hit your soft, sensitive ass on the way out; gonna cry on Mommy's apron?"

Skip blew past Michael in the hallway. Michael entered the office expecting an agitated Pug, but found him smiling. "What's up?"

"Talked to Jackson this morning. Da Judge went ballistic about Hondoya. Threatened their lawyers with contempt and slapped 'em with a second injunction. Hondoya's gator is ready to settle."

"Fantastic! The second injunction halts their marketing activities in the U.S. Let's be ready with commercial alternatives."

"You're readin' my brain!"

During the first week in June, Sean met Dave in the development lab. "Dave, look at these cut-away photos of Mathews's gas water heaters. Skip brought them from Chicago. What do you see?"

"Fiberglass. Way ahead of you! I'll replace fiberglass with IPS 10000 and see what happens!"

"Get a Mathews's water heater, tear it down, baseline the thermals. Then, install some IPS 10000 prototypes. Test against baseline. Take loads of thermal images for you know who."

"I'm on it!"

"How are your other projects?"

"Having problems with the dissipater for the Handi oven. I've tried origami techniques to fold and bend 10000 material. Looks like shit."

"Other ideas?"

"See those cooking trays on the bench?"

Sean examined them. They comprised multi-layers of metal alloy shaped in various forms. The edges were reinforced tight spirals.

Dave continued, "Those edges provide structural integrity. If we did this with multiple IPS 10000 layers, we could form multi-dimensional parts."

"I'm skeptical." *Very clever. These trays are produced in large quantities so unit costs are low. Got a hunch this can pass thermal and rigorous vibration tests. Market opportunities are unlimited for appliance applications with unusual dimensions. This could be my silver bullet patent.*

"Dave, the concept needs testing. It doesn't look patentable; there must be a ton of prior art."

"Understand. Say, need to update you on Korea. Michael's friend wants me there for two weeks for customer calls and training."

"Michael okay with it?"

"Absolutely!"

"Give me the travel dates. You can start the Hondoya Appliance Analysis when you return."

Later Sean wrote his notes and disclosures describing invention possibilities. Once Dave completed testing and proof of concept, he planned two patent applications.

"Sharon! Get in here!"

"Yes, Pug?" Sharon stood at the door and adjusted her glasses.

"It's show time for the new location! Notify management and the board."

The phone rang; Pug picked up. "Hey, sweetie."

Sharon sighed and waited. *Marcy needs a life. What's the latest family crisis?*

Pug put down the phone. "Billy's got the sniffles. Okay, back to the agenda. Find me a good steak house for the board dinner."

Sharon returned to her desk. *Maybe I should call Marcy and ask her to weigh in on the restaurant choice.*

The following day, Pug was reading Sharon's daily summary when a small voice shrieked, "Grampy!" Skip and Billy appeared at the door.

Pug stood and opened his arms. "You got a big hug for Grampy?" Billy jumped into Pug's arms. He winced as his sore shoulder absorbed the impact.

"Hey Pops, Michelle's got a headache. Babysitting Billy today."

"Grampy, can I sleep with you and Grammy tonight?"

"You betcha! Sharon, get some cookies, the books and puzzles. Hold my calls."

Skip disappeared. Pug's office became a noisy, hide-and-seek playground. Puzzle pieces and toys cluttered the floor.

From her desk, Sharon watched the circus. *Skip's left. Wife's got a headache. Grandpa's babysitting, and Grandma will call any minute now.*

Two weeks later, Bruce and Rich joined Michael, Skip, Sean, and Pug for the management meeting. They all assembled in the building lobby where Pug announced,

"Before we start, Doc will give the Denver guys a quick tour of my new digs. Next year by this time, the building will be full with engineers, development equipment, a tooling shop, and prototype manufacturing. We'll be looking for extra space."

After the tour, they convened in the gigantic conference room. Pug had purchased an enormous new table and twenty matching chairs. A hand-carved checkers set rested in the center of the polished table.

"Puggy, we gonna play checkers?" Rich asked.

"Rich doesn't understand symbols," Pug replied.

"Symbols?" Sean looked puzzled.

"Doc, checkers means wham-bam-thank-you-ma'am."

"Oh, so sorry, kind master. I way too slow today." Sean bowed.

Bruce laughed. "So, where'd you get it?"

"Bought it at a crafts fair in the Castro from the Log Cabin Republicans."

"You know who they are?" Rich asked.

Everyone laughed except Bruce.

Pug barked, "Okay Porky, joke time's over!"

"Where's the agenda, Puggy?" Rich asked.

"It's between my ears! Bruce, show Porky the financials."

Standing at the overhead projector, Bruce thought, *If I get beyond slide two…*

The first slide showed IPS's audited income statement. "Numbers for 1994 are spectacular! Sales finished at fourteen million with post tax profits of two-point-eight million. Our sales to Appliancorp and Gen Appliance led the way providing seventy percent of our profits."

Pug interrupted, "Hey guys, '94 bonuses will be outta sight! Sorry Bruce, didn't mean to steal your thunder."

Bruce fumed. "Enough about '94. Let's look at 1995's plan." His second slide showed a projected income statement. "Early signs show slower order rates. I reduced the sales forecast to eighteen million. Still solid growth over '94."

"Too low!" Pug shouted. "The investment banker needs twenty million!"

Sean scribbled in his notebook.

Looking directly at Sean, Rich asked, "What's happening with Appliancorp? At this rate, '95's a disaster!"

"Look, you know monthly fluctuations happen, inventory adjustments, etc. If you know more, enlighten us," Sean answered. *Thanks for the question, asshole!*

Bruce warned, "IPS undertook considerable new spending not in the 1994 run rates. If incremental sales don't materialize, we'll have serious..."

"Won't happen," Pug interrupted.

"We need to conserve cash." Bruce paused, hoping the suggestion resonated.

"Hey, enough financials; '95's banked. Let's get to important stuff. Doc, tell us about the technical stuff."

Before Sean could begin, Pug interjected. "What's happening on recruitment? Your numero uno priority!"

"Technical talent's scarce. Silicon Valley internet startups take all the good engineers. Starting salaries are out of sight."

"Why not advertise in the Midwest?" Rich asked. "We're in the appliance business... duh. Bet there's a ton of cold weather warriors who'd give their right nut to join this country club."

"For once Porky's got a good idea," Pug said. "You call my cousin Louis in Chicago?"

"Not yet," Sean replied.

"Well, do it! He owes me big time."

"Our sales manager is unhappy with the sales candidates he's found."

"I'll light a fire under both their asses. Am I the only one who makes things happen?"

Bruce, Sean, and Rich exchanged bemused glances.

Stunning everyone, Pug announced, "Prior art searches have started for the Lawrent lawsuit."

"But we haven't budgeted legal costs," Bruce said.

"Has the board approved?" Rich asked.

"No sweat. Jackson's doing it on contingency. Only expense is out-of-pocket like Xeroxing, note taking, you know, minor stuff."

Bruce added, "But what about the experts' fees?"

"Told Jackson to get 'em reduced."

"So how long for this 'no-cost' litigation?" Rich asked.

"The lawyers complete discovery in three months, then get a court-directed judgment. Dexter-Foresmen's financial expert says IPS could get thirty-five million plus."

Michael noticed Sean fumbling with something in his coat jacket.

Pug continued, "More good news: the Denver court slapped Hondoya with a second injunction, and the Jap court backed my patent."

Sean asked, "Any updates on that Singapore company that opposed the APO patent?"

"Pug, be careful," Michael interjected. "There might be more opponents."

"Jackson's not worried, so I'm not."

Sean leaned back in his chair. *Michael's not brain dead after all.*

"Hey Michael, now you've interrupted me, report on Korea."

Michael omitted comments on the Korean personnel's lack of competence, especially the senior sales consultant. He extracted brief points from his trip report focusing on the Handi dissipater project.

Sean followed with an update on the US business outlook concluding, "Pug's twenty million dollar forecast looks solid."

Rich frowned. "IPS hasn't hired any sales guys, and Marken's gone!"

"When sales guys start, orders'll explode," Pug said. "Enough about technical. Rich, talk about Denver. Keep it short, Porky. It's lunch time, and I know you're hungry."

"Production at the plant is operating three shifts," Rich said, scowling. "We're outta space. No way can I support the '95 forecast."

"Bruce'll do a capital plan. Give him your input so I can decide priorities!"

Bruce shrugged.

"Nice you gave me a heads-up!" Rich yelled. "Lead time for some equipment is nine to twelve months!"

"I'll figure it out... like I always do."

Sean smirked. *Rich, just you wait. Asshole.*

They adjourned for lunch. Marcy had prepared a buffet. She greeted everyone and handed Bruce her invoice for five hundred dollars. Bruce thought, *This much for sandwiches, potato salad, and cookies?*

Sean skipped lunch, returned to his office, and summarized notes from the recorder.

That evening, Pug hosted management and the board at Alfred's Steak House in San Francisco. Over cocktails, Pug worked the room making sure everyone mingled. He came to the bar where Jun stood.

"Good evening, Mr. James."

"Where's Kenji?"

"Kobyashi-san authorized me to represent his interests."

"Never told me!" Pug growled. "You can't vote at the meeting. The company bylaws say only elected directors can."

Jun gave Pug a folded document. "This letter appoints me as Kobyashi-san's legal representative."

"Until my lawyer reviews it, you can't vote." He left Jun nervously lighting a cigarette.

At dinner, Pug tapped his wine glass. "Hey guys, welcome. Enjoy the meal. Tomorrow you'll hear nothing but good news."

The waiters poured more wine and served steaming bowls of lobster bisque and Caesar salads. Bruce distributed a one-page agenda.

Darin announced, "We just got an agenda twelve hours before the meeting! I got a great idea. Weather forecast says tomorrow's perfect for golf!"

"Ted, after eating that twenty-four-ounce steak, you'll be too bloated to swing," Pug snapped.

"Listen, management's here. Do the status reports tonight. We can discuss red-meat items over breakfast, done by nine, and on the first tee by ten. Do I hear a motion?"

"If that's how you do business in Seattle, no wonder your company ain't makin' money."

"We all like golf," Michael said. "Let's plan a golf day for the next board meeting."

Over an after-dinner cognac, Pug told Michael, "Fieldsy, thanks for killing Ted's dumb golf idea."

"You two come from the same family?"

"Ted came from crazy James side. Me, I favor Mom's side, the Deckers."

The group assembled in the conference room the next morning.

"Sharon, see if you can find 'Seattle Ted.' Probably hooked up with that bar gal."

Rich couldn't resist. "Guess Puggy stopped supporting Republicans." He pointed to the table's center. "Checker set's gone."

Pug ignored him. "Let's get started."

After approving minutes from the Las Vegas meeting, Bruce gave the financial update. Anticipating Pug's interruptions, he kept the presentation brief. Status reports by Sean, Michael, and Rich followed. Pug called a break and headed to his office. Fifteen minutes later, everyone returned to find Darin drinking coffee, his feet resting on the shiny new conference table.

"Nice of you to show, Ted. Meeting started two hours ago," Pug scowled.

"What's the big deal? Based on your agenda, I didn't miss anything. By the way, this building looks awfully big for a development lab."

"What's your point?"

"My point, Puggy, is a development lab should be close to manufacturing operations. Last time I checked it's still in Denver. Sure this building is only for development?"

"Right now I'm talking legal stuff." Pug stiffened his shoulders and tapped the agenda on the table. "Jun, leave the room."

Jun froze.

"Why does he have to leave?" Darin asked.

"Jap Tech doesn't support my Hondoya injunction. Jun, leave the room! I'll call ya when I'm done with Hondoya."

Jun, clutching his stomach and shaking, hastened to the door and closed it behind him.

Pug, angry and red-faced, shouted, "Ted, if you can't support me when there's serious shit like Hondoya litigation, then you leave too!"

"This is crazy," Darin said, shaking his head.

Pug quickly summarized the Hondoya litigation status then told Sharon to get Jun. Jun, agitated, returned and slumped in his chair.

"Dexter-Foresmen filed papers to sue Lawrent," Pug said.

"The board hasn't approved," Darin said.

"No need. We pay nothing unless IPS wins."

"I don't believe in free lunches. What's the contingency per cent?"

"IPS pays out-of-pocket only, but no gator time. They get forty percent when we win."

"That's huge." Darin sat back in his chair.

"Duh, when Lawrent sees their huge liability, they'll beg to settle. No way they wanna judge deciding damages."

Michael asked, "What did Jackson estimate for these out-of-pocket costs?"

"We're looking at two hundred K max, chump change given the '95 outlook. We can win forty million for a two-hundred-thousand-dollar bet."

Michael scanned his notes from the day before. *Yesterday it was thirty-five million.*

"Sounds like a lottery, but I'm no lawyer," Darin joked.

"You're right about the lawyer part. For those slow on the uptake, sixty percent of forty million is equal to an IPO with no SEC hassle."

"How long will litigation last?" Michael pressed.

"Jackson says less than six months, shorter with a pre-trial settlement. Jackson filed the papers in Chicago."

"Why not Denver or San Francisco?" Sean asked.

"Hafta to file where actual infringement occurred."

"Lawrent Appliance won't settle without a long fight," Darin declared.

"Ted, your comment is duly noted. Can I have a motion for the lawsuit?"

"Why the fuck bother? You already filed the documents. Have you considered the negative impact on Gen Appliance?"

"As Rhett said to Scarlett, I don't give a rat's ass."

Michael asked, "How about a commercial settlement?"

"Lawrent's not interested," Pug replied.

Sean and Rich exchanged confused glances.

The meeting adjourned without a vote.

Pug met with Michael for a post mortem. "So whadya think of the meeting?"

"Could have treated Jun more diplomatically," Michael said.

"It's time Jap Tech stepped up and defended my patent."

"When Asians lose face, they don't forget."

"Gimme a fuckin' break. They started it with Pearl Harbor, and I'm finishing it with Naga-sushi."

"Yeah, they lost the military war, but not the economic one." *Naga-sushi?*

"Can't wait to get Kenji and Ted off my board."

OSAKA

Two days later, Kenji found Jun waiting outside his office. Jun stood: shoulders hunched, his thin body quaking.

"Ashi-san, are you ill?"

"Mr. James humiliated me." Jun related the embarrassing confrontation.

"Ashi-san, patience. Revenge comes in due course. Besides Hondoya, what other legal matters were discussed?"

Jun summarized the Lawrent lawsuit and Pug's mention of the Singapore company opposing IPS's Asian patent.

"Dr. Yamura informs me that MMc Ltd. has licensed its Sing 1000 patent rights to Takinami-Sing, Inc., a wholly-owned subsidary of Gano-Nippon."

"We must closely monitor these developments."

"Hai! Tell me, Ashi-san, about IPS's new products."

"Dr. O'Leary discussed a new invention by Dave James. It's called multi-dimensional IPS 10000 dissipater."

"Tell Dr. Yamura to keep Research Appliance informed."

"Hai!"

"What about IPS's finances?"

"Cash declines at alarming rates. Mr. Bruce Hargett is very worried."

"When you talked to Marken-san, what did he report?"

"Lawrent may become TADA's competitor with its Gano-Nippon alliance. Its TAI products may disrupt our marketing agreements."

"Gano-Nippon still purchases our 10000 materials. We must explore cooperation possibilities. Anything else, Ashi-san?"

"Marken-san remains concerned about Seamus's problem."

Kenji sighed. "Very troubling, Ashi-san. Shiganari and I will talk."

SOUTH SAN FRANCISCO

A week after the board meeting, Jackson called. "Pug, good news! The Denver judge set a hearing date on the second injunction against Hondoya."

"How much is Hondoya gonna pay me?"

"The judge'll be tough. Other good news—Judge Harrington has been assigned to the Lawrent case. He won't tolerate delays or frivolous motions."

"Isn't it too early for a judge?"

"No, a judge rules on discovery disputes, addresses pre-trial motions; and, most importantly, decides what IPS patent claims mean."

"What the hell did you just say?"

"Patent claims construction is a matter of law for the court rather than a fact question. The judge will decide the meaning of patent claims and instruct the jury."

"Jury? Who's talking about a jury?"

"The defendant can always request a jury trial."

"Ain't fair."

"I know. Say, do you want to file for IPS 10000 patents in Brazil, Mexico, and Eastern Europe? We're ready to proceed."

"Let's blanket the planet!"

"One more thing. Could you tell Bruce to catch up paying our invoices?"

"No problem."

By May 1995, IPS owned patents in twenty-two countries with fifty-five applications pending. Bruce maintained a monthly spreadsheet of patent disclosure filings, patent office actions, and granted patents. Dexter-Foresmen's year-to-date billings were two hundred and fifty thousand.

Phase I of discovery began June, 1995. Jackson deposed everyone associated with the invention and marketing of IPS 10000: Pug, Sean, Rich, Bruce, and Marken sales reps. His goal was to portray IPS as a small undercapitalized company that discovered a revolutionary technology.

Before his deposition, Pug boasted, "Don't have to remember lies when you tell the truth."

Pug described the IPS 10000 invention in personal terms and embellished the company's struggle to survive. Sean and Rich testified about the invention process and their marketing efforts to introduce the technology. Bruce outlined economic costs incurred for development and commercialization. He presented convincing evidence of lost revenues after Lawrent's infringement began. Marken personnel described customers' rapid acceptance of IPS 10000 as an innovative advancement in dissipater technology.

The first round generated little controversy. Lawrent's lawyers limited questions to clarifications and minor technical objections.

At the conclusion, Jackson said, "Off to a good start! Pug, you showed real passion about IPS. Keep it up when you testify in court!"

"So this legal rigmarole'll go fast?"

"Let's hope so, but don't count on a court-directed verdict. Judge Harrington granted Lawrent's motion for jury trial." Jackson detected Pug's anger. "Don't worry. We'll dumb it down for jurors."

Pug scowled and shook his head. "If IPS is David, they better convict Goliath."

Sean, at home, read e-mail messages from Larry Judson. Attachments contained transcripts of Phase 1. He annotated his comments where appropriate, sent his reply, and locked copies in his safe.

He relaxed with a tall Sapporo. *At my billing rate, I'll declare independence by March 1996.*

ASHEBORO

Sean arrived at Green Tree Country Club and found Larry Judson at the practice range. The twosome made an interesting contrast: Sean—tall, carrot-colored hair, and fair skin; Larry—short, dark, and suntanned.

Larry worked five years in General Appliance procurement before joining Lawrent. He developed a profitable business specializing in fiberglass thermal dissipaters. His political connections positioned him as CEO within fifteen years. The company's sales grew from $45 million to $125 million under his tenure.

They teed off; both drives landed in the fairway.

"With Marken gone, Lawrent has no real sales competition," Sean said as he placed his driver in the golf bag.

"But IPS hired some great new sales guys." Larry winked.

Larry's second shot sliced into the trap, pin high. Sean's second landed thirty yards in front of the green. Larry asked, "Why all these lawsuits?"

"Pug loves patent battles."

"Does that mean no commercial talks?"

"Yep!"

At the fifth hole, Larry's drive landed two feet from the pin. "Great shot!" Sean said. He drove the green, landing ten feet from the hole.

"What's motivating you, Sean?"

"To leave IPS when the time's right." Sean birdied while Larry missed an easy putt.

"Understand. Here's something to think about," Larry said as they strolled towards the sixth tee box. Sean listened without comment. When they arrived at fifteen, Larry concluded, "Our global strategy requires a long-term relationship with IPS's technology, both in North America and in Asia."

"Asia?"

"Yes, Lawrent is in merger talks with Gano-Nippon."

"Interesting!"

"We'll discuss this and your involvement at dinner. Three holes left. Want to win your money back?"

"You're on!"

"Think Pug will sue General Appliance?" Larry asked.

"Don't know, but he's predictably irrational."

When they retired to the nineteenth-hole bar, Larry did not flinch when Sean requested more money.

Later that evening, Larry called and updated a former General Appliance colleague who said, "Our general counsel will contact Jason & Jones. And, by the way, this call never happened."

CHICAGO

Pug and Jackson returned to Chicago for July's Phase II depositions. Jackson's team deposed customers regarding approval and use of both IPS 10000 and TAI. Exeter employees gave positive feedback about IPS 10000 and were negative about TAI products. General Appliance and Appliancorp praised TAI as a cost-effective, technically acceptable alternative.

At the conclusion of Phase II, Jackson told Pug, "General's depositions suggested they encouraged Lawrent to develop TAI, but everyone was coached to avoid specifics about the secret vendor meeting."

"Yeah, no one remembered shit!"

"It's important we show what happened at that meeting. Reinforces IPS's claim of intentional infringement."

"The meeting happened after General demanded our cost data," Pug said.

"A few months before IPS 10000 sales began declining?"

"Yeah, middle of '94. Picked up steam in '95. IPS 10000 sales will be off by five mil. Appliancorp and General only used TAI once the new specs disqualified IPS 10000."

"Pug, you never discussed the cost data requests with me," Jackson said. "We could have explored a compromise. Are there any written records of conversations between IPS and General? It would strengthen our conspiracy theory."

"Sean didn't do notes! IPS saved the bastards a ton of money compared to Lawrent's old prices. Think Lawrent's bribing General?"

"Could have a private investigator look into it. Could be expensive."

"Do it!!!"

"Pug, I know you're frustrated. When you depose OEMs, you involve more lawyers. Delays the process."

"When do we depose the Lawrent assholes?"

"In three weeks. By the way, Judge Harrington denied our request for an injunction to stop Lawrent's TAI sales. The judge ruled IPS didn't prove beyond question it would suffer irreparable harm."

"Christ on a crutch! Do I have to go bankrupt first?"

When his home phone rang, Sean clicked the remote and paused the film, *Osaka Orgy*.

"Sean, you get the Phase II transcripts?"

"Yes. Be careful in Phase III. An attentive judge can spot contradictions with Phase II statements."

"How about a confused and compliant jury?"

Sean chuckled. "Understood. I'll send instructions on the TAI patent for your technical manager. Thanks for the last deposit."

"You're welcome. One more thing—our lawyers don't have a need to know."

Sean clicked off the recorder and returned to the film.

SANTA BARBARA

After passing the Mathews project to Sean, Skip concentrated on Sunshine Toaster. He scheduled a Santa Barbara sales call. Wearing a new thousand dollar, custom-tailored suit and five hundred dollar Italian loafers, compliments of his newly-issued IPS credit card, he met Annie to preview his presentation.

"Thanks for arranging this meeting, Annie."

"Happy to help. Working with vendors allows me learn another aspect of the business."

"What are your usual responsibilities?"

"Marketing—product literature, print and TV advertising, trade shows—like Chicago. The meeting starts in 15 minutes, so let's look at your slides."

"Okay. Could you join me for dinner to discuss your engineers' feedback?"

Surprised, she hesitated then said, "That would be nice."

That evening, at a French bistro, Skip lifted a glass of Bordeaux and proposed a toast. "To the start of a successful relationship between IPS and Sunshine."

"Everyone's impressed with the IPS 10000 material. They want to test it on our new model prototypes," Annie replied.

"Fantastic! I'll send samples when I get back. Enough about business. What do you do for fun?"

Annie took a sip of wine. "Love to read. Right now I'm hooked on family sagas. Maybe one day I'll write one!"

"How do you like working for your dad?"

"Okay, I guess." Her eyes glanced away.

"Anyone special in your life?"

"Randy Burr, Sunshine's national sales manager."

"I believe I met him at the trade show."

"Father thinks he's doing a great job."

As they were leaving the restaurant, Skip said, "When your tech guys finish testing, please visit IPS and present their results."

"I look forward to that. 'Night, Skip."

Driving back to his hotel, Skip could not stop thinking about Annie. *What does she see in dandy Randy?*

SOUTH SAN FRANCISCO

Using IPS 10000, Dave created proof of concepts for multi-dimensional devices. He incorporated unique edges providing structural integrity and dimensional flexibility. The prototypes confirmed Sean's hunch that IPS 10000 could revolutionize dissipaters for water heater applications and many other appliances.

Dave presented Mathews prototypes and test results to the IPS management team. When finished, Pug asked, "So guys, is this a bingo, bango, bongo, or what?"

"Dave's on to something," Sean said. "Let's get him in front of Mathews's technical group."

Skip jumped to his feet. "No friggin' way! That's my customer!"

"You presenting technology is a goddamn joke!" Dave shouted. "With your people skills, Mathews's techies will eat you alive!"

"Both of you shut the fuck up! I make decisions here!" Pug yelled.

No one spoke until Michael asked, "Okay, what now?"

"Doc, make sure Jackson files for patents. I see at least three, maybe four. No one talks to Mathews until I say. Skip found Mathews, he'll take the lead."

Dave slammed his chair against the table. "You just pissed away my invention." He stormed out.

"He's a chip off the old Pork," Pug laughed.

"At least Dave didn't threaten to resign," Sean added.

Skip looked around and grinned. *So who's number one son now?*

The meeting adjourned. Sean and Michael departed.

"Skippy, stay here!" Pug ordered.

"Now here's what you're gonna do... "

Skip exploded. "Hey, this isn't like my first sales call. Duh!"

"Shut the fuck up! You're not screwing up this account with your non-tech brain! Remember I'm the message! You're nothing but a messenger!"

Michael headed to the lab and found Dave slamming things against a lab bench. He waited until Dave stopped. "Look, I know you're upset. Think about Handi. Your multi-dimensional ideas fit perfect! You passed thermal and vibration tests with no sweat. When we go to Korea, you lead the charge."

Dave kicked the lab bench. "Skip doesn't deserve my invention!"

"Skip's missionary marketing found the opportunity."

"He's only good at two things: taking money from mommy and screwing women."

"Take it easy. Tomorrow we'll talk about Korea. You need some kimchi and beer to settle the nerves, okay? Trust me!"

"Yeah, okay. Thanks, Michael. By the way, when you got time, I'll tell you about my newest idea."

"Look forward to hearing it." Michael returned to his office. *Can't let Pug defeat him.*

In the morning, Skip came to work with five coffees and a dozen Krispy Kremes. He distributed them stopping last at Michael's desk. "Got one left. Want some real coffee instead of Sharon's crap? Too bad her coffee's not as good as her hooters."

"Never heard coffee compared to breasts. How much do I owe you?"

"Forget it!"

"You spend a fortune keeping us in coffee and treats. Here's five bucks."

"Nah, got it covered. What did you think of Davey's tantrum?"

"When you invent something, it's your baby, your mistress, your mother. You don't let go."

"Like Pops, he suffers from PPS."

"PPS?"

"Proprietary Paranoia Syndrome."

"I'd call it Passionate Protective Syndrome."

"Always the diplomat. Dave doesn't have the political chops to get business. Technology isn't everything. Someone has to sell and, most important, have sex with the customer. Hey, forgot to tell you, I met one of your old MatraScience buddies at the Chicago show. Here's his card. Biltgood's a potential customer. They have lots of divisions, and all need new insulation to replace fiberglass."

Michael looked at the Biltgood business card. "I know this guy. I'll set up a meeting for you."

"Looks like IPS has the technology, and you have the politics."

"You're a fast learner. I'll call him tomorrow."

"Not yet, I'm too busy with Mathews. Say, I could use some assistance."

"Use Sharon. She's underutilized."

"She's okay for Pops but not me. You know why Pops hired her?"

"No."

"Mom insisted on interviewing all the candidates. Sharon was the only one she approved."

SAN FRANCISCO

That evening, Michael poured Ellie a glass of chardonnay and recounted the past two days.

"Dave's and Skip's competitiveness borders on jealously, sometimes rage."

"Not unusual in a family business."

"I can mentor both sons."

"How so?"

"By giving Dave more marketing exposure and Skip more appreciation of technology. One—or perhaps both—will learn how to balance politics and technology when commercializing new products."

"Be careful; remember your surname is not James."

"Yeah, I know, and blood's thicker than water. By the way, I think Marcy is keeping a close eye on Pug after the Tiffanee fiasco at MatraScience."

"How's that?"

"Apparently, she had the final say on Pug's latest secretarial hire."

TOKYO

Pug, Michael, and Jackson flew to Tokyo in August. They met with Hondoya's chief legal officer.

Hondoya's lawyer opened the discussions: "Hondoya desires to settle lawsuits in North America and Japan and to purchase an IPS 10000 license."

"Will Hondoya acknowledge its unauthorized use of IPS 10000 technology which causes considerable losses for Japan Technologies and for IPS?" Jackson asked.

"Mr. Huntley, Hondoya cannot be responsible for suppliers' actions." He looked directly at Pug. "Our procurement officers are ready to solicit direct quotes from IPS—if legal matters are resolved."

"There is no commercial relationship unless we settle the lawsuits?" Jackson asked.

"To show good faith, our procurement officers will provide sample drawings and specifications for dissipater systems used on current Z2 and future Z3 appliance models."

After conferring with Pug, Jackson concluded, "IPS looks forward to receiving Hondoya's proposal."

As participants adjourned, Hondoya's attorney approached Pug. "Mr. James, I trust we can find consensus."

"I'll keep my powder dry until I see your written proposal."

"We too want no explosions. Hondoya is unhappy with the Osaka dissipater yakuza. We urgently seek alternative sources for our dissipater components."

Next morning at Hotel Dai-ichi, Pug, Michael, and Jackson met for breakfast. Pug tore into his sausage and cheese omelet while Michael and Jackson spooned oatmeal and munched dry wheat toast.

"Eating breakfasts like that, your cholesterol level must be over 400," Jackson told Pug.

"Yeah, yeah. So whadya think about Hondoya's proposal?" Pug asked between mouthfuls.

"Commercial matters are your call. So far, they're offering IPS an opportunity to compete. Nothing more."

"Still pissed about their infringement."

"Hondoya has plausible deniability."

"Jackson's right," Michael added. "The yakuza comment suggests a mafia-like group controls the supply of dissipaters. However, I suspect Hondoya is more involved than it admits."

Jackson nodded at Michael's point and gathered up his briefcase. "Need to get to Narita. We'll talk soon."

Pug ordered more coffee. "Hondoya expects IPS won't quote," he said. "I looked at their sample drawings. They want systems: heavy attachments, that kinda thing, not just thermal dissipaters."

"What are you saying?" Michael asked.

"Let's speed up Dave's Appliance Analysis."

Later, an Osaka-based lawyer referred by Jackson joined them in the hotel lobby. Research Appliance Device had begun supplying IPS 10000-like materials to Japan's OEMs. These materials infringed IPS's Japanese and APO patents. But unlike Nippon Tooling, Research Appliance still purchased large quantities of Japan Technologies's 10000 materials for which Japan Technologies paid IPS a significant royalty.

Pug asked, "Should we take 'em to court?"

"Mr. James, Mr. Huntley and I recommend sending a courtesy letter. It implies IPS will enforce its intellectual property rights. This allows negotiation before legal action. If you don't formally advise a potential infringer, it indicates IPS will not enforce patents."

Pug slapped his palm to the table, "Done! Draft me a letter! Michael and me gotta another meeting."

When the lawyer left, Michael asked, "He doesn't know about your meeting?"

"He'd wanna come and charge me for listening. Until I know what Research Appliance wants, why get lawyers involved?"

"Good luck. I'm off to Seoul."

SEOUL

Michael dined at Seoul's Grand Hyatt's restaurant and recounted the Japan visit and Pug's update about the Research Appliance meeting.

Hondoya meeting was inconclusive. What are the implications for IPS and Japan Technologies? Research Appliance (Japan Technologies's customer) and Nippon Tooling (Japan Technologies's former tool shop and now competitor) are both infringing—but using different tactics.

Michael sipped cognac and read a fax from his MatraScience Korean colleague.

Finally, some encouraging news. He paid the bill and headed to his room and phoned Sean.

"Dave had productive visits with Korean appliance OEM engineers, built prototypes with sample material. In my colleague's garage, no less! Their tests, along with our test data, confirmed IPS 10000 is superior to other available alternatives. They love the multi-dimensional flexibility."

"I trained Dave well!" Sean boasted.

"Handi Appliance will do thermal trials. If 10000 passes, we can expect requests for quotes."

"Yeah, but they'll want a local manufacturing source. Won't import forever, given the weak Korean won."

"My guy is already screening potential licensees. He's done more in two months than the kimchi bozos did in two years."

Sean laughed. *You can thank Pug for hiring the Korean doofuses.*

SOUTH SAN FRANCISCO

When Dave returned, he rushed to Sean's office. "Dr. O'Leary! What a trip! Koreans drink and smoke you under the table! Michael's buddy made me an honorary Korean."

"Enough about fun. What about business?"

"Michael's buddy is first-class: mechanical and understands thermal transfer. Introduced me to key engineering guys at Handi Appliance. Saw all kinds of heat and noise problems. I'll support him from here with testing and samples. He'll get us a ton of business... with our technology and his relationships." Dave saw Sean's smile. "Did I say something wrong?"

"Not at all," Sean replied. *Dave gets it.* "Glad you're back. Pug called from Japan. Get the AA started. Hondoya sample parts will arrive along with drawings. Give me a project plan. Top priority!"

"Piece o' cake!"

"I like your spirit."

Dave scurried to the lab and made notes, his ideas coming faster than he could write:

Appliance Analysis (AA):

1. Take Hondoya parts, measure, and examine composition. Baseline tests to establish minimum thermal and acoustics metrics.

2. Buy Hondoya models. Tear down, reassemble, and operate them. Baseline how parts perform.

3. Get help from California, Chicago, and Denver; brainstorm solutions using IPS 100 and 10000. Use multi-dimensional ideas from Mathews and Handi. Build prototypes and test thermal and acoustic performance, both installed and uninstalled. Compare to baseline data from 1. and 2.

4. Cost existing parts to determine targets. Do same for prototypes and compare to targets.

5. Summarize technical and economic data to choose best solutions. Do PowerPoint presentation.

He estimated sixty days assuming no Pug interruptions.

The following week, Michael found Dave bent over a lab bench bending a piece of 10000. He wore rumpled jeans, his shirt hung out, his hair a tangled mess.

"Hey, Michael. What's up?"

"You look... wasted."

"Spent last night jamming in North Beach. Then headed to Japan Town, talked Japanese and drank Sapporo."

"Heard you're working brutal hours in the lab."

"Uh, there's Tina, you know."

Michael turned to go. "I want to hear about her, but I got a Pug meeting."

"We got drunk and eloped."

Michael halted. "What? We have to talk. After work!"

Dave folded the 10000 piece in half and nodded.

In his office, his feet propped on the desk, Pug scanned *Remodeling Digest*. He felt recharged after spending three days with Suzi in Kyoto.

Sharon interrupted. "Darin's on the phone."

"What's up, Ted?"

"Great news, Puggy! My investment banker is doing a secondary stock offering while the price's still high."

Pug rolled his eyes and frowned. "What's the offering price?"

"Twelve bucks a share. It'll be mid-thirties by year end."

Pug swallowed anger. "Great." *Can't believe the asshole's luck.*

"Puggy, keep those 1000 shares I sold you at ten dollars a share! Hope this call ain't recorded," he laughed. "Always happy to help family."

Pug bristled. *Fuck you, Ted! Dad and Rich got free shares.*

"Say Puggy, my lawyers told me to resign all my outside directorships—too much potential liability. I'll miss helping you. Gotta go, got another call."

Darin hung up and thought, *Time to update, Mr. K.*

Pug slammed the phone down and stared at his mother's picture. "Mom, you and me always knew when Cousin Ted lied—just like Dad. Good riddance! Nobody'll miss him... 'cept slant eyes... and maybe Rich."

He reached for the photo of the Las Vegas meeting. With a magic marker, he drew a big X on Darin's face. "One down; one to go!"

He phoned home. "Sweetie, guess what?"

"Hold on a minute while I dry off Billy."

"What are you doing?"

"Michelle left him with me. Had to bathe him. Still not toilet trained. There, Billy, all clean. Sweetie, what were you saying?"

"Ted resigned from the board."

"Hallelujah! Billy, you hear that? Cousin Darin has left the building!"

"I'm putting Michael on the board, ASAP. Coming home early to celebrate."

Pug saw Michael in the hallway and motioned him to come into his office.

"Michael, remember my board seat promise? Well, you're now a director."

"Thanks, but don't shareholders have to elect me?"

"Details, details. As major domo, I have the first word."

A few minutes later, "Jackson's on the phone," Sharon announced.

"Hey, gator! What's up?" Pug asked.

"Pug, five more firms have opposed the Asian patent."

"Wait a minute! Michael needs to hear this." Pug punched the speakerphone.

Jackson repeated the news. "First there was Takinami-Sing..."

"That pipsqueak Singapore company!"

"And now Hondoya and Nippon Tooling. No surprise."

"Wait a fuckin' minute!" Pug yelled. "Hondoya wants to settle the Colorado and Japanese lawsuits and do a commercial agreement. Why start another war?"

Jackson explained, "Applies more pressure on IPS to settle."

"Okay, okay, who are the others?"

"There's Sumato-Metal, a special alloy supplier, and then there's Research Appliance and Gano-Nippon. IPS may have six battles."

"Sounds like gator talk for more bucks," Pug snapped.

"It depends."

"Michael, see what you can find out."

"Once we review their filings," Jackson continued, "we have six months to respond, and each adversary has three months to reply. The APO court in Singapore sets a hearing date for final arguments and renders a decision."

"So, this could be many months?" Michael asked.

"Yes, I'll call after we examine the documents." Jackson said goodbye and hung up.

His brow furrowed, Pug hunched over his desk. His left hand massaged his forehead while his right hand caressed the silver Baoding balls.

Michael said, "Japan Technologies's quarterly royalty statements show Gano-Nippon and Research Appliance still buy IPS 10000."

"Why would Jap Tech's customers get involved?"

"Remember what I said: business relationships are never transparent."

"Yeah, yeah. How about these others?"

"Sumato-Metal is Japan Technologies's special metal alloy supplier. Looks like a key vendor joined this lawsuit."

"What does all this shit mean?"

"I hate to tell you this, but IPS is fighting a keiretsu."

"A kudzu?"

"Good metaphor for a cartel."

"Why's this krit-zoo fighting us? And what about Takinami-Sing? Why are they involved? Who are these guys?"

"You sound like Butch Cassidy talking to the Sundance Kid. I'll go to Japan and figure this out."

"We'll both go!"

"Pug, let me work it. It's why you hired me. Save yourself for the more important stuff."

"I want this fixed now! When we go, we'll stop in Europe."

"Europe?"

"By flying in one direction, we can travel business class 'cuz it's cheaper than round trip coach to Japan. Besides I wanna meet European lawyers to talk patent coverage."

Michael marveled. *One moment we're discussing kudzu; next, we're saving bucks in Europe.*

Pug yelled instructions to Sharon, then complained, "Damn, I'm dizzy."

"You need to see a doctor," Michael insisted. "You've had too many of these dizzy spells."

"I'm okay. This James boy don't run to doctors."

SAN FRANCISCO

That night, Michael told Ellie, "Finally, I have a challenge where I can contribute."

"What's that?"

"Fighting an Asian kudzu."

"Come again."

"Kudzu: Pug-speak for Japanese cartel. Let's hope Pug lets me use my expertise."

"About time," Ellie added.

CHICAGO, HARTFORD, AND ASHEBORO

During September, Lawrent's and IPS's lawyers took depositions in three locations: Illinois for technical, Connecticut for marketing, and North Carolina for Lawrent's top executive. In the technical depositions of engineers listed as the TAI inventors, one engineer inadvertently mentioned General Appliance's involvement. Jason & Jones deposed three other engineers to refute his testimony. Lawrent's sales personnel reconfirmed General's positive comments about TAI products and denied attending General's vendor meeting. Larry Judson's testimony was vague, with frequent 'I do not recalls' and adamant denials of any technology espionage.

At Phase III's end, Pug and Jackson headed to the Charlotte airport. "Damn it, Jackson!" Pug erupted. "You said discovery would take four months max! Seven months, and you haven't deposited the experts!"

"Lawrent delayed the depositions when they introduced the Singapore company prior art which predates IPS 10000. We petitioned the judge to rule on inadmissibility. He took four weeks to finally affirm our position."

Pug shook his head in disgust. "Those bastards'll use it in court."

"The judge will instruct jurors to ignore foreign prior art in their deliberations," Jackson said.

Pug growled, "Damn it! Lawrent's infringing, not us! How strong's our claim that TAI is a copy cat?"

"We'll know after we depose the experts. In any case, all the products Lawrent sold before TAI definitely infringe."

"Yeah, but Lawrent claimed it didn't sell much pre-TAI stuff."

After Jackson departed, Pug called Michael. "Lawrent hired a private investigator to spy on me and Marcy."

"Why do that for a civil patent suit?" Michael asked.

"Bastards are scrambling to find anything to win."

Thought you told me Jackson hired a private investigator to spy on Lawrent? Strange... almost sounds paranoid.

SOUTH SAN FRANCISCO

"Dave, want me to turn off the lab lights?" the engineer asked.

"No, got tests running. See you tomorrow."

Dave finished thermal measurements and cleared his desk. He turned to his new computer. Pug's neighbor had installed the company's first router and file server in October.

Why didn't Pops let me do it? I know this stuff. Okay, let's test how secure his network is.

Dave tried accessing the file server, but the firewall blocked him. He hacked into the router by clever trial and error. The neighbor had used his wife's name as the password.

The guy's got abs-so-fucking-lute-ly no imagination! Dave added his host into those allowed to access the fileserver. Through the file server, he located the directory for human resources. Inside the HR directory, he accessed "payroll." Security settings were off.

Pops has no idea how dumb his buddy is.

Payroll records flashed on the screen. *What's this shit? Skippy gets forty thousand more than me? That jerk-off does half the work I do.* He printed a list of employee salaries for both South San Francisco and Denver.

Hmmmm... let's see what Doc's up to? Spends umpteen hours in front of his computer. No fucking way it's only patent searches and recruiting.

Returning to the router, he enabled logging in order to track IP addresses Sean visited. He'd return later to see what addresses Sean accessed in the meantime.

A few nights later, he discovered Sean had accessed the US patent office address and various job-search sites. He noted requests for thermal and acoustic information from universities and government research groups.

Sean also visited unusual addresses. Dave typed them into his web browser. Soon he stared at names like *LustyThighs, HotAsianLadies, AsiaPornoFun.*

Astounded, Dave realized he'd stumbled into the world of Japanese pornography. Sean's e-mails described orders and shipment logistics.

Shit! This is sick! No wonder he wanted all this memory and processor speed.

Conflicted and confused, Dave turned away from the computer and tried to make sense of what he'd discovered.

Guy's fuckin' brilliant... I've learned so much from him... he's let me do my thing... but, fuck, this is really weird... he's actually selling and distributing this shit.

He closed the websites and noticed another suspicious file on the file server. He tried to access it, but it was password protected.

Getting late... I'll work it another time.

He shut down the computer, hit the lights, and headed to his car. Realizing he hadn't eaten since breakfast, he stopped at Hooters. Three beers and two orders of wings later, he drove home.

I'll sit on this... until I need something... like a big, fat, fucking raise...
and recognition for my hard work.

The next day, Dave, dressed in wrinkled jeans and sweatshirt, entered Michael's office and closed the door. He brushed straw-blonde hair from his forehead. "What does Sean do all day on his computer?"

"Ummmm... patent research and job searches. Why do you ask?"

"Think he's ever been to Japan?"

"Who knows? Frankly I'm just happy he lets you work on my projects. What's the AA status?"

"Phase II starts soon. Going faster with Judith. She's a fast learner. Thanks for letting me hire her."

"Thank Sean too. Join us for lunch?"

"Can't. I'm monitoring lab tests."

"Okay, walk with me to Sean's office."

They found Sean staring at the computer.

"Same oh, same oh," Dave whispered.

Michael stood at the office window and gestured. No response. He rapped the window. "Hey, get your nose out of that computer!"

Sean looked at his watch. "Let's not take too much time. This prior art research drives me nuts."

"Let's get sushi at Yamamoto's."

"Bring me take-out and say hello to Kamiko," Dave quipped.

"Sure, back in an hour," Michael replied.

Dave watched them leave then hurried to his computer. Earlier, he'd found a sticky note under Sean's keyboard. Scribbled on the note was a cryptic combination of letters, numbers, and symbols: *glhq%K:ft8z*. It looked like a password for the blocked file.

As Sean started the car, he turned off the audiotape but not before Michael recognized Japanese being spoken.

"How do you like your Lexus?" Michael asked.

"Thought Japan's quality would be better. Next car will be a Cadillac."

"That'll make Pug happy."

"Yeah, his economic theories go in one ear and out my ass."

At the restaurant, they ordered green tea and edamame.

"When do interviews start?" Michael asked.

"Pug's Chicago cousin Louis finally identified three engineers. He'll send them after checking references."

"Super! It'll be good to have more people to fill the space. You pleased with Dave so far?"

Sean took a sip of tea. "He's bright, as innovative as Pug, and equally impatient."

"I hear you. He's helped my Korean colleague get the first Handi approvals. Involving him allowed me to bypass our do-nothing bozos Pug hired."

Sushi arrived. Sean fumbled with chopsticks to mix wasabi into soy sauce.

Michael asked, "You want a fork?"

"Yeah, otherwise I'll starve."

"How about joining me next time I go to Japan?"

"Never been there. I'd need to get a passport."

Michael made a mental note. *Call Tokyo.*

Dave accessed Sean's restricted files. The first contained information about Singapore patent procedures and included a copy of an issued patent, Sing 1000.

Who the hell's Seamus McCord?

The second file contained information for filing other patents in Japan and Thailand. Dave read the information identical to his lab notes on Handi and Mathews. The third file, titled J2, contained documents about litigation and prior art from Japanese and Singapore sources. He transferred the files to a zip disk. He heard Sean and Michael in the hallway and closed the screen as they entered the lab.

"Here's your sushi. Kamiko says kennichi wa," Michael said.

Dave laughed. "I bet she did."

Sean continued working in his office until early evening. The phone rang. A caller speaking Japanese said, "Dr. O'Leary, I represent the

American Commercial Attaché in Tokyo. I am conducting a survey of American companies interested in doing business in Japan."

Sean replied in English, "You've got the wrong number." He hung up.

That evening, Dave closed the door to his home office, sat at his computer and opened the zip file. He focused on J2. A sub-file captured his attention:

-Commercial settlement not possible; CEO won't budge. L & GA have no alternative.

-Delay depositions to bleed opposition.

-Grease the jury.

Dave jumped to his feet and swift-kicked the wastebasket. It clattered across the room.

He shouted out loud, "Why?"

Tina appeared at the door, one hand on her expanding belly. "What's goin' on?"

"Leave me alone!" Dave shouted.

"Okay, okay, I'm outta here!" she said, closing the door.

Furious, he slammed the chair against the desk. *What he's doing is so wrong!* He paced back and forth, clenching and unclenching his fists. *But he never interferes. He's taught me so much.*

He sank to a chair. *Should I tell Michael? At least, he'd listen.*

Next morning, Michael stood at his office window and watched dense fog blanket the Bay Area. *A keiretsu fog is smothering IPS patents in Asia. Six opponents have sent messages to IPS and to potential competitors. They want control of this technology.*

Michael saw Pug in the doorway. "Pug, if Japan Technologies and Nippon Tooling are enemies, theoretically Kenji should support IPS to prevent the patent's invalidation. Otherwise, its exclusive license becomes worthless."

"Tell me something I don't know."

"Perhaps Kenji wants us to believe they're adversaries."

Pug, arms folded, leaned his good shoulder against the doorframe. "Okay, Mr. Anulytical, whadya thinking?"

"Like the old Arab proverb, 'the enemy of my enemy is my friend,' Kenji considers us the enemy. And since Nippon Tooling is also our enemy, they remain friends. In politics, one sleeps with strange bedfellows," Michael said, thinking out loud.

"You just make that up?" Pug sank into a chair. "Sharon," he hollered over his shoulder. "Bring java!"

"Why would Japan Technologies's customers join the opposition?" Michael wondered.

"More infringers drive down the price of 10000."

"But lower prices hurt Japan Technologies's profits and market share."

"Duh. And my royalties! Why's Sumato-Metal sticking their nose in this?"

"They're like a friend of the court, or in this case, the appliance cartel. It supports its customers. I'll confirm after talking to my Asian colleagues. The real mystery is Takinami-Sing."

Michael launched his investigation. Over a two-week period, he made numerous calls to his contacts in Asia including a former Singapore colleague:

"Mr. Soh, thank you for your prompt reply about Takinami-Sing. What can you tell me about the inventor of the Sing 1000 patent?"

"I met Seamus McCord at an industry trade conference in Thailand. He spent considerable time with Japanese businessmen during the meetings."

"What did this McCord fellow look like?"

As Mr. Soh talked, a distinct image flashed through Michael's mind. He thanked Mr. Soh and turned to notes he had assembled:

TAKINAMI-SING:

– – *Singapore-based distribution company wholly owned by Gano-Nippon.*

– – *Acquired a thermal dissipater patent in 1992 from MMc Ltd. Copy of Sing 1000 patent attached.*

SUMATO-METAL:

– – *Special metal alloy supplier to Japan Technologies, Research Appliance, Gano-Nippon, and Takinami-Sing, and all major OEMs- Hondoya, General Appliance of Japan, and Niota.*

– – *Owners include Bank Hanjokani and a 10% interest held by undisclosed private investor.*

– – *Company owns 5% interest in Nippon Tooling and Research Appliance Devices.*

RESEARCH APPLIANCE, GANO-NIPPON, and NIPPON TOOLING:

– – *All Tier 1 suppliers to Japanese appliance OEMs.*

– – *Except Nippon, all purchase IPS 10000 materials from Japan Technologies. Prior to split, Nippon Tooling manufactured dissipater tools for Japan Technologies.*

– – *Several cross ownership interests exist; undisclosed private investor owns 35% of Nippon Tooling and 20% of Research Appliance.*

AKAMI-THAI:

– – *Thai-based manufacturing company. Supplies thermal and acoustic dissipater components to Japanese OEMs located in Thailand and also exports to Japan.*

– – *Major customers include Tier 1 suppliers (Research Appliance, Gano-Nippon) and OEMs. (Hondoya, etc.)*

– – *Research Appliance owns 85% of this company and 15% owned by undisclosed private investor.*

BANK HANJOKANI:

– – *Principal bank for all opposition participants.*

– – *Provides affiliates with considerable financial resources.*

– – *Owns minority interests in each member.*

Michael sketched a relationships schematic. At the end, he wrote:

CONCLUSION:

– – *IPS is fighting a deep-pocket Japanese keiretsu.*

– – *Who is or are the undisclosed private investors? Kenji's Brunei Trust? (Need to confirm).*

– – *IPS should rethink legal and commercial options before continuing expensive litigation.*

– – *If Japan Technologies has special relations with Hondoya, then the others (Research Appliance, Nippon Tooling, etc.) probably do as well.*

– – *Are Asian and US lawsuits connected?*

– – *Is Seamus McCord the guy I think he is? Need more concrete proof.*

– – *Things have changed since I did my graduate thesis on Japanese keiretsu. Need to do some more research…*

SAN FRANCISCO

Michael and Ellie enjoyed an evening at La Pergola, their favorite Italian trattoria in North Beach. The waiter poured Santa Margarita pinot grigio. They savored the light, fruity wine they discovered when they visited Tuscany.

"Sweetheart, are you enjoying IPS?"

"Pug's personality makes work fun. He's a bee trying to pollinate every flower."

"How does he keep track?"

"Photographic memory. Remembers what he asked you three months ago as if it were yesterday. When we all get together, Pug-speak guarantees lively meetings."

As they enjoyed the pasta course, Michael continued, "IPS is like a big family."

"Isn't it difficult making decisions when family's involved?"

"Not so far. Pug keeps me involved in all key decisions."

"I had lunch with Marcy. She's so thrilled you're part of IPS. Says Pug really respects you."

"Nice to hear."

"Marcy's coming around about Dave's Tina. Thinks the marriage will survive."

"I'm glad Dave finally told them." Michael took a long sip of wine. "I think Marcy's accepted Tina now that a baby is on the way."

"She's always wanted more grandkids. She and Pug love spoiling Skip's son."

SOUTH SAN FRANCISCO AND CHICAGO

In November, the attorneys deposed technical and financial experts in San Francisco and Chicago.

Pug monitored the testimony of IPS's financial expert. Using Bruce's internal accounting data, Lawrent's SEC 10K data, and independent market studies, the expert showed significant declines in IPS profits and market share. The losses coincided with Lawrent's increased revenues and profits derived from its TAI dissipater business.

IPS's technical expert, a seasoned mechanical engineer, testified IPS 10000 patents were unique and represented state-of-the-art advances in thermal dissipater technology. He demonstrated how Lawrent's TAI patent relied on IPS prior art. He cited examples of Lawrent infringement: selling material directly to General Appliance before and after the TAI patent issued. This testimony strengthened the links between engineers at General Appliance and Lawrent. In Chicago, Lawrent's technical expert, Dr. Berry, explained and defended the TAI patent, but his rambling answers to specific questions were weak and inconsistent.

When Chicago depositions concluded, Pug and Jackson headed to O'Hare and relaxed in American Airline's Admiral Club. Pug nursed a Pat Henry while Jackson drank Perrier. "Jackson, you gotta try something stronger than that sissy water."

"Alcohol and triathlons don't mix," he replied.

"Whadya think of Dr. Berry? Couldn't Lawrent afford a better expert? Guy's asleep at the wheel. Probably won't live to see the trial. Is Lawrent just goin' through the motions?"

"If so, the judge will demand a pre-trial settlement."

"Can't wait to see treble damages. That'll make for a great holiday."

"One more issue. Judge Harrington ruled on our request claiming Lawrent directly infringed. After looking at discovery evidence, he ruled direct infringement had not been proved."

Pug reacted, nearly toppling his beer. "How much goddamn proof ya need for chrissakes! Sonovabitch!"

"Calm down, Pug! When comparing Lawrent's TAI products and processes to IPS claims, there's no exact or literal match."

"What the fuck! He wants a polaroid carbon copy?"

"The judge believes elements in Lawrent's thermal dissipaters, while not literally identical to IPS claims, are interchangeable with what's claimed."

"Speak English, dammit!"

"It means Lawrent's dissipaters do the same work in substantially the same way to accomplish substantially the same results as IPS 10000."

"Chrissakes! Infringement is infringement!"

"Pug, the judge thinks there's enough evidence to prove Lawrent's infringement. That's all you need to worry about."

"Jeezus, why didn't you say that in the first place?"

"I see the judge's reasoning. First, there are two valid patents, IPS 10000 and TAI, and they're not identical."

"Duh, we know they're not the same!"

"Pug, let me explain."

"Lawrent's patent is recent and doesn't cover the entire period in which IPS claims infringement. Lawrent presented insufficient evidence to refute infringement before the TAI patent issued. This'll be a question of fact for the jury to decide."

"Shit! There you go again with the jury crap!"

"Pug, we're stuck with jury trial whether we like it or not. Lawrent's request to invalidate IPS claims will be a question of fact for the jury. But Lawrent will have a higher standard of proof, because a patent is presumed valid. It will have to establish invalidity and unenforceability by 'clear and convincing evidence.'"

"Don't we have the same standard?"

"No, because the judge says to prove infringement, we have to present a 'preponderance of evidence;' a lower hurdle than 'clear and convincing.'"

"Cut to the chase, for chrissake. What about damages?"

"Willful infringement equals treble damages."

"Jackson, that's the first time any of this makes sense!"

"We'll talk after the New Year. You and Marcy have a great Thanksgiving."

TOKYO

On their December 10 thirteen-hour flight between London and Tokyo, Pug alternated complaints about smokers and comments about the flight attendants' tight skirts. He squinted at a flight attendant's nametag.

"Setsu, where ya from?"

"Kyoto, she answered softly."

"Koto! A beautiful city with beautiful women, like you!"

Embarrassed, she retreated to the galley.

"Pug, if you're going to hit on Asian ladies, know your geography. It's pronounced 'Key-o-to.'"

"Yeah, my key will open her oto."

"A hundred yen says you can't."

"You're on!"

After meal service, Pug yawned and dozed. Michael listened to Vivaldi and reflected on the last two days. *The U.K. stopover was a ruse to get some English nookie. Pug committed IPS to a three-year lease for a London apartment. Patent lawyers never showed. Blamed Sharon for the screw up.*

Pug stirred after two hours; Michael nudged him awake. "Pug, look at my schematic of relationships among the cartel's companies. We know about the vendor-customer ties, but what's really interesting are ownership linkages."

"Whadya talking about?"

"We don't know the owners of each firm, but it appears one or more investors are involved. Several firms have unidentified owners, similar to Kenji's investment in IPS. Combine cross ownerships with OEM special relationships, and you see how customers like Hondoya get more than products from vendors."

"You mean like Jap Tech's bribes?"

"Yes, the OEM big shots get them."

"Probably met some of them when I first introduced IPS 10000 to Hondoya."

"Remember their names?"

"That was seven years ago. They were all named san."

Michael smiled. "When we return, see if you can find their business cards."

"What about that mystery company? Takawho-Sing?"

"Takinami-Sing has a patent similar to ours."

"Who's the inventor?"

"Seamus McCord."

"Never heard of him. I'm hungry for some Setsu." He lifted his bulky body out of the seat and headed to the galley. When he returned, he handed Michael a hundred-yen note.

Michael grinned. "Told you. Let's discuss the meeting agenda."

"Yeah, yeah, Hondoya's got to cut bait before we fish."

"That's why it'll be a short meeting. In Osaka, we'll confront Japan Technologies followed by another secret meeting…"

TOKYO

They arrived at Narita, taxied to Tokyo, and checked into Dai-ichi. At registration, Michael asked, "See you at the restaurant in an hour?"

"My gut's acting up. Gonna skip dinner. You mind?"

"Not at all. Get a good night's sleep."

Pug headed to his room. He showered, splashed on Old Spice, and left. He returned at 5:00 a.m.

At breakfast, his blood shot eyes worried Michael. "You okay?"

"No. I was in and out all night."

"In and out?"

"You know, the bathroom." Pug made quick work of eggs, sausage, and toast, washed down with four cups of black coffee.

"Think we'll see a proposal from Hondoya?" Pug asked as they walked to the headquarters. "I want something in writing!"

"We'll be ready. Sean tells me Dave needs only a few more weeks to complete the AA."

SOUTH SAN FRANCISCO

Dave bought or borrowed Hondoya appliances and removed every thermal and acoustic dissipater. He documented physical characteristics and performed stand-alone tests. He reinstalled each dissipater and measured thermal and noise performance while operating them under various conditions.

Judith Kramer, his new assistant, was a significant help. Her calm demeanor softened his impatient edge. Her mixed-race heritage appealed to Dave. She taught him Japanese customs and introduced him to Buddhism. They often conversed in Japanese.

TOKYO

Hondoya presented the settlement offer. The lawyers proposed a three-year commercial agreement with renewal options and unrestricted IPS access to all engineering groups. IPS could quote all thermal dissipater projects for the new models and running changes on all existing models. In return, IPS would cease lawsuits in Colorado and the Japanese courts. Hondoya requested reimbursement for its Japanese legal expenses.

At a meeting break, Pug and Michael assessed the offer. "Let's go for it," Pug said.

"Why pay their legal costs?"

"No big deal. Think of all the business we'll get based on the AA."

"Pug, getting real orders takes a long time!"

"Fieldsy, you got no balls! I want their written offer."

OSAKA

The following day, Pug and Michael arrived at Japan Technologies's offices.

"Mr. James, Kobyashi-san sends his regrets," Jun said.

"Sure he does!" Pug snarled. "I only booked this appointment a month ago. IPS's been fighting your battles with Hondoya!"

"Mr. James, patent legal matters are IPS's responsibility."

"Don't insult me!" Pug snapped. Michael placed his hand on Pug's shoulder to calm him. Pug continued, "Why are you guys causing this APO opposition?"

Michael winced. Jun looked bewildered.

"I do not understand," Jun replied, avoiding eye contact.

"And not only that, Jap Tech is doing illegal practices!"

Michael grimaced. The one-way argument prompted Michael to suggest a break. Jun excused himself.

"We're outta here," Pug yelled as he headed to the door. "Can't trust anything he says. Wouldn't look me in the eye."

"You talked so fast, he couldn't respond."

"Nothing but a sushi-snacking, sake-sipping sucker."

Previous covert meetings with Research Appliance produced no progress. Pug had instructed the Osaka lawyer to send the cease-and-desist letter. Within two weeks, Research Appliance filed a suit in

Osaka claiming IPS threatened serious economic harm. The local court agreed and granted an injunction against IPS and imposed fines and market restrictions. Outraged, Pug fired the local lawyer and hired a Tokyo-based attorney.

After the first meeting, the new lawyer assured them, "Mr. James, the national courts will overturn the Osaka court's ruling. Research Appliance has political influence in Osaka but not Tokyo."

Afterwards Michael told Pug, "The new lawyer's words are reassuring, but he's motivated by the novelty of the appeal—not who wins."

"Fieldsy, for godsakes, lighten up! Jackson says this guy's top rate."

"Yeah, and so's his retainer. Thank god we're still talking with Research Appliance."

The day after seeing Jun, they met with Research Appliance's CEO. Three hours later, they boarded the train to Narita.

"God, I hate secret meetings!" Pug groused.

"I agree. Did you buy the CEO's rationale for their injunction?"

"Fuck no! At least he agreed we're only making the lawyers rich."

"What did you think of their commercial offer? They want IPS to quote on a three-year contract for at least fifty percent of its requirements for 10000-type products."

"Yeah, but why not one hundred percent now?"

"Pug, Research Appliance has to phase the changeover from Japan Technologies to IPS."

"Well, I cut to the chase when I told him to put the request in writing."

"But what about the caveats that we resolve the legal matters in Osaka and cancel our appeal?"

"If we get the commercial deal, the legal stuff's peanuts. 'Sides, I love the idea of stealing business from Kenji."

"Pug, you know what they say about revenge?"

"Yeah, Marcy told me it's like a dish of cold cuts."

Michael shook his head and chuckled.

OSAKA

Kenji conferred with Dr. Yamura in his office.

"Dr. Yamura, I am preparing to meet Mr. Darin James. Interesting that he resigned from the IPS board. What are the results of your investigation?"

"Mr. James's company specializes in aerospace and defense communications. Revenues of approximately eighty million come from defense contracts. During the past two years, the company has had significant losses."

"The company's stock price?"

"Shares currently trade between twelve and fourteen, down from a recent high of twenty-nine dollars."

"How does the market justify the current price with no profits?"

"The current equity market is receptive to companies with major government contracts and strong political influence in Washington, D.C."

"Interesting. What about his personal situation?"

"After the IPO, Mr. James's net worth amounted to twenty million, but recently declined very much. He has sold several thousand shares."

"Why?"

"The first divorce settlement was very expensive, and he maintains an extravagant lifestyle with considerable debt: large mortgages on two Seattle houses, a Colorado farm, and stock margin obligations. His company stock is pledged as collateral."

"He will have serious trouble if the company's stock value declines more or if he loses his position."

"Hai! Also the US Securities Exchange Commission is investigating insider trading by company officers."

Darin joined Kenji at the conference table. "Mr. James, it is a pleasure to welcome you to Osaka. I trust your flight went well."

"Good to see you, Mr. Kobyashi. The Japan Airlines flight was excellent." Darin surveyed the office. "Your office is elegant."

"You are most kind. Mr. James, tell me, what is on your mind?"

"Our discussions are confidential?"

"You have my word," Kenji said as he pushed a hidden button to engage a recording device. Cigar and cigarette smoke filled the office. Kenji's assistant coughed as she poured tea.

"The first matter involves the Lawrent lawsuit," Darin said, "which could have severe financial consequences for IPS and your equity investment."

"I understand, but I am not sure what I can do to stop this litigation."

"Perhaps some solutions will surface. I'll ask Rich James to monitor the legal activities and to keep us informed."

"Thank you. What other issues do you wish to discuss?"

"Puggy plans to close Denver."

"That does not make sense. Why take such action?"

Darin removed a second Cuban from his breast pocket. Lighting it and exhaling, he said, "I agree. Here's more for you to consider..."

After two hours Kenji concluded, "Ashi-san will expect Rich James's call." He looked at his watch. "It is time for dinner, Mr. James. We have reservations at the Comfort Station."

Suzi served them in a private dining room. Darin's eyes locked on her as she poured Gekkeikan sake. Beginning to feel the effects of warm sake and jet lag, he said, "Mr. Kobyashi, my private investigator tells me Sean O'Leary secretly consults for Lawrent. Competitors who steal proprietary information destroy the value of exclusive licenses and shareholder value."

"Dr. O'Leary pursues a dishonest and dangerous course."

"Can't be trusted." Darin watched Suzi refill his cup.

After dinner, they relaxed with cigars and Johnnie Walker Blue at Kenji's club. Darin was pleased when Suzi joined them.

After several more rounds, Kenji said, "Mr. James, I will now say good night. Your information has been most helpful, and I look forward to meeting again. Have a good evening."

Kenji departed. Darin and Suzi continued drinking.

Kenji and Jun met the following day. "Mr. Darin James's visit was most informative, yet his motives are suspect."

Jun scanned notes from Dr. Yamura's report. "His financial problems present interesting opportunities."

"Hai! And he knows too much. Instruct Dr. Yamura to take care of him. Jun, expect Mr. Rich James's call. Shiganari and I will address the O'Leary matter."

REDWOOD CITY, CALIFORNIA

A holiday party for employees and spouses took place at Café Baronni in Redwood City. After dinner, Pug stood and tapped his wine glass.

"Wanna wish everybody happy holidays and a prosperous 'ninety-six. Ninety-five's been rough with the legal messes and Lawrent stealing our business. Lawrent's gonna write us a nice big check, so IPS can develop new technologies. Next year's Katy-bar-the-door!"

Everyone cheered. Marcy beamed. Pug kissed her as he sat down.

After dinner, Michael and Ellie watched the guests dance. "Not sure the James boys are happy," Michael whispered.

"Skip's bored, Michelle's depressed, and Dave ignores Tina. I sense a family implosion."

"Things should get better for Skip. I did a budget for his personal finances," he said.

"Marcy claims Skip's always broke. Where does his salary go?"

"Not sure. Bruce says Skip's still behind on filing expense reports."

"That doesn't sound good."

"I haven't given up on Skip, but he's taxing my patience. Dave, on the other hand, shows a lot more promise. If I had to bet, he'll succeed while Skip flounders."

1996
SOUTH SAN FRANCISCO

IN THE FIRST WEEK OF the new year, Pug flipped through Dave's AA status report on the first two phases.

Dave waited patiently for Pug's reaction. *Got thumbs up from Sean and Michael. Will Pops agree?*

"Remember my MatraScience network analysis idea?" Pug said, tossing the report aside. "Today you're gonna learn about rainstorming." Pug retold the MatraScience skunk works story and concluded, "When you invent, you're the alpha dog. Now here's what you're gonna do."

Dave shrugged. *My father, a patented asshole.*

AA Phase III required more personnel. Pug ordered everyone to support the project. Dave assembled resources from South San Francisco, Denver, and Chicago. Over the next two weeks, the staff studied results of Phase I and II and brainstormed IPS solutions for thermal and acoustic applications. The solutions became "proof of concept" prototypes for testing. Dave required three alternative solutions for each application. Sean supported Dave when requested; otherwise, he kept a low profile.

Michael asked Maurice Oshima to find Japanese consultants to study Hondoya's parts and to estimate target-manufacturing costs. Rich's team estimated costs for manufacturing IPS prototypes. Dave challenged him to beat the target costs by at least 15 percent.

Meanwhile, Skip faced three obstacles: his wife, Annie's fiancé, and Pug. He ignored his wife and told himself, *Randy Burr will self-destruct. How to convince Pops to hire Annie?*

On a visit to Sunshine, he noticed Annie's glum mood. "Something bothering you, Annie?"

"Family problems."

"Hey, you're talking to an expert on family stuff."

"You have it so good at IPS."

"What's your father done now?"

"At today's meeting, he announced Randy's promotion to vice president of sales and marketing."

"I don't follow..."

"He never once considered me. Said women don't belong in executive ranks. It's time I quit Sunshine."

"Hey, if you decide that, maybe I can help you find a job."

"Skip, thank you... that's very kind of you."

Excited and happy, Skip returned to Sunnyvale. *Annie's free to join IPS!*

OSAKA

Jun walked into Kenji's office and announced, "Kobyashi-san, the Hondoya commercial agreement is ready. It allows IPS personnel to visit the engineering group—with no limitations."

"Instruct Hondoya's oven department to select an appropriate project and involve Nippon-Soft-Dev."

"Hai! Dr. Yamura has another concern. Gano Nippon requested legal assistance regarding Lawrent," Jun continued.

"A Lawrent victory will assist us in Asia, but a Gano-Lawrent alliance could become a problem. We cooperate, but with caution! Tell Dr. Yamura to send the Sergeant Sacker file to Gano Nippon's CEO. He will know what to do."

SOUTH SAN FRANCISCO

In February, Pug and Michael reviewed the completed Appliance Analysis. "Whadya think of Dave's work?"

"Like father, like son. Dave's proofs of concept are impressive."

"Sharon! Get Dave in here!"

Dave arrived with Judith.

"You guys joined at the hip?" Pug asked. Dave's sneer conveyed a *fuck you*.

"Congratulations, Dave!" Michael interjected. "Your solutions are great. I like your new idea, 'Design Freedom for Cost and Technical Improvement.'"

"Thanks, IPS technologies give engineers design freedom to achieve thermal, acoustic, space, and weight improvements—and best of all—cost reductions."

"So Dave, what's the next step?" Michael asked.

"We'll summarize technical and economic data, choose the best solutions. Judith's doing a PowerPoint presentation. When Hondoya's ready, I'll go to Japan..."

"Not so fast," Pug interrupted.

"But..."

"But nothing! Hondoya negotiations are above your pay grade."

"Then raise my pay!" Dave shouted as he stomped out. Judith, embarrassed, followed.

"Pug, you took the wind out of his sails!" Michael said.

"Ain't got experience with high-level people."

"He's got to learn sometime."

Michael returned to his office and found Dave pacing and furious.

"You believe this shit? First Mathews and now this!"

"Easy now. We'll arrange more visits with Hondoya until they request you to present. Remember, patience and long-term view are crucial."

Dave continued to pace but more slowly. "Guess you're right." Calmer, he brushed hair from his eyes. "Sounds like an okay plan." He took deep breaths. "Why can't he trust me like Sean does?"

"Your dad finds it hard to delegate. I'm working on him to ease up."

"Thanks, Michael, I appreciate that."

The next day Skip introduced Annie to IPS. She presented test results showing IPS 10000 thermal performance on Sunshine toaster prototypes. "I'm happy to announce all tests proved positive," she said. "Dr. Ramirez is very pleased with IPS materials."

Skip added, "Sunshine's ready to place orders for its new models."

Later, Michael and Pug discussed Annie's presentation. "Sunshine a good opportunity?" Michael asked.

"Chump change," Pug said.

"Could lead to other applications."

"Yeah, but Skip should push Mathews faster. More potential."

Michael smiled. "You've seen the Mathews people Skip brings to IPS?"

"Yeah... why?"

"Duh..."

Pug laughed. "That's why Skip wants to hire her. Today was her audition."

"You can't be serious!"

"Skippy deserves some extra perks for the Mathews project. You gotta admit, hiring Annie would brighten up this place."

"Yeah, but right now we don't need the extra overhead."

TOKYO

Dave spent most of March visiting Hondoya's engineering departments and informally showcasing the AA project proof of concepts. His linguistic skills and sales confidence grew. Hondoya's engineers appreciated his willingness to solve thermal problems. The oven department group requested he develop a multi-dimensional thermal dissipater based on the Handi prototype. Hondoya's engineers introduced him to Nippon-Soft-Dev's design engineers who would assist customizing the new dissipater for other Hondoya appliance applications.

SEATTLE

At Darin's company party, a booze-induced argument flared in front of employees, guests, and board members. Sylvia accused Darin of infidelity. The next week they separated, and Sylvia filed divorce papers.

But Darin had bigger problems. The company's financial performance failed to meet the board's and shareholders' expectations.

Rich called Darin. "Sorry to hear about you and Sylvia. Hope you guys can reconcile."

"She's a historical footnote. Besides, I filed first. So how you and IPS doing?"

"Shitty and '95's a disaster. Sales down to eight million, losses close to a million and a half. Appliancorp and Gen Appliance orders vanished."

"Why?"

"Lawrent's recaptured the General business, and '96 looks worse unless…"

"Unless what?"

"IPS wins the lawsuit."

"Sounds like another Puggy 'Hail Mary.'"

"Yeah, I feel like I'm on the IPS Titanic, and the ship's sinking fast."

"Stay close to your life boat."

"What life boat?"

"The Denver plant. Change of subject: you uncovered any dirt on Fields?"

"Not yet."

"Keep digging. No room for him in our future. And the redheaded asshole will be history soon."

"I hear ya," Rich added.

CHICAGO

The litigants convened in early March at Chicago's historic federal courthouse. With everyone assembled, the judge set the trial ground rules and asked for remaining motions.

Jackson began: "Your Honor, we respectfully request all prospective jurors associated with the appliance industry be excluded as this could prejudice their judgments."

Judge Harrington replied, "In the jury pool voir dire, all jurors denied any current relationships with the appliance industry or with either party to this lawsuit. Plaintiff's motion denied. Next motion."

Jackson's assistant rose. "Your Honor, plaintiff requests dismissal of defendant's motion to discipline Mr. Huntley. Plaintiff's counsel disclosed to the patent examiner all material information and known foreign prior art in accordance with their discovery dates."

Lawrent's attorney started, "Objection..."

The judge interrupted, "Court rules for plaintiff. The discovery evidence provides no basis to support defendant's motion. Mr. Huntley followed all disclosure rules." He continued, "I see from court records that settlement discussions have been inconclusive. Any possibility for a pre-trial settlement?"

Jackson replied, "No, Your Honor. Defendant's offers are totally inadequate given financial damages suffered by plaintiff."

Lawrent's lawyer indicated IPS rejected all its settlement offers.

Judge Harrington glared at the Jason & Jones table. "Disappointing. Court sets trial for April 20, 1996."

As they left, Lawrent's attorneys handed Jackson an envelope. The enclosed letter contained a new offer. Pug read it and slammed his fist to the table. "This is insulting!"

"Pug, no downside to one more meeting."

"Tell 'em we'll see 'em in court!"

Dexter-Foresmen's lawyers arrived from Washington, D.C. and San Francisco. The entourage numbered twenty and occupied most of the twenty-fourth floor of Chicago's Renaissance Hotel.

Jackson called Pug. "Based on witness lists, amount of discovery evidence, and allowing for unexpected delays, the trial should last five, maybe six weeks."

"Marcy and me are gonna be there from start to finish!"

"That's great! Your presence will personalize it for the jury. See you in Chicago."

Sean strolled into Pug's office. "Pug, when am I scheduled to testify?"

"Not sure, but be there Monday."

"I know most of the Gen Appliance witnesses. I can detect their lies. Does Jackson expect a big win?"

"Yep! There's no victory for substitutes."

Sean smiled. "Sounds like Arthur Mac's speech."

"Quit twisting my words!"

On day one of the trial, Pug marveled at the majestic courtroom with its ornate oak moldings, carved paneling, antique benches and tables—testament to the building's dignified history. He told Marcy, "They don't build 'em like this anymore."

The legal teams arrived. Four Jason & Jones partners sat at the defendant's table. Behind them, a junior attorney sorted documents from a large packet with Japanese postmarks. Behind the rail, ten legal assistants occupied the first two rows.

Jackson and two senior partners took seats at the plaintiff's table. Other staff sat behind, filling three rows. Pug sat behind the rail and Jackson's chair. Marcy and Sean joined him in the first row.

Sean nudged Pug. "See those three guys in the third row? They're General Appliance's legal beagles."

Pug passed a note to Jackson. *Why are General's gators here?*

Jackson scribbled an answer. *To make sure they don't incur any liability.*

Pug wrote back. *Who's the blonde babe behind Lawrent's lawyers?*

Jackson's responded. *Lawrent's jury consultant.*

Judge Harrington, stern-faced and business-like, entered. Jury selection was first order of business; and since he had ruled against IPS's previous motion, the process began.

Jackson handed Pug a note. *Candidate pool looks good, mostly blue collar and minorities. Score one for David!*

Both sides exercised their allowed challenges. One candidate, Mr. Sacker, took considerable time to vet. Sean watched Lawrent's chief litigator scribble notes for the jury consultant. She gave an okay sign. When Jackson finished questioning Sacker, Pug—red-faced and furious—passed a note to Jackson. *I don't like this guy. Get rid of him!*

Jackson addressed the judge. "Your Honor, I ask Mr. Sacker be excused. Two of his previous employers have vested interests in the outcome of this trial."

"Overruled."

"Objection."

"Objection noted. This candidate has not worked in the appliance industry for fifteen years. If the defense has no objections, this juror is accepted."

"No objections, Your Honor."

The jury selection process continued for three days until jurors and alternates were approved. Judge Harrington declared the jury impaneled. The judge ordered the trial date to commence next Monday.

Pug grabbed Jackson by the arm and demanded, "Get Sacker off the jury! You can't trust him!"

"Pug, what are you talking about?"

"I just want him off the jury!"

"You heard the judge overrule us. Besides, Mr. Sacker denied any prior or current relationships with any parties to this lawsuit. I have no other basis to challenge him. Look at it this way, his engineering background will help the non-technical jurors."

Furious, Pug left the courtroom.

That night in the hotel room as they lay in bed, Marcy asked, "What's bothering you?"

Pug grunted, "That asshole Sacker. How the hell did Jackson let him on my jury?"

"Honey, did you tell Jackson what happened in Viet Nam?"

"Shoulda put a bullet in the bastard." He rolled over and began to snore.

His erratic sleep and breathing worried her. Often when breathing in, he did not exhale for what seemed like minutes.

On Monday morning, the judge ordered Dexter-Foresmen to present opening statements. Jackson outlined the history of IPS 10000 and its rapid acceptance in North America. Evidence would show Lawrent conspired to steal IPS's innovative technology and market share causing severe financial harm to IPS and that Lawrent infringed IPS's patents before and after the TAI patent issued.

Jason & Jones's lead attorney described Lawrent's successful history of manufacturing and supplying thermal dissipaters. Lawrent, unlike IPS, did not rely on any one technology. The facts would prove Lawrent invented its own thermal dissipater technology and demonstrated Lawrent practiced its own patents. The jury would hear expert testimony proving IPS 10000 patent was invalid and therefore Lawrent did not infringe.

Judge Harrington instructed plaintiff to call first witnesses the next morning.

That evening, Pug phoned Rich. "Jackson wants you up here the day after tomorrow. Anything else happening?"

"Darin's divorce is final."

"No surprise. Who's his latest bimbo?"

"Name's Amber."

Pug's testimony captivated the jury. He described his small, struggling company and its revolutionary technology. Jackson's questions elicited how distraught Pug became when he realized Lawrent copied IPS's intellectual property. Cross-examination was brief, and nothing refuted Pug statements.

He returned to his seat and whispered to Marcy, "Softball questions! Pretty hard to challenge my truth."

She patted his leg. "You were terrific. The jury hung on your every word."

Next, Sean testified. He described the invention's novelty, not obvious even to those schooled in the art. He stated his detailed searches revealed no prior art. Rich discussed processes needed to manufacture the material including techniques not found in prior art. Both stressed positive customer responses when introduced to IPS 10000. From their statements, Jackson developed a timeline which demonstrated IPS 10000 preceded Lawrent's TAI by many months.

With IPS 10000's history established, Jackson called witnesses from Marken and Exeter who corroborated IPS being first to market this technology to OEMs. Exeter witnesses suggested Lawrent's products were clever copycats. Jackson then asked General Appliance and Appliancorp witnesses to explain General's supplier meeting. Their answers were vague and unconvincing. Jackson's pointed questions elicited responses that supported the conspiracy theory. Judge Harrington overruled frequent objections from Jason & Jones.

Jackson asked the last General Appliance witness, "Isn't it ironic General Appliance prevented IPS from qualifying for its new specification? Yet Exeter considered IPS 10000 a revolutionary advancement."

"Objection your honor!" Lawrent's counsel said, "Is that a question or a rhetorical statement for the witness?"

The judge declared, "Sustained. Let's recess and resume at 2:00 p.m."

At the noon recess, Pug called Michael, "Jackson's doing great! Da Judge is in our corner."

"By the way," Michael said, "Hondoya's official commercial settlement document arrived. Hold on, Skip wants to talk with you."

He handed the phone to Skip. "Hey, Pops. What about Annie?"

"We'll discuss it when you and Michael come to Chicago. Gotta go." He heard the click.

Michael asked, "What about Annie?"

"Thought Pops told you. With my Mathews's workload, I need administrative and marketing support. Can't find new customers if I'm stuck with paperwork."

"Use Sharon. She's never busy."

"Dave's got an assistant!"

"And he's got a full plate. Let's discuss in Chicago. On another subject, Bruce said you're over nine months behind filing expense reports."

"I'll do them tomorrow."

"How are you doing with the budget I prepared? You should have enough money to get by. Unless, you didn't give me a complete list of spending."

"I gave you everything Michelle found."

Michael looked dubious. *And Billy ate the credit card receipts?*

When the trial resumed, Jackson questioned the IPS experts. The technical consultant maintained Lawrent infringed with products sold before and after the TAI patent issued. Lawrent had more incentive to sell non-TAI versions given their lower production costs. Obtuse accounting records made it difficult to verify exact product mix and costs. The financial expert gave convincing data showing monetary damages IPS incurred on lost sales between 1995 and into 1996. Judge Harrington once again overruled Lawrent's objections.

Jackson leaned over the rail. "David's in the driver seat. Goliath had a weak cross exam."

Jackson concluded at the end of week three. The judge ordered a four-day recess.

Sean phoned Bruce. "I want to exercise my 60,000 stock options."

"You sure?"

"The way this trial's going, I have a hunch IPS's book value will skyrocket. You know how Pug sets share price value with his two-and-a-half times net book. Higher price means more taxes."

"I hear you."

"So, how much will I owe IPS?" *I mean how much will Kenji owe?*

"If we use Pug's twenty dollar per share, you'll owe IPS two hundred and forty thousand... and, you'll owe one hundred and forty thousand dollars in taxes to the IRS and Colorado."

"I'll Fed-Ex the checks tonight."

Bruce pondered Sean's decision. *I better exercise my options. Sean's hunches always pan out.*

When court resumed, Jason & Jones presented their case which lasted two weeks. The defense focused on refuting intentional infringement and proving IPS 10000's patent was invalid. Defense witnesses contradicted earlier testimony by IPS witnesses. Jackson's cross-examination highlighted inconsistent statements when compared with discovery evidence.

Dr. Berry, grandfatherly and aided by a cane, took the stand as Lawrent's final expert witness. His reputation among appliance thermal engineers had long passed. He stated TAI patent claims did not infringe and further testified why the IPS patent claims were invalid.

He withered under Jackson's aggressive cross-examination that exposed rehearsed explanations, incorrect statements, and faulty logic.

The judge overruled defense objections and allowed Jackson to pummel Dr. Berry.

The trial adjourned for a three-day weekend.

Michael and Skip arrived on Monday evening and met Pug for dinner at Onassis, the hotel's Greek restaurant. As the waiter filled their wine glasses, Michael asked, "Where's Sean?"

"Gone," Pug replied.

"Gone?"

"Quit."

"No two week's notice?"

"Didn't want him hanging around. Knew he'd never move to San Francisco."

"I'm really surprised. Guess I better get cranking on his replacement," Michael said.

"Hope you're faster than Sean. If I hadn't stepped in, we'd never hired the three new engineers. I'm hungry, let's order."

The waiter brought an assortment of Greek specialties. Skip asked, "Pops, when can I hire Annie?"

"Whadya think, Michael?"

"She's qualified but we can't afford her right now. Let's wait until the trial's over."

"Pops, I wanna make an offer."

"Michael decides."

"But we agreed!"

"Remember what Winston Churchill said about…"

Skip frowned. "Dictatorship?"

"You want to get into Annie's panties, get Fieldsy's okay." Pug winked at Michael.

On Tuesday at breakfast, Michael watched Pug devour scrambled eggs, hash browns, thick sausage, and two cheese Danishes.

"Amazing your arteries function," Michael said, sipping orange juice.

"Gonna talk arteries or Hondoya? Whadya think of the proposal?"

"We've discussed it for six months. Now they're in a rush to sign?"

"Hondoya knows Lawrent's gettin' its legal ass kicked. They wanna settle… before we win. The value of my patents only goes up."

"But Hondoya offered no substance. In return for an ambiguous three-year commercial agreement with no commitments, they want us to one, discontinue the legal battles in Colorado and Tokyo, and two, reimburse them for legal expenses in Japan. Coincidently, the amount is identical to Hondoya's payment after our Colorado victory. Three, they still oppose our APO patent. Four, to add insult, they don't acknowledge past infringement. If we beat Lawrent, our U. S. position strengthens. Let's wait. We hold all the cards."

"You're forgetting Jap Tech isn't selling to Hondoya, so the coast is clear. My AA shows we got huge opportunities."

"Pug, quit dreaming! It'll take years to develop profitable business, and we don't have a manufacturing base in Asia."

"Fieldsy, with award money from Lawrent, we'll have plenty. I'm signing before Hondoya changes its mind."

"But Japan Technologies has the exclusive license."

"Got it covered. Remember the license clause… if Jap Tech can't sell direct, IPS can. And if we don't put this legal shit behind us, we'll never do business with the largest Japanese OEM."

"Jackson needs to review the document."

"He's busy beating the shit out of Lawrent. I'm signing the document."

SOUTH SAN FRANCISCO

Michael instructed Bruce to wire $150 thousand to Hondoya. Hondoya and IPS executed and exchanged a three-year commercial agreement and settled all Colorado and Japanese legal matters.

Dave plopped on the corner of the Michael's desk. "Boy, you look serious. What's up?"

"Thinking about the Hondoya agreement."

"Pops says my AA is our roadmap for quoting on lots of business."

"Sales calls and quoting are easy. Do you think our competitors will sit idle?"

"What's different from how we do business in North America?"

"First, it takes a long time to develop deep political relationships like Japan Technologies's. Second, we have no troops in Japan. Parachuting is expensive, not to mention inefficient."

"Hey, I'll live in Japan!"

"Now... that's an interesting thought!"

Michael recalled his conversation with Dave about the business cards Pug collected at his first Hondoya meeting:

"What do you make of this Shiganari Okazaki card? I can't make any sense of his job function. Is he chief engineer?"

"Did some snooping. He was in engineering once, but this dude's now executive chairman of Hondoya."

"Say, are you serious about Japan? It takes time for an American to adjust, and it won't be a vacation."

"Yeah, I know, but my Japanese is getting better—and I'm real comfortable with Hondoya's techies. The Nippon-Soft-Dev group's been a real help, like having a local tech support team."

Michael tapped his pencil on the desk and nodded. *Hell, why not Japan? And it gets Dave away from Pug.* "If Pug's right and we beat Lawrent, then money won't be a problem to relocate you."

CHICAGO

Lawyers completed closing statements in week six. Judge Harrington issued instructions to the jury and excused them. Lawrent's lawyers gave Jackson a new settlement offer.

Jackson told Pug, "Wait until the jury's verdict then Lawrent will make another offer before damages are decided. They're running scared and so is General Appliance."

"What's that mean?"

"General Appliance's lawyers claimed IPS supplied material for its field trials, and this granted it a de facto license. They need another rationale for using IPS 10000-like products from sources other than IPS once Lawrent loses this lawsuit."

"We got 'em by the short hairs!"

Later that afternoon, Pug called Michael. "Fieldsy, begin the Japan plan."

"We'll need five million."

"No problem-o. Opened a new bank account called Lawrent. Deposits start very soon. Our team's going out tonight for a big celebration. See ya!"

APRIL 15

The next day, Jackson and Pug met in the courthouse cafeteria to await the outcome.

"How long'll the jury take?"

Jackson replied, "My guess is no more than eight to ten hours. After the jury digests the weak testimony from Lawrent's star witness, this should be a slam dunk."

"You really creamed that old codger with your cross examination. So how much will the jury award for damages?"

"Let's think conservative. High end could be as much as thirty to forty million, but I'll go with twenty million. Not bad for six weeks work."

"You mean, six weeks plus nine months of expensive discovery!"

"Touché!"

Six hours passed, and the judge summoned the lawyers to review a jury question.

Judge Harrington said, "Mr. Sacker, the jury foreman, has requested an answer to the following question: 'If the jury determines the IPS 10000 patent claims are invalid, isn't Lawrent's infringement irrelevant?' Gentlemen, this is the answer I will provide: If the jury determines the original IPS patent claims are invalid based on the facts presented, then the jury can conclude infringement did not occur."

Two hours later, the jury announced it had a verdict. From his front row seat, Pug watched each juror. All avoided eye contact. Judge Harrington studied the verdict, and then read, "The jury finds Lawrent

Appliance did not infringe the IPS patent. Six IPS 10000 patent claims are declared invalid."

The judge removed his glasses and remained silent for a full minute. "I will issue a summary ruling affirming the verdict. IPS can appeal to the Federal Circuit Court of Appeals. The court thanks the jury for your service." He slammed his gavel. "Court adjourned."

Pug clinched his fists and yelled, "No!" Marcy burst into tears.

Jackson said, "Pug, you saw the judge's reaction. He totally disagrees with the verdict. We'll request a judgment not withstanding jury verdict."

"Dumb-ass jury invalidated my patent! That Sacker guy fucked me!"

"Pug, we'll talk to the jurors to see what happened."

"Yeah, yeah. Thank god I signed the Hondoya agreement. Marcy, we're clearin' outta this dump."

NAPA VALLEY, CALIFORNIA

Dismayed and angry, Pug cancelled Denver and San Francisco victory celebrations and returned to California. He and Marcy drove to the Silverado Resort in Napa Valley. As they strolled the vineyards in the May afternoon sun, he rubbed his neck and grimaced.

"Honey, your neck still bothering you?" Marcy asked.

"Trial was a pain in the neck. Asshole Sacker screwed me over! Told Jackson to get the SOB off the jury, but he didn't listen."

"I want you to see a doctor. You haven't slept in six weeks."

"Talk about a roller coaster! In Vegas, we had two million in the bank, looking to sell twenty million in '95. At fifty-five bucks a share, I was worth twenty-five million!"

"Honey..."

"Now everything's crap! Those General Appliance bastards gave our profitable business to Lawrent. Jackson cost me a million and a half for his free contingency. We're outta cash. Now I gotta spend more gator money fighting sake-sippers and the Lawrent verdict!"

"Sweetie, we'll get through this."

"I'm calling my army buddies about Sacker!"

"Honey, you don't know what happened in the jury room."

"Sacker had somethin' to do with the verdict! Jackson shoulda listened to me and kicked him off the jury!"

"But, honey, you never told Jackson the whole story... what happened in Vietnam."

"For chrissakes, how could I? It was a secret mission, still classified. Sacker betrayed his team, had to get rid of him... shoulda got him a dishonorable discharge!"

"Well, Jackson did his best."

"He didn't bet his firm like I did!" Pug paused and took a deep breath. "One day he'll pay for this!"

Marcy kissed him on the cheek. "Honey, things'll get better, and you still have me."

She took his arm, and they walked to the inn's restaurant.

SOUTH SAN FRANCISCO

With Pug out of the office, Michael took the opportunity to call Jackson. "Hey Jackson, want to catch up now that the trial's over. Sorry we couldn't talk more during the course of it."

"Michael, thanks for checking in. Yeah, I would have appreciated your active involvement on a real-time basis."

"Thought that's why Sean O'Leary was there."

"Well, if that's what his role was, he kept pretty quiet most of the time. Then he surprised everyone and suddenly resigned!"

"Yeah, that was strange. Anyway, give me your thoughts on the verdict."

Jackson paused. "To be candid, it was a complete surprise. You should have seen the judge's expression when he read the verdict. Everyone was stunned."

"Jackson, you can't predict how a jury thinks."

"Say, do you know a guy named Joe Sacker? He was one of the jurors."

Michael thought for a moment. "No... why?"

"Well, Pug went ballistic when I couldn't get him excused from the jury."

"Don't know anything about him..."

"After the trial was said and done, I told Pug we should interview the jurors to understand what happened. He said no way. Didn't want to spend more money."

"How did you and Pug leave it?"

"We didn't discuss it. Off the record, he said some pretty nasty things to me and my colleagues before departing in a huff."

"Pug's reaction is understandable. He bet his company's future on this trial. It was a terrible disappointment."

"Hey, tell him to join the club. My firm made a major commitment with the contingency agreement. We have nothing to show but two million of unbilled fees."

"When the dust settles, Pug will come around and recognize your effort."

"But to tell you the truth, Michael, I'm very frustrated with Pug. You and I worked with him a long time at MatraScience and now at IPS, but lately..."

"What are you saying, Jackson?"

Jackson paused as if collecting his thoughts. "Okay, during the deposition phases, Pug made several unsubstantiated claims that we could never investigate or verify."

"Like what?"

"He claimed Lawrent was spying on him and Marcy to get some dirt for the trial."

"Pug mentioned that. So what happened?"

"We could not find any evidence to support his claim. But he did tell us to investigate Lawrent's connection with General Appliance to see if there was anything illegal."

"What did you find out?"

"When we got the investigator's proposal and fee charges, we opted not to pursue it."

"Why not?"

"Would have cost IPS another fifty thousand. Pug complained daily about the out-of-pocket cost for experts and charges IPS was paying per our contingency arrangement. Frankly, Pug acted very irrational at times. Bottom line, we decided to forgo incurring more fees. And there's more frustration with how Pug treats our firm."

"Explain."

"When we call IPS to find out why our invoices haven't been paid, Bruce Hargett says Pug's put a hold on them. Then I have to argue with Pug or call you to get them paid. We have invoices over 150 days past due!"

"As you know, cash is tight. Let me see if I can get you guys on a more regular payment cycle."

"Thanks, and remind Pug we're not a bank and need to pay our bills too."

"Understand. When Pug returns, I'll arrange a three-way meeting so we can work a plan to move forward on a number of legal matters."

"That'll be great, Michael. Thanks for listening to me rant."

SAN FRANCISCO

That evening, Michael updated Ellie who observed, "I don't envy Jackson. Pug demands legal services yet constantly interferes in the process."

"True. Pug insists on wide patent coverage but never balances the costs/benefits."

"Can you intervene… insert some common sense?"

Michael sighed and shook his head. "I'll try, but Pug thinks patents and all intellectual property are his sole purview."

Ellie chuckled. "You know the old saying when a wannabe lawyer represents himself."

"He's got a fool… maybe an asshole… for a client."

KONA, HAWAII

Kona Village on the big island of Hawaii was special: secluded, peaceful, and relaxing. Sean sat on the lanai of his hale and enjoyed the warm sun. He opened a tube of sun block and rubbed a thick layer on his chest and shoulders.

His thoughts were conflicted. *First vacation in… how many years? At least eight. How did I get into this craziness?*

He gazed at the peaceful lagoon and inhaled the warm air. He finished applying sun block to his pale legs, tossed the tube on a chair, and lit a Marlboro. *Guilt? Hell no! Kenji, Shiganari, Walter… they betrayed me!*

He ground the cigarette in an ashtray, donned a baseball cap and sunglasses, and headed to the beach. As he walked along the black volcanic sand, his heart ached. *Natsuko! Natsuko! I miss you so! What happened? Why?* He walked faster. *My obligations to Kenji are cancelled.*

Grief and anger overwhelmed as he returned to the hale. *I have to think of my future.*

He retrieved his recorder and tapes from a briefcase and listened to recorded conversations. He lit another Marlboro and called North Carolina.

"Larry, it's Sean. Got your message."

"How's Kona?"

"Perfect antithesis to chaos. What's the trial fallout?"

"Waiting for the judge's verdict affirmation. The longer he delays, the better."

"What can I do for you?"

"Would Pug consider selling IPS?"

"Depends...'96 will be disastrous. If Lawrent starts taking IPS's Exeter business, vulnerability increases."

"Already on that. What about the Hondoya commercial agreement?"

"Japanese don't like foreign suppliers."

"Our Asian colleagues tell us IPS and Research Appliance are discussing cooperation."

"I'll check into it."

"You get our transfers?"

"Yes. Thanks for the bonus."

"You earned it. General Appliance and Lawrent are extremely grateful for your services—especially the heads up about Sacker. He kept that dumb jury in the palm of his hand."

"Well, Larry, you managed to get him on the jury. No small feat."

"Amazing what offshore money in the right pockets can do, isn't it?"

Sean said goodbye and pressed the recorder stop button.

SEATTLE

In Seattle, Darin read his laptop notes. *Outed the doctor. Kenji understands more than he admits. Questions: Is O'Leary conspiring with anyone else? Does Kenji know about O'Leary's porn habit?*

His secretary interrupted with a call.

Rich's excited voice announced, "Lawrent wiped our proprietary ass big time!"

"Wow, bet Puggy's pissed."

"Yeah, he blamed the stupid jurors, then the incompetent judge. Now he blames his lawyers for mishandling the trial."

"So nothing's his fault? What next?"

"He called an urgent meeting at the California country club."

"Two words: protect Denver!"

TOKYO

Two weeks after the trial, Hondoya requested Dave present the AA technical results. Michael engaged Maurice Oshima to handle market-related matters. Maurice's experience lent credibility. Hondoya officials praised the presentation. The procurement officer accelerated work on the multi-dimensional dissipater and initiated several new projects.

Michael, Dave, and Maurice met for a post-meeting libation in the Dai-ichi lounge. "By my count, we got projects worth over fifteen million," Dave said. "Pops should see me in action."

"Your dad needed time off. Your presentation's a great start." Michael took a sip of wine and cautioned, "Don't book revenues yet. We've just begun a long journey. MatraScience needed five years before receiving its first order."

Maurice nodded. "Amen to that!"

SOUTH SAN FRANCISCO

After three weeks working on home remodeling, Pug returned to the office in June and summoned Bruce, Rich, and the sales manager to San Francisco. Michael, Skip, Dave, and Sharon joined them in the conference room.

"For a guy slammed by a legal two-by-four, he's pretty upbeat," Michael told Rich.

"Yeah, he's fixing that wreck of a house—gutted the basement— putting in a wine cellar, exercise room, god knows what all…"

"Explains why he sold more of his personal shares."

Pug, his demeanor brusque and serious, appeared at the door and without comment took a seat.

"Hey Puggy, no Krispy Kremes?" Rich joked.

"Least of your worries, Porky! Bruce, do the financials."

Bruce fumbled with overhead slides. "Everyone knows 1995 was a disaster," he began. "Revenues declined to less than nine million with a net loss of one-point-two million. It's easy to understand—increased start-up expenses in Chicago, San Francisco, Asia, Europe, and Mexico, and very significant legal costs for lawsuits."

"Wait a minute!" Rich interrupted. "Wasn't this supposed to be free?"

"IPS paid all out-of-pocket costs which amounted to a million and a half," Bruce answered.

Pug pushed away from the table. "Taking a pee break."

Rich whispered to Michael, "Code for Puggy's changing the subject."

"Understandable," Michael said. "By the way, Bruce doesn't have much spark. Something wrong?"

"Boyfriend problems."

"Does Pug know?"

"And what if 'Mr. Empathy' did?"

The group reassembled, and Rich noted, "Too bad Dr. O'Leary ain't here to 'defend' his '95 sales forecast. What happened to the twenty million?"

"Shut up!" Pug barked. "Let Bruce finish without your cyclical comments."

"Sorry, I'll be less cynical."

Bruce continued, "Ninety-six started with sales running below last year's rate and operating expenses higher due to legal bills in the first five months. At this pace, all profits and cash reserves from ninety-three and ninety-four will be gone. Questions?"

Pug looked around the table. "Guys, this is a no-rainer. We hunker down 'til the storm passes."

"Reducing expenses yes, but how about increasing the top line?" Michael asked.

"Look, revenues'll come. For now we cut!"

"Makes sense," the sales manager added, "but don't cut sales expense."

"Last two weeks, I had a scheme. Like Marty King. Rebuilding my basement from scratch gave me a vista." Pug looked at the sales manager. "We're closing Chicago. Starting over. Can't afford the overhead with current sales. We'll save seven hundred thousand a year."

"Pug, you'll kill sales. We hired three new guys after we fired Marken."

"Those new guys aren't worth shit! Not one new order in six months. They were supposed to hit the streets running. All I see are their fuckin' expense reports."

"But you approved each new hire recommended by your Chicago cousin!"

"They're history! If you wanna stay, move your ass to San Francisco."

"How do I cover Chicago?"

"Simple... bring Marken back and manage their asses."

Rich leaned forward and banged his fist on the table. "Puggy! This is bullshit!"

"Sean mismanaged them. Never gave them goals, never measured progress, never held anybody accountable. And Michael, you're shutting down Korea."

"What about the Mexican team?"

"Gone!"

"What about Europe and Tokyo?" Bruce asked. "With no sales revenues, we can't afford the administrative overhead."

"Europe and Tokyo are investments, like development. We need presence in Europe and Asia. The Hondoya agreement'll bring sales."

Michael frowned. "IPS doesn't need world-class headquarters from day one. Get sales first, then add overhead."

"Offices stay! From now on, I approve all travel and entertainment spending. Company cars are cancelled. If you wanna keep yours, give Bruce a check for the book value or the company'll sell it."

Bruce asked, "You want every car cancelled?"

"Yeah...'cept for any position whose salary is below seventy thousand."

Rich thought, *Let's see. Who does that leave?*

Pug continued, "Bruce, fire the new engineers. They're losers."

"But I thought you said development was an investment?"

"These guys can't invent shit! I'll run it until Michael finds Sean's replacement."

Bruce nodded. *Since Sean never hired them, I guess I can fire them.*

"Pug, you realize these engineers passed their three-month probation period. Your cousin won't refund his agency fee." *Thank god we haven't paid him yet.* "And what about all the unused space in this building? Couldn't we rent it?" Bruce asked.

"I don't want outsiders near my proprietary stuff. Take all the cuts we've agreed, and lemme know the annual savings. Do a new sales forecast for '96."

"What should I use for sales?"

"Grow sales at twenty per cent, same as the forecast in *Appliance Weekly*. With better management of Marken, twenty per cent's a slam dunk."

Rich turned to the sales manager. "You agree?"

"Hey, who am I to say we can't..."

"See, he's on board, Porky. You can learn a lot from him."

"I'll keep that in mind, Puggy."

The meeting finished, Bruce gathered his overheads and walked out with Rich. "Damn glad we got our two cents in to solve this latest crisis," Bruce said.

"Two cents? Puggy coulda phoned in this meeting."

"He wants face-to-face consensus."

"Bullshit! You mean steamrolled consensus!" Rich noted Bruce's furrowed brow. "You getting another migraine?"

"Wouldn't you after this meeting?"

"Guess you'll postpone relocating to SFO?"

"Pug insists I move now."

Rich thought, *Darin's right... Puggy's gonna close my plant.*

DENVER

In early July, Pug visited Denver and headed straight to Bruce's office. "You set a moving date yet?"

"I can't move until we have an MIS system that integrates both sites."

"Your boyfriend would enjoy the Castro."

"Pug, you said cut costs, not increase them."

"You're in SFO no later than January '97. End of discussion! Don't study MIS to death. Dave can help. He needs some overtime bucks."

Bruce watched Pug depart. *He gave me my first real job, more responsibility and salary… now it's payback.*

CHICAGO

Pug and Michael flew to Chicago to assess the verdict's impact on IPS's customers. At the rental car counter, Michael asked, "Sure you want to rehire Marken without interviewing others?"

"When I poured the foundation for my new porch, it hit me. For concrete, you need the right balance between water and cement. Never had the right formula with Marken."

"How do you figure?"

"Sean ignored them. Too busy playing golf."

"If Walter realizes Marken's the only candidate…"

"We need experienced feet on the street now, and Marken knows us!"

"Marken's sales people are technically inept."

"Keep that opinion to yourself!"

They rented a Chevrolet sedan with satellite navigation. Pug entered the destination. "Let's see if this system's any good." The GPS did not include construction detours. The estimated thirty-minute ride took an hour and a half.

Walter Marken greeted them in his office. At six feet five, he was an imposing figure. Impeccably dressed, he looked every bit the successful executive.

Pug began, "Walter, thanks for seeing us on short notice."

"Pug, Michael, always good to see former clients. What brings you to Chicago?"

"We closed our office."

"Not sure I understand…"

Michael gauged Walter's reaction. *Inscrutable… this guy would survive in Asia.*

"Sean caused customer problems…'specially at General Appliance."

"Pug, you're absolutely right. The last few months we represented IPS, Sean was never available for important sales calls. We could never locate him… it delayed our project quotes and responses to inquiries. The office joke was you could only reach Sean at the nineteenth hole."

"That's why I fired him. Time to build a new foundation. Think IPS can get back into General Appliance's good graces?"

"I won't bullshit you. Sean really pissed off Dan Teller. But we can start over now that Sean's gone."

"Now you're talking."

"Pug, there's been one change. We increased our commission rate to six percent for exclusive relationships. We've added more technical resources."

"Six percent? Need to think about that."

They shook hands, and Pug and Michael departed for Appliancorp. In the car, Pug mused, "I knew Sean never worked that hard. Marken confirmed it. Bet Sean lied about General Appliance and Exeter. He's the reason we got kicked outta of General Appliance."

"Six per cent commission is pretty steep."

"If they do their job and our guy manages 'em, they're worth every cent."

"What about Walter's requirement for a five-year contract? If they don't perform, it will be an expensive buyout for any booked business."

"It'll be less expensive after I fire our sales manager."

The navigation system instructed a right turn at the light. Pug drove into a dead-end. "So much for the latest fuckin' technology. What kinda idiot mapped this friggin' thing?"

"Why didn't Marken contact us about Sean?"

"Hey, if they complained, they risked getting canned."

"Ironic, IPS fired Marken in 1995 instead of Sean. Did you notice the picture on Walter's wall? The one with the two Japanese and two Americans?"

"No."

"Kenji has a similar one in his office. One of the Americans in the photo looks familiar, but from a different generation."

"Who cares?"

"Curious, that's all." *Coincidence. Or something more?*

As they finished the last two sales appointments, Michael remarked, "Each customer seems pleased about Sean's departure and positive about rehiring Marken."

"Let's get a new rep agreement signed before Walter raises it to seven per cent."

ASHEBORO

Sean traveled to Asheboro. He and Larry met for breakfast at the clubhouse.

"What's happening with your former employer?" Larry inquired.

"Ninety-six will be worse than ninety-five. Company's in total chaos."

"Is your information source reliable?"

"You bet." Sean grinned. "My source hides in the closet. Say, how's Lawrent's merger with Gano-Nippon?"

"Proceeding smoothly," Larry answered. "By the way, sources tell me General Appliance of Japan wants to replace Hondoya as the lead OEM."

"What do you have in mind?"

"Help us fight IPS's legal appeals. And then acquire IPS technology." Sean lit a Marlboro and leaned in. "Sounds intriguing... then what?"

"What do you want?"

"To return to Japan."

"Your technical credentials and knowledge of Asia fit perfectly to manage the post-merger entity. Let's get to the first tee, and I'll fill in the details. Think you can win today?"

"Take your best shot." As Larry paid the bill, Sean headed to the men's room to change the recorder tapes.

SOUTH SAN FRANCISCO

By mid-August, Michael found Sean's replacement. Bill Arrow arrived like a cleansing breeze with his pleasant personality, lively curiosity, and disciplined work ethic. An experienced mechanical engineer, he had worked at three Fortune 500 companies, including five years at Mathews.

Bill accompanied Skip to Mathews for a project update. The technical manager told them, "Our new electric water heater model must be energy efficient without using fiberglass."

"I invented the perfect solution," Skip assured him. "I'll let Bill explain."

Bill placed a slide on the projector. "Our new product called Multi-Dimensional Finished Part 10000 can fit many applications."

He presented test data and prototype samples.

"This could work. I love the dimensional flexibility," the technical manager said.

"How would you like to proceed?" Skip asked.

"We'll establish a development project. IPS can participate in our internal design reviews. With successful proof of concept, we can introduce it at the Chicago trade show. Give me a proposal by next week."

They returned to brief Pug and Michael. Before Skip could finish, Pug interrupted, "Reminds me how I solved customer problems at MatraScience."

"But this time, the customer pays for the development," Michael said. "Skip, ask for a fee based on estimated hours to complete."

"You tell them IPS owns all patents and proprietary data!" Pug insisted.

"But Pops, what if we use Mathews's ideas?"

"No inventing in front of them. Show me your notes after each visit. Understand? Bill, make sure Skip doesn't fuck up."

Skip frowned. *Thanks for your vote of confidence, asshole.*

Dave knew Bill's arrival would rock his world. Sean had ignored the Judith relationship despite office gossip. When rumors reached Marcy, she confronted Pug.

"Tina called. She's heartbroken!"

"What's her problem now?"

"Dave and that... that lab technician."

"Tell Tina to mind her own goddamn business."

Disgusted, Marcy headed to Starbucks to meet Ellie who listened to her anxieties about the sons.

Later that evening, Ellie told Michael, "Marcy says Dave's having an affair with his assistant."

"She should worry more about Annie."

"Annie?"

"Skip's new marketing squeeze."

Ellie rolled her eyes. "IPS is a family soap opera. Why couldn't you run the company and keep Pug in the development lab?"

"Don't think that hasn't occurred to me."

The following day, Pug and Michael lunched at Hooters.

"I see why Dave loves this place. Look at the knockers on these waitresses."

"Dave's close to getting the first Hondoya order," Michael said.

Pug grinned. "Can't wait to shove that order up Kenji's ass."

"Do it after the shipment. Better yet, after we get paid."

"Fieldsy, you happy with Dave's work?"

"Absolutely!"

"Some day he'll be my skunk works manager."

"Bill's doing a fine job supporting him."

"Not what I hear. He won't let Judith work full-time for Dave."

"But Bill has multiple projects and only one lab tech."

"Hondoya's our top priority."

After lunch, Michael stopped by Bill's office. "Has Dave complained about not getting enough technician help?"

"Judith already works full-time for him. It's a reporting issue. If I got another tech, then Judith could report to Dave."

"Sets a bad precedent."

"Well, this is a family-owned company."

"The James family owns a big share but not fifty-one percent."

The next day, Dave took Michael to Hooters. Dave eyed a curvy waitress. "Wish I'd noticed her before Tina got herself pregnant."

"We need to find a new restaurant. This place is distracting," Michael said. "How are your Hondoya projects?"

"If I got more support, I'd have the order by now."

"What's the problem?"

"Bill's not completing the testing and lab samples fast enough. I've apologized to Hondoya for missing my promise dates. In Japan, that's embarrassing."

"Have you discussed this with Bill?"

"He's wasting too much time on Mathews."

"I'll see what I can do."

For the first time, Skip enjoyed work. He had a real customer, a supportive ally in Bill, and a gorgeous assistant who accompanied him everywhere. After an all-day meeting at Mathews, Skip and Annie drove back to San Francisco.

"Annie, you look under the weather. What's wrong?"

She choked back tears. "Randy and I are having problems, and it upsets Father."

"Anything I can do?"

"I don't think so."

"It's been a long day. Let's get a quick bite." *Does she know Randy's queer?*

"Don't you need to go home?"

"Nah. Michelle and Billy are in Oregon with the crazy in-laws."

The Mathews design, development, and test program concluded with a final presentation in Santa Barbara. The technical manager stated if both companies agreed on licensing and unit price, Mathews would place a major stocking order.

A week later, Mathews's executives arrived at IPS. Skip and Annie gave them a tour. Later, everyone assembled in the conference room.

Mathews's vice president of purchasing opened the meeting. "We want a three-year exclusive license to market and manufacture our electric water heaters installed with IPS thermal dissipaters. We expect a reasonable unit price with annual price reductions as volumes increase. If any similar thermal dissipaters are sold to other customers, Mathews expects rebates or royalties."

Michael thought, *Easy Pug.*

Pug barked, "Our patented technology is what makes your water heater perform. It's a big market, and Mathews doesn't own it. Exclusive means you don't want us selling to competitors. You need to pay me for lost profits."

"What's your price for a three-year license?" the vice president asked, his annoyance evident.

"Half a million."

The Mathews's team looked stunned. The tech manager mouthed at Skip, *What the fuck?*

Michael intervened, "Let's review each point." He highlighted differences: Pug wanted $500 thousand up front. Mathews considered $150 thousand acceptable and wanted the development fee rebated. Mathews, given its technical input, wanted royalty sharing. Pug considered this non-negotiable. Mathews suggested a starting unit price three dollars below Pug's thirty-three dollar number.

As tension escalated, Michael proposed a break. The IPS group retired to a separate conference area. As the door closed, Pug snapped, "No way that kike buyer's stealing my technology for thirty pieces of silver!"

"Pops, you never let him finish before interrupting!"

"Look Skippy, you got zero negotiation chops. Someday you'll see the wisdom in my value."

"If I live long enough."

"Keep your mouth shut. This ain't no fuckin' democracy!"

"Let's start with the easy one," Michael interjected. "Mathews isn't committed to royalty sharing. They know we're a technology company and sell licenses. So let's maintain Pug's position on no sharing. Bill says Mathews didn't contribute any significant ideas. Dave did all the innovative work before Mathews saw our technology. You agree, Bill?"

"That's fair. Their tech manager agrees. He claims the procurement guy loves to posture."

"Okay, one down. Let's talk about the up-front fee. Pug, not sure how you arrived at five hundred thousand. First time I heard that amount. We should have talked before the meeting."

"See why I wanted a pre-meeting," Skip interrupted.

"Shut the fuck up, Skippy. Go ahead, Michael."

"What I'd suggest is we offer a rebate each year if, and only if, they achieve a certain volume. Then they have an incentive to sell the hell out of the product."

"I like that," Pug said. "Listen up Skippy, and learn from us masters."

Michael continued, "Finally, whether we give them cost reductions in later years will depend on how they respond to the rebate issue. We force them to decide where to take risks. Let's see how confident they are in their volume projections."

"So what'll this kike go for?" Pug asked.

"Educated guess is he'll accept an initial license fee closer to, say, two hundred and fifty. Then we give them a fairly high starting unit price with yearly rebates only if they achieve minimal volumes."

"You see, Skippy? Michael's read my brain."

"Will Mathews go for this?" Michael asked Bill.

"The procurement chief wants to squeeze us."

"Done!" Pug declared. "We'll demand three hundred and fifty K and a unit price of thirty-five."

Michael added, "Give Mathews the option of annual fee rebates or unit cost reductions based on yearly volumes."

"If they don't meet target volumes, I'll cancel for non-performance," Pug said, slamming his palm to the table.

"And no royalties," Michael added. "But let's not talk non-performance yet."

The group reconvened, and Michael presented the counter. The Mathews team caucused. Within an hour, they returned with their counter: $250 thousand up-front and no rebate. They agreed to a higher starting price in the first year followed by aggressive unit price reductions in later years. Royalty sharing was ignored. The final bonus: Mathews would place a huge stocking order after tooling and production processes were ready.

SAN MATEO

After the meeting, Pug rushed home to celebrate. He popped open a bottle of Pat Henry and toasted Marcy. "Sweetie, my negotiating skills saved the Mathews deal."

"That's nice, sweetie," Marcy said.

Skip's earlier call and angry version of events conflicted her thoughts.

SOUTH SAN FRANCISCO

Pug bounded into Michael's office. "Got a great idea!"

"What now?"

"Dave now works for you! Needs more sales experience."

"That leaves Bill short-handed."

"No problem. Told him to hire a new engineer and another lab tech.

One more thing, I'm promoting you to executive VP. You're my right-hand guy. So if anything happens, the board's got a succession plan."

"You planning to leave?"

"Nah!"

"Don't the board and shareholders have to approve?"

"Hey, I'm the only vote that counts!"

"Didn't expect this."

"With me, expect the unexpected! By the way, I'm raising your salary twenty thousand 'cuz you got lots more to do."

Michael smiled. "Thanks, Pug."

That night, Marcy and Pug dined at their neighborhood Mexican café. She pushed a lime slice into her bottle of Corona Light. Pug peeled at the label of his Pat Henry.

"Fieldsy's now my official constigulatoria."

"Right on, Don Pug-leone," she giggled. "How did Rich and Bruce take the news?"

"Bruce and Bill liked it. Rich's opinion don't count."

SAN FRANCISCO

Michael shared the news with Ellie while enjoying their evening wine and snacks.

"Can IPS afford an executive VP?" she asked.

"Pug wants a succession plan. Maybe he senses my frustration with recent cost-cutting and no growth."

"Doesn't look like either son can step up."

"Dave could, if Pug got out of the way."

"And Skip?"

"Skip has some great marketing instincts but little else. Pug is tough on both sons, but Dave can handle it better. If I had to pick one, I'd back Dave."

SINGAPORE

Michael, Pug, and Jackson arrived in Singapore for the Asian patent opposition hearing beginning October 9. Michael invited Maurice Oshima to observe. His recent performance at Hondoya convinced Michael he added value.

Three judges from Japan, Korea, and Singapore would examine IPS's patent and review the six opponents' legal arguments and Dexter-Foresmen counter-arguments. Everyone expected a full two days.

The meeting convened at the APO offices located near the historic Raffles Hotel. Besides IPS's contingent, each opponent arrived with his patent counsel. While they waited for the judges, Michael whispered, "Pug, what's that old saying about alligators and swamps?"

"Uhh... when you're up to your ass in gators, hard to remember to drain the swamp."

"Count the alligators in this room."

Pug glanced around. "Eleven?"

"Make it fourteen when the judges arrive."

On day one of the hearings, each opponent presented new information. Jackson argued each point. Heated debate centered on the validity of specific patent claims. When Gano-Nippon and Sumato-Metal introduced information from Lawrent's trial, the judges declared it inadmissible.

That evening, the IPS team dined at Jumbo, a restaurant on Singapore's Gold Coast. At a huge outdoor table, they drank Tiger beer and enjoyed warm breezes wafting off the ocean. Waiters brought platters piled high with chili crab and stir-fried vegetables.

"We'll prevail if the judges are objective," Jackson said, tucking a napkin under his chin. "The opposition provided no new compelling data."

"I dunno... they kept talking about the US patent," Pug said, licking chili sauce off his fingers.

"I agree," Michael said. "Maurice, any background talk?"

"The two Hondoya lawyers looked very confident. I think they and the Japanese judge have a close relationship."

"It's outta our hands," Pug said. "Let's drink beer and pray to buddy."

"You mean Buddha?" Maurice asked. Everyone laughed.

On the second day, the chief judge opened the session. "The court has reviewed and considered all submitted arguments pertaining to the Asian Patent Office patent number 4321456 granted to International Protected Solutions, Inc."

Michael leaned close to Pug. "This can't be good."

"The court rules against International Protected Solutions, Inc." The judge continued, "Concerning the validity of its IPS 10000 patent, sufficient information has been presented to invalidate patent claim numbers two, four, five, eight, and eleven. Prior art existed in Singapore and Japan and negates the novelty aspect of the current patent. The court's formal decision issues in ninety days."

The judge gaveled the session closed. Hondoya's chief lawyer approached and offered his hand. "Mr. James, the decision did not favor IPS; perhaps commercial work can continue without further legal interference."

Pug bristled. "You won round one." As they turned to leave, he snarled, "Whole thing's rigged!"

"Their decision was unanimous," Jackson said.

"Jackson, the Jap judge was just like Sacker!"

Jackson looked at Michael with a "what-can-I-do?" expression.

"Need to get back to the hotel and pack," Michael reminded Pug. "We have to get to the airport."

"I'm staying another day."

"Oh, okay... see you in California." *Who does he know in Singapore?*

In the Raffles Hotel limo to Changi Airport, Michael asked Jackson, "What's our legal recourse?"

"After receiving the court's written decision, IPS has six months to prepare its appeal. The opponents have three months to respond, and then IPS has one month to reply. The court will set the final hearing date."

"Meanwhile, what's the status of the Asian patent?"

"Still valid. If IPS wins the appeal and if opponents continue to infringe, IPS can sue for damages."

"The game's rigged against the patent owner."

"If we prevail on appeal, we can get court injunctions to stop the manufacture and sales of infringing products."

"As Pug says, 'life ain't fair.' Hondoya's offer to license the technology looks pretty good now."

"At least IPS has the commercial agreement."

"Jackson, at the rate business develops in Japan, we'll be retired by the time the first products ship. By the way, how's our Multi-Dimensional FP 10000 application doing in Japan?"

"Work in progress—we pay the maintenance fees while the patent examiners review. Our Japanese attorneys haven't found any prior art so far."

"Jackson, we desperately need this patent, especially if we lose the IPS 10000 appeals."

"Right. Michael, I need help on another matter. IPS is behind again on its payments."

"I'll see if we can catch up. Cash is really tight."

SOUTH SAN FRANCISCO

A month later, Jackson called with good news. The US patent office granted IPS a patent for Multi-Dimensional Finished Part 10000. Dave and Sean were listed as co-inventors. IPS also received two new patents for water heater dissipaters.

Research Appliance presented a written proposal in late October.

"Finally, something to chew on," Pug remarked.

"Research Appliance wants lower prices than Japan Technologies's," Michael said. "We can't give a ten percent discount and absorb freight and duty. We'll lose our ass."

"We'll be manufacturing in Asia before the first shipment in January 1998!"

"Maybe, but what about Research's demand to settle the Osaka legal matters as part of the commercial deal? Why pay their legal bills? Let's call it a draw."

"Fieldsy, you don't listen. They want our Multi-Dimensional FP 10000, and the best part is we take business from Jap Tech! Think like a chess player."

"But your checker tactics kill us in the meantime."

"I'm signing their memo of understanding."

OSAKA

Kenji and Dr. Yamura met at Kenji's rustic country home. Kenji invited only close associates to this retreat. After a day of hunting, a crackling fire in the stone fireplace welcomed them. They enjoyed a fine venison dinner prepared by Kenji's chef and relaxed afterwards in the smoking room.

Dr. Yamura said, "Accessing James family innovations is a constant challenge. We cannot alert competitors or American regulators."

"Hai! In Japan, it is much easier with Nippon-Soft-Dev's assistance."

"I have discussed Thailand-based manufacturing with Research Appliance. It will ensure reliable low-cost manufacturing of standard two-dimensional and the new multi-dimensional thermal dissipaters."

"Excellent!" Kenji lit a cigarette and exhaled. "Another problem: Lawrent seeks war on two fronts with its Gano-Nippon alliance and its attempt to buy IPS."

Dr. Yamura nodded and poured himself another glass of cognac. He needed no further instructions.

1997
SOUTH SAN FRANCISCO

J UDGE HARRINGTON'S AFFIRMATION ARRIVED IN April prompting Jackson's call to Pug.

"Dammit Jackson, why'd it take the judge twelve months to rule?" Pug asked.

"Pug, we expected him to reverse the jury's decision and that takes time. Instead it looks like our case went to the bottom of his priorities."

"What now?"

"File an appeal."

"On what grounds?"

"The judge made incorrect rulings on our motions and misapplied the law to the facts. His jury instructions were incorrect."

"How much and how long?"

"About one hundred thousand dollars and nine months. There's no discovery since facts are established. The appeal involves only procedural errors and questions of law."

"Jackson, we're broke. Dexter-Foresmen's gotta bankroll the appeal."

"Sorry Pug, we've already lost two million in unbilled hours."

Pug slammed the receiver and yelled for Michael. "Damn fuckin' Jackson! Won't do a contingency! That jury verdict can't stand. Otherwise my US patent is kaput. It'll destroy my APO appeal!"

"Pug, instead of throwing money down the drain, let's discuss a commercial settlement like you did with Hondoya and Research Appliance."

"Fuck Lawrent. They're different."

"You're way too hard on Jackson."

"I got Bill auditing the legal bills."

Sharon appeared at the door. "Mr. Satir is on the phone."

Pug gave Michael a "who's-he?" look and hit the speakerphone.

"Pug James."

"Mr. James, my name is Joseph Satir. I represent the Thailand Industrial Development Board. How are you today?"

"Sure you got the right number?"

"Yes, sir. Our agency recruits American firms to establish operations in Thailand."

"Unless you got money, you're wasting my time."

"Financing is one of our many services provided for qualified companies."

Michael joined in. "Mr. Satir, this is Michael Fields. What types of companies?"

"Those creating new jobs in Thailand via technology transfers."

Pug thought for a moment. "Doesn't cost to listen if you buy lunch. Come by Thursday."

"Thank you. Look forward to meeting you."

Pug leaned back. "Ain't chaos wonderful? I was thinking about Asian manufacturing and outta the blue comes this call!"

The following week, Joseph Satir presented his agency's programs. After the presentation, Pug said, "This all sounds good, but I don't trust free lunches."

"Mr. James, IPS should contact other Bay Area companies who've worked with our agency. Then visit Thailand as our guest and examine what these companies accomplished. We'll introduce potential Thai partners, review your business plans, execute agreements, and arrange funding."

After Mr. Satir left, Michael cautioned, "There's always strings attached to free money, but Thailand has attractive export/import agreements with Japan. And the ASEAN free trade zone will open more markets in Southeast Asia."

SOUTH SAN FRANCISCO

On their third visit to Thailand in July, Pug and Michael met a potential business partner, Akami-Thai, located sixty kilometers south of Bangkok. Akami-Thai's ready-to-use facilities matched the operational needs of IPS. Its management expressed interest in an alliance. Pug and Michael returned to California encouraged that Asian manufacturing was a distinct possibility.

In late August, the Thai Industrial Board audit team inspected the Denver plant and then visited San Francisco. The auditors examined IPS's business plan prepared by Michael and Bruce. Afterwards, the team traveled to Japan to discuss commercial contracts with Hondoya and Research Appliance.

In September, the Thai Board announced its decision.

As Michael entered Pug's office, he heard an angry bellow. "Those Thai assholes want a guarantee for their fuckin' free money!"

Michael scanned the agency's letter. *IPS business plan financials and projections are insufficient unless IPS provides collateral.* He tossed the letter on Pug's desk. "Bottom line, IPS has to kick in more," he said.

"For chrissakes, what about the investment we'll make and the commercial contracts? Don't they count? Hondoya and Research said the Thai Board liked the commercial deals."

"Let's see if additional data can change their minds. Remember, Research Appliance owns eight-five percent of Akami-Thai. Maybe they could lobby on our behalf."

"The Thai Board can go pound their fuckin' rice cakes!"

"Pug, this is an initial offer. We've spent too much time and money to quit now."

"Those assholes never planned to give us money."

Michael informed a disappointed Mr. Satir.

When the news reached Denver, Rich called Darin. "Told you this'd happen after we sent the Thai auditors that 'extra information!' I'll make sure Puggy finds out his right-hand man screwed him over with that letter about IPS's financials."

"Cousin, you done good! Soon the Denver plant'll be ours!"

SAN FRANCISCO

Michael and Ellie visited Ristorante Siena. Giacomo's friendly greeting and the ambience reminded them of their Tuscany vacation.

"This restaurant's charming," Ellie said, looking around.

"Yeah, it's okay."

Ellie folded her hands on the tabletop and peered at Michael. "Okay, what's bothering you?"

"Can't put my finger on it. Ever since the Lawrent fiasco, IPS appliance business has gone to hell. Marken hasn't generated any new business. IPS's Asian patent is invalid. Thailand rejected our business plan."

"Won't the two commercial contracts help?"

"We won't see sales or profits until '98. Without an operations base in Asia, we'll lose money on every shipment to the region."

"Sweetheart, just imagine if you were in charge. What would you do?"

Michael took a long sip of wine. "I wouldn't do stupid stuff." The antipasto arrived. "This looks delicioso. Now I understand why Pug thinks he's in 'frenzy' when he's here."

"Frenzy?"

"Pug's word for Firenze."

Ellie re-filled their wine glasses. "No more Pug-speak. Let's enjoy this wonderful chianti."

DENVER

Rich's frustrations at work and with Pug were compounded by his wife's hospitalization in September and mounting medical bills. Darin's problems also increased. His board of directors complained about company losses and SEC investigations. His second wife threatened more legal action after receiving anonymous photos of sexual indiscretions in Japan.

Rich and Darin met for their annual October hunting trip. Instead of tracking deer, they waited in a heated deer blind drinking shots of Jack Daniels with Coors chasers.

"You wouldn't believe the shit Puggy's dumped on me: new process start-ups, production and shipment of Research Appliance's stocking order, answering his hourly micromanaging questions. He's driving me nuts," Rich growled.

"You have enough workers?"

"Hell no! Puggy won't allow permanent hires 'cuz he's still dreaming about his fantasy Asian manufacturing site."

"Using temps ruins quality, productivity, creates chaos."

"I'll show him chaos," Rich said, stifling a laugh.

A buck strolled nearby. Darin raised his rifle and fired. The animal scampered away. "Shit!"

"Puggy'll lose his ass on the Research Appliance business."

"Why's that?"

"He's priced the business too low. Research wants ninety separate parts, shipped to three separate overseas locations in just-in-time mode. It's a goddamn logistics nightmare!"

"What's your plan?"

"Manufacturing variances and quality certification. Smoke and mirrors."

In late afternoon, they called it quits and drove to the cabin and continued drinking.

"Looks like November to December will be a perfect storm," Darin slurred.

"When manufacturing gets crazy, there's lots of metal alloy scrap, missing inventory, etc."

"Bank that plan, Cousin."

1998
SOUTH SAN FRANCISCO

I N JANUARY, BRUCE PREPARED FINANCIAL results for November and December 1997 and sent them to San Francisco. Pug grabbed the phone and yelled, "Bruce, your numbers suck!"

"What do you mean? We finally made some profit!"

"Material costs are too high. Mathews's business shoulda made a ton more money!"

"Our accounting system doesn't track costs by products. It's why we need a new MIS system."

"Stop with the MIS shit! What caused the two hundred and fifty thousand dollars of negative material variances?"

"Rich blames plant inefficiencies, too many temps, but..."

"I want you in SFO tomorrow."

"I can't. I'm preparing for the year-end audit."

"Get your ass on a plane! Fuck the audit!"

The second week of February, the audit partner called Michael. "Bruce tells us the audit schedules and interim year-to-date numbers aren't ready."

"What about completing the audit?" Michael asked.

"We'll reschedule for April."

When Michael relayed the news, Pug ranted, "Bruce needs to juggle more balls!"

"Pug, that's not fair! Bruce has been working full time on your material variances analysis."

"I don't give a shit!"

"Sharon says he's stressed about boyfriend problems and the weekly commutes from Denver," Michael argued.

"I'll show Brucie some real stress."

Later that same week, Bruce sat in Pug's office. He unfolded spreadsheets on Pug's desk. "We've analyzed every material purchase, job order, scrap sale report, and rechecked the physical inventory. Can't find reasons for material variances."

"Yeah, yeah. By my count, there's at least one hundred thousand dollars of missing inventory. Can't disappear in thin air. Unless…"

"Unless what?" Bruce asked.

"Unless someone's stealing!"

Michael looked stunned. "You're kidding. You agree, Bruce?"

"Not sure. We did write off the unfavorable variances, the ones previously capitalized to… uh… improve the monthly numbers for Mile High."

"Typical accountant bullshit! Why isn't Rich helping you? Too busy stealing?" Pug yelled.

"He's under a lot of pressure at home given his wife's medical problems," Bruce insisted.

"All the more reason to steal," Pug muttered.

That night, Pug told Marcy. "Can't trust Rich. He's drinking, banging that plant floozy, burning the candle at both ends and worst of all he's Ted's lap dog."

"Sweetie, after all we've done for him, I hope you're wrong."

"Rich is acting more and more like Dad."

"Do you think Darin is influencing him too much?"

"Who knows? From now on, I'm watchin' him like a hawk."

In late March, Bruce flew to California to review preliminary 1997 financial results for the April audit. Revenues increased to $12 million driven by Mathews and Research Appliance stocking orders. Despite profits of $500 thousand, cash remained tight due to funding huge accounts receivables and inventories for the Research Appliance business.

"Bruce, before the auditors start," Pug ordered, "re-check the material usage rates."

"Cost of sales is correct. The auditors verified the beginning and ending inventories, and I personally re-checked purchases three times."

"What else you got?"

"Heard some plant gossip. Oh, forget it. Not important." *Pug wouldn't believe the rumors about Rich and his production supervisor.*

Bruce headed to the break room where Sharon was brewing coffee. She poured him a cup. "Bruce, you don't want to move, do you?"

"Pug needs a spreadsheet flunky next door—on call, twenty-four, seven. Three sixty-five."

A few weeks later Rich called. "Puggy, I've been thinking about how to make Research business more profitable."

"Talk at me."

Pug listened to Rich's suggestions, ended the call, then yelled, "Fieldsy, gotta minute?"

When Michael arrived, Pug announced, "Let's outsource Research production to Japan."

"What?"

"Here's the deal. IPS subcontracts production to Jap Tech but stays the customer interface: order scheduling and invoicing. Production's a piece o' cake 'cuz Jap Tech still has the tooling. No duty and freight costs for IPS. Pure profit for us."

"Denver should keep the production volume in-house. At least it contributes to fixed overhead," Michael replied.

"Did you see how bad the variances were the last few months? Mathews saved our butts. Every time I suggest improvements, Rich fights me. Don't have the time to do his job too."

"Do we really know how much we're losing?" Michael asked.

"I will after outsourcing Research. But here's where I'm brilliant. It's temporary until I find my Asian site close to Research Appliance."

"Pug, let's run some numbers first."

Pug rose from the chair. "Forget it! Already told Rich to get moving."

Michael left with a puzzled look. *One minute Rich is stealing from*

IPS, and the next he trusts Rich to implement outsourcing. Is Pug thinking straight?

Rich contacted Jun who asked, "IPS signed a three-year contract with Research Appliance, and now you want Japan Technologies to manufacture?"

"Yes, sir."

"Most unusual. We require a guaranteed three-year contract to quote firm prices."

"I look forward to your proposal. Puggy said to do whatever it takes."

In two days, Rich received Japan Technologies's proposal for the ninety parts. He compared IPS's manufacturing costs versus Japan Technologies's prices and adjusted for duty and freight expense.

Time for my Excel voodoo I do so well. Soon the Denver plant will be worthless, and Puggy'll have to accept my offer.

During an April staff meeting, Pug declared, "Bruce, I want the accounting function in SFO now! Tired of everybody having his own set of numbers. Rich's separate databases constipate our computer. When's the new MIS system ready?"

"I need more time with Rich's people."

"Wrong answer! You're closing '98 with a new system."

"Pug," Michael interrupted, "he can't implement a new system without Rich's cooperation."

"Michael's right," Bruce said, his eye twitching.

"I'll make this easy. A few weeks ago, I talked to the Denver auditor. He recommended a simple upgrade, minimal retraining, a lot cheaper."

"You're joking!" Bruce said. "The Denver accountants don't know our current situation."

"Upgrading is always an option. Let Bruce do the analysis first," Michael argued.

"Discussion over!"

Pug's simple MIS upgrade morphed into a debacle. Bruce groused about Rich's non-cooperation, and Rich complained about Bruce's incompetence. The slow progress angered Pug. He studied software manuals, sketched flowcharts, and enlisted Dave's help. Dave argued to start over from square one. A frustrated Pug halted the project.

Michael sat in his office and pondered the mess. *A total nightmare: Pug interferes, Rich won't cooperate, and Dave should be selling. Instead, he's developing a website with Judith. Ellie's right, this is a family soap opera.*

The annual shareholders' meeting convened on May 15. Skip took center stage to announce, "IPS's 1997 profits came from water heater dissipater sales to Mathews. This year will be even better; first quarter 1998 orders are spectacular!"

Michael listened while recalling last week's meeting between Pug and Skip.

"Mathews's second quarter orders suck!" Pug said.

"Pops, the first few months Mathews stocked big box retailers," Skip insisted. "Mathews waits for customers to pull them out of the stores. Takes time."

"Don't insult my intelligence! I know retail! Mathews needs to advertise."

"They've been in business for eighty years. They sell four hundred million a year of all types of water heaters. They know what they're doing."

"Maybe Mathews underestimated marketing a new technology not part of its normal gas water heater business," Michael said.

"I'm not waiting for those assholes," Pug yelled. "If they don't start showing progress, I'm pulling the license!"

"You can't do that!" Skip yelled.

"Oh yeah? Try me!"

Michael remembered his next day conversation with Skip:

"Pops thinks he can tell Mathews how to sell."

"Visit Mathews and brainstorm new marketing approaches to increase demand."

"I don't have enough hours in the day."

"That's why you hired Annie."

"She's overloaded."

"Doing what? She travels with you to trade shows and printing houses and every time you visit Mathews. Don't you have some other new customers to contact?"

"I'm looking at Kenton-Aerocon."

"Quit looking and start closing!"

After the shareholders' meeting, Skip and Annie ate at a French restaurant in San Francisco's Marina District. Skip poured glasses of Charvin Chateauneuf du Pape.

"My father's favorite," Annie said, taking a sip.

"Cheers! The shareholder presentation was fantastic! Your PowerPoint slides were superb," Skip said. "By the way, how are things with Randy?"

Annie replied, "I think we've resolved our issues. The wedding's set for next month."

"That's great." *But you're making a terrible mistake.*

"Skip, you don't seem pleased with the Mathews project. So, I've been thinking about how to improve sales to Mathews. Could IPS afford some trial advertising? Once Mathews sees the benefits, they'll continue it."

"Could work. Can you handle the advertising copy, design work, and support?"

"I thought you'd never ask."

Skip smiled and refilled their glasses. "Michael's pressuring me to bring in new customers. Says I can't rely on just Mathews and Sunshine."

"Makes sense. What do you have in mind?"

"Thinking about talking with Kenton-Aerocon. Bob Kenton called several times wanting to get together."

"What's stopping you?"

"Well, I don't want my new customers to end up like Mathews… you know, where Pops interferes and messes it up for me."

"I understand. It's what Father did to me at Sunshine. So what do you want to do?"

"We need to think strategic, and most of all, keep my dad out of the mix. He can't know what we're doing."

"Just tell me how to help."

"Don't worry, you'll be the center of anything I do. And this time, we'll have a contingency plan."

"Thank you for having such confidence in me."

In July, Annie developed an advertising program for the electric water heater. Pug liked giving her ideas on advertising strategy. Doing the work in-house, she kept out-of-pocket costs under $200 thousand.

The following week, Dave rushed to Michael's office and handed him a square of IPS 10000 material. "Michael, look at this!"

Michael examined the piece, turning it over and back again. "Looks like corrugated cardboard except it's our alloy material. How'd you do this?"

"I took layers of our base 10000 material and ran them through reverse grinders to make these deep peaks and valleys."

Michael noted large spaces between the layers. "I bet this would be a good insulator with these large air gaps. How are the thermals?"

"Much better than the fiberglass used in ovens or in construction."

"And totally recyclable. Have you written disclosures?"

"Bill's calling Jackson tomorrow."

Michael reexamined the sample. *Dave's done it again!*

Two weeks later, Bill sent Jackson patent paperwork for Aerolation 10000.

In early August, Jackson called. "Pug, the D.C. Court of Appeals reversed the Lawrent verdict."

"Finally! When do I get my treble damages?"

"The court did not reverse the infringement decision because of the TAI patent. However, the IPS patent has been validated. Now you can file for a new, stronger patent utilizing information found during discovery."

"We can't afford... Oh, forget it."

Later, Pug relayed Jackson's message to Michael.

"Let me get this straight," Michael said. "IPS starts with a valid patent and spends two million suing for infringement. IPS loses the patent—and worse—market share because we pissed off General Appliance. Two years later, the patent's revalidated, but no infringement, no damages, and market share's still gone. Did I miss anything?"

"Yeah, Jackson says the patent's like a silver bullet 'cuz it's been adjecated and can't be challenged."

"Adjudicated or whatever, customers still buy Lawrent's TAI."

"After IPS files for a stronger patent, we can go after those bastards again!"

Michael sat back in his chair. *He's got to be kidding! He hasn't learned a damn thing!*

Pug phoned the Denver investment banker and asked Robby Benton to join the conversation.

"Hard to believe it's been four years since we talked IPO."

"Yeah, too bad lawsuits got in the way. So how's business?" the banker asked.

"Lost the first patent battle with Lawrent but won the appeal. Patent's now bulletproof."

"Sounds great. What can I do for you, Pug?"

"Companies wanna buy my appliance business. Had calls already from Research Appliance and a New York investment banker."

"Who's the client?"

"Lawrent."

"Could make it a bidding contest, depends on the financials," the banker said.

"Super idea," Robby added.

"Appliance sales have been growing since '96, I got a great story, and sales forecasts for '99 are outta sight."

"When can I have the financial data?" the banker asked.

"I'll get Michael and Bruce crankin'."

Pug yelled for Michael. "Hey Fieldsy, my investment banker called."

"What did he want?"

"Research Appliance and Lawrent wanna buy my appliance business."

"Lawrent?"

"Their agent's sniffing around."

"You said you'd never deal with Lawrent."

"I'll use 'em to raise the price of poker for Research."

Michael, taken aback, asked, "Shouldn't we understand if Research is serious? They know us and use our technology. If we don't like their offer, we can pursue others."

"Look, it's Hail Mary time! I want outta this crappy appliance business and just focus on my skunk works and new technologies."

Michael and Bruce prepared data for the investment banker. They constructed pro forma numbers to depict historical and forecasted sales and profitability of a stand-alone appliance business. Pug insisted they use overly optimistic sales forecasts.

Michael shook his head as he reviewed the numbers with Pug. "I never thought your inventive skills applied to numbers," he said.

"Whadya talking about?"

"We've invented the last three years of appliance sales—'95 to '97—to look profitable. We've allocated all sales, research, and administrative expenses to the non-appliance business. Then we ignored all the one-time, nonrecurring costs. Future business can't be this profitable."

"Look, we gotta show results without irreverent clutter."

"Potential buyers will consider the data irrelevant if they can't reconcile to our audited numbers."

The investment banker's offering memorandum went to prospective buyers recommended by IPS. The banker waited for initial responses before circulating to his private client list. Only Research and Lawrent requested the full package. Pug authorized only Research to receive it.

Research's due diligence lasted one month and required several conference calls. Finally, the CEO announced Research Appliance would not make an offer because of other acquisition priorities.

"So whadya think?" Pug asked Michael.

"CEO thinks he's the only game in town. He didn't buy your line about other interested buyers, so he'll wait for a lower price."

"It's eighteen million or fuck off!"

"Pug, it's too high given it excludes the technology."

"Look, I'm selling the appliance business. Technology stays with IPS."

"The banker thinks twelve million is more reasonable."

"What the hell does he know? Time to shit or get in the pot. Bastard hasn't brought one new prospect."

"Careful, we owe them a seventy-five thousand dollar retainer."

"So let 'em sue me!"

A week later, Michael found Pug sporting a big grin. "Last weekend, I landscaped the backyard. Got back to nature."

"And this means…?"

"Time to go basic and long-term."

"How about the here and now?"

"Details, details. Producing finished parts as a Tier 2 supplier won't ever work. Why? No critical mass!"

"Most companies want to be Tier 1. Look at what my Korean colleague's done with his Tier 1 licensee."

"IPS can be the Johns Mansville of dissipater insulation. We'll sell tons of easy-to-make base material for all customers, even competitors."

"Pug, we don't have the production capability, let alone the customers."

"We'll hold a vista meeting with Dave, Skip, Bill, Ryo, and Maurice-san."

"Oshima-san?"

"I gotta visit Jap Tech, so we'll meet in Osaka."

"Why not Rich and Bruce?"

"Septics not invited."

OSAKA

Michael prepared data for the strategy session. Two weeks later, they assembled in a conference room at Hotel Sakura.

Michael remarked, "Pug, you look rested. Hotel Sakura's beds must be better than Hotel Osaka's."

"Kenji and me talked strategy the last two days."

"Aren't we here to formulate a strategy?" Dave asked.

"Here's the agenda," Michael interrupted. "The first topic involves a quick overview of our past marketing strategies."

"IPS needs a back-to-basics material strategy; gets us outta this shitty finished parts business," Pug declared. "IPS can produce high volumes of low-cost proprietary materials."

"IPS has no manufacturing processes," Bill reminded. Michael gave him a thumbs up.

"And no customers," Dave added. He high-fived Michael.

"Don't worry. I'll build it, and they'll come."

Dave pressed. "Customers want finished parts. Who'll design and test? It's hard enough being a Tier 2 supplier. Your strategy makes us Tier 3: bottom of the supply chain."

"Davey, my son, someday you'll have my vista. IPS can charge a fee for technical services like I did to Mathews."

"What if IPS's special metal supplier copies and bypasses us?" Bill asked.

"Duh… not if we patent the process."

"I'm selling finished parts using my website," Dave insisted.

"Look! You will do what I say! This ain't no fuckin' democracy!"

Dave frowned at Skip. "Wipe that shitty grin off your face!"

The conversations grew more heated and less productive for the next few hours. Finally, Michael suggested an early break for dinner. At the robatayaki restaurant, noise and commotion overwhelmed Pug's attempts to convince anyone about his new strategy. Instead, they focused on food, beer, and tomorrow's flight home.

The next day all departed for Narita except Pug.

While waiting for his flight, Michael called Jun. "Mr. Ashi, I'm interested in Japan Technologies's reactions to Pug's materials strategy."

"Mr. Fields, excuse me, what strategy?"

"The one you and Mr. Kobyashi discussed with Pug a few days ago."

"Mr. Fields, we have not talked with Mr. James for some time."

"My apologies. I must have incorrect information." *Why did Pug mislead me?*

SAN FRANCISCO

When Michael returned to San Francisco, Ellie met him at the airport.

"What a wasted trip! Everyone disagrees with Pug's latest strategy. He won't listen to our objections! But there's a bigger problem I can't figure out."

"What?"

"IPS is fighting a Japanese keiretsu intent on hurting the company."

"That sounds like one of Pug's conspiracy theories."

"Maybe. What I can't figure out is why the cartel hasn't already killed us."

"Honey, what's IPS's legal entity status?"

Michael registered surprise. "Did I miss some segue?"

"Bear with me…"

"IPS is a Colorado C Corp."

"Never reincorporated in California?"

"No."

"Delaware incorporation allows more flexibility and stockholders have interesting rights."

"Sweetheart, you're talking above my pay grade."

Exeter Appliance, IPS's most profitable customer since 1995, ceased operations. Festering union relationships exploded into a four-month strike. Orders for IPS products stopped in August and remained zero through November. Two more months would elapse before the supply chain normalized. And without Research's business, IPS had little in-house production. Worse, IPS lost money on every subcontracted order. The yen strengthened against the dollar adding to the misery. IPS was unable to meet Japan Technologies's 30-day payment terms because Research paid IPS in 90 days. IPS became more indebted to Japan Technologies.

Pug's frustrations mounted. "I've been looking at Rich's prices to Jap Tech. He betrayed me!"

"That's a strong word. Right now, Japan Technologies acts as our second banker," Michael counseled.

"That makes two asshole bankers."

DENVER

Despite increased commercial and financial problems, Pug focused on the material strategy and new products for non-appliance markets. He ordered Rich to find a new building since the lease on the current one expired at year-end.

In October Rich found a location, and Pug approved a new lease. Rich spent $300 thousand on leasehold improvements financed with working capital line of credit. The move occurred in late November. Pug surveyed the consolidated operations along with the obsolete inventory, production chaos, inefficient machine utilization, excess staffing, and poor morale.

He called Michael. "Firing Rich's ass tomorrow!"

"Come again?"

"Remember the huge materials shortage last year? I knew Rich and his production supervisor were diddling me. Didn't know how, but they did."

"Who'll run Denver operations?"

"Bill."

The next morning, Pug confronted Rich. "Remember every time you threatened to quit? This time, I'm keeping your keys."

"You telling me I'm fired?"

"End of discussion."

"Wait a minute... gimme a chance to buy the plant."

"Get the fuck out! And the Ted you rode in on!"

IPS finished 1998 with revenues of $12 million and record losses of $1.6 million. It had negative working capital and increased long-term debt due to restructuring liabilities. Since 1994, the company had lost $2 million in equity.

-And 1999 looked even more daunting.

1999
DENVER

Business stagnated throughout 1999. Exeter orders remained weak, and IPS captured no new customers. Dave blamed Marken's incompetence. Skip appeased Pug with optimistic Mathews and Sunshine forecasts that never materialized. Privately, Skip blamed Pug's interference as the real cause for no new sales.

In the first quarter, IPS cancelled the Research Appliance contract and let Japan Technologies resume direct relationships. With 1998 losses and a disastrous first 1999 quarter, the accountant's audit of 1998 financials indicated IPS had a 'going concern' problem.

Michael met with Mile High to discuss renewing the line of credit. The banker asked, "I just received the auditor's financials draft. Where's the opinion page?"

"Ninety-eight was a bad year: Exeter strike, restructuring, etc."

"What happened to Mathews?"

"Electric water heater sales stalled after introduction despite IPS advertising."

"What about the base business?"

"Not enough to offset other shortfalls."

"Pug told me the Research Appliance contract would grow the business."

"Rich negotiated a terrible contract for outsourcing production. It's why Pug terminated him. Can we talk about the one-year credit renewal?"

"Not without an auditors' clean opinion!"

"Without the renewal, the auditors will issue a qualified opinion. The loans are collateralized; your risk is minimal," Michael argued.

"The company generates negative cash flow, and Pug's personal loan is secured by worthless stock. If we renew, the terms will be more stringent."

SOUTH SAN FRANCISCO

Michael returned to California and headed to Pug's office. Looking exhausted, Pug slumped at his desk. Michael delivered the bad news. "Mile High's the only option, Pug. No other bank will touch IPS... or you."

Pug gripped the arms of the chair, and snarled, "Fire the goddamn accountants! This going-concern shit delayed Mile High's renewal!"

"Auditors were just doing their job. Our numbers don't lie!"

"IPS gets first-rate bills for a third-string audit. Fire 'em!"

"Okay, but let's get the clean opinion first."

After Michael dismissed the accounting firm, he and Bruce reviewed, screened, and recommended three second-tier firms.

When Pug announced his choice, Michael called Ellie. "I'm up to my eyebrows in Pug shit!"

"What did he do now?" Ellie asked.

"He overruled my recommendation for a new accounting firm and chose the worst of three choices."

She laughed. "Pug believes in the 'my way or the highway' management. Anyway sweetheart, you have great material for case studies. By the way, the business school at San Francisco State called today."

"Finally!"

SAN FRANCISCO

Ellie invited Gordon Orlio to dinner at Ristorante Siena.

"So this is Mr. Pug's favorite restaurant?" Gordon asked. "You know, he still owes me ten thousand for my work defending him on insider trading charges."

"Yes, I know. I'm sorry I ever referred him to you." She gestured to Giacomo.

"Giacomo, I'd like you to meet Gordon Orlio." The two men spoke Italian; Ellie studied the menu.

After placing orders, Gordon said, "Small world! Giacomo's from Calabria, same as my family! Anyway, what's on your mind, beautiful lady?"

She smiled and took a sip of wine.

Gordon listened at length. "I've heard enough," he said. He pulled a legal pad from his briefcase and wrote. "Send me this info. I'll review, and we'll discuss. By the way, your Delaware idea is clever. I trained you well."

Ellie glanced at Gordon's notes and thought, *Uh, oh,... privileged information.*

"Thanks, Gordo. Michael doesn't need to know."

"We have attorney-attorney privilege."

DENVER

The second quarter of 1999 found Bill supervising Denver operations under tough conditions with limited resources and the strain of weekly commutes. When Pug arrived in late spring, they walked through the plant, stopping at each press.

"We need to eliminate down time between production runs," Bill observed.

"Remember my material strategy idea?"

"Yeah, but never really understood it."

"If we could produce multiple layers simultaneously, we'd become the Johns Mansville of dissipater insulation." Pug pulled sketches from a folder. "Look at these. Came to me when I remodeled Marcy's office. Whadya think?"

Bill studied them. "Looks like the paper feeds from old computer printers... the ones that print and stack."

"Bingo! Now imagine producing multiple layers in the same way and then folding 'em into a pile. Then, feed the piles into presses. And here's the eureka: No more time-wasting shutdowns and setups."

"It'll take special equipment."

"Bingo again! Special means patents and trade secrets."

Bill arranged with equipment manufacturers to review specs for the new equipment. The selected vendor insisted on advance payments, which delayed progress given IPS's cash shortage.

SOUTH SAN FRANCISCO

Pug summoned Michael and Bruce. "We need cash. Any ideas?"

"Sell inactive patents, or better, license more companies to use the active ones," Bruce suggested.

"No one'll pay me what they're worth."

"We ask potential licensees for too much up-front money before business develops," Michael argued.

"Stop! I invested big bucks for these babies. No one cut me slack. I need to recoup now! Not ten years from now!"

"The only sources of cash are profitable sales growth and commercializing patents. What else do we have?" Bruce asked.

Pug grinned. "This building! I've looked at commercial property appreciation. It's a bundle of untapped silver waiting to be mined!"

Michael understood. "I'll call some real estate firms."

"Already did it."

When Pug left, Bruce said, "Pug must really be in a bind."

"You don't know the half of it… and don't ask about the other half."

The real estate broker confirmed substantial appreciation, and the property sold in August.

IPS negotiated a three-year leaseback for the bottom two floors with the new owner occupying the top floor.

Proceeds from the sale allowed IPS to retire the building loan, to reduce short-term obligations, and to net cash of $500 thousand. IPS paid the equipment vendor to finish the secret project. The 1999 revenues of $9.3 million showed an operations loss of $1 million. The building sale gain was sufficient to produce an overall profit of $350 thousand.

DENVER

Pug and Bill spent Christmas and New Year holidays testing the new process and solving manufacturing bugs. Jackson filed a patent application for IPS High Volume Low Cost Process (Hi-Volow).

Later Michael visited Denver to examine the new equipment and watch the material being produced. The unique equipment produced multiple layers of metal alloy neatly stacked onto pallets.

"Bill, got to hand it to Pug! Everybody scoffed at his dream."

"I know. What surprises me is how it simplifies and improves speed, efficiency, reduces waste and overall costs."

"We're missing one little thing."

"This a trick question?"

"Customers. Remember Pug said, 'If I build it, they will come.' Where are they?"

"I guess Skip and Dave have to make real sales calls on real customers."

"Do I detect a hint of rhetorical sarcasm?"

"Sorry, I meant, it's the customers' duty to order our material without exception."

"Maybe changing our name to IPS-Johns Mansville will help."

"Mansville will sue for trademark infringement."

"Pug's kind of company," Michael joked.

2000
SOUTH SAN FRANCISCO

"**L**ET'S TALK ABOUT GETTING ORDERS for Hi-Volow material," Pug announced at January's staff meeting.

"Remember that Thai firm you and Michael thought might be a partner?" Dave asked.

"Bingo! Akami-Thai! I'll give 'em a call!" Pug exclaimed.

"What if they don't have the right equipment to use Hi-Volow?" Bill wondered.

"We'll rent 'em our spare press," Pug said.

"Why start with international customers?" Michael asked. "Let's find a US customer. Dave, you must know some company... or how about you, Skip?"

Pug snapped, "Lawrent's not stealing my idea! Bill and me are headin' to Thailand."

An agreement with Akami-Thai was finalized in February. IPS agreed to ship pallets of Hi-Volow material to Thailand, to absorb the duty and freight costs, and to lease a press to Akami-Thai. The material arrived in April. Bill stayed for two weeks to assist the start-up.

OSAKA

Two months later, Jun sent Kenji a brief status note:

Kobyashi-san, Research Appliance is pleased with the quality and efficiency of the Hi-Volow. When combined with the Multi-Dimensional

Finished Part technology, TADA has a cost-effective and proprietary position. The first application will be the thermal dissipater for Hondoya's new models. Shipments start next quarter. Then we can export to Korea for Handi.

SOUTH SAN FRANCISCO

Pug and Michael met in Pug's office.

"Marken's been our rep since '96! No new business since we rehired 'em! Dave says they're worthless. No way they're selling my Hi-Volow! Fire their asses!"

"There's no money for a buy-out."

"Tell Bruce to stop commission payments to soften 'em up."

"Okay, but who calls on customers?"

"Details, details. By the way, I'm firing our sales manager too."

Pug summoned Bruce. "Whadya working on?"

"Payroll conversion for your MIS upgrade. If I don't finish, no one gets paid!"

"Give it to your assistant. Need you for my licensing model."

"What?"

Pug smiled, "How do you think IPS'll sell Hi-Volow material?"

"Asking customers to buy it?"

"Noooo! My licensing model will! Brucie, starting now, you're on this full-time!"

Pug never fully explained his licensing scheme. His daily iterations confused everyone. The model seemed predicated on complicated assumptions and intricate formulae. But to Pug it was simple: He wanted a multi-phase licensing program that let licensees pick and choose a phase depending on their market objectives and manufacturing capabilities. Pug created a menu of different prices and fees for each phase.

Skip and Annie watched the project unfold. "Annie, let's prepare a PowerPoint presentation to market Pop's new program. He promised me a commission for each sale."

"Let's pare it down to basics; it's kind of intricate. I was wondering… have you thought more about Kenton Aerocon investing in IPS?"

"Only after they commit to a license." He leaned closer and spoke in a confidential tone. "The license is step one to set the hook for Kenton and my dad. Step two is to wait until IPS is desperate for a cash infusion, and step three…"

"Is to get Kenton to invest!"

"As Pops says, bingo, bango, bongo!"

Annie looked around to ensure they were alone. "Skip, you've made me so happy these last few months."

"Once you said you and Randy were through, I've thought about nothing else but you and me…"

She smiled; her deep blue eyes locked on his handsome face. "When do you want me to activate our harassment contingency?"

"I'll find the right time… for you to approach Bruce and drop the bomb. Knowing how Pops thinks, your time at IPS will be very short."

Michael's analysis indicated IPS owed Marken $1.5 million for early cancellation. The net present value of this income stream was $900 thousand.

Pug reviewed Michael's spreadsheet. "No way!"

"Pug, it's moot. There's no cash."

"Give Exeter a nice discount for faster payment and take the rest from the bank line."

"That's a recipe for financial insolvency. Let's pay in installments."

"You're giving me a headache. Marken's history! Don't go higher than four hundred K."

"And if they don't agree?"

"They can sue me!"

CHICAGO

A few weeks later, Michael met with Walter Marken. He accepted the $400 thousand with little objection. At the meeting's conclusion, Michael asked about pictures in Walter's office: one of two Americans and two Japanese, and another of General MacArthur.

"I spent time there after the war as part of the occupation forces to restructure industries," Walter explained.

"Travel there often?"

"Once a year. We rep several Japanese companies."

They shook hands. Walter added, "Michael, I appreciate your prompt resolution of this matter. Who knows, maybe you and I can do business again."

Michael thought, *This was too easy. And what did he mean by "do business again?" Need to do some background research on Walter.*

SOUTH SAN FRANCISCO

Bruce wired Marken the money. When he showed Michael the confirmation, Michael warned, "Tighten your seat belt. We're out of buildings to sell."

Bruce tugged at his tie. "Right, the patents are the only assets not pledged."

"Pug will never sacrifice the family jewels."

"You got that right."

SEATTLE

Skip and Annie met Bob Kenton in his office at Kenton Aerocon. "So Skip, what's this new concept you're raving about?"

Skip smiled. "Well, I developed a new licensing program." Annie gave the PowerPoint presentation.

"Looks innovative," Bob said. "Not sure I fully understand it, but it looks like a staircase: each step progresses towards an integrated marketing and manufacturing capability using IPS technologies."

"Bob, the important point is it leads to closer cooperation. When can you visit San Francisco?"

"Two weeks?" *That will give me time to consult with Darin.*

"You got it!"

In the taxi to the airport, Annie said, "You look pleased."

"Sweetheart, if Kenton bites, we're set."

She kissed him. Skip was ecstatic. The Kenton deal was in motion, and Annie had filed divorce papers.

"How did your dad take the news about Randy?"

"He was disappointed but wants him to stay with the company. I'm so happy I left Sunshine." She paused and looked lovingly at Skip. "I have a surprise for you."

"What?"

"I'm two months pregnant."

He turned to her and whispered, "Annie, that's wonderful." He pulled her into his arms and held her tight. "Once we get Kenton-Aerocon underway, I'll file for divorce and we'll be together."

SOUTH SAN FRANCISCO

When Bob Kenton arrived at IPS, he requested a private meeting with Pug. "Kenton-Aerocon wants an exclusive license for Aerolation technologies and materials. Our aerospace and construction contacts and your technology make a great partnership," he said.

"Skip says you got good sales guys, but lemme cut to the chase. I hate exclusives. Up-front talk is big, but follow-through sucks. I just fired an exclusive rep for non-performance."

Bob paused. "Pug, without exclusivity, anyone can steal the business."

"My licensing model lets you start as a non-exclusive sales licensee, then you add a manufacturing license when business takes off. You become exclusive by being first to market and first to manufacture. A Hi-Volow license always gives you the lowest costs."

Bob looked skeptical. "You're asking for a large license fee while Kenton funds all the sales and marketing. We've invested large sums to establish sales presence and customer relationships... like your technology investment. It's counterintuitive to our business model. Who else has bought these licenses?"

"We got an appliance licensee already at Phase three... and several others in final negotiations. If Kenton's as good as Skip says, you'll get your original investment back in no time."

Skip joined the meeting. "Pops, let's give Kenton a discount since they're first in North America."

"Remember Winston Churchill's democracy speech?" Pug glared.

Bob looked confused. *Winston Churchill?* Rather than ask, he said, "Okay Pug, I'll think about your proposal."

After Bob left, Pug yelled. "Skippy, shut the fuck up when you don't know what the hell you're talking about!"

"Whatever you say, Pops." Skip left, slamming the door.

Four weeks later, Skip and Annie skipped through the office hallways demanding everyone's attention. Michael, Bill, Dave, and Bruce heard the commotion and joined them. Pug appeared at his office door and said, "Skip, tell 'em."

"I got a three hundred and fifty thousand dollar check from Kenton-Aerocon!" he shouted. "Kenton bought two Phase I Aerolation licenses, one for aerospace and one for construction. When we're at the Hong Kong trade show, we'll negotiate the manufacturing phases!" Skip announced, clearly pleased with himself.

"Kenton proves my model works," Pug boasted. "Dave, start contacting Tier 1 appliance customers!"

Dave, hands shoved in his jean pockets, headed back to the lab.

At home that evening, Pug popped a Pat Henry and told Marcy, "Babe, we got our retirement annuity."

"Retirement?"

"With my licensing royalties, we'll be sailing first class on the USS Silver Lining!"

The next day, Dave met Pug to discuss the appliance business.

"You gonna let Skippy beat you?" Pug asked.

"What are you talking about?"

"The Kenton deal! I'm tellin' you to sell my license model to your customers!"

"My customers don't want Hi-Volow product or licenses."

"Goddamn it! IPS is through with finished parts!"

Dave stormed away and headed to lunch with Judith. "Your dad upset you," she said.

"Everything's going to shit! You and I worked our butts off in '99 to meet our sales plan and prepare a good forecast for 2000. Did he give us credit? Hell no! He said the programs started before we got involved. Skippy-poo's missed forecast caused the 1999 disaster."

"Why can't your dad see this?"

"My friggin' overpaid, protected brother always gets a free pass."

"What are you going to do?"

"I don't know. Maybe Michael has some ideas."

SOUTH SAN FRANCISCO

Every week, Pug threatened to close Denver, despite Michael's and Bruce's objections.

Bruce argued, "IPS has no cash to close Denver—let alone start up a new plant!"

"And Mile High won't renew the credit line if it gets wind of this," Michael added.

A dark look crossed Pug's face. "Mile High's history!"

"Moot point," Michael concluded, "since we have no cash."

DENVER

In June, Pug flew to Denver to meet the Mile High banker. Entering the office like a bulldog, Pug demanded, "Okay, where's the paperwork to renew my credit line?"

"Just got the 1999 auditor's report. What's your rush?" the banker replied.

"Look, damn it, I sold the building and retired your friggin' note!"

"The balance sheet's better. But why did IPS borrow more on the credit line?"

"Bruce didn't tell you? Bought out Marken's contract, saved over a million bucks."

"And who's selling in Chicago?"

"Our own people."

"Wait a minute. You tried that in '95."

"I got a new licensing strategy and program. Customers are excited. Already sold three."

"Look, that's the future," the banker stated. "When you adjust for the one-time property sale in '99, your base business lost money like in 1998. The first months of 2000 showed more losses."

"You haven't listened to one damn thing! I fired our lousy sales rep, got full-time sales guys, and started a new licensing program!"

"You need more equity! And a new bank!"

"Michael's searching for a California bank."

"Anything else I should know?" the banker asked, checking his watch.

"Business as usual," Pug said, trying to control his anger.

"How's the new plant manager doing?"

"Bill's installed my new Hi-Volow manufacturing process. I supplied material to our first appliance customer. It'll revolutionize how customers use IPS materials."

"Okay, but the loan committee's concerned with IPS's insufficient cash flow and the company's undercapitalized."

"So, what about my line?"

"The loan committee bumped the interest rate by two percent for the additional risk. Second, available credit line is reduced. Third, working capital collateral requirements are higher. Fourth, no more delays in receiving monthly financials! Finally, and most important, no more surprises! Am I clear?"

"Already talked to Bruce about the late financials. Don't understand your second and third items."

"The bank's reducing the total credit line to one-point-five million and asking for additional collateral."

"But I've never missed an interest payment!"

"Until your operations show revenue growth, sustainable profit, and positive cash flow, the bank requires more security."

"How about my personal note?"

"We'll renew it, but the interest rate will increase by four percent."

"Message received." *Asshole!*

"Good! Tell Michael to find a California bank now."

Pug, furious and red-faced, stormed out.

SOUTH SAN FRANCISCO

When Pug returned, Michael asked, "Everything okay?"

"I got the six-month renewal. By year end, Mile High's gone!" Pug turned and yelled, "Sharon, tell Bruce to get in here!"

Bruce rushed in, spreadsheets tucked under his arm, notepad in hand.

"We're closing Denver," Pug said. "I want all operations here by fourth quarter of 2000."

"I did another what-if analysis on a close-down scenario. Bottom line is…," Bruce stammered.

"Only way to build cash is to grow sales and profits," Michael said, completing Bruce's thought.

"You two don't get it! Think what IPS saves by consolidating: travel, facility rental, lower phone costs. I could go on and on."

"What about the restructuring liabilities?" Michael argued. "Where does the cash come from in the meantime?"

"We're not studying this to death. I wanna close-down plan on my desk tomorrow!"

An angry edge to his voice, Michael said, "Closing Denver and starting up new operations will be another financial disaster, worse than 1998."

"And we can't survive another disaster," Bruce added.

"Don't care what you septics think."

The following week, Michael stood in the door to Pug's office. Pug, his eyes fixed on his mother's picture, fiddled with the silver Baoding balls.

"Pug, got a minute?"

"Sure. Anything beats thinking about Ted and Rich."

"What about them?"

"Trying to dump Dad on me for Thanksgiving… again."

"Pug, need to talk. I told Sharon to hold your calls."

"Uh, oh. Sounds serious."

Michael eased into a chair and took a deep breath. "I've been offered a full-time teaching position at San Francisco State, starting January 2001."

The silver balls fell from Pug's fingers, clunked loudly, and rolled to the edge of the desk. "You can't leave! It's why I made you executive VP!"

"An offer like this doesn't come around very often."

Frowning, Pug hollered, "Geez, at least wait until we consolidate in California!"

Michael nodded. *Don't know if I'd survive.* "Wish I could, but can't pass this opportunity. Pug, think of it as changing roles, not leaving. I'm glad to consult for IPS and stay on the board, if that suits you."

"Yeah, okay." Pug spun his chair around and looked out the window. "Yeah, go consult."

Michael walked outside the building and called Ellie's cell. She answered, "How'd it go?"

"Okay, I guess. Pug's upset."

"Michael, you did the right thing. Now we have some flexibility."

SAN MATEO

Emotionally drained and nagged by a stiff neck and blurred vision, Pug headed home. He pulled into the driveway, turned off the motor, and stared at the house. The one-story ranch, at the end of a wooded cul de sac, cried out for more renovation.

So much to do... new porch, front door, roof. Never enough time or money. One of these days... god, my neck's killing me.

He hoisted himself out of the car and shuffled into the house. In the kitchen, he found Marcy slicing vegetables. She wiped her hands on a towel, opened the fridge, and handed him a Pat.

"What's wrong?"

"Talked with Ted and Rich. Guess what?"

"No, he's not coming for the holidays!" She stepped back and leaned again the refrigerator. "Your father ruins Thanksgiving for everyone!"

"Not that. Would you believe Michael's quitting? To teach?"

Marcy relaxed somewhat. "Well, he's often talked about that."

"He betrayed me on the Thailand deal. Goddamn it! All I've done for him! Rescued him from MatraScience and made him executive VP for chrissakes!" Pug took a long swig of beer. "But chaos is wonderful."

"Huh?"

"Michael told me to hire a strong finance assistant for Bruce, but I'm way ahead. I'll hire a good guy and fire Bruce. Already got my cousin Louis headhunting. Not paying Michael's salary means I can hire a new CFO and... my own patent guy."

SOUTH SAN FRANCISCO

The next morning, Pug sat at his desk, rubbing his neck and shoulder. Sweating, he felt as if walls were closing in on him. His chest and heavy waistline rose and fell with labored breaths.

Another fuckin' holiday with Dad!! Gotta relax! Breathe in 1-2-3. Breathe out 1-2-3.

A sharp, burning pain raced up his neck.

Relax for chrissakes!

He opened the silver music box and looked around his sanctuary. As the familiar tune played, he gazed at his wall of fame: twenty-two silver-framed patents surrounding a University of Colorado diploma in mechanical engineering. Certificates from engineering honoraries hung alongside. The Las Vegas picture and bank wire had disappeared.

On the credenza lay two books, gifts sent on his birthday. He read the anonymous note: *To Pug James with best wishes on your fifty-six-year milestone. It signifies one's achievement of wisdom. Too bad you didn't read the* Art of War *and* The Peter Principle *before commencing your IPS journey.*

He grabbed the Baoding balls and glanced up at the wall and the alligator cartoon. He smiled. *Ted, the alligator mouth!*

Dave burst in. Dressed in jeans, sneakers, and a Colorado University sweatshirt, he plopped into a chair. "We need to talk."

"About my licensing strategy?"

"No. I accepted a great job with a Japanese software design company."

Pug was stunned. He grabbed a tissue and dabbed at his damp brow. "Leaving IPS? What about all the opportunities I gave you in technology, sales, international? How many twenty-six-year-olds get that chance?"

"You never let me make any decisions."

Pug stiffened. "You don't know one-tenth the shit I do to keep this company from going belly up! Don't tell me how to manage!"

"All I wanted was a chance to develop and sell real products! Not licenses and Hi-Volow crap."

"Skip proved the strategy works," Pug yelled, his fist pounding the desktop.

"Proved? Kenton hasn't sold one dollar of product. And why? 'Cuz Skippy's too busy screwing Annie."

"Who Skip fucks is none of your business!"

"It is when you pay him forty thou more than me!"

How in the hell does he know Skip's salary? Neither spoke. Dave stared out the window. At last, Pug asked, "What's so great about this Jap company?'"

"I can use my computer and language skills. They're sending me to Tokyo. Getting in on the ground floor, and I get a signing bonus."

"Takin' a big risk."

"Coming from you, I guess that's a compliment."

Goddamn, just like me. Proud of you, Son. "Grass ain't always greener, but if you yen for slant ass, go for it."

Dave stood and ambled to the door. "Pops, just so you know, the wrong son's quitting. Oh, and someday, ask me about Dr. O'Leary."

Pug did not respond. *He'll be back begging for his job.*

SAN MATEO

That evening, Marcy was inconsolable. "Why Japan? Can't he work here?" she asked between sobs.

"Not at the money they're offering."

"I'll talk to him."

"No! Let him be." Pug popped open another Pat Henry. "Kinda funny, I wanted Dave to set up our operations in Japan. Like a condom in Kenji's camp."

"Condom?"

"You know, like a 'Trojan in Kenji's camp.'"

Marcy frowned. "Sometimes I worry about your mind."

SAN FRANCISCO

Dave sat at a bar in Japan Town and called Michael. Swigging a Sapporo, he updated him.

"Congratulations!" Michael said. "Sounds like a great opportunity."

"Thanks, Michael, for encouraging me to explore my options."

"You'll enjoy living in Japan. Nippon-Soft-Dev's gain is IPS's loss. Hope you checked the company before signing on." *I'll call my friend at the commercial attaché.*

"Been working with their people on Hondoya's projects. We got great chemistry."

"Tina going with you?"

"She decided it's better for her and the baby to stay here."

Michael paused. "Understand. Dave, you leave behind one hell of a legacy."

"Legacy?"

"Yes! First, you converted two–dimension 10000 technology into formed multi-dimensional shapes. IPS can sell more product capabilities like Mathews and Handi. Then you leveraged the technology with the AA project. Second, you became IPS's resident acoustics and vibration expert, expanded its materials beyond thermal applications. Third, you helped launch the Korean business. Fourth, you invented Aerolation, which opened construction, and aerospace markets. Hopefully, Kenton will exploit it. If IPS could ever market, we could eliminate all fiberglass insulation."

"Yeah, but where's the new business? You know Pops thinks the patent is the only mission."

"Sean once said, 'IPS fights patent battles but loses commercial wars.'"

"Michael, I'm telling you something I never told Pops. You're good at big picture stuff and diplomacy." Dave took a deep breath, then blurted details of what he'd discovered about Sean's internet searches.

Astounded, Michael listened as Dave described Sean's computer files. He sat back in his chair. *Porn! Knew it had to be something other than patent searches and recruiting. Is that the whole story? Dave seemed hesitant, as if he had more to tell.*

2001
SOUTH SAN FRANCISCO

MICHAEL EXPECTED FEWER PUG DISTRACTIONS as he began teaching and part-time consulting in January. He devoted one day a week to IPS. His first task was to locate a less risk-adverse California-based bank.

After a few weeks, he updated Ellie. "Finding a new bank is impossible. The dot-com disaster has scared bankers. Focus is profits, not optimistic forecasts. They like IPS technologies and forecasts, but…"

"Let me guess. When they see the 2000 results with the restructuring losses, they get nervous," she said.

"Five have already said no thanks."

"What's your plan?"

"Keep looking. May have to ask Mile High for another extension. Bruce and I are preparing an investment package to raise debt. Investors will receive twelve percent interest, conversion rights and warrants to purchase stock at three dollars per share. The five-year projections show investors could see net book value as high as nine-and-a-half dollars a share. That's a twenty-three percent return."

"Honey, I'm not optimistic given this economic environment. Or Pug's forecasts."

Michael and Bruce completed the private placement memorandum for debt. The executive summary explained Pug's licensing model. Lawyers required full disclosure of prior years' losses. The financial projections used Pug's assumptions for licensing revenues.

During a school break, Michael marketed the memorandum in Colorado, Arizona, California, and Illinois with a goal to raise three million. First stop was Colorado to meet with VenCapOne. Robby pledged $300 thousand. Another investor transferred $50 thousand from an IRA. In southern California and Arizona, Michael visited wealthy, sophisticated investors. All declined.

When Michael returned home, Ellie asked, "How'd the meetings go?"

"Terrible! Everyone questioned IPS's history of negative cash flow. They challenged the warrants' value since IPS has no clear exit strategy. Bottom line, they all have better investment opportunities."

"So why did VenCapOne invest?"

"Doesn't make any sense, but beggars can't be…"

"Choosers. Is Pug buying any debt?"

"No, but he has raised some short-term unsecured debt at eighteen percent interest. Some MatraScience friends bought one hundred thousand and Marcy pledged fifty thousand from her IRA. Jackson sent fifty thousand. Pug forced us consultants to convert unpaid invoices into short-term notes. He coerced the special metal vendor to exchange overdue payables into a one-year note."

"What other financing possibilities does IPS have?"

"Have you heard of a firm called Patent Financing, Inc.?"

"Yes, it's a new company funded by wealthy Silicon Valley entrepreneurs. Company has a reputation of bottom feeding for intellectual property on the cheap. Where'd you hear about them?"

"Robby mentioned it when I told him about problems finding a new bank."

"If they get serious, let me know. Have you talked to Pug about Delaware?"

"Yes, but it's got to be his idea."

The night before the March board meeting, Pug, Michael, and Robby Benton met for dinner. Michael previewed his presentation.

"I've contacted five banks about credit/loan proposals. Each requested the same information: three years' audited results, current and subsequent years' projections for income statements, cash flows, and balance sheets along with receivables and payables. They all questioned prior losses and forecasts and disliked our negative working capital and the one-point-five million of unfunded long-term restructuring liabilities. The 2000 financials showed revenues of nine million down from 1999 and a huge loss of two-point-two million."

Pug interrupted, "Thought California bankers were ass kickers when it comes to risk."

"Banks get very nervous about poor financial history," Michael responded.

"But you gave them the reasons! Are they deaf, dumb and blind?"

"Michael, what's the status on the debt?" Robby asked.

"VenCapOne came through, but we only raised one hundred thousand from non-related parties."

"Bottom line?"

Michael looked at his spreadsheet. "We got four hundred thousand for debt and about two hundred and thirty thousand in one-year notes. Vendors converted two hundred and fifty thousand of accounts payable to short-term notes. We're still short by two million to get through 2001."

Pug stared at Michael. "Any ideas?"

Michael did not answer.

Pug continued, "VenCapOne agreed to pledge more collateral for the bank's line of credit. IPS'll pay fifteen percent on the pledged amount. Oh, and by the way, Robby's joining my board."

Michael thought, *Robby never told me about the collateral pledge. Now he's on the board? What the hell is going on?*

At the meeting, board tension was palpable. Mile High's banker, who had invited himself, strolled in.

Michael presented his report, then Pug spoke: "My cost cutting, restructuring, and materials strategy'll make 2001 profitable."

"I only believe audited actuals with clean opinions," the banker responded sarcastically.

Pug ignored him. "With the debt proceeds and some short-term financing, we'll keep our heads above water, but we need Mile High's full credit line."

"IPS lacks sufficient working capital to support a full line," the banker said.

"VenCapOne will pledge nine hundred thousand dollars in collateral as a guarantee," Robby added.

The banker looked out the window and then at Pug. "VenCapOne's collateral may get the loan committee to grant a six-month extension." A stern look crossed his face. "But I will not tolerate any more surprises like this recent move!"

Everyone expected Pug to explode. "Yeah," he muttered.

As the banker was leaving, Pug said under his breath, "Thanks for the renewal, asshole."

Pug and Marcy ate lunch at Margaritas after the board members departed.

"Sweetie, IPS needs to win the lottery. Only way to climb outta this hole," Pug said between bites of an enormous burrito. "Now that I fixed the bank problem, I'm gonna fix the Jackson problem."

"But he loaned you fifty thousand!"

"IPS had to pay it back to Dexter-Foresmen. Jackson blackmailed me for fifteen percent interest on his friggin' note. I'm hiring an in-house gator to handle patents and reorganization."

"Honey, sometimes I can't keep up with you."

"Trust me, babe. I know what I'm doing."

Pug called an emergency board meeting for late April. Michael scanned the room. "Where's Jun?"

"Golfing with Kenji. Let's get to work. Sharon, tell Don Wagner to come in. I want everybody to meet my new CFO."

Michael and Bill exchanged surprised looks.

A small trim man entered. Dressed conservatively, he exuded confidence with a firm handshake and direct eye contact. Pug summarized his credentials and asked him to remain for the rest of the meeting.

"What happened to Bruce?" Michael asked.

"He'll stay 'til Don fires him," Pug snapped.

Pug ordered Skip to talk about marketing status. Since Dave's departure, he now carried the title of worldwide sales manager. Skip gave the usual spiel: heavy on colorful overheads and optimistic projections with little substance. Bill followed with an operations and technology update.

Pug returned to the main topic. "Mile High gave us six more months. If they force a workout, I'll tie up their asses in California courts. Anyway, I'm working several angles to raise more cash. First, to make it easier to find a new bank, debt holders will take lower interest rates and stretch out their notes by two years."

"They're already subordinated behind everybody except shareholders," Michael said. "We need new equity, not reshuffling debt chairs." Bill gave him a mock salute.

"Michael, you're a great straight man. You made my second point. My investment banker's looking for new equity."

Michael stared with a "here we go again" look. "Who besides insiders would invest in IPS?"

Pug's forehead wrinkled. "Septic!"

"Sophisticated investors will demand significant ownership and board seats. So you're prepared to cede control?" Michael questioned. He didn't wait for Pug's answer. "When will new business start? The stuff Skip talks about at every meeting? It's been months since Kenton bought two licenses."

"Look, finding new customers takes time. Skip, tell 'em the problems with those construction customers you and Kenton visited."

On cue, Skip mentioned recent sales calls and the many obstacles.

Pug interrupted, "Okay, let's face it. We need cash now. How 'bout you, Michael?"

Michael said nothing. Pug sighed and tapped the table with his pen. "I'll call Kenji too."

"We're not fixing the lack of sales," Michael argued.

"After I fix cash, I'll work on sales," Pug replied.

Michael frowned at Skip. *Any ideas Skippy?*

The meeting ended, and Pug followed Michael to his office.

"Okay, when you gonna approve my compensation plan?"

Michael answered, "You're asking for several things: increased base salary, IPS assuming your personal loan, paying your key man insurance, and additional options."

"Yeah, tax guys say my salary's too low with all my responsibilities."

"I'll get a pay expert to evaluate," Michael suggested.

"Tax guy already did. Look, if you can't, I'll do it myself!"

"Stop! You want a compensation evaluation or a rubber stamp?" Michael's anger shocked Pug. "Don't take too long," he muttered.

SAN FRANCISCO

That evening, Michael vented to Ellie. "I'm tired of the same excuses. New business never happens. Skip's full of horseshit. Now with more so-called responsibility, he complains he can't handle all the work."

"Why can't Kenton get the aerospace and construction business started?" she asked.

"Have no idea. Bob Kenton seemed like a heads-up guy when I met him."

"So, tell me about this Don Wagner?"

"Don't get me started! If he's any good, he'll quit before Pug fires him." Michael popped open a bottle of chardonnay and muttered, "Thank god, I got my teaching gig."

Michael, worried and frustrated, summarized his thoughts on Pug's compensation:

– – *IPS's results suck! Wish I made $170K for running an insolvent company. A pay cut's in order.*

– – *Pug argues he's had no raise for three years—his contribution to save cash. He's the only employee without a pay raise. A simple 5% a year would net $205K by now.*

– – *Claims he's the CEO, CTO, and CFO. But he's hired a CFO, and Bill's acting CTO.*

– – *Shareholders received no returns for 15 years.*

– – *James family enjoyed nice incomes for a long time. Skip uses expense reports to supplement lifestyle. The family gets at least a half million in salaries, benefits, and other perks.*

– – *The accountants recommended IPS assume Pug's personal bank loan. What are these guys smoking?*

– – *Ellie said Section 143 of the Delaware Corporations Code permits directors to approve a loan to an officer or director if reasonably expected to benefit the corporation. Pug claims he'll use future bonuses and salary increases to pay it back.*

– – *Pug wants 100,000 options at $1 per share while price is at rock bottom. Everyone else has underwater options. Options should be granted for outstanding performance (which hasn't occurred since '94.)*

– – *I can only support a small salary adjustment.*

SOUTH SAN FRANCISCO

Morning barely began when Pug's phone call interrupted Michael's breakfast. "Hey, Fieldsy! What'd you decide?"

"I'm getting some insurance quotes and…"

"The accountants say I'm underpaid, so the salary's a no-rainer."

"Hard to support a salary adjustment given the last three years' results."

"If I hadn't saved IPS, you wouldn't have this consulting gig! How 'bout the loan?"

"Mile High will never approve this."

"Not their call!" Pug hung up before Michael could reply.

Pug immediately called Robby. "Michael stiffed my comp proposal."

"Pug, what are you talking about?"

"He's angling to bill IPS more consulting hours. By the way, auditors want Skip to clear his advances. If he could refinance his mortgage, it'd help."

"I know some sub-prime guys, but they charge high rates."

"Skip wouldn't be in this mess if credit card companies hadn't screwed up his credit score."

"Let me see what I can do. I'll call you later."

Pug's next call was to his 401K administrator.

"What can I do for you today, Mr. James?"

"What's my account balance?"

After checking Pug's security information, the administrator replied, "Your balance is four hundred and seventy-five thousand dollars."

"Cash me out!"

"But Mr. James, you realize…"

"Yeah, yeah, I'll owe taxes."

"Yes, at least twenty percent for federal and six percent for state. Are you sure?"

"Send the paperwork and don't withhold taxes!"

Sharon arranged a May board conference call. Pug ordered her to exclude Jun.

Pug began: "Hey, sorry for short notice. Don, Bill, and Sharon are on the line too. So are Michael and Robby. Bill finished his audit of Dexter-Foresmen. Tell 'em what you found."

Michael's thoughts swirled. *Why is Pug offloading an audit to Bill? Pug gave Jackson carte blanche. He and Bruce should do the audit. Is he setting Bill up?*

Bill shuffled his notes. "Pug asked me to check Jackson's invoices since the Lawrent verdict. I found examples of high charges for patent filings and maintenance fees, especially international ones."

Pug chimed in. "Overbilled big time!"

"Give examples," Michael requested.

Pug interrupted before Bill could reply. "I'll cut to the chase. Jackson overcharged IPS at least forty percent."

"What's the total damage?" Robby asked.

Bill began, "I haven't finished..."

Pug yelled, "At least five hundred thousand dollars! Asshole already recovered twenty-five percent of his so-called unbilled fees."

"Did you challenge Jackson?" Michael asked.

"You won't believe what he charged for filings in Asia, and it gets worse. Tell 'em, Bill."

"The Japanese patent office informed us the annual filing fees were delinquent. They cancelled the application for our multi-dimensional patent," Bill explained.

"Can't you pay the delinquent fees?" Robby asked.

"No appeal," Pug answered.

Michael was incredulous. "How could this happen?"

Bill replied, "Jackson blamed it on administrative confusion between the patent office and Dexter-Foresmen's Tokyo affiliate."

"His fuck-up cost me my most important Asian patent," Pug continued. "Worst part is another firm already got a similar patent."

"Who?" Michael asked.

"I'm firing Dexter-Foresmen. Let me introduce Ken Lee, my new vice president and general counsel."

No one realized another person was on the call. Ken introduced himself, and Pug announced, "He's got his law degree from UCLA. He'll handle our patents and licenses. No more outside gator firms and their phony bills."

"When did he start?"

"Few weeks ago."

"Doesn't IPS owe Dexter-Foresmen over three hundred grand?" Michael asked.

"It'll be a hot day in hell before Jackson gets that."

"How about Jackson's loan to IPS?" Robby asked.

"It's his parting gift. If we cancel the debt, we book it as income. Right, Don?"

"I'll check with the auditors," Don said.

"That's it for now." Pug ended the call.

SAN FRANCISCO

Michael waited until evening to call. "Bill, this Dexter-Foresmen mishap is a shock."

Bill cleared his throat. "Jackson's been in Pug's cross hairs since the Lawrent verdict. The final straw was the loss of the Japanese patent and the alleged cover-up. I talked with Jackson offline. He admitted lax supervision but vehemently denied any intentional cover-up."

"What about the billing charges?"

"They're high, but Pug only extrapolated the very worst examples."

"So this whole brew-haw-haw was staged to fire Jackson and hire Ken Lee?"

"Afraid so."

"Tell me about Ken. Why the big title?"

"Pug wanted more than patent counsel."

"Will Pug sue Dexter-Foresmen?"

"Pug forgot to tell Ken that before he joined IPS."

Michael thought, *Ken's in a no-win situation. And just what IPS needs... another lawsuit.*

DENVER

On a weekend, Michael flew to Denver to meet Robby Benton at Denver International Airport. VenCapOne now owned the third largest stake in IPS.

"Robby, let's keep this discussion confidential," Michael said. "I have concerns about Skip. He hasn't paid back advances, and he uses the company credit card for personal expenses: groceries, restaurants, home improvement, etc."

"Son of a bitch! And I got him refinancing to clear all that debt!"

"Skip's got other problems. He's accused of sexual harassment."

"Do I want to hear this?"

"Apparently he's threatened Annie Burr."

"Does Pug know?"

"Bruce told him. Pug accused her of seducing Skip. IPS could face a major lawsuit now that Pug fired her. To make things worse, she's pregnant."

"I'm afraid to ask... anything else?"

"Pug won't make Skip accountable for sales results, yet refuses to get involved himself. Skip's brought in zero new business."

"I should withdraw VenCapOne's pledged collateral. Let Mile High be the bad cop," Robby said.

"Then the company goes bankrupt and your equity and unsecured debt are worthless, not to mention my unpaid invoices. One more thing, you'll love this, Pug distorts the monthly financials he gives Mile High."

"Oh, shit."

"Pug forced Bruce to capitalize manufacturing variances to improve monthly results. At year-end, the auditor adjustments produce a loss. He started this in '99."

"What's Don doing?"

"Too early to tell. It'll be a good ethics test. If he passes, his days are numbered."

"Mile High will be pissed about this!" Robby fumed.

"Right now, Pug has no real shareholder pressure given his thirty-nine percent ownership and Kenji's passive twenty-five percent."

"Anything else?"

"Pug's ordered Don and Ken not to talk with us."

"That doesn't sound good for us."

Before flying back, Michael left a long voice mail for Ellie: "I met with the vested associate and planted the seeds. He seems concerned, not sure it's genuine. Suspect he's linked to Mile High. Here are our alternatives:

– – Key investor withdraws collateral pledge, bank forecloses, then vultures step in.

– – Find new investors or creditors who provide money for majority control; Pug won't agree.

– – Implement the Delaware option to get 51 percent plus control by stockholder consent without a meeting."

TOKYO

Sean returned to Japan in June after a long absence. Settled aboard Japan Airlines, he reflected.

Natsuko! I'm coming back. I've tried to forget, but my heart won't let me.

The flight attendant, offering a flute of champagne, interrupted his thoughts. "May I get you anything else, Mr. O'Leary?"

"No." *Doctor O'Leary to you, babe.*

He refocused. *First, I'll the repair the damage caused by Lawrent's gaigin ineptitude with Gano-Nippon.*

Then I'll find Natsuko… if it's the last thing I ever do.

OSAKA

Sean spent a productive week in Tokyo with Gano-Nippon executives before heading to Osaka. On a whim, he called Dave at Soft-Dev and invited him to dinner. They met at the Comfort Station. A lovely companion accompanied Dave.

"Sean, great to see you! Nani, meet Dr. O'Leary, my boss at IPS." Sean surveyed a stunning young woman who was an exquisite meld of Asian and American heritage.

"Pleased to meet you." Sean shook her hand and gazed, transfixed. *Extraordinary: green eyes, auburn hair. Astonishing! She's like Natsuko, but taller.* His mind raced as he compared her every gesture, her every word to Natsuko's. His heart pounded.

At dinner, he attempted to concentrate on Dave's comments, but his eyes gravitated to Nani. Finally, he asked, "Where do your parents live, Nani?"

"Dr. O'Leary, when I was very young, my parents died in an automobile accident in Kyoto. I was adopted by a kind man, Kobyashi-chan. He has seen to my welfare and education."

Sean felt as if he had been kicked in his mid-section. Lightheaded, he managed to say, "I'm sorry for your loss."

Dave said, "Yes, Kenji Kobyashi sent Nani to good schools and mentored her. He introduced us—kind of by accident. But I'm grateful it happened!" He smiled at her.

As dessert was served, Sean apologized for the onset of a terrible headache. He excused himself and returned to his hotel. *I have to think this through. Nani is so like Natsuko. My mind's playing tricks on me.*

At the hotel bar, he ordered Glenlivet straight up, opened a pack of Marlboros, and reconstructed the past twenty-five years.

Nani's age correlates with the year Natsuko disappeared. Was she pregnant? Kobyashi-san and Okazaki-san never approved of Natsuko because she was "just a bar girl." Did they pay her to leave Osaka? If Nani is Natsuko's child, why did Kenji adopt her?

Kobyashi-san and Okazaki-san insisted I go to America to become TADA's eyes and ears. They said that's what my father would have wanted. Marken-san encouraged me to date American girls. It all makes sense now. They all betrayed me!

The next day Sean arrived at Kenji's office. A startled Kenji stood and took a moment to speak.

"Seamus, this is indeed unexpected! Please sit. May I offer tea?"

"No!" Sean spoke in rapid and angry Japanese. "Kobyashi-san, permit me to speak the truth."

"Your father, Hafferty-san, would expect no less."

"Last night I met Nani."

Kenji's face remained impassive.

"How ironic Nani's parents died in a Kyoto accident... like my parents. So tell me, who are Nani's mother and father?"

"It is unproductive to revisit painful history."

Sean reached in his briefcase and pulled out cassette tapes. "Speaking of painful history, listen to these recordings of my past conversations with you, Okazaki-san, and Marken-san."

"What is it you want, Seamus? An apology? You must apologize for the disappointment and shame you brought: disobeying instructions, collaborating with Lawrent, stealing secrets from your employer, and most of all, your disgusting addiction!"

"And what about you? You took Natsuko from me, hid my daughter, and ruined my life!"

"Seamus, what do you want?"

"You decide what is appropriate. I await your decision. If acceptable, you will never hear from me again, and Nani will never learn the truth." Sean bowed and departed.

Stunned, Kenji turned and walked shakily to a wide window. *Seamus, I treated you as a son, but I could not allow you to be associated with Nani's mother. I had great plans for you... but you dishonored your father and me.*

He took a linen handkerchief from his pocket and dabbed his eyes. *I will not allow your betrayal and addiction to harm Nani's future and my legacy.*

He phoned Shiganari. Choking back tears, he said, "Dear friend, I must unburden my heart."

Shiganari listened as Kenji spoke of his disappointment in Seamus. "Nani is part of Hafferty-san," he said. "I was obligated to protect and raise her... out of respect and loyalty for him."

"Indeed," Shiganari responded, "we are both obligated to Hafferty-san. It is fitting and right you have taken excellent care of his granddaughter."

Kenji, still emotional, said at last, "It was very difficult. Many Japanese objected to Nani—her parentage—*konketsu*."

"But, dear friend," Shiganari said, "you persisted, giving her every advantage for an excellent education. Those same people who objected now praise her beauty and intelligence."

"Yes, that is true, but a problem remains. What about Seamus? How do we respond to his threat—the tape recordings?"

"We agree to Seamus's demands. Let us be generous. Generosity. Who knows? It may help resolve his personal demons."

"I will instruct Dr. Yamura to settle this most unfortunate situation."

SOUTH SAN FRANCISCO

"Robby's on the phone," Sharon announced.

"Robby, how ya doing?"

"Not good. VenCapOne's going into receivership. The pledged collateral for IPS has declined by five hundred thousand." Robby paused. "Sorry, Pug, but Mile High'll ask IPS to find new collateral. By the way, I might have a possible solution for you. You ever heard of Silverado Valley National? It's a bank specializing in undercapitalized technology companies."

Pug slammed down the phone and pondered this latest setback.

On June 20, Sharon announced, "A representative from Patent Financing, Inc. is on the phone."

"Pug James here."

"Mr. James, I understand your company needs a California-based bank. We'd like to tell you about our services."

"You a bank?"

"We finance technology companies with strong intellectual property."

Pug invited its representative to with meet him, Don, and Ken. After the meeting, the three discussed the pitch.

"These guys for real?" Pug asked.

"Well-connected," Don replied.

"Their client list and bank partners are first class," Ken said.

Don tapped his pen on the table. "Okay, let's summarize. First, Patent Financing, Inc. guarantees long-term financing using clients' intellectual property as collateral."

"Finally! Somebody not afraid of patents."

"Second, it partners with a local bank and guarantees working capital loans."

"Once patents are pledged, there's no more collateral," Ken cautioned.

"Time I got some return from my patents!"

"One of the potential bank partners is Silverado Valley that Robby mentioned. But we should look at other banks," Don added.

"Don't bother. That's why I hired you two. You can out diligent anybody. If Patent Financing guarantees long-term financing, the bank don't matter."

Over three weeks, Patent Financing evaluated the patent portfolio and estimated potential commercial value of all active patents. Silverado Valley analyzed IPS's financial condition.

When their joint proposal arrived, Pug called a meeting. He gestured to his wall of patents and exclaimed, "They valued the active patents at ten million bucks. Whadya think, Ken?"

"My Korean ancestors say: Never look gift kimchi in the mouth."

Don laughed. "So the valuation's too good to be true?"

"I don't know how they arrived at ten million. IPS's active patents generate only five hundred thousand a year in royalties, and they're declining since Japan Technologies pays less each year."

Pug could not hide his excitement. "Easy, they saw potential with the Aerolation, multi-dimensional, and Hi-Volow patents. All that matters is Patent Financing lends twenty percent of that ten million."

"Don't forget," Ken said, "Patent Financing discounts the two million with their upfront fees and costs of three hundred thousand. IPS gets one-point-seven million for a two-million-dollar loan. Even though they didn't value inactive patents, they're part of pledged assets. I don't like that."

"Pug, did you see Silverado Valley terms and conditions for financing the working capital?" Don asked.

"So what?"

"Their fees are higher than Mile High's! They won't allow IPS to use fixed assets for other financing or sale/leaseback agreements. And they want all the subordinated debt holders to defer all interest and principal payments."

"If the sub-debt guys don't go along, tough shit! What have they done for me lately?!"

"Patent Financing wants to approve all management bonuses and compensation," Ken added.

Pug sighed, "If that's the price to dump Mile High, I'll live with it. When we get new licensees, I'll retire all this shitty debt."

"So what do you want Ken and me to do?"

"Get the papers ready for the board's rubber stamp." Ken looked concerned. "Ken, lighten up! I'm kidding! Just fix the papers to cover my ass."

"I'll fed-ex the documents so the board reviews before the call," Don said.

Three days later, Pug opened the board conference call. Don updated the financial status and summarized the new financing proposals. Pug asked for questions.

"What other alternatives did you consider?" Robby asked.

"No one else will loan money against patents," Pug said.

"I don't see Patent Financing putting actual money into the deal. They're only providing a letter of credit to secure the IP loan and the working capital loan," Michael said.

"What's your point?"

"The point is they're charging a lot of money for a letter of credit."

"And what's this about sub-debt holders waiving future payments?" Robby said.

"Patent Financing wants to ensure its principal and interest income aren't usurped by other debt payments or shareholder dividends," Don said. "They'll waive it if company cash flow is positive after IPS meets other obligations and ratios."

"With Mile High, debt holders got interest payments—although late," Robby said.

"Our options are zilch. This deal gets Mile High out, once and for all," Pug argued. "Robby, you oughta be in hog heaven 'cuz VenCapOne gets back its collateral. Silverado relies only on Patent Financing's guarantee."

"Yeah, Pug, we're out of options," Robby sighed. "I move to approve the deal."

"Wait. I have a question," Michael added. "What are Silverado's terms?"

Don answered, "First, IPS must maintain adequate cash flow to cover its fixed charges to Silverado and Patent Financing. Second, IPS provides annual audited financials and submits timely monthly financials."

"Same as Mile High's," Pug bellowed.

"IPS is always late. Can IPS meet the cash flow coverage and will Silverado be as lenient as Mile High?" Michael asked.

"Do I hear a second to Robby's motion?" Pug asked.

Pug declared the motion passed. Ken and Don exchanged perplexed looks.

"Ken, you've vetted the legal clauses?" Michael asked.

"Of course he did!" Pug snapped. "Why'd ya think I hired him?" He turned to Don and Ken. "Get this damn deal ready for my Henry John!"

SAN FRANCISCO

That evening, Ellie listened as Michael related the latest developments.

"IPS signed a bargain with the devil," she said. "Silverado makes clients adhere to loan covenants. The Patent Financing angle is a new twist, but Pug's taking a huge risk with the cross-default provisions."

"He loses all his precious intellectual property, not to mention the company. Whoever ends up owning the patents might actually commercialize them."

"You're starting to sound like... what does Pug call it? A septic? How long can IPS stay afloat with this deal?"

"Six months maybe less. This debt-chair shuffling provides no new funds."

"Why would Silverado and this patent company take IPS as a client?"

"My gut's bothered me about this whole process. IPS's financial history sucks, the forecasts are overstated, and the ten-million-dollar valuation reminds me of dot-com revenue projections. Feels like one of Robby's back room deals."

"What about Pug's pledged stock?"

"Bruce said Pug got his shares back from Mile High. He cashed out his 401K."

"Interesting. Let's open some sauvignon blanc and speculate what's in Pug's digital brain."

SOUTH SAN FRANCISCO

As Sharon prepared for another conference call, she asked Pug, "What do I tell Michael and Robby?"

"The usual."

"You mean cash?"

"Yep!"

Today Pug wanted no witnesses including her. Once the operator confirmed the participants, he began, "Hey, got a news update. Bill quit."

"What?" Robby asked.

"He's working for a chink company that manufactures cheap water heaters. And there's more. He screwed up the annual contract for the special metal alloy purchases. Now IPS's paying higher spot market prices."

"But you always personally negotiated that," Michael argued.

"Fieldsy, you're two years outta date! But here's the real kicker—Bill fucked up our patent database because Jackson ran rings around him. Ken's sorting out the mess."

Robby asked, "Who'll run operations?"

"Production manager. He'll handle daily stuff. Skip'll oversee him."

"Doesn't Skip have enough work growing sales?" Michael asked.

"He's hired a new sales engineer in Chicago. Skip'll stay here and watch operations for me."

Michael was incredulous. *Another excuse to increase Skippy's salary.*

"Okay, that's it! Oh, don't forget, if anyone knows where IPS can get more cash, let me know."

"Wait a minute," Robby said, "Do you mean IPS exhausted funds from Patent Financing and Silverado?"

"Don told you we paid off the restructuring debt. Current receivables and inventory are too low, so credit line's small. Barely meeting payroll. Gotta go. Marcy and me are closing on a beach house in Santa Cruz."

Michael mulled over Pug's announcements. He dialed Bill's home phone. "Heard you quit."

"Want the long or short version?"

"I got time."

"Six months ago, Pug refused to sign the annual metal alloy contract. He gambled that prices would decline. Told me to wait. I reminded him every week as prices rose. Now it's too late. Then Pug accused me of working for a Chinese company. An ex-Mathews employee wanted supplier contacts for his new company in China, so I helped introduce him."

"Listening to Pug, you'd think you worked full time for them. So why did you screw up the patent data files?"

"He said that? I spent the last few months showing Ken where to challenge Jackson. Pug doesn't want me around when he sues Jackson."

"I see why he fired you."

"Fired? Then he'd owe me severance. We had a big blow out. I told him IPS would always be a poorly-run family company."

"What did he say?"

"Blamed me for bad mouthing IPS to employees. I accused him of hypocrisy since he let Dave moonlight and Skip abuse the company credit card."

"Wow!"

"That's when he told me to get the fuck out of his office. Still waiting for severance. And Michael, there's something else you should know."

"What's that?"

"Ever wonder how Pug got the money to purchase the Santa Cruz vacation property and the golf course membership?"

"Enlighten me."

"I suspect he's stealing special metal alloy material and reselling to scrap dealers. Then he revises interim numbers, creates a smoke screen until the year-end audit. That's why Bruce always capitalized those material variances."

"Explains why he never fired Bruce."

The board met on September 20. Pug rushed into the conference room with his customary bravado.

"Before we get started, I wanna go on record," Pug said, slapping his notes to the table.

"What are you talking about?" Robby asked.

"This chicken-shit attack on my country. Bush should just bomb all those Mideast bastards and piles they call countries. They've always betrayed us."

The board members sat in stunned silence.

"Okay, said my piece," Pug said. "Let's get started. Gotta lot to cover."

"Is there an agenda?" Robby asked.

"You bet! Cash! But first, everybody's gotta know somebody broke into the building and stole our computers."

"What do the police say?" Michael asked.

"Oh, they filed paperwork for our insurance claims."

"Any suspects?"

"Kenton-Aerocon."

Michael noticed a red-faced Sharon staring at her notes, avoiding eye contact. He thought, *She looks embarrassed.*

"When I told Kenton to go fuck themselves, bastards sued me. I countersued for five hundred grand—what they owed us for all the free work we did," Pug declared.

"How are the lawsuits related to the break-in?" Robby asked.

"Simple! Kenton needed information for their lawsuit."

Skip interjected, "It's why they only targeted Don's and my office."

"Right," Pug said, "Don's got the financial shit, and Skip's got the marketing stuff. But not gonna get our shorts in a knot over this. We'll find other licensees. Kenton's worse than Marken. Let's get to the real stuff—how to raise cash! Ken looked at our patents and found more phony bills from Dexter-Foresmen. He hired Chatham & Weiss to sue them."

Michael leaned back. "Pug, aren't they the... oh, never mind." *Same law group that filed the insider trading class-action suit against you and MatraScience?*

Pug continued, "Chatham & Weiss says IPS has a strong case for overbilling, fraud, cover-up, professional misconduct, and other stuff."

Michael looked at Ken. "Why Chatham & Weiss?"

"The firm has an excellent record against deep-pocket opponents," Ken replied.

"For all the money we paid Dexter-Foresmen since 1989, did we ever question or challenge their invoices?" Robby said.

"Bill screwed up! That's why I fired him."

"I thought he resigned," Robby said.

"Didn't discourage him. Jackson lost my Japanese patent for the multi-dimensional patent. My new gators say he's unethical. When Jackson loaned IPS money, he made IPS pay Dexter-Foresmen's phony invoices. Big time conflict of interest! He'll lose his gator license."

Michael and Robby exchanged weary glances.

"Once Chatham reviews the evidence, we'll ask the board to approve," Ken said.

"How much can we sue for?" Robby asked.

"A lot!" Pug insisted. "Already got a financial expert to estimate how much revenue IPS loses without a patent."

"So, Chatham's doing this on contingency?" Michael questioned.

"I'll decide after discovery," Pug replied.

Michael pressed, "In the meantime, where do we get cash to fund discovery?"

"I'm asking vendors and creditors for delayed payments. We'll discuss other stuff over lunch."

Between bites of a Reuben sandwich, Pug presented his latest idea. For a minimum investment of $100 thousand in preferred stock, an investor would earn a dividend rate of 22 percent while the lawsuit unfolded. After victory, the investors could receive up to two times the original investment depending on the lawsuit's outcome. The preferred shareholders could also convert their shares into common stock with attractive terms.

"Whadya guys think? Pretty nifty, huh?" Pug shoved the last of the sandwich in his mouth and wiped his hands on a napkin.

"Sounds like a litigation lottery to me," Michael joked.

"Good one!" Robby added.

"Laugh all you want. When bucks roll in, I'll be the one with the first laugh."

November's morning sun warmed the East Bay horizon. Pug turned to his desk, sat down with a sigh, and stared at his mother's picture.

"Pug, Rich and Darin are on the phone," Sharon announced.

"Tell 'em to cool their jets. Fax this to Kenji." He handed her a letter marked "Urgent and Confidential."

"I'll e-mail."

"No! He needs a hard copy to wipe his slant-eyed butt!"

Sharon, looking fresh in a rust-orange blouse complimenting her hair, shrugged and headed to the fax room. Despite being Pug's executive assistant for six years, she could not tell serious from joking when it came to Kenji or Darin. Working for Pug was never dull.

As Pug reached for the phone, he glanced at a photo of his grandchildren. *Ted ain't got what I got when it comes to family.* "Hey, guys."

"Been waiting five minutes! Don't have all day!" Darin's nasal tone resonated self-importance.

"It's snowing, and I gotta buy snow tires," Rich growled.

"Hello to you too! So who's taking Dad for Christmas?"

"Gosh, Puggy, Dad's anxious to visit your family. He's got the air ticket—our annual holiday present to you and Marcy."

"Hold on, got an urgent call," Pug put them on hold.

"What's so urgent?" Rich asked. "He's always interrupted by something sooooo important."

"Last time Marcy called about the grand kiddies."

"Hear she calls at least ten times a day."

Pug rejoined the call. "So where were we? Oh yeah, Dad's been with us for the last three Christmases. We need a break."

"I babysit him the entire year!" Rich yelled.

"I would," Darin smirked, "but leaving for Asia the next day. You don't want to disappoint him, at his age and poor health."

"This ain't fuckin' fair!"

"Well, Puggy, I don't give a fuck what you think!" Rich hung up.

Pug slammed the receiver. Darin smiled at the simultaneous clicks. Fights with Pug always invigorated him, but lately personal problems were taking a toll: the second divorce and loss of his CEO position. The board accused him of conflicts of interests, indiscreet actions, abuse of company expense accounts, and misuse of the corporate jet. He accepted an exit package in lieu of a messy lawsuit.

SAN MATEO

Pug and Marcy met his dad at the airport. In the car less than five minutes, he blurted, "Have you seen Darin's stock price? Gave me a hundred shares for my birthday."

"That's swell, Dad." *Has he told you he was fired?*

"He's helped Rich start his new business."

Marcy and Pug stared straight ahead. She read Pug's thoughts. *Obviously the old coot forgot how we helped Rich.*

"Puggy, when's your company going public? So far you're nothing but talk."

Pug clinched his jaw as they sped towards San Mateo. Once home, Marcy pulled Pug aside. "No more! He will not ruin another holiday!"

At Christmas dinner, Skip's son Billy sat next to the old man and grabbed at his hairpiece.

"Leave my hair alone, you goddamn brat!" He slapped Billy who screamed. Michelle grabbed the wailing child and left.

Marcy yelled, "You horrible man! Get out of my home!"

"Dammit, Dad!" Pug yelled. "You've ruined another holiday!"

Furious, Pug booked his father's return flight that evening. After turning him over to Southwest Airlines, Pug skipped to the parking lot. "Thank god, free at last!" he shouted.

At home, Pug settled into his recliner, watched the film *Patton,* and consumed a six-pack of Pat Henry.

In the morning, he woke with blurred vision in his left eye. On his way to work, he stopped at Marcy's optometrist. After an exam, the doctor said, "Pug, you have an inflammation near the optic nerve. You need to see a specialist. Today!"

"Can't you give me something for this?"

"Here's the name of a neuro-ophthalmologist. See him immediately."

Pug endured numerous tests over the next four weeks. He told no one about his diagnosis of arterial ischemic neuropathy of the optic nerve. His doctors advised him to lose weight, lower his blood pressure, and control cholesterol. If he didn't, he risked a heart attack or stroke. He was told to start additional blood pressure and cholesterol medicines. His partial vision loss would be permanent.

2002

SAN MATEO

By February, Pug resumed his normal routine. Marcy had taken a cooking class to prepare more healthy meals which would help him lose weight.

Marcy yelled, "Pug! Dinner's ready! Want another Pat?"

"Yeah, babe. By the way, I'm leaking my reorg ideas."

"How much does Michael know?"

"He'll never see my big picture with all my twists and turns. Lettin' him think he'll make big consulting bucks while I pick his brain for free."

"But, Pug," Marcy said, handing Pug a beer, "Michael was always your best employee… and friend."

"Yeah, 'til he put a Thai knife in my back. Then he delayed my compensation package and forced me to cash in my 401K." Pug took a swig from his third Pat Henry.

"Oh, forgot to tell you," Marcy said, "we're baby-sitting Billy while Michelle's in Oregon and Skip's traveling."

Settled at the dinner table, Pug buttered a roll and took a big bite. "Wish Skip was as good at… at least I showed that slut the door. That dick-tease started it all. Her sex harassment claim was pure blackmail."

Marcy scowled. "Annie and her little Joey aren't exactly out of the picture. I'm afraid Michelle will leave Skip and take our Billy away to Oregon."

"Goddamn it, I pay Skippy over a hundred grand a year! Gave him another salary pop after Bill quit."

"He never seems to have any money. Where does it go?"

"Who knows? I don't know why he keeps pushing his stupid Kenton scheme. Now he wants the bastards to invest in IPS." Pug shoved a forkful of salad in his mouth. "I know how to get rid of Kenji."

Marcy looked confused. *Again, turning on a dime. Annie and Kenton one second, then Kenji the next.*

"IPS lost the second appeal on the Asia patent. Chalk up another Jackson screw-up. Now IPS's got no patent protection in Asia, and Jap Tech won't have to pay royalties. But I figured a way to keep milking Kenji's tit."

"You've lost me."

"Told the Jap I'd sue his customers' butts if I catch any of their 10000 material in countries where the patent's still valid."

"But how do you get rid of them?"

"Here's why I'm so smart. He'll pay a reduced royalty to keep me from suing customers in the US. He can't risk it with my bulletproof US patent. I'll sweeten the offer with a one-time discounted payment for all future royalties. In return, he gives up his shares and board seat. Bingo! IPS gets cash, and the Jap's outta my hair."

"Honey, with those shares retired, we'll have more than fifty-one percent control, won't we?"

"Bingo again!"

"Now I understand why you don't want Kenton's investment."

"Triple bingo! In the meantime, I gotta figure out how to raise short-term cash."

"How's the preferred offering?"

"Way short of the three million, but I gotta super scheme to make real money."

"You mean the internal licensees and the 'S' partnership?"

"Yeah! Another reason I don't want Skip screwing around with Kenton."

After dinner, Pug relaxed in his recliner and looked at three articles in the *San Francisco Chronicle*. The first described the intricate web of relationships between Enron and its special purpose entities. The second article exposed the Rigas family shenanigans at Adelphia Cable. The last showed Bernie Ebber's conflict-of-interest loans from WorldCom.

Pug thought, *Enron and WorldCom guys deserve jail. Rigas family didn't do nothin' wrong.*

SOUTH SAN FRANCISCO

The following week, Pug found Michael in his office. "You busy?"

"Finishing a project. Why?"

"Guess who called?" Pug eased his heavy frame into a chair opposite Michael. "An ugly, red-haired, nicotine-breath, four-eyed, golf-playing Irish asshole."

"Looks, smells, sounds like Sean O'Leary."

"He asked about the next shareholder meeting."

"And why would he care? Unless he's still upset after exercising all those stock options he can't sell."

"He's probably still fronting for Kenji," Pug sighed. "He introduced me to that slant-eyed asshole. Anyway, I got a new idea."

"Shoot." *Here comes another crack-pot-off-the-wall scheme.*

"Nobody's willing to pay IPS a fair price for the cash flow and all my intellectual property 'cept me. I'm the only one who believes in my company."

"But you don't have the cash."

"Who needs cash when you got credit? Sharon'll type up my ideas."

Thirty minutes later, Sharon appeared at Michael's door. "Urgent delivery!" She handed him Pug's plan.

Michael scanned ten pages. They included a diagram of Pug's concept embellished with bullet points. After a cursory review, Michael summarized key points and questions:

— SSFO's 'S' corporation buys working assets and licenses from IPS. *What's a SSFO 'S'? Where does the 'S' get the money to buy assets? Who owns it?* Purchase price = 4 or 5 X 'preformed earnings.' *Preformed?*

— IPS continues as a 'C' Delaware corporation owning the IPS patents. Continues licensing third parties using Pug's licensing model. *Where does all the debt go? 'C' or 'S'? Sounds like an Enron Special Purpose Entity.*

— 'C' corporation does share buyback and underwater options now good. *Where does 'C' get the funds, and explain why options are good? What happens to tax-loss carry-forward? Are 'C' and 'S' really necessary? What is he doing with this legal entity shuffling?*

No sooner had Michael written his last thought, Pug appeared. "Pretty nifty, huh?"

"Not sure I understand."

"Fire away!"

"What is 'SSFO S?'"

"Stands for 'South San Francisco S Corporation.'"

"Why do you want to use a subchapter 'S' corporation?" Michael asked.

"Because the profits go directly to the owners avoiding double taxation."

"And the losses too?"

"You're such a septic!"

"Better skeptical now then too late. Why not make IPS a subchapter 'S' instead of creating an additional company?" Michael asked.

"Way ahead of you! Talked with my tax accountants. IPS has to stay a 'C' corp. Got too many shareholders, and 'sides we got an ineligible foreign sake-sipping shareholder. If IPS converts to an 'S,' I lose the tax-loss carry-forward credit."

"Where does 'S' corp get funds to pay for the purchase?"

"No problem! IPS sells the assets to the 'S' and takes my personal note, a seven-to-ten-year payback at nine percent interest."

"So you own the 'S?' How's the note secured?" Michael asked.

"Wake up! No need for collateral! The 'S' cash flow'll retire principal and pay interest."

"Based on the last three years, it may be hard to pay off that note. Did you run five-year sales and cash flow projections?"

"There you go getting anulytical."

"Sorry for being anal. So, remaining IPS shareholders have no ownership in the 'S?'"

"No need. They got my personal note as payment for the assets. Ownership of IPS won't change."

"Who runs the 'S?'"

"Me. So everything's arm's length, I won't stay president of the 'C.' Been thinking. You could be president, part of your consulting gig. I'll decide important stuff like patents and licensing, since I'm still the largest C shareholder. By the way, tax guys liked my idea about reincorporating in Delaware for the 'C' corp. Ken's filing the paperwork."

"Makes sense," Michael said, drawing lines through his notes. "So how do you set a purchase price? I don't understand this 'four or five times preformed earnings.' That's a new term."

"This is where I'm really brilliant. It's those earnings before interest, taxes, and other nonrecurring crap."

"You mean earnings before interest, taxes, depreciation, and amortization?"

"Yeah, yeah. Shit-can stuff that muddies up real earnings."

Michael paused. *Exactly how companies like WorldCom got in trouble.*

"Pay attention!" Pug continued. "Four or five times preformed earnings will be basis of my note. Simple, ain't it? We use the same valuation formula to value IPS 'C' corp shares. Then IPS buys back shares. Time I returned money to original investors like you and me, and you know the best part? It'll make the "under-water" non-qualified options have value!"

"Where will 'C' corp get cash for the buybacks or dividends?"

"You're not too swift. IPS will have my note payments for principal and interest. Also it'll get royalty payments from Jap Tech and other licensees including my 'S.' With all that cash flow, IPS can buy back its shares."

"Your concept is creative. You should patent it. Will Kenji go along?" Michael asked.

"Nobody'll ever pay the price I set. If Kenji wants to outbid me, be my guest."

Michael tried to concentrate as Pug expanded on his plan. *Talk about conflicts of interest. Who wouldn't want to do a no-cash purchase of IPS now all the hard shit's done and the cash flow's improving?*

"Why create separate companies?" Michael asked. "Do it virtually. Real cash flow only comes from profitable sales growth and new licensees. Your plan does nothing to increase them."

"Legal separation creates arm's length to set real values," Pug declared.

"Your family owns forty percent of IPS, and you're establishing the four-five times 'preformed' earnings. That's not arm's length." *Shit, he's got me saying 'preformed!'*

"Gotta move fast. Longer we wait, more expensive the values get, and the more taxes we'll pay if we exercise options after the fair market value exceeds the option price."

"Let me study it." *At least Delaware's launched.*

SAN FRANCISCO

Ellie watched Michael gulp a large glass of red wine as they sat in the family room.

"Another rough day?"

"Pug's restructuring plan is a ruse to siphon valuable assets and leave garbage to the rest. He and Enron's Andy Fastow attended the same business school."

Michael poured another glass. "Nice evening. Let's sit outside." They moved to their favorite place, the porch overlooking Presidio Park.

"Pug's acting irrational."

"He's lost his moral compass," Ellie said. "If he's doing anything improper..."

"You can't convict someone for thinking that. He wants me to analyze his proposal. When I do, he'll change directions making my work obsolete."

They sat in silence. Ellie sighed and said, "When you're around Pug, he seems so genuine, so sincere..."

"That's his disingenuous secret. His candid, seemingly-honest comments and outrageous opinions are clever smoke screens."

Ellie refilled glasses. "What drives him to act this way?"

"A genetic disease called *Darin-itis...* or *Ted-itis*?"

Ellie laughed. "And Marcy's the horrific enabler claiming everyone's against him."

"Dave was smart to leave." He offered more wine. Ellie cupped her glass. He poured the rest into his.

"Pug's family is a Shakespeare tragedy. King Pug, an insecure soul poisoned by a cousin's jealousy and father's paranoia, is trapped in a web of self-inflicted co-dependency. Queen Marcy forgives him for Tiffanee and now blindly swallows his spin. The real tragedy: IPS will never have value with Pug in charge. Give me six months without Pug..."

Ellie laughed again. "You sound like the 'bard of the business school.' Your case studies will be positively literary!" She departed to the kitchen to prepare dinner.

Michael grabbed a legal pad and drafted a metaphor-rich letter. *Time King Pug got a surprise message.*

SOUTH SAN FRANCISCO

With his feet on the desk, Pug read the *Chronicle's* business section. He glanced up to see Michael at the office door. "Hey Fieldsy, you read this Enron shit and WorldCom crap? Those crooks oughta be shot!"

"And Adelphia too!"

"Not even close! The Rigas family built their cable company from scratch!"

"Whatever, I looked at your proposal. I'll have Sharon type my notes."

"Whadya think?"

"Bottom line, you don't need multiple legal entities. Don could keep separate books, distribute the money, and do the share buybacks. Keep it virtual and lawyer-free."

"No way!"

"I ran a five-year projection assuming the sales and license fees grow ten percent a year. You can't pay off your note. You'll barely make interest payments let alone the required principal and royalty payments owed the 'C' corp." *Not to mention the 'C' Corp has no collateral backing the note.*

"You don't get it! Look, I made it even better. First, Ken'll incorporate IPS in Delaware, and it'll be my, I mean, IPS's holding company. He'll set up an 'S' corp in California. The holding company'll pay my salary and expenses and the accounting-legal stuff. That way, the 'S' has more profits to pay the principal and interest faster. Second, so lotsa cash doesn't go back and forth, I'll pay my personal note back with the share proceeds from the holding company share buybacks."

"Whoa, slow down! You lost me."

"Do I hafta draw pictures? When 'S' corp makes a payment of principal and interest to IPS, it's like paying me since I'll own thirty-nine percent of that payment. Follow? Thirty-nine percent of 'C' corp's cash would be available to pay down my personal note. So, do the math! You get the payment valued by dividing the 'S' corp payment by the inverse of my ownership percent. For every dollar 'S' pays 'C' corp, it's really worth one dollar and forty-two cents. One dollar divided by point sixty-one, the inverse. And when 'C' corp buys back my shares, I'll use 'em to pay off the note even faster. So you see, the 'S' corp personal note disappears quicker."

Michael was speechless. *Jesus Christ! This is Enron shenanigans and confusion squared!* He shoved his hands in his pockets, sighed, and said, "Okay, I'll run the numbers with your new tweaks and see how it looks against five-year projections."

"You gotta accept my concept before doing more anulytical voodoo."

"Difficult when the concept changes every hour."

"Fieldsy, focus on the big picture, which is getting money to the shareholders! Got another brilliant idea. To encourage us option holders to exercise underwater options, we'll loan them the money."

Michael shook his head. "Pug, IPS has no cash to loan anyone."

"The option holders sign a note. Since the options are underwater, there's no tax liability. If we wait, the price of the IPS stock will go up and force us to pay taxes."

"But if the stock doesn't increase, then the option holders will owe the money," Michael argued.

"There you go again! No confidence! There's another advantage to exercising options. Kenji has to invest more cash to keep his ownership at twenty-five percent."

"Fair point." *Assuming Kenji's stuck on stupid.*

"I'll go to Tokyo and show him what happens after the options are exercised. Since you and me got the largest blocks, we'll exercise them before I leave."

Michael returned to his office and dialed Ellie. "You won't believe the latest!"

She listened, said goodbye, and thought, *Delaware's commenced. Captain James rearranges the equity and debt chairs while the iceberg looms. He has an unhealthy capacity for self-delusion. For deceiving himself about harsh truths.*

I need to move fast. Pug's plan will harm all non-family shareholders.

SOUTH SAN FRANCISCO

Pug relaxed in his office and scanned an article on installing bathroom fixtures. Marcy was away. When she returned, he'd have to tell her about the flooded basement and his botched plumbing repairs.

"Darin's fiancée is on the phone. Says it's urgent," Sharon announced.

"Weird," Pug said. "Hello, Sylvia. I mean, Amber?"

"Darin told me to call. Your father passed away."

Pug thanked her and slammed the phone. "Asshole couldn't call? Sharon! Get me on the next flight to Denver and book me at the Monte Carlo!"

He rushed home, packed, and left Marcy a note.

DENVER

Six hours later he arrived at Denver International, drove the rental car west on Pena Boulevard to I-70 west. Early evening traffic slowed; he marveled at the view of the silver-lined Rockies. As he approached downtown, he recalled his last trip to Denver when he met with Mile High's banker.

"Mr. Pug James! To what do I owe this honor?"

"To say good riddance!"

"Look Pug, Silverado National is a much better bank for IPS."

"You didn't have to push me off the cliff! You're no better than those bastards at Farm Ridge National!"

"You're out of line! I told you to find a new bank after your surprise move from Denver. You're damn lucky Robby stepped up!"

"Goddamn it! You forced me to pledge my intellectual property!"

"That's your problem. Not Mile High's!"

"Suppose you want my personal note paid too?"

"You took the words out of my mouth."

"Here's my check for the loan. Gimme my stock certificates! Now!"

SAN MATEO

Marcy returned home late Friday night after an exhausting week at the Los Angeles design show. She read Pug's note.

World's a better place without the old bastard. She poured Jack Daniels over ice, gathered the mail, and headed to the family room sofa.

What's this? She opened a manila package labeled "Japan and Singapore."

A videotape? She turned on the VCR, inserted the tape, and froze. Scene after scene labeled as to location and time—Osaka, Tokyo, Kyoto, Singapore—showed Pug intimacies with a much younger and pretty Asian woman.

Marcy, trembling and sick to her stomach, wept.

FARM RIDGE

Pug arrived at the Decker farm. He found Rich and Darin chatting with relatives in the party room on the barn's second floor. The room reeked of alcohol and cigar smoke. Conversation ceased as Pug approached.

"Look who's here!" Darin announced.

"Hope Dad's death didn't interrupt the weekend remodeling," Rich slurred.

Pug ignored Rich and addressed Darin, "No one bothered to tell me until what's-her-name, Ambient, called."

"Rich, tell him."

"Dad was sick ever since he returned from California."

"Whadya talking about?"

"He complained Skippy's kid kicked him. You shoulda seen the bruise."

"He slapped Billy!" Pug raged.

"Besides the physical abuse, Marcy treated him bad," Rich said, drunkenly waving his beer glass. "Doc said the stress caused a massive stroke."

"He treated Marcy like he abused Mom," Pug yelled.

"Always bringing your mom into this!" Darin yelled back.

"Look, if you're gonna dump on me and her, I'm outta here. When's the funeral?"

Another cousin took Pug aside and told him the family would receive visitors at Olinger Mortuary on Saturday morning with the funeral scheduled for early afternoon. The ashes would be inurned at Crown Hill Cemetery. Pug thanked him and left.

Pug could not reach Marcy. *She oughta be home now.* After a few more attempts, he went to bed but lay awake, his mind spinning.

The following day, a small group gathered in the mortuary chapel. After the minister's prayer and brief remarks, Darin delivered the eulogy:

"Family and friends, thank you for coming. Uncle Darin would appreciate your presence. As his namesake, I'll offer some thoughts about his wonderful life. He would be eighty-four this year. He relished that milestone as he outlived my father. Darin James was a survivor, and his positive attitude kept him active. I am proud to be his namesake."

Pug glowered at the stained glass window behind Darin.

"He worked hard at the railroad providing Amelia a decent, comfortable living. He was caring, a loving father and faithful husband. A bedrock. He put family first especially after Amelia's death. His generosity allowed me to attend college."

Pug fidgeted. *Dad paid Ted's tuition but not mine? If anyone kept the family together, it was Grandma Decker.*

"Uncle Darin and Aunt Amelia were married for seventeen years before she died. He missed her dearly."

Pug smoldered. *Horseshit!*

"In 1985, he completed thirty-five years of loyal service and looked forward to a quiet retirement. Unfortunately, a vacation in California took an unexpected turn. He couldn't return for several months. He was never the same."

You fuckin' son of a bitch! Now you're blaming me for his loony-bin time! Pug stood, lowered his head, and walked out. All eyes followed. Darin resumed, "We'll all miss him. May he rest in peace."

Rich strode to the lectern, hugged Darin, and said, "You're all invited to the cemetery for the inurnment and then to the James's family farm. We'll celebrate Dad's life."

At the gravesite, mourners shivered. The temperature dropped to 18 degrees.

When Rich tried to place the urn into the vault, the box proved too large. A cemetery technician was summoned. Forty-five minutes passed as the technician improvised to make the box fit. When the urn was at last in place, Pug announced, "Stubborn to the very end! Not going down without an argument!"

The group re-assembled in the Decker barn. They feasted on an impressive spread of food and drink. Pug grabbed a Pat Henry and found himself face-to-face with Darin.

"Puggy, first time you've seen the place since I remodeled. I named it the 'Darin James Farm,' in Uncle Darin's honor."

"How much?"

"Two-hundred grand in this room alone." He gestured toward an antique oak bar. "Got that for fifteen grand. Everything's first class."

"You bring the family here?"

"Used to. Sylvia won't let the kids come. You know I caught her cheating. Got photos to prove it."

Pug stared in disbelief. *Geez, Ted, I'd like to see those.* "So she got the kids?"

"Seattle courts favor the wife even if she cheats."

Pug opened another Pat Henry and took a long swig. *Ted, you're so like dear old Dad.* "Quite a eulogy, Ted."

"It was heartfelt."

"That's good to know 'cuz I couldn't figure who the hell you were talkin' about." Pug gulped more beer.

"What's that supposed to mean?"

"Last time I checked, when someone dies, you don't tell a bunch of fuckin' lies. If you can't say something honest, you should shut up. You forgot to mention Dad's drinking problem, his cheatin' on Mom, his crappy personality. Should I go on?"

"If you hadn't put him in that mental zoo, I wouldn't be giving a eulogy today," Darin yelled. The room grew silent; everyone stared at Pug and Darin.

"That's it! You fuckin' asshole!" Pug's fist landed a sharp blow to Darin's right eyebrow. Darin fell back against a table. Cousins rushed to restrain Pug. Others held Rich from attacking Pug.

Pug, his face beet-red, snarled, "Now you got matching scars for your lying eyes! I'm outta this goddamn fuckin' showplace!" He stormed out.

At the hotel, he threw things into his carryon, checked out, and drove to the airport. His only thought: *Colorado's in my rear view mirror.*

SOUTH SAN FRANCISCO

On Monday, Pug found Skip waiting at his office door.

"Whadya doing here so early? It's only nine."

"How was the funeral?"

"Waste of time. Say, where's your mother?"

"I don't know, but we need to talk."

"Make it quick. Got lots on my mind." In pain, Pug lowered himself into the chair. Skip sat opposite.

"You thought about Kenton?"

"Yeah, for all of five seconds."

"Come on, Pops! You know IPS needs money. Give them a chance to look at our numbers and make an offer!"

"I don't trust those bastards! Supposed to be a first-class

organization. Haven't sold shit, then a lawsuit. Now they wanna invest? Gimme a fuckin' break!"

"They cancelled the lawsuit!"

"Only after I countersued."

"Jesus, Pops, they gave us three hundred and fifty thousand on a handshake, and you accuse them of bad faith?"

Pug stood and yelled, "This ain't no fucking democracy!"

"Fuck you and your dictatorship!"

"Get the fuck out of my office!" Pug sank back into his chair and yelled, "Not wasting any more time on your half-baked, half-assed fantasies! Why I ever paid you a commission..."

"Go patent your 'fucking democracy' speech!" Skip yelled, slamming the door. He stormed down the hallway.

Perspiring, Pug rose from the chair, his legs weak. He grabbed the desk and bent forward. A sharp pain stabbed at his neck. His vision blurred.

"Sharon, get me Excedrin! Quick!" He slumped back in the chair.

Sharon moved as fast she could. "Pug, you look terrible! Should I call a doctor?"

He gulped three tablets and downed the glass of water. "No, I'm okay." He sat for a few minutes and stared at her breasts. "Just need a minute."

Sharon returned to her desk but watched Pug through the glass.

He took deep breaths and waited a few moments. Recovered somewhat, he dialed Marcy. When she did not answer, he left a message: "Sugar, remember about Skip and Kenton? Well, now I'm sure! Skip's betrayed me! My own son! Tell ya more tonight."

He idly shuffled papers. *Skip pushes a stupid deal behind my back while knocking up Annie. Dave's gone to Japan. Sean, Jackson, Michael, and Bill screwed me. Not to mention my asshole brother and cousin.*

"Sharon, tell Don to get his ass in here!"

"What do you need?" Don asked as he entered.

Pug said, rubbing his neck, "You fixed the numbers?"

"Working fast as I can, but you keep interrupting."

"Oh, blame me, why don't ya! Your revisions better improve profits, or I'll be looking for another CFO."

Don returned to his office and documented Pug's instructions for auditors and the bank's examiners. He reread his resignation letter.

LOS ALTOS, CALIFORNIA

Skip drove south on Highway 280. He loved the scenic drive, but he couldn't relax. He grabbed his cell and speed-dialed. "Sweetheart, I'm on the way."

"I thought you left for Seattle."

"I got a few hours before the plane leaves."

As he entered Annie's driveway, he noticed a green sedan parked nearby. The occupant looked vaguely familiar. Skip parked behind the house and opened a patio door. Annie greeted him with a passionate kiss.

He sighed and kissed her again. "Where's our Joey?"

"In Belvedere with Randy." She gently nudged him. "You look like the weight of the world's on your shoulders."

"I got Pop's democracy speech—again. Says he can't trust Kenton. No way this ends like Mathews."

She poured him a glass of wine, and they relaxed in the family room. He handed her an envelope.

"There's another two thousand in here. How much have we saved so far?" he asked.

"Close to one hundred thousand dollars."

"Once the Kenton deal goes live, we'll be set," he said. She snuggled close and kissed him with urgency. They moved to the bedroom. An hour later, Skip showered and left.

Annie opened her laptop and added the following entry:

– – *S to show financials to B without P's approval.*

– – *B's investment commitment is function of company's appliance cash flow and market potential for company technologies.*

– – *S blames P for all delays. Be patient S says. I'm concerned. Can S make it happen with B?*

– – *Keep the harassment as contingency.*

Annie saved the notes to a floppy and locked it and the envelope in her floor safe. She positioned a rug over it with a pair of shoes on top.

SAN FRANCISCO

Skip drove north on I-280. *Can't go home. Need to think. Gotta clear my head. Need to talk with Michael about Kenton. Not sure I want to go to Seattle. Will Annie stick with me if something goes wrong?*

He dialed the Sheraton Hotel and booked a room for the night. Twenty minutes later, as he passed the exit for IPS, he called Michael's number and left a message to call back.

He arrived in the City, checked in, and later drove to Scoma's for dinner. Back at the hotel, sleep was impossible. His mind raced. Worries about Annie, Michelle, and his fight with Pug kept him tossing and turning. He glanced at the clock. Twelve a.m. came and went. He got up, grabbed a Perrier from the mini bar and watched five minutes of TV porn. He dressed and headed to the garage. The clock on the dash read 12:45. He drove to Van Ness, followed the signs to the 101 freeway and headed south toward the 280 exit.

TOKYO

Kenji, Shiganari, and Dr. Yamura met at Kenji's apartment. Kenji had returned from a TADA meeting in Seoul. He opened a fresh bottle of Johnnie Walker Blue and poured each a drink. Three cigarettes ignited simultaneously, and Kenji proposed a toast.

"To our health and fortunes, gentlemen."

"Hai! Hai!" Shiganari and Yamura responded.

"Dr. Yamura, thank you for your excellent analysis on Mr. Pug James's proposal. Please share your conclusions with Shiganari."

"As you recall Okazaki-san, the APO appeal confirmed the Asian IPS 10000 patent is invalid. Japan Technologies has no further royalty obligations to IPS. The license terms are quite clear on this. However, Mr. James invented a new theory. He claims sixty per cent of Japan's appliances are exported to the United States where the IPS patent remains valid. He threatens to block OEM exports with court injunctions."

Shiganari smiled. "As he did with Hondoya."

Dr. Yamura continued, "Hondoya and other OEMs can seek court injunctions to stop this legal harassment. But Kobyashi-san reminded me of Mr. James's unpredictability."

"Hai! How do we prevent Mr. James from suing in American courts? Lawsuits and discovery reveal matters best kept private," Kenji added. "We do not want special relationships publicized nor European and American market plans disrupted. Since IPS is a California-based company, we must not allow local and state politicians to get involved. TADA requires a contingency plan. What are your thoughts, Dr. Yamura?"

"First, Japan Technologies pays a reduced royalty rate in return for releasing its exclusive marketing and manufacturing rights in Japan, Asia, and Hondoya worldwide. Second, Japan Technologies will retain a non-exclusive right to make and sell IPS 10000 in Japan. Third, in return, IPS will not sue customers for exporting appliances to American or European markets. It is important we keep the reduced royalty linked to exclusivity and nothing else."

Kenji added, "Mr. James desperately needs cash. He wants my equity interest in IPS and my resignation from the board."

"How can he do that with no resources?" Shiganari asked.

"He proposes a generous discounted value for all future royalty payments if I agree to a one-time advance payment."

"I see. He wants majority control," Shiganari said.

"Dr. Yamura will reply to Mr. James as he outlined and nothing more."

"Excellent. How did the TADA meeting go?"

"According to plan," Kenji replied. "In addition to legal matters, we reviewed new materials developed by IPS for next generation thermal and acoustic dissipaters including Aerolation, multi-dimensional parts and integrating plastic composites for more applications. TADA must not lose access to this creativity."

Dr. Yamura nodded, "Hai! Nippon-Soft-Dev has access to the son's creativity. I have hired Oshima-san to smooth the son's sharp edges and to develop his managerial talents."

Kenji added. "Our challenge is to retain access to the father's creativity."

Kenji refilled glasses. "Another matter of concern. Gano-Nippon terminated its TADA affiliation."

"The Gano-Lawrent alliance prefers confrontation."

"We must prepare for global war."

APRIL 14, 6:00 P.M.
SAN MATEO

PUG'S HEADACHE AND NECK PAIN intensified as he drove home. The day's events consumed him: his company's insolvency, Skip's betrayal, and conspiracies poised to destroy him. He parked the SUV in the garage. As he opened the door to the kitchen, his only objective was an ice-cold Pat Henry. Standing between him and the refrigerator was Marcy, her arms folded across her chest. Her face registered fury.

"You fucking moron!" she yelled. "You're worse than your idiot dead father! Get the hell out of my house!"

Pug stood paralyzed, his mouth agape. "Whadya talking about?"

Her voice became a growl. "How many Asian sluts have you fucked since Tiffanee? Get out!"

"Wha... what?" He'd never seen her like this.

Her angry voice lowered. She spat words through her teeth. "You better get checked for syphilis!" She stormed away.

Shocked and stunned, Pug had to think. *Maybe I can reason with her tomorrow. Right now, gotta find a hotel and a real stiff drink.*

APRIL 15
LOS ALTOS

THE 911 OPERATOR RECEIVED A frantic call at 7:30 a.m. A sobbing voice pleaded for help at 1259 Lowlands Circle in Los Altos. Responding officers entered the one-story ranch and found a female prostrate on the bedroom floor. Severe bruises on her naked body indicated a violent struggle.

Two homicide detectives debriefed first responders and questioned neighbors. No one reported screams or commotion. One neighbor remembered an unfamiliar late model green sedan parked nearby the previous day. Another remembered a SUV in the victim's driveway the previous afternoon. No one recalled either driver.

Inside, detectives examined for evidence. As the coroner's team prepared to transport the body, the lead investigator said, "Terrible. Young woman and all…"

"Yeah, such a shame…"

The detectives questioned the woman who placed the call.

"Ma'am, what's your relationship to Ms. Burr?"

"Friends since grade school," she replied, trembling and distraught.

"And why were you here today?"

"We meet weekdays at 6:30 to go to the gym. Annie never missed a workout. Today she didn't answer my calls, so I came here. When I saw the newspaper on the lawn, I got worried. I knocked, no one answered, so I opened the door."

"How were you able to get inside?"

"We share keys for emergencies."

"Who else has keys?"

"Probably her parents, maybe her ex."

"What happened after you entered?"

"I walked in, called her name. When she didn't answer, I thought maybe she overslept. So I checked the bedroom and found her." She sobbed.

"We know this is hard, ma'am, but we have to ask these questions. Did she live alone?"

"With her two-year-old son."

"You mentioned an ex-husband?"

"Randy Burr. He lives in Belvedere."

"Where's the son?"

"With him this week."

"This week?"

"They share custody."

"Any other relatives nearby?"

"Her parents live in Atherton, but they're vacationing in Indonesia."

"Is Ms. Burr employed?"

"She was between jobs."

"And her last employer?"

"She worked for IPS in South San Francisco."

"Can you think of any reason someone would harm her?"

"No! Everyone loved her." She pulled another tissue from her pocket and blew her nose.

"Take your time, ma'am. What is Ms. Burr's relationship with her ex-husband?"

"They argued a lot, but nothing serious."

"What kind of arguments?"

"Things like taking care of Joey. This week Randy wanted to leave town. Annie refused to change her plans."

"Was Ms. Burr seeing anyone since the divorce?"

"She never mentioned anyone."

"Here's my card. Call us if you think of anything else."

MONTEREY

Skip arrived at Monterey at 8 a.m. and registered at a bed and breakfast he and Annie frequented. His wrinkled clothes, day-old beard, and uncombed hair made an odd spectacle. Exhausted, he headed to his room.

Worried thoughts plagued him. *Been under Pop's thumb ever since high school. My breakout years, '94 and '95. Found Mathews and met Annie. Pops screwed up everything... never trusted me. Now he's wrecking my Kenton deal. Not going to happen.*

He slept fitfully.

SOUTH SAN FRANCISCO

"It's J-Man in the Morning!"

Pug rolled toward the sound, his arthritic shoulder radiating pain. *Where the hell am I?*

Head throbbing, he squinted at the clock radio. Nine o'clock.

He listened to the sarcastic patter of "J" Jefferson, popular shock jock, something about the ninetieth anniversary of the Titanic sinking... and a news item about President Bush. The J-Man shouted, "What an effing moron!"

The words slammed Pug. He remembered. He was exiled in a fetid smoker's room in a Burlingame hotel. The alcohol fog lifted, and Marcy's verbal tsunami pounded his brain.

You fucking moron!

Pug closed his eyes and breathed through his mouth, trying not to inhale the room's stench. *Gotta get up. Gotta get going.*

He dragged himself into a cold shower. Dizziness came and went. He toweled himself and stared at the mirror. Thick stubble salt-and-peppered his chin.

Nauseous, he steadied himself and pulled on yesterday's wrinkled Dockers, crumpled polo shirt, and fragrant socks. He swung his right arm back and forth to relieve numbness.

Bypassing his usual artery-clogging breakfast, he grabbed a cup of lukewarm coffee from the hotel lobby. Juggling the cup and his briefcase, he unlocked the door to the SUV and eased in his aching body.

Heavy fog blanketed the Bay Area as he drove north on Highway 101; poor visibility slowed traffic. He turned up the radio.

"So tell me about your book," J-Man asked his first guest, a historical fiction author.

"The title is *What Was the Captain Thinking?* It's about the 1912 disaster from the captain's point of view."

J-Man joked, "I read where one passenger said, 'This ship can't sink!' Another said, 'But the iceberg's cut the hull, water's coming in, sharks are circling, and the captain's nuts!'"

The novelist laughed. "J-Man, there's an element of truth. The captain made irrational decisions and put the ship at risk."

"Why didn't the crew mutiny?"

"Actually, the captain's executive officer conspired to take over."

"Did the captain go down with the ship?"

"He escaped at the last minute."

"You're kidding!"

"That's why it's called historical fiction."

Pug braked as traffic came to a halt. *God, my head hurts. Everything hurts.*

J-Man's second guest was a well-known political pundit promoting his memoir. "Okay, your new book, *Dad: My Mentor.* Tell me about it…"

"I describe my father's work ethic and values, valuable lessons I share with my two sons."

"Aaaah, now you're getting mushy," J-Man joked.

His head pounding, Pug hit the mute button and thought about his father's funeral and fight with Ted. His vision blurred. *My old man never shared anything with me.*

Shaking his head, he turned up the volume. At a station break, a local announcer said, "This just in: Los Altos police report an apparent homicide in Los Altos. More later…"

J-Man's third guest had written a *New York Times* column arguing Japanese appliance manufacturers are the only ones who get it when it comes to innovation, low cost and quality. He insisted Hondoya, Japan's largest appliance maker, acquire Exeter to rescue the American appliance business.

Pug shouted, "Bullshit! Japs never got it! All they do is steal my technology!"

J-Man changed topics. "You're something of an expert on corporate scandals. What's happening with the Adelphia Communications mess?"

"Adelphia is tragic. Besides illegal business practices, there's a special twist. The Rigas family treated Adelphia like their personal piggy bank."

"So they had their hands in the corporate cookie jar?"

"Good one, J-Man. A title for my next novel."

"Pay me royalties, or I'll sue your ass," J-Man intoned.

Pug grimaced. Acid reflux burned behind his sternum. *What's the big deal? Rigas took all the risks! He deserves every single silver dollar!* Pug silenced the radio.

Today's commute from the hotel to his South San Francisco office took a full hour. He exited the freeway and hesitated at the intersection of Paul and Silver Streets. On a sunny day, the impressive IPS building reflected a silver sheen. Today, fog kept it a dull gray. Pug pulled into his parking space and shuffled to the basement entrance.

Eleven o'clock. Neck pain, blurred vision, dizziness plagued him.

Sharon met him at the office door. "Morning, Pug. Here's the daily summary and today's mail."

"Shitty day!" he growled. "Listened to radio crap about icebergs, fathers, and Japs."

"Get you coffee and... a razor?"

"No smart-ass jokes! Get me a triple-leaded espresso. Skip call?"

"Sorry, okay, and no. Pug, what's wrong?"

"Damn! That makes twenty-four hours. He always checks in."

"He left no itinerary. He seemed upset yesterday."

"Yeah, him and me fought about Kenton crooks."

"I'll leave a message for him to call."

"Hold all my calls."

"Including Marcy?"

"Especially her."

Sharon smiled. *No interruptions from Mrs. Pain-In-The-Ass.*

She jumped as Pug slammed the glass door to his office. The vibration caused the painting of the Colorado silver mine to list at an angle. He reached to straighten it. Grabbing at his sore shoulder, he shuffled to his desk, sat down heavily, and opened the silver music box. He leaned back and listened to the familiar tune.

Later, Sharon returned with coffee. "Get you anything else?"

"Shut the door! Let's look at your summary." His skin was pale, clammy.

"Ready?" she asked. An uneasy feeling enveloped her.

Pug's eyes seemed frozen. Perspiration wicked along creases in his forehead. "Uh... what?"

"I said, 'Are you ready?'"

"Your memo's giving me a friggin' headache. Get me Excedrin."

Sharon hurried to her desk and dropped two tablets into her palm. Suddenly, the receptionist rushed to her side and whispered. Sharon gasped and sank into her chair.

Pug scanned the summary's litany of problems: cash shortage, vendors threatening collection, Silverado Valley Bank's credit line termination, Kenji's rejection, and Dexter-Foresmen's countersuit. The last two items meant no quick cash. He ransacked the mail and reached for an envelope marked "Confidential," postmarked Chicago with no return address. On the front and in bold type was "For the Eyes of Mr. Pug James Only."

Weird. He read the unsigned letter. *What goddamn hell is this? CCs to Kenji, Michael, and Robby? What's this shit comparing me to Enron and WorldCom crooks?*

His mind raced. As the shredder devoured the paper, he opened another envelope postmarked Seattle. Each side read, "Photos—Do Not Fold or Bend." Pug stared at the contents:

Dear Puggy,

Enjoy these pictures from Osaka, Kyoto, Tokyo, and Singapore. Hope Marcy enjoys the action version.

Best regards.

Beads of sweat rolled off his scalp as he flipped through pictures. Vision blurred, images flashed in and out. Pain, crushing and relentless, pounded him. The pictures fell from his hand as his right arm went numb.

Sharon entered. "Pug, I got terrible news…"

Pug slurred, "Tiffanee… meet me… at the Turtle." He slumped, his head crashed on the desk.

Frantic, Sharon shouted, "Call 911! Call 911!" She checked his pulse. *Thank god, he's breathing. What's this? Oh my god!* She slid the pictures into the daily folder along with the summary.

Paramedics arrived and commenced emergency procedures. Pug lay ashen and unconscious on the stretcher. Sharon and the staff watched the ambulance pull away.

Sharon dreaded calling Marcy. "Tiffanee, it's Sharon. I have bad news."

Marcy took an interminable time to respond. "Tiffanee?"

"Oh, Marcy… I'm so sorry! It's been a nightmare!" Loud sobs followed.

"Calm down. What's wrong?"

"Pug's in an ambulance, on the way to the hospital. Paramedics think he had a stroke or heart attack. They're taking him to St. Joseph's in Burlingame. Should I call Skip and Dave?"

Marcy didn't answer.

"Before he collapsed, he said something about Tiffanee's turtle."

Marcy replied in a measured, icy tone, "He'll remember if he comes to his senses."

Sharon, her heart hammering, returned to Pug's office and re-examined the photos. *What do I do?*

SAN MATEO

Marcy hurled the phone at the kitchen counter. *Tiffanee was his last thought?*

Strands from her bleached, shoulder-length bob fell across her eyes. Her once-pretty face showed the effects of time, alcohol, and stress. She tucked hair behind her ear as tears filled her sad blue eyes.

Who'll look after IPS? I co-signed all those personal guarantees.

She opened a fresh bottle of Jack Daniels and filled a large tumbler. She watched the amber liquid cascade over ice until it overflowed. Wandering into the family room, she glanced at the VCR with the disgusting tape. Her mind catalogued past and current betrayals. *Why didn't I divorce the bastard in 1986?*

Marcy's fifty-eighth birthday was two months away. Today she felt eighty. The whiskey eased tension but not the angry heart.

BURLINGAME

Sharon, shivering from jangled nerves and icy air conditioning, sat in St. Joseph's visitor area.

Please don't let me be the one to get the bad news.

She saw Michael approach. His calm demeanor reassured her. They embraced.

"Office called; told me about Pug. What happened?"

"Not sure," Sharon said, fighting tears, mascara smudged beneath her eyes. "Paramedics said stroke or heart attack. He's been in emergency room for two hours. What if he dies?"

"Pug's a survivor. Where's Marcy?"

"She should be here by now."

Sharon fidgeted with her handbag and pulled out a manila envelope. "Michael, I don't know what to do with this. It's all in here except for some document Pug shredded." She began crying.

"Sharon, what's wrong?"

She blew her nose and sobbed. "Annie Burr's been murdered."

"Oh no!" Michael exclaimed.

"Mrs. James?" They turned to a tall man in hospital garb. "I'm Dr. Simmons from Intensive Care."

Sharon looked embarrassed. Michael spoke, "I'm Michael Fields, Pug James's colleague. This is Ms. Manzi, his assistant. Mrs. James should be here any minute. How is Pug?"

"He's in a coma, but vital signs are stable. Were either of you with him when he collapsed?"

"I was," Sharon answered.

"Did he exhibit symptoms like dizziness, slurred speech, or complain about headaches?"

Sharon replied, "Just before he collapsed, he looked very pale and asked for Excedrin. He did slur his words."

"Does Mr. James take any prescription medications?"

"I know he has hypertension," Michael said. "Don't know about his meds."

"Here's my pager number if Mrs. James wants to contact me."

They thanked the doctor and walked to the parking garage. Sharon whispered, "Michael, when I phoned Marcy, she... she seemed cold, as a matter-of-fact. Not upset."

"Probably in shock."

"Maybe so." She hugged him and said goodbye.

Michael sat in his car and opened the envelope. Sharon's summary memo was a bad news avalanche.

Enough crap to give anyone five strokes! Photos? Good grief! I shouldn't be surprised.

Michael called Ellie. "Captain James hit an iceberg."

"Iceberg?"

"His silver-lined ship is sinking. Captain's disabled. Sharks are circling."

"What happened?"

"Stroke, maybe heart attack."

"Oh, my god. And the sharks?"

"Lawrent, IPS's bank, Patent Financing, Kenton, Japan Technologies, Jackson... you name it. All of them want a piece of IPS. And there's another problem... someone photographed him in bed with some Asian babe."

"Blackmail? What else can go wrong? Hurry home; we've a lot to discuss."

"Marcy left a message on my cell. Wants to meet tomorrow," Michael added.

SAN FRANCISCO

At home, Michael sat at the kitchen table, opened his briefcase, and reread bullet points in the daily summary and jotted notes:

    – – Daily cash problems and vendors threatening collection actions.

    – – Litigation lottery status: Only $750 thousand raised versus the $3 million goal. Dexter-Foresmen's counter suit is bad omen.

    – – Kenji accepted the reduced royalty rate but rejected Pug's other proposals on stock and board seat.

    – – Silverado Valley Bank's notice of default expected in 30-60 days.

    – – Kenton's offer to invest in IPS looks suspicious.

    Lawrent still stalking.

He jammed the notes into the briefcase and snapped it shut. *Who took the photos and why?*

MONTEREY

Skip checked his phone and returned Michael's call.

"Hey, Michael. It's Skip."

"Thank god you called!"

"What's wrong?"

"Bad news. Steel yourself." Michael paused, "Annie's dead... murdered..."

Skip choked, could not speak. At last he said, "Guess the police will want to talk to me."

"Probably to all of us. Skip, there's something else."

Skip interrupted, "They'll think I'm involved."

"What are you saying?"

"The police will find out."

"Find out what?"

"I've been seeing Annie since she left IPS."

"Not sure I understand. For now, stay put. I'll get back to you."

Skip collected himself and dialed Kenton's Seattle number. "Bob, change in plans. I have to stay in California."

"What happened?"

"Annie Burr died." His voice cracked.

"That's terrible. Sorry to hear that. Anything I can do for you?"

"Can you handle the sales calls?"

"No problem. By the way, has your dad changed his mind?"

"No."

"So, what do we do in the meantime?"

"Bob, IPS is in serious trouble. Revenues are stagnant. IPS needs a huge cash infusion; otherwise, the bank seizes the assets. I'll send you some confidential information. Let's talk after you review it."

"Okay, Skip. One last question, is two million still enough?"

"Three would be better."

"Again, sorry about the bad news."

"Thanks, Bob."

Somehow he managed to prepare a package and mark it "confidential." He deleted all references to company name and products and dropped the package into a mailbox.

SEATTLE

Bob reflected on Skip's call. *Consider plan B without Skip. The preliminary analysis indicated cash flow from restructured appliance business can pay back our original investment and fund new startups. With Kenton's standard operating ratios applied to IPS sales, profits increase by a country mile. The bonus: the huge tax-loss carry-forward can reduce other tax liabilities. Most exciting is IPS technology. With no Pug interference, we can now grow sales in aerospace and construction. Later, we sell the appliance business to Darin James for a nice markup.*

BURLINGAME

The next day, Michael and Marcy met in the hospital's coffee shop. Pug's vitals had improved, but he remained unconscious.

"How you holding up, Marcy?"

"Okay, I guess. The doctor says Pug may never fully recover." She cradled a mug of coffee in her hands. "I must consider IPS's future without him."

"Don't say that."

"Michael, there are certain things I can't…" She swallowed hard and looked down. "Let's just say, Pug should not run IPS."

"But he still owns the major share. He or his proxy will have a controlling vote on the board and management."

"Not if his ownership share decreases."

"I don't understand."

"What I'm about to say nobody else knows including Skip and Dave. I'm divorcing Pug." She paused. "I need your help to protect my interests. Skip's a terrible disappointment, and Dave abandoned his family."

"What do you want me to do?"

"You're the only one who can save IPS."

"That's a full-time commitment. I'll have to talk with Ellie."

"I know she'll agree when she understands what happened."

After Marcy left, Michael left a voice mail for Ellie. "She's either desperate—or angry the family gravy boat is sinking. Saw a side of her I never knew. No longer the sweet, passive airhead-enabler we've grown to love."

SOUTH SAN FRANCISCO

"Set up an emergency board conference for tomorrow. Tell Jun it's mandatory," Michael instructed Sharon. "Marcy will represent Pug. Let me know when it's confirmed."

"Okay. I notified Dave about Pug. Called Darin and Rich. Left messages on Skip's cell, but he hasn't called back."

"That's strange. What did Darin and Rich say?"

"Darin said never count Pug out."

"Good old, caring Ted. And Rich?"

"He actually sounded concerned."

On the conference call, Jun listened from Osaka and Robby from Denver. Michael, Marcy, and Sharon sat in Pug's office.

"Hello, everyone," Michael began. "By now, you know about Pug. Marcy has the latest medical update."

Marcy, in a soft but firm voice, thanked the group for their expressions of sympathy. "I'm sorry we're talking under such circumstances. The doctors say Pug suffered a major stroke. He's in a coma, some possible paralysis. Soon they'll transfer him to Stanford University Hospital's stroke center. Pug often said if anything happened to him, he wanted Michael to assume CEO duties until he returned. Considering Pug's condition and IPS's problems, I've asked Michael to serve as acting CEO."

Robby asked, "What about your teaching, Michael?"

"I'll request a leave of absence." Michael paused. "If there are no further questions, do I have motion to accept Marcy's request?"

Robby motioned for approval, and Jun seconded.

"The motion carries. Thank you. I'll prepare an action plan. Sharon will schedule our next conference call."

The group expressed their best wishes to Marcy and said goodbye. Robby remained on the line.

"Robby, you know the Silverado Valley people," Michael said. "Could you request extra time regarding the line of credit and long-term note? It would help IPS right now not to scramble for a new bank."

"Glad to help. Our first concern is Pug's recovery."

After Robby disconnected, Marcy said, "Be careful, Michael. Pug said Robby has serious financial problems and isn't dependable."

Michael walked her to her car. They hugged. "I'll do my best to save IPS for all its stakeholders."

OSAKA

Jun met with Kenji after the conference call. "This is truly an interesting development. And you said Mr. Fields wants to come to Japan?"

"Yes, Kobyashi-san."

"Excellent. Have Dr. Yamura complete background checks before he arrives."

"Hai!" Jun had never seen Kenji so pleased.

SOUTH SAN FRANCISCO

Michael returned to Pug's office and locked the door. When he opened the desk drawer for a pencil, he found several unfilled prescriptions. *Why am I not surprised?*

He reviewed action bullets he compiled since Pug's collapse:

-*Visit Kenji.*
-*Rehire Bill Arrow to do AAs and sales?*
-*Cost reduction.*
-*Revisit Pug's restructure & reorganize for more savings.*
-*Reduce admin overhead ASAP.*
-*Preempt adversaries.*
-*Kenton-Aerocon proposal, post Skip?*
-*Lawrent's offer?*
-*Make licensing model work. How?*
-*Settle with Jackson.*
-*Follow-up Robby and Silverado, with caution.*
-*Shareholder Action Plan (Role for Don Wagner?)*
-*Check Skip's files for damaging material.*
-*Visit customers and vendors.*
-*Pug's future role, post-recovery?*
-*Monitor Darin and Rich.*
-*What is Dr. O'Leary up to?*
-*Talk to Dave.*

DUCK, NORTH CAROLINA

Sean called Larry Judson at his Duck vacation home. "Good morning, Larry. Heard Pug James had a stroke?"

"Who's running IPS?"

"Michael Fields's the acting CEO."

"What do you know about him?"

"He was executive VP before resigning. Still on the board."

"Sean, now's the time to strike. I'm calling Lawrent's investment banker. Time to take IPS out!"

Sean clicked off his recorder. *Time to cash in my US insurance policy.*

Larry made two calls: Lawrent's investment banker and Gano-Nippon's CEO.

The alliance of Lawrent and Gano-Nippon was creating serious competition for TADA and challenging its stranglehold on the Japanese thermal and acoustic dissipater market. Hondoya no longer dictated all technology innovation and procurement decisions for OEMs. General Appliance of Japan was leading the effort to replace Hondoya as lead OEM. The retirements of Kenji and Shiganari had opened the floodgates.

Two days later, Larry opened an information folder from Gano-Nippon Tokyo. The contents stunned him. *No way Lawrent can send Sean to Japan with this personal baggage.*

He opened another package marked "Personal and Private." It contained cassette tapes and a note that stated, *Larry, listen to this. I await your offer. Sayonara.*

Larry listened to conversations between Sean O'Leary, Lawrent personnel, and General Appliance executives about damaging references to bank wires, perjury during discovery, jury tampering, and conspiracy to destroy IPS.

He agonized. *This risks everything I've built for Lawrent! And the Gano-Nippon alliance!*

He dialed his lawyer.

PALO ALTO, CALIFORNIA

From San Francisco airport, Dave drove straight to Stanford Hospital. He arrived at Pug's room to find a nurse attending his father. Shocked by Pug's comatose appearance, he asked her, "How's he doing?"

"As well as can be expected."

Dave stood close and placed his hand on Pug's. "Hey Pops, just arrived from Tokyo." Pug did not acknowledge. "My work in Japan's going great! Got two promotions! Boss tells me I'm in line to manage the entire operation. Nippon-Soft-Dev assigned a senior executive to mentor me. Remember Oshima-san? Anyway the best news, I met this wonderful lady, a real beauty. Can't wait 'til you meet her."

Pug's eyes remained closed. "Better go now. See you tomorrow." He closed the door.

In the hallway, he bumped into Michael.

"Dave! No one told me you were here! How's he doing?"

"Hard to tell…"

"Can we get together before you return to Japan?"

"Sure, call me at the Burlingame Hyatt," Dave said. He hugged Michael. "Thanks, man, for all you've done. You were right about Japan. It's been a blast."

"Knew you'd like it."

They parted, and Michael entered Pug's room. He drew up a chair and sat close to the bed.

"Pug, not sure where to start. Looks like you shredded my letter. Did you think I wouldn't connect the dots when you bought the beach house and club membership? Always wondered how you got the money. Your penchant for litigating rather than commercializing always baffled me. IPS licensees commercialized the technology while you squandered it. But I must admit, banging the cute Japanese lady and god knows who else… takes the prize. You outdid your dad, Ted, even Doug Aldrich."

Michael stood and sighed. "I'm going now. I've got a load of work to remodel IPS."

When he reached the door, he turned and said, "Your life's a tragedy, straight out Shakespeare."

LOS ALTOS

The detectives reviewed the coroner's official report. Cause of death: Suffocation. The deceased's nostrils, mouth, and lungs contained a fibrous material. Time of death was between three and seven a.m. Evidence containing semen and fibrous matter was sent to the California Bureau of Investigation. The Santa Clara district attorney requested expedited processing.

The two detectives sat in their cramped office and reread the coroner's report, preliminary lab findings, fingerprint samples, and printouts from computer disks found in the victim's home.

"What we got so far?"

"Why would someone keep one hundred thousand in cash along with love notes?"

"Someone with dark secrets."

"Ms. Burr's quite the writer."

"Her friend said she loved writing. She's provided lots of clues. "Who are 'S, B, and P?'"

"Good question. And what about her note about the 'harassment contingency?'"

The detectives drank coffee and studied their notes. "What about her ex?"

"He's a suspect without a butt-tight alibi."

"Reading Ms. Burr's graphic descriptions of sex with S gave me a..."

"Everything gives you a woody."

They pored over crime lab reports.

"We know she had intercourse a few hours before she died based on semen samples. She was also pregnant."

"Yeah, what about the fibers in her nose and lungs?"

"Similar to samples of some kind of insulation found in her desk."

"Any clear fingerprints?"

"Several. Last count, five different sets besides hers."

They examined her life insurance policy. "Ex-husband's the beneficiary. Randy could be richer by five hundred thousand. Possible motive?"

The detectives outlined their investigation plan:

– – *Re-interview neighbors.*

– – Visit IPS and interview Pug James, Michael Fields, Skip James, Dave James, Sharon Manzi, Bruce Hargett.

– – Contact IPS customers with whom Ms. Burr worked.

– – Meet with parents, ex-husband, friends.

The district attorney grew impatient when no immediate suspects emerged. Local newspapers editorialized about snail-like progress. Each day, the DA reviewed the detectives' meticulous notes taken from interviews with various people at different locations.

Ms. Burr's parents:

– – Ms. Burr's father angry about beneficiary designation, son-in-law's sexual orientation, and motives for marriage.

– – Parents surprised about Ms. Burr's pregnancy.

– – Thought daughter was happy working at IPS until she complained about sexual harassment.

Randy Burr:

– – Randy Burr's house owned by his partner, Josh Baker.

– – Two cars in driveway, A SUV (Burr's) and green sedan (Baker's).

– – Mr. Burr denied paternity for Joey and unaware of second pregnancy.

– – Mr. Burr and partner at Belvedere home between midnight and 7:00 a.m., November 5.

– – Mr. Burr confirmed ex-wife's complaints about sexual harassment at IPS.

– – Mr. Burr appeared ignorant about life insurance.

– – Request Mr. Burr's DNA and Joey's.

IPS Personnel:

– – Checks on IPS website and D&B services revealed Company products use fibrous material (IPS 100). Company has terrible credit ratings. Silverado Bank claims Company's insolvent.

– – Unable to interview Pug James (in hospital), Dave James (in Japan), and Skip James (in Seattle).

Michael Fields:

– – Michael Fields (interim CEO) confirmed Ms. Burr's employment between 1996 and 2000; her supervisors were Skip James and Bruce Hargett. Said Ms. Burr was friendly, well-liked, and demonstrated excellent computer skills.

– – Denied she was sexually harassed while at IPS. Management

restructuring was reason for supervisor change. Indicated her reasons for leaving IPS were childcare, long commute. He reluctantly provided access to HR file and customer contacts. Mr. Fields and wife at home between 12:00 a.m. and 6:00 a.m., November 5.

– – Fields's answers appeared rehearsed.

Bruce Hargett:

– – Bruce Hargett (HR manager) seemed genuinely shocked by her death.

– – Nervous and reticent when asked about her relationship with Skip James. Denied sexual harassment claims; showed notes from her exit interview. Said Pug James ordered the supervisory change, subsequently ordered her termination.

Sharon Manzi:

– – Ms. Manzi described close working relationship between Skip James and Ms. Burr.

– – She suspected after hours involvement because both marriages strained.

Bob Kenton:

– – Bob Kenton learned about murder from Skip James phone call. Indicated Ms. Burr worked closely with Skip James on business development projects for Kenton aerospace and construction markets.

– – Kenton's current relationship to IPS is sales licensee; hoped for expanded cooperation. Clarified reasons for initial lawsuit and subsequent settlement.

– – Indicated surprise when told about Pug James's medical problems. Claims Skip James did not mention this.

– – Kenton's reasons for zero sales implausible, different from Ms. Burr's computer notes.

Dave James:

– – Dave James disagreed with Annie Burr's marketing philosophy. Thought little of her computer or publishing software skills.

– – Offered an alternative sexual harassment theory: Claims Ms. Burr was an office gossip and caused problems for him and Judith Kramer.

– – He was in Japan when Ms. Burr died.

– – Collected DNA sample given imminent return to Japan.

Skip James:

— – Skip James came to police station after five-day Seattle business trip. Confirmed he recruited Ms. Burr. Gave numerous examples of her excellent computer and marketing skills.

– – Reasons for Ms. Burr leaving IPS consistent with explanations by Mr. Fields and Mr. Hargett.

– – Appears to be only IPS employee who saw her after she left IPS. Denied knowledge of pregnancy.

– – Claims he was in San Francisco at the Sheraton Hotel at time of murder; no witnesses.

With interviews completed, the detectives had copious notes, recordings, and forensic data. They studied them in sequence.

"You know, when you compare alibis of where people claimed to be between the evening of November fourteenth and early morning of the fifteenth, only the victim's parents have an ironclad one. Hotel records, airline tickets, passport records support their statements."

"Wish the others were as clear. Then we have what I call 'biased witnesses.' Although Pug James is in the hospital, for now we'll accept his wife's statement."

"Remember how unhappy Mrs. James acted. Couldn't tell if she was thinking about her husband's condition or something else."

"Another biased witness, Randy Burr. Relies on his boy toy to vouch whereabouts."

"Dave James and Skip James claim they were in transit or at a hotel."

"Need to talk with hotel people and see if anyone recalls Skip James."

"You buy his reasons for not rushing home?"

"No, unless there's some family dynamic we don't understand. May have to talk to his wife when she returns from Oregon."

"What does the lab say about the fibers found in the victim?"

"Same material used in the IPS 100 product."

"Motives?"

"Randy Burr has a financial one—life insurance. But nothing indicates he knew he was the beneficiary."

"From the looks of his Belvedere mansion, not sure he needs the money."

"Property records show the mansion's in Josh Baker's name. Could be Burr's sugar daddy."

"How about Dave James? Certainly no fan of Ms. Burr and had a revenge motive."

"We'll talk again if his airline ticket and passport stamps don't check out."

"How about Pug James? Any motive?"

"Can't think of why he would want her dead or have her killed unless…"

"Unless what?"

"He was trying to cover up or protect somebody."

"And then we come to our boy, Skip.

"His answers were peanut butter smooth with a dollop of nerves. Had most contact with the victim. But from everybody's input, their relationship seemed cordial."

"What do you make of these floppies found at her house? Any ideas?"

"*S* is most likely Skip. *P* could be Pug."

"How about *B*?"

"*B* is definitely Bob Kenton. The company wanted to get in bed with IPS, but for some reason Pug James objected. Remember when we talked to Sharon Manzi, she referred to an argument between Pug and Skip; thought it involved Kenton. Looks like *S* and *P* disagreed about *B*."

"And if you combine it with Ms. Burr's frustration about slow progress, maybe she was ready to blow the whistle. This gives Skip motive or perhaps Pug."

They outlined next steps: "First, we visit the Sheraton in San Francisco and confirm Skip's stay. Second, we'll request DNA and fingerprints from Skip, and if necessary, from Randy, the son and Pug and compare with those at the crime scene and of the unborn baby. Third, we recheck alibis. Have a chat with Marcy James and Randy's beau."

They moved quickly. At the hotel, the desk clerk recognized Skip's photo but found no record of a Skip James. Paul James, however, had registered and was seen leaving about 12:45 a.m.

Follow-up with Josh Baker reconfirmed Randy Burr's alibi. Dave James provided airline tickets and passport documents to establish his location. Marcy James re-confirmed Pug left their house at 8 p.m. She was uncertain where he spent the night in question. She confirmed they had separated earlier that day.

SOUTH SAN FRANCISCO

A week later, the detectives arrived at IPS unannounced. The receptionist, distraught and nervous, escorted them to Skip's office. Sharon and other staff exchanged worried looks as the detectives closed the door behind them.

"Mr. James, we have additional questions."

Skip stood and crossed his arms, then uncrossed them. He pushed hair off his forehead.

"I... I answered all your questions."

"Corroborating facts, Mr. James. You stayed at the Sheraton Hotel on the night of November fourteenth, is that correct?"

"Yes."

"Hotel records don't show a Skip James registered. Did you use an alias?"

"There must be some mistake... oh, I remember now... I paid in cash."

"You have the hotel receipt?"

"I threw it away before going to Seattle."

"We showed your photo to hotel employees. They recognized you, said you checked in that evening."

"I told you that."

"The hotel person claims the picture was Paul James."

"I don't understand." Agitated, he shoved hands into his pockets and rocked from one foot to the other.

"Now tell us again where you were between the late hours of November fourteenth and the early morning of the fifteenth. The hotel clerk said Paul James left the premises around 12:45 a.m."

Skip dropped his hands to his sides. "I left the hotel and drove around until checking in for my flight."

""Did you go to Los Altos on the morning of the fifteenth?"

"Look, this is ridiculous!" He began to perspire.

"Yes or no, Mr. James."

"No!"

"One more item, the DNA samples you provided match hair and semen samples found at the crime scene. In fact, they also match those of Ms. Burr's unborn baby and her son. Do you still maintain you were not at her home on the morning she was murdered?"

"Look, I want a lawyer. I'm not answering any more questions."

The detective said calmly, "Mr. James, you're under arrest for the murder of Annie Burr and her unborn child."

Skip had requested counsel; they didn't bother Mirandizing.

The officers handcuffed Skip and led him, crying, from the office. The staff stared in disbelief.

"Call Marcy," Michael told Sharon. "He needs a good lawyer."

LOS ALTOS

Skip was booked and taken to a holding cell. He felt as if he were sleepwalking, ambulating in a nightmare. He said nothing as officers processed paperwork.

In the morning, the detectives reviewed the case. "We got the prime suspect, with no alibi and a strong motive."

"Yeah, he had his dick between a rock and a hard place. His wife didn't have a clue, and now the 'other' woman's dead."

"Anyway, there are loose ends to tie down. The DA and police chief want a slam dunk conviction."

"At his first court appearance, he can ask for a public defender. In a case like this with all the publicity, there's no way the DA will agree to bond. This boy's a flight risk."

"Yep! First degree murder. It'll be a no-bond hold."

"How about his family? Any signs they're helping?"

"Not yet. His dad's in the hospital. His mother hasn't called, and my guess the wife's not anxious to save his bacon."

"Let's see how he responds when we do follow-up chats."

"Need to talk to Skip's wife. She's filed for divorce and is moving to Oregon."

"What should we do about Pug James?"

"He'll be transferred to the VA hospital. Until the doctors give clearance, we're on hold. Besides he isn't going anywhere. Nobody can verify where he was that night and early morning."

Skip's arraignment went fast. The public defender entered a not-guilty plea. As expected, the judge denied bail. He noted no member from the James family attended. Skip's sworn statement indicated he had insufficient resources for counsel. Investigations of his finances revealed no equity in his home, extensive overdue credit cards, and a family with no visible means of support. The trial date was set for six months later.

MENLO PARK

Dave oversaw Pug's transfer from Stanford Hospital to the Menlo Park Veterans Hospital. Pug's physical condition and speech improved. However, he remained combative and accused nurses and staff of undermining him at every turn. The doctors told Dave his father's mental state hampered recovery. Pug needed mental as well as physical therapy.

Dave exited the Bayshore Freeway onto University Avenue and headed toward Stanford University. He passed handsome homes along University Avenue and entered Palm Drive. Ahead, Stanford Chapel's mosaic façade came into view. He turned into the medical complex, parked, and entered the hospital to await Pug's discharge. A nurse appeared pushing a sullen and medicated Pug in a wheelchair. After signing the release and getting Pug into the car, Dave suggested a short drive around the campus and old Palo Alto.

"How you feeling, Pops?"

"Meds... sleepy."

"How's your right arm?"

"Quacks... don't know shit."

"Let's stop at Stanford Shopping Center for a cold drink and hang for a few minutes."

Dave found parking then struggled to get Pug into the wheelchair. At a table outside a coffee place, Dave ordered two iced teas. The sun felt warm and comforting.

"How Japan?" Pug asked, struggling to form the question.

"Great! I'm chief operating officer of Nippon-Soft-Dev."

"What I want you do I-P-S," Pug said. His speech was hesitant and weak. "Defeat bas-tard Ken-ji. Why you quit me?"

Dave didn't argue. *He's forgotten.*

"Right, Pops."

"...Ti-na?"

"We're divorced."

Pug's eyes welled. "Take care...your mo-mother. C-can't take care of her-herself."

"How long will you be at the VA hospital?"

"Lock up like my old man." Pug began to weep.

"Look Pops, everything'll be okay. Where's your patented optimism?"

"Dead."

Dave looked at his watch. "Dr. Tower wants us by two o'clock."

As they drove towards Menlo Park, Pug said, "Keep close Mi-Michael... good man. I get back, I make up... to you."

"Okay, I promise."

"Watch your-self. Don't trust Ken-ji. Screwed me."

Dave wanted to say, *Pops, you don't know the half of it. You should have worried more about Sean O'Leary.*

"Pops, Kenji's no longer a problem."

"Huh?"

"Retired. Ashi-san runs Japan Technologies."

"Oh..." Pug began to cry. "Skip... threw a-away... on that slut."

"Pops, I've married a great lady I met in Japan."

They arrived at Menlo Park Veterans Hospital, and Dave wheeled Pug to admissions. He remembered Pug's detailed description of committing his grandfather here years before. *Is craziness in my DNA?*

As Dave said goodbye, Pug held onto him. "Nev...nev-er told me wife's name," he said.

"Her name is Nani."

"Fa-miliar."

"Bye, Pops, see you later."

As Dave exited the parking area, workmen were applying a new coat of grayish stucco to the building exterior. The building seemed to take on a silvery sheen.

PART III
THE RENEWAL
(MAY 2002)

MENLO PARK

Weeks later, Michael entered the lobby of the Menlo Park Veteran's Hospital. He headed to the reception desk and asked to see Pug James. The receptionist looked at her watch and laughed, "At this time of day, you'll find him with the maintenance crew."

"But he's a patient!"

"Oh, he's impatient all right!" she laughed. "Here's where you'll find him." On a visitor's map, she highlighted the maintenance area.

Minutes later, after several turns, a long hallway walk, and a steep flight of steps, Michael was in the basement. He pushed open a door and found Pug directing two workers.

"Fixing this boiler's a piece o' cake," he heard Pug say. "Do this..."

Pug turned and saw Michael. "Hey, Fieldsy! Fixin' the hospital's heating!" The mechanics smiled in agreement.

"When you're finished, let's talk." Michael noticed Pug had lost a lot of weight. He moved and spoke slowly, but his "can do" attitude was there.

"Be there soon. Guys, get some IPS 10000, wrap it around the pipe. Close with a stainless steel clamp." Five minutes later, Pug emerged, wiping his right hand with a towel. He shuffled; his right leg dragged. They headed outside to a patio.

"Pug, how's it going? You look good."

"Right side's weak, getting' better every day. On real strict diet and exercise plus butt-load of pills."

"This time, be sure and take them."

Pug gave a lopsided smile but seemed near tears. "You're my... only visitor since Dave... Marcy filed for divorce. Picked a great time to kick me when I'm down..."

Michael thought, His *speech is slow—but he's thinking clearly.* "So what are your days like?"

"First week pure hell. Quacks ask me same questions over and over. They think I'm crazy, so I change answers to confuse them!" He laughed.

"Pug, cooperate. Otherwise..."

"Right. Dad was here six months. Can't let him beat me!"

"So what else keeps you busy?"

Pug retrieved a small notebook from his jacket and thumbed through pages. "My nighttime work." He showed Michael pages of sketches, notes, mathematical equations, and hypotheses on solving thermal problems.

"Looks like your old lab books from IPS."

"You remember!" Pug said. "Problems. Never had time to solve at IPS."

"Any good ideas so far?"

"Remember my vista from the '95 AA, for an all-in-one dissipater? Now possible with the metal alloy-plastic composite!"

"Thinking's good therapy. Why were you in the boiler room?"

"Told Dr. Tower I'd fix mechanical problems. Run the maintenance crew. Like Dirty Harry. I maintain their day!" He laughed again.

"As you would say," Michael chuckled, "one hell of an anthology."

"Careful or I'll subsize this conversation!" They laughed. Michael was pleased Pug-speak had returned. He paged through the notebook while Pug got Cokes from a machine. They reminisced. An hour flew by.

"Pug, need to go. What say I stop by soon?"

"Any time, Michael. Do me a favor?"

"Sure."

Pug became emotional. "Get Dave to come back and help IPS. Don't want him to end up like me."

"Pug, I'll talk with him. He seems very happy in Japan."

They shook hands, and Pug watched Michael disappear.

On his way out, Michael stopped at Dr. Tower's office. The office door was open. He knocked and said, "Dr. Tower, sorry to interrupt. I'm Michael Fields, colleague of Pug James. Can we talk?"

"Mr. Fields, please come in."

"I just saw Pug."

"My most interesting patient! Had a similar case many years ago."

"Dr. Tower, I've known Pug since 1979. I know your 'other case' was his father. I know Pug's entire background, his problems—maybe I can help with his recovery."

"It troubles me I haven't seen any family members, no local support."

"Doctor, I understand doctor-patient confidentiality; but under the circumstances, would you tell me how long he'll be here?"

"Our maintenance department hopes he's permanent!"

Michael chuckled. "When I saw him today, he was in the basement helping technicians fix the heating."

"You weren't supposed to see that!" Dr. Tower laughed.

"Pug loves solving problems, fixing things."

"Exactly, it's why we have him helping. His attitude and mental state have improved. He has a clever, active mind—constantly thinking. You asked me how long? Okay, let me back up a bit. When he came here, he suffered from 'circle of failure.'"

"Meaning…"

"It's a phrase to describe Pug and his father. I'm writing a research paper on this topic."

"What does it involve?"

"Pug's paranoid delusions combine with an unusually creative imagination…possibly hereditary. His father was very negative, a fatalist. Yet Pug is a fanatical optimist. Both have unrealistic expectations, fantasies, and an unwillingness to accept reality. For Pug, this results in poor decisions which lead to disasters and setbacks. He becomes more and more paranoid and blames others. He's caught in a circle of self-inflicted failure."

"Wow, you've summarized IPS's last fifteen years. Paranoia and delusional thinking… that was Pug!" Michael thought for a moment and asked, "So, how long?"

"Depends on how he does with medications and counseling, how his behavior and attitude stabilizes. It's important he remain in a controlled environment."

"Controlled?"

"Where he can work independently using his creative mind. Somewhere he feels successful, doing things like repairing our heating system."

"Doctor, appreciate your honesty. Talk with you soon."

As Michael drove the Bayshore to San Francisco, he talked with Ellie on his cell and outlined his ideas.

"Brilliant, darling! Very creative! And here's really good news! We have forty-one percent approval to elect a new board of directors without a stockholders' meeting—the beauty of the Delaware option! We need the Brunei Trust shares to get above fifty-one percent."

"Have all US shareholders been contacted?"

"Yes, except for the James Family and Bob Kenton."

"The ball's in my park. Hello Japan, hello sixty-one percent, and hello new board."

OSAKA

Michael arrived at Kenji's office. Jun was already there.

"Mr. Fields, Jun and I appreciate your comprehensive advance notes on IPS."

"The summary should bring you current."

"I see IPS faces many financial challenges," Kenji observed.

"Yes. Silverado Valley Bank and Patent Financing have started their workout. That will force the company into bankruptcy. IPS has very little time before the company's assets and patents are seized."

"That is unacceptable. Jun informs me IPS intellectual property is pledged as security."

"Correct. That means Patent Financing will own IPS patents and technology."

"Mr. Fields, that must not happen. There are two—maybe more—firms wanting to purchase or destroy IPS. This means others see long-term value in IPS. What are your plans?"

"First, I'm requesting Silverado Valley and Patent Financing for more time by showing a turn-around plan for growth and positive cash flow," Michal explained.

Kenji glanced at Jun. "Please continue."

"Using this same business plan, I'll contact all interested buyers to determine their interest and how we might work with them—if they're interested in investing and/or accessing our technologies. I won't limit discussions. I'll contact Lawrent, Kenton-Aerocon, and others. I want to find what our adversaries are thinking. As an interim step, I think we can interest them in licensing agreements that allow them to use the technologies. Pug's original three-phase licensing model offers creative options, but with one important difference."

"What is that?"

"I'll structure win/win relationships. Pug demanded huge front-end fees before business materialized. Pug never negotiated."

"I couldn't agree more, Mr. Fields. Be careful of Lawrent," Kenji warned. "They are affiliated with Gano-Nippon. Treat their inquiries with utmost caution."

"I have short-term actions to raise cash—such as selling some country-specific dormant patents for a one-time discounted fee. Another action involves restructuring the company to eliminate high overhead costs."

"Excellent! IPS's administrative expenses were always excessive."

"High salaries and expenses of family members caused that excess," Michael stated. "With Pug and his older son gone, we can reduce the cash drain. I estimate six to seven hundred thousand dollars of savings."

"Impressive. Please continue."

"I've already met with Dexter-Foresmen and proposed a lawsuit settlement. IPS's litigation position was ill considered."

"Mr. James's legal actions always disappointed us."

"I have several other minor actions which are summarized in this attachment—you can read at your leisure. I'd like your assistance in re-engaging Marken Company. I believe you have a special relationship with Marken-san."

Kenji and Jun smiled. "That should be no problem. I would be most happy to assist."

"Thank you. Are there other questions or issues I can address for you?" Michael asked.

"One matter," Kenji said. "My investment trust has received a letter requesting support to hold a shareholders' action without a meeting. Please explain."

"As I understand, some key shareholders have requested an election of a new IPS board without holding a meeting. If fifty-one percent per cent of stockholders agree, then a new board with new directors can be elected. This allows the new board to restructure the company and move forward."

"How many have agreed?"

"About forty percent."

"Interesting. So if my trust were to vote in favor of this action, there are enough votes?"

"When Pug pushed to change the corporate legal structure from California to Delaware, he planned to acquire the company's valuable assets and leave other shareholders with worthless equity stakes in a holding company."

"Mr. Fields, we have discussed many subjects today," Kenji said. "Let's adjourn and continue over dinner."

"One more item," Michael said. "I've started a new skunk works. It's a controlled way to capture Pug's creative brain." He described a new development lab with Pug working on new technologies.

"Very intriguing," Kenji remarked.

At dinner, Kenji continued, "Mr. Fields, I am impressed with the quality of your plans. You give credibility to the American phrase, 'it is never too late.' I respect your candor. I will assist your endeavors."

Michael listened as Kenji outlined various actions.

After dinner, they adjourned to Kenji's bottle club. "Mr. Fields, may I call you Michael?"

"Of course, if I may call you Kenji."

"Agreed. Michael, you have found a way to control, yet access Mr. Pug James's inventive brain. I have nurtured a similar opportunity."

Kenji described Dave's role at Nippon-Soft-Dev. He spoke of his vision for Dave to oversee a global corporation. IPS was integral to his plan. "Michael, I am in your debt. You mentored Dave while at IPS and supported his desire to work and live in Japan."

When Michael heard Maurice Oshima would assist Dave's management development, he was delighted and impressed. "Kenji, I never realized the depth and breadth of your operations. I would consider it an honor to help realize your vision."

"Thank you, Michael! Your participation is valued and appreciated."

On his return flight to San Francisco, Michael entered notes on his laptop:

1) At the appropriate time, Kenji will vote his trust's shares allowing Ellie to implement the shareholder action plan. A new board and new management team will operate IPS without James family involvement until Dave is ready. Kenji agreed to support a generous exit strategy for all remaining shareholders.

2) Kenji's plan for global operations with Dave in charge indicates his long-term strategy to dominate thermal and acoustic dissipaters markets. With Pug's creative brain controlled and focused, he will provide new technologies to insure new products and technologies are available. Dave will duplicate his father's efforts in Japan before he assumes the global CEO role.

3) Kenji and colleagues will keep Lawrent, Gano-Nippon, Kenton-Aerocon and other predators off balance while we position IPS for the consolidation phase with Japan Technologies and into TADA.

Kenji has resolved the Dr. O'Leary problem. I avoided specifics after Kenji refused to elaborate.

4) The Silverado/Patent Financing threat will be neutralized with a short-term cash infusion from Brunei Trust. They will be soon replaced with other financing alternatives. Very intrigued about the Walter Marken, Mile High Bank, and VenCapOne connections. Kenji's tentacles reach long and deep—perhaps even to Silverado and Patent Financing.

6) Complete all action items from last board conference call as it relates to Bill Arrow, Jackson Huntley, customers, vendors, and Marken.

7) Some unknowns: what are the plans of Darin and Rich? Who is Dave's wife? Someone Kenji knows?

CONCLUSIONS: Kenji is truly a chess master—plotting moves far ahead of adversaries, covering all the bases. Pug remained immersed in real and imagined conspiracies. Based on what Dave and I learned about Sean O'Leary, I'm convinced he was Kenji's first choice to run the global empire. But betrayals and addiction intervened. When I praised General MacArthur, Kenji knew I had unlocked a secret. I let him retain a perceived advantage. But there are things he won't acknowledge. I suspect his "adoption" of Dave and his happiness with the marriage holds the key to that puzzle.

Michael shut down the computer and relaxed. He knew Ellie would be pleased. He agreed to Kenji's five-year employment contract with a nice signing bonus and options. An important part of the assignment involved assisting Dave's transition into his global responsibilities. Ellie and Orlio had legal work to finish.

Michael reflected on events. *Politics and technology are finally balanced.*

BURLINGAME

Nursing a Pat Henry, Pug sat at the far end of the restaurant's mahogany bar. He couldn't believe the changes since Tiffanee liaisons, twenty years before. Gone were cold salad forks and green goddess dressing, replaced by overpriced Italian-style cuisine. *It was called the Velvet Turtle. Now sounds sorta Italian, rhymes with Sausalito.* This spot held special memories of earlier victories. He loved those days—inventing new solutions and products by day—bedding Tiffanee at night.

He thought about his dad and Darin. *You two got what you deserved. Dad went to his grave a bitter old man, and Ted's back in Denver with his tail between his legs. He and Rich deserve each other.*

Pug swigged from the bottle and glanced at the overhead TV. He jotted ideas on a bar napkin. He had two solutions to the first technical problem on Michael's list using an idea for a lightweight high-temp plastic co-molded with IPS 10000. He felt adrenalin rising, excited to begin his experiments.

He paused and thought of Michael. Like 1986, Michael gave him another chance. This time, circumstances were profoundly different—his marriage dissolved, half his IPS shares gone to Marcy, his new regimented life.

He recalled when Michael took him to the new lab for the first time. They drove from Menlo Park to the new site. He remembered every detail:

"Hey, Pug! You and Dr. Tower finished?"

"Yeah, I'm officially on mental parole, ward of Sheriff Michael Fields."

"Well, you're in for a surprise! Get in the car."

He drove north to the Bayshore freeway off the Willow Road exit. He looked at me and smiled. "Remember '86 and our skunk works discussions?"

"How could I forget?"

"Dr. Tower and I discussed your recovery. We thought you'd love solving technical problems..."

"Do my ears hear me?" I asked him.

We laughed, and Michael turned west on Highway 92 and made a quick right. We were at a small industrial park near apartment buildings. I saw a sign for Kuletos Restaurant.

I asked, "Say, didn't that place used to be the Velvet Turtle?"

"Yes, used to be Doug Aldrich's favorite hangout."

Michael parked in front of an apartment building and pointed to the top of the three-story building. "See that corner apartment to the right? Your new digs."

"Why here?"

"Dr. Tower wants you close to your work, since you can't drive."

"And where do I work?"

"Follow me," he said. He took me across the street and unlocked the door to a building with a small sign on the door.

"Sign says 'PSW II.' What's that?"

"You'll know... soon enough."

Followed him into a front office and then to the back rooms where there's a small lab with test equipment. Recognized a thermal camera, heat pipe with propane gas connection, vibration tester, workbenches, and tools.

"What's this?" I asked. "This where I'm gonna work?"

"What the doctor ordered. Welcome to PSW II."

"So what's the catch? What I gotta do?"

"Very simple. Rule number one: Take your meds. Dr. Tower warned you what happens if you forget."

"Don't remind me!"

"Rule number two: Work only on technical problems I assign. No freelancing. Here's the list of the first ten projects. I'll see you have enough money to cover expenses to operate."

Looked at the list. Thermal, sound and space problems.

"Rule number three: Don't talk to anyone, including family, about your new job or for whom you work. If someone asks, tell them you run a contract development lab. It's all here in the confidential employment agreement."

"No family, so no problem. So who's my boss?"

"I'll be your official and only contact. And rule number four: Provide a weekly status report on your progress finding solutions to the problems on the list. And rule number five: No moonlighting in the stock market!"

"That's it?"

"One more thing. You'll get a generous salary. Any commercial successes resulting from your work, you get a nice piece of the action. We'll discuss details later."

"I operate solo?"

"You'll start with three assistants. Stay focused on big issues and don't sweat the details. Assistants do the heavy lifting. Pug, I have to leave now. Here's keys to the lab and your apartment. Lock up, and I'll see you tomorrow. By the way, your luggage and stuff is at the apartment. Try some of the restaurants nearby. I hear Kuletos is not too bad. See ya."

I looked around the lab. Then it hit me.

PSW II stands for "Pug's Skunk Works II." I sat down on a lab stool and cried.

Pug finished his second Pat Henry and made notes. He had five bar napkins filled with sketches and ideas. *Those assistants better be good. Gonna crank their asses.*

He stood up, tossed a ten-dollar bill on the counter, and started towards the dining area. He glanced at the other end of the bar. A familiar face smiled back.

"Tiffanee?"

"Pug, I knew that was you!" She stood to hug him. "How've you been?"

"Great! Oh, had a little health go-'round. Talk a little funny now, not the Speedy Gonzales I was, but I'm back, good as new. Gosh, it's good to see you, Tiff. Hey, join me for dinner!"

For three hours, they ate, talked, and laughed. She had married a lawyer for a commercial real estate firm specializing in properties in the Mission District. His workaholic personality provided a comfortable lifestyle, and he soon became a multi-millionaire investor. Tiffanee raised their children by herself and saw little of him. His unexpected death left her devastated. The children, now grown, had their own families. No amount of financial security could hide her loneliness.

Pug told her about his many business triumphs since MatraScience. He extolled his latest venture, PSW II.

"Pug, your skunk works sounds wonderful."

"Thanks, Tiff. After I... uh... sold my company, I was gonna retire and play golf, but it's not in me. I have to be inventing and creating. It's in my Levis."

"Levis?"

"You know... jeans."

"Oh, genes! Always loved your way with words!" She laughed her infectious way.

"Tiff, my apartment's just a short walk away. Join me for a nightcap."

"Pug, I'd love to. I want to hear more about how you Pearl Harbored Japan when you owned IPS."

~ End ~

ABOUT THE AUTHOR

S. J. Fairchild grew up in a family business and observed dysfunctional behavior and its impact on business decisions. During his business career, he lived and worked in five states, Europe, Asia, and Australia. His senior management responsibilities included finance, sales, marketing, product development, manufacturing, and international business. Senior management positions in both public and privately-owned companies provided him with first-hand experience in operating successful enterprises, both domestic and foreign. He utilized lessons learned from his own family's business.

S. J. Fairchild lives with his wife, Katherine, near Chapel Hill, North Carolina.

Contact S. J. Fairchild at fairchildsj4@gmail.com or visit him at www.fairchildsj.com.